GIVE A DOG A BONE

A Dr. At Mystery

by

JAMES HOSEK

Copyright © 2015 James Hosek

Published by Balmoral Books

All rights reserved.

ISBN: 1505500079
ISBN-13: 978-1505500073

Other Books by James Hosek

A Really Good Day

Visit me at
jameshosek.wix.com/author-blog

Dedicated to my mother, Sylvia Hosek,
the best mom and grandmother in the world,
and who convinced me to do my own house calls

PROLOGUE

Bang. Bang. Bang.

That had to be gun shots, I thought. Even slightly muffled through the heavy door to the building's atrium they were loud. That was the door that Chicago Police Officer Marcy Avers had disappeared into moments before.

I didn't remember diving to the floor. I did remember thinking how good a job Henry, the janitor, did at keeping the marble tiles so shiny.

My mind was racing. What was going on in there? Did Marcy shoot someone? Did someone shoot her? Were we in danger here? I was a veterinarian. I did house calls for pets, not police shoot outs. The bump on my head from earlier in the evening was throbbing again. Part of me was thinking someone might need help in there. The sane and rational part of me kept me glued to the floor.

Charlie, the doorman, was still standing up, a confused look on his face.

"Get down, Charlie," I told him. Charlie took my suggestion immediately. The third man in the lobby, an agent from the Public Health Department, here to enforce a quarantine, hit the ground as well.

I was lying in front of the reception desk and couldn't see the atrium door from where I was.

"What was that?" asked Charlie.

"Gun shots," I said.

"Who was shooting?" asked the guy from the Public Health Department.

"How the heck should I know?" I answered, a little perturbed at the stupidity of the question.

"What do we do?" asked Charlie.

"Stay down," I suggested.

Outside, the recently arrived television news crews had their cameras pointed at us through the large glass wall and doors. One of the reporters had crouched down, probably her own reflexive response to the sound of gun shots. This was probably being broadcast live. The whole thing had become a big news story and I was trapped in the middle of it.

I really wished I hadn't gotten out of bed this morning. What had started with a sick dog, two dead dogs, a deadly disease, an annoying cop, and a crazy smuggler had progressed to a situation where I was now in fear for my life on television.

But I did get out of bed this morning. It all started with that early morning phone call from Sheila . . .

CHAPTER 1

I'll start by saying that I am not a morning person. I say this unashamedly and even proudly. Nothing against morning people. I am just not one of them.

I was jarred awake by what I thought was the sound of my alarm. My right arm shot out with a reflex practiced from years of routine and flopped on the top of my clock radio in the general area of the snooze button in response to the noise. I loved my snooze button. Whoever invented the snooze button was owed my undying gratitude. Did I mention I am not a morning person?

Before I could drift back to unconsciousness for another ten minutes I heard a ring.

That wasn't right. My alarm clock didn't ring.

Ring.

I let the lid on my right eye open. The glowing red numbers taunted me with the ungodly time of 5:35. 5:35 a.m.

Ring.

Someone was calling and didn't realize that I still had a good hour and a half of sleep left.

Ring.

I thought it might be my mother. Ever since she moved from Chicago to California to live with her sister, she never did figure out the whole time zone difference. Some days she'd call at dinnertime hoping she hadn't woken me, other times she'd call me at midnight and ask me what I was having for breakfast. She just couldn't grasp that Chicago was two hours ahead.

Ring.

It could be Sheila. If it was Sheila I would have to answer. It would probably be an emergency. Most of my patients took their emergencies to the emergency clinic. That was what they were for. But Sheila would be the one to either tell them they needed to go in at the ungodly hour of 5:35 a.m. or tell them it could wait until later in the day when I could stop by and see to their medical needs.

Ring.

I let my hand crawl to the phone sitting in the recharger. I pulled it off before it could send another of its annoying rings to resonate in the bones of my skull. It almost fell to the floor as I brought it over to my head.

"Hello?" I grunted.

"Good morning, Atty," said Sheila's way too cheerful voice.

"It's the middle of the night," I corrected her.

She ignored my remarkably lucid assessment of the time.

"You have an emergency."

"That's what the emergency clinic is for," I said, knowing she knew that too, but I said it anyway.

"It's Darla," she answered.

That woke me up. Well, brought me up another level of consciousness. "For real?"

Mrs. Jeffries, Darla's "mom" called at least once or twice a month for me to come check on some "serious" ailment of Darla's. Mrs. Jeffries was a hypochondriac and by association so was Darla. Any cough, sneeze, or fart required a medical workup. Darla was actually one of my healthiest patients despite everything Mrs. Jeffries did to her. All in the name of love.

"Sheila, it's five..." I cranked open my right eyelid for an update from my clock-radio, "thirty-seven in the morning. Can't it wait?"

"It's 5:27, you always set the clock ahead ten minutes, remember?" she said.

Right. The one last psychological trick I played on myself to let me sleep an extra ten minutes in the morning. You'd think my body would have caught on by now. Stupid body.

"What's the problem?"

"I think she's dying. Apparently she's been crying all night. Mrs. J. has been too afraid to call thinking it could wait, but I don't think it should. I really think you need to see her. I don't want to think of Mrs. Jeffries going to the emergency clinic on her own with Darla."

I tried to digest everything Sheila had just told me.

"Are you still awake, Atty?"

"I'm here. Need to go see Darla," I reiterated.

"I told her you'd be there in half an hour."

It would take me ten minutes to drive to her condo on Lake Shore Drive. "I'm not a morning person," I told her, hoping to get a little more time.

"Morning is a state of mind," she said.

"Which state is that, South Dakota?"

"Very funny. Get up. Darla needs you."

"On my way," I assured her and pushed the off button on the handset.

I tried to open both eyes, but they were putting up a really good fight. They knew their contract didn't call for this early morning work and they were determined to make sure I honored it. I tried one at a time; first the left, then the right. It was the unexpected aid from their ally, my mouth, in the form of a yawn that caused me to close them both at the same time.

Ring.

This time I had the phone to my ear in a second. "Hello?"

"Get up, Atty," said Sheila.

"I am up," I said.

"Right, 'Mr. I'm not a morning person.' I bet you went right back to sleep after I hung up."

I snuck a peek at the clock. 5:41 a.m. "You know, if you just slept over here, you could just wake me up with a kiss instead of annoying me over the phone."

Sheila make a puckering sound. "Now get up," she almost shouted. "You need to get over there."

"As you wish," I said. The line went dead. No more playful flirting. No more witty bantering. No more Sheila.

Sheila had been my phone service for nearly two years. I found her ad on a bulletin board at the Jewel-Osco. She offered twenty-four hour call service for what seemed like too low a rate. I called her and found out that she had about half a dozen clients and actually made a pretty good living at it. All I had to do was forward my business line to her and she took care of the rest. I tried her for a week then wondered how I ever got along without her.

The weirdest part is that we have never met. All I know is the smooth, sexy, (well, sexyish) reassuring voice on the other end of the phone. I imagine it belongs to a devastatingly beautiful blonde, young and fit, way out of my league. I often wondered if some of the pretty women I passed in the grocery store when doing my shopping were her. Part of me didn't want to know the truth. The dream of her was too good to lose.

For all I knew, she was a three hundred pound redhead drinking Diet Pepsis and Miller Lites while reclining on a Lazy Boy in her muumuu and bunny slippers.

I fought up to a sitting position. I rolled my neck around, feeling, more than hearing, the cracks of my cervical vertebrae as they slipped back into place. There were still some cobwebs obscuring part of my brain, but a hot shower and a hotter cup of coffee would clear them away.

I stood and swayed on unsteady legs that had more than a little sympathy for my eyes. I took a deep breath, let it out and made my way to the bathroom. It was still dark outside. This wasn't right. This wasn't right at all.

I flipped on the lights in the bathroom and squinted against their blinding glare. It was like staring into the sun. I turned the hot water tap. It would take about a minute for the hot water to start flowing. I stared into the mirror. There he was: Oliver Platt. Dark hair that curled at the back of my head, round face, well cultivated sideburns. I had been told over and over again how much I looked like the actor. Some people even told me I sounded like him. It was the sideburns, I told myself. Without them I looked like no one.

I took care of my full bladder then checked the hot water. I splashed my face for a quick lather and shave then stepped into the tub for a quicker shower.

I wrapped myself with my robe and headed for the kitchen, anxious for my first cup of coffee. It took me almost a minute to figure out that the coffee machine wasn't set to turn on until 7 a.m., my usual wake up time. That sucked. I hit the start button and figured I'd be better off spending the time getting dressed rather than waiting for the machine to drip enough artificial energy to fill a cup or two.

I almost tripped over Beaker heading for the bedroom. The silly cat had no sense of danger. I could quite easily crush him with a misstep. He squeaked at me and reminded me I had something else to do before getting dressed. He needed food.

I don't know if 'need' is the proper verb to describe Beaker's consumption of the dry kibble he enjoyed. He was always hungry, but never got fat. I could fill the food bowl four times a day and he'd keep his slim figure. What I wouldn't give for his metabolism. I had settled into my thirties weight. A good twenty-five pounds over what my doctor called ideal.

I attributed his amazing super power to the severe trauma he suffered shortly before he adopted me. I had found his shattered body in my alley when taking out the trash one Wednesday night. I had heard a squeaky cry and followed it to find him half hidden behind a garbage can. His fur had been matted with blood. His limbs had been twisted in unnatural positions and a gash in his belly revealed gravel-encrusted intestines. I had figured the best thing at that point was to go get my medical bag, draw up some pink juice, as I call the euthanasia solution, and put him out of his misery.

He had squeaked again. I had put my hand near his head. He managed to lift his chin over my finger and began to purr. It had been a pathetic purr, highlighted by blood bubbles forming on his nose, but despite all the pain he was in, he had been telling me he wasn't ready to give in.

I had carefully transferred him into a cardboard box, shot him full of antibiotics and painkillers and drove him to the Chicago Veterinary Specialty Center on Addison. One of the techs, Allie, had helped me work on him in a marathon surgery session we thought would never end. Apart from cleaning up his abdomen and sewing it back together, I had put two pins in his right rear leg and one in his left front, wired his lower jaw back together, and put another hundred stitches or so in the lacerations that covered his body.

We didn't think he'd make it through the surgery. When he did, we didn't think he'd wake up. And when he did and squeaked his high-pitched meow, Allie dubbed him Beaker after the hapless assistant to Dr. Bunsen Honeydew of Muppet Labs fame.

It had been three years and no sign of his injuries remained without taking an x-ray. I figured some brain trauma had flipped a switch in his pituitary gland giving him his super-metabolism and often wondered how I could bottle that.

I grabbed a scoop of his food and filled the bowl. He settled in front of it, happy that I could be of service.

I stumbled back to the bedroom and got dressed in my usual. A pair of khakis, white shirt and tie, argyle socks and my ever comfortable Sperry Topsiders, the leather softened to the point where my feet slipped in without having to undo the rawhide laces. I pulled on a brown tweed sport coat and headed back to the kitchen.

Two Pop-Tarts were devoured without ever seeing the warm red coils of my toaster and they started feeding sugar to my bloodstream along with the caffeine from two cups of the coffee, the second accompanying me to my office as I gathered up everything I thought I would need. Ideally, I'd return home before starting my regular appointments at 9 a.m.

I looked over at my printer. A copy of my itinerary for the day was sitting in the tray. On top of it was a short note from Sheila, "Mrs. J. Is Waiting. Get Going." it read in large block letters. What a gal, she could nag me electronically as well.

Sheila had set up the remote access to my printer. She kept my schedule on some online calendar program and made sure it appeared in printed form. She said I could access it on my phone as well, but I preferred the hard copy. She hadn't got me texting yet, but was working on it. She sent me messages and my giant fingers kept me from sending anything intelligent back. "Okay" usually ended up as "POKJAYU." Seems kind of silly when I can just speed dial her and talk directly.

Don't get me wrong, I use technology; heck, I even need it, but really? When did we get to the point where texting replaced talking? Probably around the time that cameras replaced cops writing tickets.

I slipped my laptop from the charging cradle on my desk and unplugged my portable printer. Both went into my black computer bag stocked with paper, labels, rabies tags, park district tags, business cards and some pens. I also unplugged my smartphone and slipped it into my pocket. I used to have a nice simple flip phone, but Sheila had insisted on the gadget and I admit it had some advantages. The Domino's Pizza app was my favorite.

I then opened my drug cabinet with a key from my key ring and selected a few bottles of meds I might need to treat whatever Darla might be afflicted with. I also pulled out some pre-counted bottles of antibiotics and other meds indispensable when dealing with hypochondriac pet owners. The rest of my gear was already loaded in the back of my car.

I left my vaccines in the mini-fridge. I'd need them later in the day, but right now I needed to hit the road. I pulled my itinerary out of the printer from beneath Sheila's note and sat down in my chair to look over the day. Pretty routine stuff. Nothing that should get me behind schedule, although you never could tell with some clients. A simple heartworm test and vaccines update could easily turn into a "by the way" appointment. By the way, could you check out his ears? He's been shaking his head for the last week. By the way, could you shave those matts on his belly, I can't seem to brush them out. By the way, he's been vomiting for the last three days and maybe ate some socks.

I leaned back for a moment and let my eyes close. Despite the caffeine and sugar, my body still knew that this was just wrong. It was used to its routine and getting up early for anything other than an early tee time was not natural.

I suddenly felt myself jolt back to the world as I nearly fell out of my chair. My eyes were wide. I looked at my watch. Several minutes had elapsed. Sheila was going to kill me.

I carried the bags to the kitchen and set them down before putting on my overcoat. I started out the back door when I heard a ring. It was the phone. What now?

Another ring.

I left my bags in the back doorway and rushed back to the office picking up the phone on the fourth or fifth ring.

"Hello?"

"What are you still doing there?" asked Sheila.

"What?"

"Why haven't you left?"

"I was leaving, I had to come back to answer the phone."

"Right."

"Really, you can ask Beaker."

"You weren't sleeping in your desk chair?"

"No," I lied.

"You get my note?"

"Better than a love sonnet my dear, I didn't know you cared so much."

"Go, go, go," she ordered.

"I'm gone. I'd have left already if you didn't just call."

"Right. I'm watching you," she said before hanging up. Somehow I believed that she was.

Now I was out the door, locking it behind me. I fingered the little fob that was a mini remote control for my garage door opener. I never used the side door for the garage. It was locked with a padlock and I had long ago lost the key. Unlocked garages invited vandals and kids looking to steal anything useful. In my case, I had a tiny electric lawnmower to groom my postage stamp sized lawn, a plastic snow shovel, and a bicycle that I hardly ever rode.

I could hear the garage door moaning open as I walked towards the alley and then it coughed. It only took me a second to realize that while garage doors don't cough, my across the alley neighbor, Mrs. Hornby, did. Another phlegm-infiltrated heaving of lungs echoed through the crisp, cool, morning air. There would be no avoiding her. I lifted the latch and swung the half height gate open and stepped into the alley.

"Good morning, Mrs. Hornby," I said, holding up my black medical bag, "got an emergency."

"Good for you," her deep throaty voice answered. She took a drag on the Marlboro perched between the first two fingers of her right hand, held inches from her face, easier to make sure every breath contained a full dose of the carcinogenic nicotine filled smoke. "Got the grand kids over this week. Can't even smoke in my own house," she said accompanied with a rolling of her eyes and a "woe is me" shake of her head. She was wearing a housecoat and dirty red slippers. There were curlers in her hair and it was covered with a blue mesh cap.

"Love to talk, got to get going," I said, heading for the interior of my garage. She was unflapped.

"The younger one, Griffin, gots the asthma. Little rugrat can't breathe nothing that isn't air." She took another puff, the smoke dragging a hunk of her lung out with it as she exhaled with a powerful cough. "What kind of name is Griffin, anyways."

"A mythical beast, I believe," I said. I hoped she wouldn't interpret my answer as an encouragement for more conversation. "Got a sick dog waiting."

"Back in my day, we didn't worry about all this nonsense. Never heard of kids having allergies to milk or gluten, or whatever. They're going all soft and delicate. What's the world coming to?"

"Kids," I punctuated. "I'll have to see you later."

"Yeah," she said waving her cigarette hand around, "if I'm still around." Another vicious cough wracked her frame. This time she made a throat clearing noise and spat out a puddle of brown liquid onto the pavement at her feet. I felt my stomach turn. "That'll kill the weeds," she added.

I almost ran to my car. I tossed my bags onto the passenger seat of my Escape, rather than in the back hatch. I pressed the start button and fired up the car. I pulled out of the garage and hit the close button on the remote attached to my visor. I didn't wait to see it close. I waved my arm goodbye in case Mrs. H. was watching, but still couldn't get that puddle of brown fluid out of my mind.

"Play Neil Diamond," I instructed the voice-controlled MP3 player. I loved my car. I'd had it for six months now and wondered why I waited so long to buy a new one. I had driven a Saturn Vue for nearly six years. It was lime green. My new car was also green, but more of an avocado green. Still easy to spot in a parking lot. Most people nowadays went for silver cars. Lots of silver cars in the parking lots.

My previous car had made the decision for me. Driving south on the Kennedy Expressway, I heard a clunk then a grinding noise then saw the smoke and smelled the burnt rubber scent that meant the repairs were going to be more than the car was worth. I let it drift to the shoulder. Called AAA and Sheila in that order. I was in my new Ford within twenty-four hours. It wasn't that I couldn't have afforded a new car sooner. I had just gotten used to my Vue. But as soon as I sat in that Escape and took the test drive, I knew I would be driving it home.

Now Neil was crooning me with Sweet Caroline and I was cruising down Montrose Avenue towards the sunrise and Lake Michigan.

I live on the North side of Chicago in a neighborhood called Ravenswood. It used to be crowded with thousands of the black birds until the West Nile Virus swept through and they dropped like flies from the trees. Literally, they were dropping out of trees as I drove around. I'd find a dozen a week dead on my lawn. Once they were gone the pigeons moved in. There were so many I wondered if they might rename us Pigeonwood, but the original name remained.

There are a few ravens coming back. Nature has a way of restoring the balance. Likely these are as resistant to the virus as the pigeons seem to be.

Mrs. Jeffries' condo was on Lake Shore Drive. She actually had a nice view of the lake. I'd probably catch the sunrise I realized. That was kind of depressing. The sunrise and I were really not acquainted that well. I could see a long trail of construction cones along the street. No one was working, but the cones were out. In fact there weren't even any signs that work was being done. No men (or women) breaking up perfectly good pieces of blacktop with a jackhammer, with five or six other construction workers watching to make sure they did it right.

That probably wasn't fair. I really shouldn't judge those loyal street and sanitation workers. I couldn't do their job any more than they could do mine.

I made sure to keep my speed to thirty miles an hour. The lights were timed perfectly on this stretch. If you went faster you'd usually catch one red light after another and end up spending more time waiting for greens than driving.

I reached Lake Shore Drive then turned south. It was just a few blocks to Mrs. J's building. The entrance was under an overhang, protecting the residents as they got in and out of cabs or cars (or ambulances). Most of the people in the building were very old. Few, if any drove their own cars. I actually had about half a dozen patients in the building, but most of my visits were to Mrs. Jeffries.

I stopped out front. The time on my dashboard display said 6:10 a.m. I was hoping I could just leave my car there for the twenty or thirty minutes I'd be upstairs visiting my benefactor. I clicked on my blinkers and grabbed my bags from the passenger seat, then headed for the revolving glass door.

Billy, the midnight to 8 a.m. doorman, was at the desk. "Dr. At, thank God you're here. The old lady has been calling down every five minutes," he said from behind the marble-topped counter that served as the reception area's desk and sign-in area. Just as he finished the phone on his desk chirped a very annoying electronic sound.

"That's her now," he said. He picked up the phone. He listened for just a moment before answering. "He just walked in, Mrs. Jeffries, he's on his way up." He smiled at me, pressed the buzzer that would unlock the door to the elevator lobby and started to hang up the phone.

"Can't leave that car out there," said another voice. We both turned and there was Henry, the building's janitor. He had a mop and bucket that were partially holding him up. "That's a fire lane. Can't leave the car there. And he needs to sign in," he added.

"The Doc has an emergency, Henry," Billy started to explain. "I'll watch his car."

"Watch it get towed," said Henry.

"I'll move it," I said, not anxious to try and find a parking spot at this time of the morning.

"Give me the keys," said Billy, I'll pull it in at the loading Dock." He glanced at a monitor on the desk that showed the feeds from several security cameras. "No one is there right now."

I handed him the keys. "Great." I picked up the pen attached to a chain cemented to the granite counter. I scribbled my shorthand signature at the top of the day's sign-in sheet. @@. The two leering eyes that I had adopted years ago.

My first name is Atticus. Only my mother calls me that. Everyone else calls me Atty. I had taken to using At for my last name, but that's a long story. Heck, this is a long book, I'll tell it now.

My real last name is Klammeraffe. It's German. In fact it is the German word for the @ symbol used in email addresses. It also means monkey tail, but I'm not about to call myself Dr. Monkey Tail. Once I discovered this fact, I shortened it. Legally I'm still Dr. Atticus Finch Klammeraffe, but to my friends I'm Atty, and to my patients, I'm Dr. At. I have joined the ranks of the monosyllabic doctoral elite including James Bond's archnemesis Dr. No, and the campy British Sci-Fi legend, Dr. Who.

My sister had it a little easier. My mother named her Harper Lee Klammeraffe. My mother is a "To Kill a Mockingbird" fan. We never figured out if it was the book or the movie. My father never used our full names. I was Attaboy and my sister was Harley, like the motorcycle. That was what we called each other as kids. I hated Attaboy. My sister loved Harley. My mother hated both.

I didn't hate my last name. I hated spelling it all the time. So for all practical purposes I was Dr. Atty At, hence the signature. I thought it was pretty cool.

I put down the pen. Henry returned to swabbing the marble lobby floor. Billy buzzed the door to the elevator lobby once more and as soon as I made my way into the air-locked area he was out the front door and into my car. I hoped I'd turned off the MP3 player. Not that I'm embarrassed about listening to Neil Diamond or Billy Joel or even the occasional Weird Al Yankovic, but some things are better left under the dusty covering of my mystique.

I pressed the call button for the elevator and one of the four doors opened almost immediately. I stepped in and pressed the button for twenty-three, pressed the close door button, then waited. I knew from experience that these elevators wouldn't be rushed. In fact, the building's management had the elevator company come in and slow their up and down movement. There were a lot of elderly folks in this condo and they were worried that the sudden starts and stops would cause them to lurch about; a tangle of brittle bones and walkers awaiting the next batch of elevator users in the lobby.

I guess part of the deal was to make sure the doors didn't close too quickly, crushing an unsuspecting tenant in the metal slabs. Of course it had the electric eye sensor to prevent that, but apparently they were of the philosophy that you couldn't be too careful.

I pressed the twenty-three button again and the close door button as well. I pressed it several times just to be sure. This was getting ridiculous. I started for the lobby, figuring this elevator was malfunctioning and as soon as I reached the threshold the doors started to close, immediately shuddered to a stop, then opened again.

Curse you, elevator. I thought of the villains Dr. Who had encountered on his travels through space and time and couldn't remember an evil elevator among them.

I pressed the buttons again and waited. And waited. I had an idea. "Well," I said out loud, "looks like this elevator isn't going anywhere. I better try another." I started for the door, but was careful to stop short of the sensor and the door started to close. I jumped back, a huge smile on my face. A small victory, but a victory nonetheless. My smile started to fade as the numbers for the floor lit up in a slow, slow steady pattern.

I'd often thought it might be quicker to walk up the twenty-two flights of stairs, but then I'd have to walk up twenty-two flights of stairs. Elevator one, Dr. At, zero.

Mrs. Jeffries was the only one of my clients to call me by my proper name. Most of them didn't know what it was, but it came out during one of our conversations and I explained the shortening. She told me it was silly and insisted on calling me by the German name from then on.

The elevator glided to a non-jarring stop and dinged. The doors slid open and I stepped out. "It's been a pleasure," I informed it. I looked to the left. One of the cream colored doors that lined the hallway cracked as far as the security chain would let it. I saw the silvery-blue of Mrs. Jeffries' hair and the pale white papery skin of her face before she closed the door and slid the chain off. I walked towards her condo and she had the door open as I arrived.

"Oh Dr. Klammeraffe, thank you so much for rushing over. Sheila told me how concerned you were and that you would be right over and here you are. I don't know what I'd do without you."

I smiled, but then realized that something was really wrong. Normally at this stage of my visit Darla would already be jumping around at my feet, waiting for me to unload my bags and scratch her fluffy orange ears. She was nowhere to be seen. I slipped my computer bag onto the plastic slip-covered chair by the door. All the furniture had plastic covers. My grandmother had those as well. They kind of defeated the whole purpose of furniture being comfortable.

I looked around the room for my patient.

"She's in the bedroom, Dr. Klammeraffe, on our bed. She seems to have no energy at all. She was fine last night. I gave her a bedtime snack, a few of those mini-marshmallows she loves, and she seemed just fine then." Mrs. Jeffries gave a little cough in to a lace handkerchief, "Excuse me," she added. I couldn't tell if the cough was to clear her emotionally tightened throat, the first signs of an upper respiratory disease, or one of her hypochondriacal symptoms.

"Lead on," I encouraged her. She took me into a narrow hallway, then into the bedroom. She stepped in and I followed her. The shades on the window were drawn. Two lamps on either side of the queen-sized bed gave a yellow glow to the room. On the bed covered partially by a sheet, was the orange fluff ball of Darla. She looked dead.

CHAPTER 2

I watched the still form for a moment then saw the covers moving slightly with her breathing. I instantly forgot all my whining and complaining up until then. This just wasn't right. I put my bag on the floor and sat on the bed next to Darla. I touched her forehead and stroked her lightly between her ears. They felt warm. Her face wasn't right, even in the dim light. Her eyes were mere slits. The fur on her face was sticking out, her muzzle swollen.

I pulled down the sheet and looked at the rest of her tiny body. Whatever it was seemed to only be affecting her head. She stirred a little as I opened my bag. She looked at me through her swollen eyelids and wagged her tail with what must have been a reserve of energy saved just for me. I pulled out my ear thermometer and slipped a cover onto it. I gently slid it into her left ear and pressed the button. A second later I was looking at a reading of 104.2, pretty high.

I was thinking it had to be some sort of allergic reaction. Facial edema due to histamine, maybe an insect bite or sting, but I was determined to do a full exam to make sure I didn't miss anything. The worst mistake any doctor could make was jumping to a conclusion and missing some vital finding.

Her heart rate was rapid, but her lungs were clear and there was no wheezing. The swelling hadn't progressed to her airways at this time. I palpated her lymph nodes. The ones under her jaw and in front of her shoulders were enlarged, but that was to be expected. I searched through the fur around her face looking for some sort of welt or bite mark. Nothing. When I pressed on the swollen skin around her face, the impression left by my finger took several seconds to disappear.

"Doctor Klammeraffe, what is happening with my Darla?" asked Mrs. J.

"You were right to call me," I said. "When did this start?"

"The swelling around her face was early this morning. It just seemed to come on suddenly. I then felt her ears and they were so warm."

"She does have a fever. I suspect it may be an allergic reaction. The swelling is due to edema. She may have been stung or bitten by something or perhaps stuck her face into something irritating. Can you think of anything that she might have gotten into in the last twenty-four hours or so?"

"We haven't left the building. We were in the atrium for her walk. I suppose she may have gotten into something there, but she never complained about anything."

"The atrium?" I asked.

"Yes, certainly you've seen it," she said.

Certainly I hadn't. I didn't even know there was one.

"Henry takes care of it. The inside apartments look over it. There's a large skylight as well. Very pleasant place, especially since Henry fixed it up. There are lots of plants. Henry has a green thumb, you know. He's helped me with my African Violets. Gave me some sort of fertilizer that got them blooming again. I suppose there could be insects in the atrium. Once in a while a bird finds its way in when the skylights are open in the summer."

That made sense. An indoor garden could have spiders, maybe even some wasps. "I'm going to treat her with some antihistamines and cortisone for the swelling and also some antibiotics for any possible secondary infection."

"Is she going to be alright?" asked a nervous Mrs. Jeffries.

"She should be, but call me if she gets worse. I'll stop by and check on her tonight. I wouldn't be surprised if Darla was all better by then."

"Oh, Dr. Klammeraffe, what would I do without you? You are a godsend. I knew you'd find the problem."

"Well, I can treat the symptoms just fine; as to the cause, I'll check out the atrium before I leave and see if I can see what she might have gotten into."

I pulled three vials from my bags and calculated the doses for some antihistamine, steroid, and antibiotic. I also took a small bottle of antihistamine tablets and filled out a label instructing Mrs. J to give Darla a dose every six hours, then gave Darla her injections.

"It might make her sleepy," I warned, "but watch her breathing. If there is any increase in her breathing rate or she is wheezing or gasping, call Sheila immediately. I can be here in ten to fifteen minutes." Part of me said I should just take Darla with me, maybe even transport her to the emergency clinic, but apart from the fever she was not in that bad of shape and for a dog, a temperature of 104 wasn't that bad. They could normally go up to 102.5. Well, it was bad in the sense it was a fever. "And give her fluids. Water, I mean," adding that in case Mrs. Jeffries' definition of fluids didn't match mine.

"Oh, Dr. Klammeraffe, thank you so much. I will watch her like a hawk. I'm sure she will be better now that you have come." She took my hand with hers. They were cold and dry and rough. A handkerchief was tucked into the sleeve of her dress. Ready for her next cough.

I petted Darla once more and watched her tail wag. She was still too weak to lift her head and give me one of her licks, but I suspected that by tonight she would be back to her normal self. I would have to remember to have Sheila add her to my schedule. Not that I would forget, but I didn't want Sheila double-booking me with another emergency.

I loaded my bag and went back into the living room. I took out my laptop and typed up my notes and my bill. Mrs. Jeffries never complained about my bill. The closest she ever came was asking if it wasn't too low. I assured her it wasn't. I handed her the invoice and she went to her purse, sitting on the dining table and pulled out her tiny change purse. She pulled out a tightly folded wad of bills and peeled off the exact amount. Cash was nice.

"Thank you again," she said.

"No problem," I said. It was a problem, but as far as problems go, not a big one. Darla really had been sick. Who'd have thunk it?

Mrs. Jeffries showed me out and remained standing in the doorway until the elevator cab finally arrived for me. A smile and a wave preceded her departure and a cough that was mild in comparison to Mrs. Hornby, but still significant. I was sure she headed straight for Darla's side, probably after putting on a kettle for tea.

The elevator ride down was twice as long as I picked up two passengers. An elderly gentleman with a bouquet of daisies got on at eighteen and off at eight. An early morning booty call? Way to go. Another man in a dark overcoat and dark felt hat carrying a flute case got on at fifteen and made the entire trip to the lobby with me. Neither spoke to me or each other. Neither seemed to mind the slowness of the ride.

When I got to the lobby I allowed the flautist to leave first. A taxi was waiting for him where my car had been parked and Billy was ready and waiting to hold the door for him.

I looked around to see if Henry was still around. I wanted to check out the atrium to see if there was anything Darla could have gotten into, but mostly because it really had my curiosity tingling.

Billy returned and stepped behind his marble counter. "Want me to bring the car around, Doc?" he asked.

"Sure, that would be great," I said. "Have you seen Henry?"

"I think he went into the atrium," said Billy. He pointed at a metal door down the hall. "Be back in a few," he said, snatching my key chain from the desk and heading back into the building, presumably to a service entrance.

I stashed my bags behind the counter and headed for the door Billy had indicated. I had probably seen it dozens of times, if not a hundred, but never knew it hid an entire atrium. I tried the knob then stepped through. I felt like the kids entering Willy Wonka's chocolate factory. The early morning light was beginning to lighten the skylights thirty floors above. The top floors of windows on the west side were starting to get some of the light. The sound of running water drew my attention down to a fountain in the center of a magnificent courtyard. I was standing on a cobblestone path. Lush green vegetation punctuated by blooms of all colors and shades surrounded me. The fountain in the center was a topless mermaid holding up half a scallop shell, water dripping over the edges and showering her. Four fish in the corners spurted streams of water on her body as well. In the pond I saw flashes of orange, gold, and white as giant koi swam amongst colorful lily pads in bloom.

I started walking around the path surrounding the fountain. Benches were tucked in among the flowers and shrubs. There were even some trees reaching up twenty or thirty feet to accent the landscaping. I saw a man hunched over a rose bush, pruning shears in one hand, a collection of dried buds in the other. "Henry," I said, "this is amazing."

I expected some sort of rebuke. A reprimand that this area was for residents only. He stood slowly and tossed the buds onto the soil. "Dr. At. Thought you'd be gone by now."

"I wanted to check this place out. I thought Darla might have gotten into something around here. She had some sort of allergic reaction."

"That little orange thing?"

"Yeah. The pom," I added.

"That thing is all over this place. But Mrs. Jeffries always picks up after her. Contrary to popular belief, dog poop is not that great a fertilizer."

"Any spiders or wasps or bees around?"

"Spiders all over, but I haven't seen any wasps or bees. They get in in the summer, but so far no nests."

I nodded. A spider bite could cause significant tissue damage, but that might not show up for a few days.

"You did all this?" I asked.

"Part of the reason I took the job. I used to work at the Garfield Park Conservatory as a botanist. City made me retire at sixty-five. This place was a wreck. All the plants dead. The fountain pump was clogged up. Mice and rats all over. No one came in here. I insisted on being able to maintain this as part of my position as maintenance engineer. Well, janitor, I suppose."

I smiled at the self-deprecating joke. I considered Henry's work with plants. In a way we were a lot alike. We had to diagnose our patients without being able to talk with them. We observed symptoms and relied on our experience to prescribe the proper treatment. The only difference was if Henry lost a patient, he just bought a new plant. For me, they were members of the family.

"Mrs. Jeffries mentioned that you helped her with her violets," I remembered.

"Yup. They had stopped blooming on her. Sounded like they needed a little calcium and phosphorus. I had an old bag of bone meal and gave her a little. She told me they've been putting out blossoms like crazy."

"Well, thanks for letting me take a look," I said. "I really should go." I was starting to realize how tired I was. It was probably the promise of another hour of sleep more than actual fatigue that was the cause.

"Any time, Doc," answered Henry. He returned to his gardening.

I walked back out to the lobby then picked up my bags from behind the reception desk. Billy had just poured a steaming cup of coffee from his thermos into the tiny cup that doubled as a cover. Just the aroma erased some of my tiredness.

"Did you know Henry was a horticulturist?" I asked.

"Hadn't heard that. Live and let live, I say. But he sure is good with plants." Part of me didn't want to know what Billy thought I was talking about. "We're always getting compliments on the atrium. I think that's why the board wants to keep him happy. He's really not a bad guy, just a stickler for the rules." He took a sip of his coffee.

Just then my phone chirped. I pulled it out and read Sheila on the caller ID. The phone was also kind enough to display the time. 6:45 a.m. She probably just wanted to check and see how Darla was. I let it go to voice mail. I'd call her back when I got home and in my bed. She could wait a few minutes.

My keys were on the counter and the car was sitting in the fire lane, blinking its apology to any fire trucks that might show up before I got to it. I slipped my phone into my inside coat pocket and picked up my gear. "Thanks again, Billy."

"No problem. It'll be nice not to have her calling down every five minutes. I like her, she tips nice at Christmas." I smiled then headed for the door. He popped up and ran in front of me to hold the door.

I opened the rear hatch of the Escape, stowed my equipment, and then hopped into the front seat. I found myself thinking about Billy's coffee. Then I thought about what would go great with a cup of coffee. That was enough incentive for my hunger to surpass my exhaustion and I decided on a better use of my time before starting my "regular" day. I pulled out onto the street, and headed south on Marine Drive.

My phone chirped again. I hated this. I refused to be a person who drove and talked, even with one of those blue tooth thingies you could stick in your ear. I turned right onto a side street and found a parking space that I could actually squeeze my car into. Fortunately it was late enough in the morning for a few people to start giving up their treasured fifteen-foot parcels of temporary real estate to head for work. Around 4 p.m. they would start filling up again.

In winter, many of these spots, carefully shoveled out and salted to de-ice them, would be blocked off with brooms laid across the seats of a couple of chrome kitchen chairs. While this was technically "illegal", Chicago parking etiquette demanded that you respect "dibs" or risk an angry resident covering your car with a layer of ice sprayed on with a garden hose as your penalty.

The phone had stopped ringing, but there were two missed calls. Both from Sheila. I growled. It was going to be easier just to call her now rather than shudder every time the phone rang. I pressed 1 to speed dial Sheila.

"Atty, how is Darla?" she asked.

"She's got a face like a Shar-Pei, but I think she'll pull through."

"What happened?"

"I think she was stung by a bee."

"On the twenty-third floor?"

"Well, more likely outside or in the atrium."

"Oh, Henry's garden. That would make sense."

"You know about Henry's garden?"

"Hey, I talk to Mrs. Jeffries as much as you do. More probably. I know things." she explained.

"I need to squeeze in a recheck for her this afternoon."

"No problem, I'll update your schedule," she answered.

Then there was silence. An uncomfortable silence. I recognized that silence. Sheila had many silences I had come to recognize over the years. "Something else you want to tell me?" I asked cautiously.

"Uh, now that you ask..." She tricked me. Darn.

"No, Sheila. It's not even seven o'clock."

"Atty, take a deep breath."

"Not a deep breath one," I muttered. Whenever "now that you ask" was accompanied by "take a deep breath" it meant I wasn't going to like it.

"Breathe."

I knew she would wait until I breathed, so I sighed loudly into my phone.

"You have another emergency," she said. A pause. "Breathe."

I wasn't going to satisfy her this time. "What?" I asked. My voice whined. It even annoyed me. Normally I don't mind an occasional emergency. I charge extra for emergency calls. They're usually not as bad as I think and rarely do I need to take them in to the emergency clinic for further care or surgery. "It's still before eight. Can't they go to the emergency clinic?"

"Technically, you are their emergency doctor."

That didn't make any sense, unless . . .

When some of my clients boarded their pets, they left my information with the kennel as the emergency doctor. The few times I had been called by kennels about a boarding patient it was during regular office hours. I groaned. "Which one?" I asked.

"The Bark and Breakfast," she answered. "Peanuts Johnson is staying there while his family is on vacation."

I cringed. "Did he get out?" I asked. A couple of years ago several dogs had escaped the kennel, one was sideswiped by a car, fortunately with no serious injuries.

"No, nothing like that. They said he's sick and won't come out of his kennel."

That didn't sound like Peanuts. That little beagle loved people. Even slightly overweight vets with needles didn't phase him. "How long?" I asked.

"A couple of days, Betty claims."

"Why didn't they call a couple of days ago?" I asked. The question was rhetorical. The first rule of sick pets was owners never called when they needed to, Mrs. Jeffries aside. They waited to see if it would get better on its own.

"You'll have to ask Betty," Sheila answered. Betty and Kirby Cunningham were a brother and sister duo that ran the kennel. Kirby was a genuine dog lover and wanted to provide a nice place for dogs to stay, Betty was a business woman who got her way more often than not.

"Why now? I mean, it's still early. Why not wait until 8 o'clock to call like a normal client. It doesn't sound like a critical emergency."

"She said that she wanted to make sure you knew about it. I think she just wants to pass on the responsibility to you. I guess normally I'd have waited to let you know, maybe squeezed it in early this afternoon, but since you're up and they're almost on your way home . . ."

"Who said I was going home?"

"Atty Klammeraffe passing up a few minutes of extra sleep?"

"My stomach made a better offer and my tired brain made a deal for an extra dose of caffeine."

Sheila was silent for a moment. "So," she started tentatively, "you're going to stop at the Meli Juice bar for half a grapefruit and yogurt with granola?" The hope in her voice was sincere yet strained.

"I was thinking that my early morning heroics and sacrifice deserve a trip to Danny's." More silence. "Sheila, you still there?"

"Danny's?" It was her turn to whine.

"It's on the way to the Barf and Breakfast."

"That's Bark and Breakfast. Danny's should be called the Barf and Breakfast."

"What's wrong with Danny's?"

"Nothing, if you want to listen to your arteries clog and poison yourself with chemicals and caffeine."

"You make it sound so good," I teased.

"Atty," she complained, "That place is not good for you."

"Well, if you wanted to make me some granola and grapefruit, I could be at your place in no time," I taunted.

"You're not going to get to me that easily," she added.

"You'd rather see me corrode my arteries and rot out my liver, eh?"

"I'd rather see you eat a banana and yogurt."

"After this morning and in the interest of fortifying myself for a visit to the Cunninghams, I deserve one of Danny's 4-by-4 breakfasts."

"4-by-4?"

"Four eggs, four slices of bacon, four sausage links, and four deep-fried hash brown patties. A transfusion of some of Carla's coffee and I'll be ready for the whatever Bark and Breakfast has to offer. Allow me my simple pleasures," I pleaded.

She sighed. "Just get there as soon as possible."

"Aye, aye, Captain." She made a raspberry sound over the phone and hung up. I was sure she wasn't really mad, but it was nice to know she cared.

CHAPTER 3

I pulled out of my parking space with mixed feelings. It was a good parking spot with a driveway in front so I could just pull out. But I had no use for it. Easy come, easy go. I headed west then south. Danny's was on Irving Park Road in the first floor of a corner office building. The street was populated with parking meters. They had yet to be replaced with the new pay machines in the center of the block that made you put this little receipt in your window. Don't even get me started with the rates for parking. Thankfully, if there was a place worth the confiscatory parking rates of privatized parking meters, it was Danny's.

There was an empty spot just down from the diner. I pulled in and grabbed a quarter from the tray in the center console. I stepped out and was greeted by the aroma of Danny's grill, even through the plate glass windows that showed off the entire diner to any passers-by. I was about to feed the meter and noticed there was still forty-six minutes left on the display. I pocketed my quarter and smiled. It was an omen. This was definitely the right decision.

Carla, Danny's fixture of a waitress, saw me through the window and gave me a nod as I headed for the door. She stuck a pencil into her beehive hairdo then pulled out one of the large coffee mugs from under the counter. She grabbed one of the coffee pots from behind her and filled it to the rim with the steaming brew.

I pushed in through the front door and slipped off my coat. I hung it on the coat rack by the door before sliding comfortably onto the chrome stool with red vinyl seat cushion.

Yogurt and bananas tomorrow, pork and eggs today. At the far end of the grill Danny stood tending to a pile of food on the flat iron griddle. His spatula constantly pushing and flipping the eggs, sausages, and bacon until they were cooked to perfection; the eggs runny within a hairsbreadth of Salmonella; the bacon just on the edge of crispiness, dripping with the delicious, deadly trans-fats that would make Sheila faint; the sausages popping and sputtering in their own grease, browned to perfection.

To his right was the deep fat fryer. Just saying those words made my mouth water. Its job in the morning hours was to cook up the disks of shredded potatoes. After eleven o'clock, french fries took their place. I wondered if it was the same batch of fat that had been used for years, a carefully crafted mixture that could never be duplicated if the machine were to be emptied and cleaned.

To the right of the fryer were three coffee machines that were constantly brewing Carla's contribution to Danny's cuisine. There were stories about her coffee. About how some people bought it by the gallon to use as a safe and environmentally friendly paint remover. Then there was the embalmer at Weinstein's Funeral Home who accidentally spilled some on a corpse. The body jerked as if coming to life, causing the frightened mortician to run screaming from the back room.

Of the three machines, one of the pitchers had an orange top that signified decaf. I suspected that it wasn't really as advertised. I'd seen her fill all three machines from the same can of grounds. When customers asked for decaf, they got the same coffee as everyone else. They probably knew it wasn't decaf. Just a harmless self-deception.

I wrapped my hands around the large mug, letting it warm me by induction and letting its vapors diffuse into my nasal membranes, a direct path to my brain. I refused to taint the coffee with sugar or cream, well, the cream-like substance that came in tiny plastic cups in a bowl on the counter. I had once made the mistake of checking the expiration date of one of the packages. The length of time that had lapsed since its suggested use-by date corresponded to the life span of some of my patients.

"The usual?" asked Carla, her order pad poised in front of her as she pulled the pencil from her heavily sprayed hair condo. Her hand unerringly found the writing implement as though it was a part of her body. I liked that she asked. It was kind of neat to have a "usual."

"4-by-4," I confirmed.

"Four fours," she shouted over her shoulder to Danny. Danny

pulled the eggs from a carton, two in each hand. He cracked them simultaneously and let them drop onto the middle of the griddle, their translucent whites immediately congealing into irregular circles of cholesterol laden protein.

A few swipes of his spatula and he had them neatened up into four piles of sunny-side up delight. Next he pulled the sausages and bacon from their bins, laying them sputtering on the flat grill, steam and smoke sucked into the giant sheet metal hood.

The fryer beeped, announcing that a batch of deep-fried hash brown disks were ready. He pulled the basket from the fryer, shook off only a fraction of the grease, dumped it into the serving bin and showered them liberally from a large canister of salt.

While Danny responded to the name "Danny" and the place was named Danny's, it seemed that he was too young to have been the original owner of the diner. I often wondered if he just inherited the name with the diner when he took over. For that matter, Carla may just have inherited the name tag with "Carla" written on it and perhaps her real name was Juliet or Sonia. I decided that it really didn't make a difference. They were part of the experience that was Danny's; the décor, the food, the people, the conversation or lack of any. No Burger King or McDonald's could ever hope to come close.

Danny pulled a plate from a shelf above the grill and slipped a pile of pancakes along with a few slices of bacon and a smaller plate of scrambled eggs onto it. It was headed for a customer at the other end of the counter. My stomach was jealous. I sipped coffee thick enough to be a meal on its own.

A couple entered, setting the bell above the front door jingling. They took a booth and Carla lifted the section of counter that allowed her to leave the confines of the counter-grill area grabbing a few menus and a pot of coffee as she stepped over to their table. She gave them a smile with their cups full of coffee as they pondered the choices before them. Not a bowl of oatmeal or grapefruit among them.

She returned topping off my mug before slipping the coffee pot back into its slot. "You're in early today, Doc," she said.

"I had an emergency," I explained. Glancing at my watch it was 7:05 a.m. "On my way to another. Just need to get refueled for the demanding world of veterinary medicine."

"You know, I wanted to be a vet at one point. I loved horses, anything to do with them. When I went to the high school counselor and he looked at my grades I could have sworn he laughed."

"That's too bad." I stared down the grill. My meal looked almost ready.

"Ah, it turned out for the best. Married a trucker. He makes good money, is gone five days a week. After two days with him around I'm usually ready to kill him, but by the time the weekend rolls around, I'm beginning to miss him."

I noticed the customer at the end of the counter glancing my way more than he needed to. I mentioned my unfortunate resemblance to the actor, Oliver Platt, famous for his roles in *Flatliners*, *The Three Musketeers*, *The Imposters* (my personal favorite), *Bicentennial Man*, and many others. He also had a short-lived television series called *Deadlines* and appeared in *The West Wing*. As a result, there were quite a few people who knew who he was and confused me for the genuine article.

The diner took a sip from his cup and made his move. He slid off the stool and walked toward me. He stood by my shoulder. "You're him, aren't you?" he asked. Carla chuckled and headed over to take the order from the couple in the booth. She'd seen this happen before and I think secretly got a kick out of it.

"I'm me," I confirmed. I found that if I creatively answered the questions that the people who confused me with Oliver asked, I never had to lie.

"I knew it," he said. "My wife is never going to believe me."

"Are you a fan?" I asked.

"Are you kidding? Our favorite is "The Ice Harvest". It is hilarious. We have it on DVD." I had seen the movie. Oliver was pretty funny in it.

"I like that movie too." Once again, the answer, while not a lie, did nothing to dissuade my fan's misidentification.

"My name is Arnie, Mr. Platt."

I took his outstretched hand. "Call me Ollie." Why not.

"Are you working on a movie here in Chicago?" he asked.

"Yeah, a remake of Charlie Chan." I squinted my eyes to convey an Asian appearance and did my best, "Ah, so."

"Wow," he said. "They'll remake anything these days."

"Tell me about it."

"Um," he said with a little hesitation. I know what was coming and motioned for Carla to come over. "Could I trouble you for an autograph?"

"Sure." Carla tore a blank order sheet from the top of her pad. I pulled a pen from my jacket pocket.

"Can you make it to Arnie and Emily?" I scribbled a signature with a recognizable O in the first word and P in the second following the inscription, "to my friends, Arnie and Emily." I handed it back to the Platt-ophile.

"Thank you," he said. "My wife will never believe this."

Not if she has any brains, I thought. He walked back to his stool. He sat down, waved his trophy and smiled.

Danny walked over with a large white plate heaped with my breakfast. "I don't think you look anything like him," he said.

"Bless you, Danny. That's the nicest thing anyone has said to me today."

"I'm talking about Charlie Chan. You're a dead ringer for Platt." He wiped his hands on a greased stained towel tucked into his apron then returned to the grill.

"Don't you ever feel bad about doing that to people?" asked Carla.

"If I have to look like him, he owes me a little fun," I explained.

"I doubt he sees it that way. And what makes you think they'd cast him as Charlie Chan?"

"Who would you like to see in the role?"

"Leonardo DiCaprio," she answered with hardly a moment for consideration.

"Leonardo DiCaprio?"

"Hey, I got a soft spot for him."

"He'd be a terrible Charlie Chan."

"Yeah, but he's so cute."

Couldn't argue with that. I dug into my plate of ambrosia.

Fifteen minutes later I settled my check with a large tip after finishing my third cup of paint-thinning corpse-reviving brew. The diner was starting to get busy. I sighed, slipped my coat off the rack and headed outside with a wave to Danny and Carla. I dreaded my trip to the Bark and Breakfast. I was feeling much better with my own breakfast in me, but I still dreaded it.

The kennel was a mile south near Belmont and Lincoln Avenue. I made it there in about ten minutes. The traffic was beginning to get as thick as Carla's coffee. I hated driving during rush hour. Actually, it was more like rush three hours. From six-thirty to nine-thirty everything slowed down. My car was still playing Neil Diamond. "Ain't No Sunshine" was up. Perfect for my mood.

A few minutes later I pulled to the back of the kennel's building and slipped into one of the spots reserved for their customers and employees. At the back door Betty Cunningham was just making her way back into the building with three dogs on leashes. She stopped to drop several blue plastic bags into a can near the rear entrance. She saw me as I got out. "Dr. At. So nice of you to show up. I called about half an hour ago."

"Traffic," I explained not wanting to remind her that the dog had not been doing well for days at this point.

"Come on in," she said, dragging her three charges behind her. I followed. The racket from the barking and the smell from the kennels hit me like a migraine. "Pete" she yelled, her voice penetrating the din like a police siren. "The doctor's here."

A teenage boy appeared, a Cubs cap covering his long blond hair and he wiped at a runny nose with a stained cloth of his long-sleeved t-shirt. "I still got to feed the dogs in the VIP suites," he whined.

"Take Dr. At to see Peanuts Johnson."

"That beagle that hasn't been eating?" he asked.

"That's the one," she answered.

I got most of the conversation over the barking. Part of it was lip reading. I followed the kennel worker to another section of the "pet motel."

As we left the main section and the door closed after us, the noise was attenuated to a tolerable level. "This way," directed Pete.

There were two levels of cages in this room, the top filled with small dogs, the bottom cages were twice as wide and accommodated the larger pets. Peanuts' "room" was at the far end on the top. Pete opened up the latch and pushed at the bowl full of kibble near Peanuts' head. "Breakfast, doggie," he said.

I looked at Peanuts for a moment, then at Pete. "Has Betty seen this dog?" I asked.

"Sure, I tell her about all the animals that aren't eating."

"I assume he hasn't been getting out for walks either," I said after doing my initial assessment of his condition.

"Naw, he doesn't want to get up," said Pete.

GIVE A DOG A BONE

It didn't surprise me at all.
Peanuts was dead.

CHAPTER 4

I didn't know what to say. If I could tell the dog was dead standing six feet away, I wondered what was going through the heads of the people working here. They probably figured it was less work if the boarders didn't want to partake in an occasional meal or walk.

"Is he sick?" asked Pete. "I've been giving him his pills, at least when he was eating," he added.

Peanuts had been on a thyroid hormone supplement. Even if he had been off it for a few days, he wouldn't end up like this. I could feel a blast of sarcasm, totally inappropriate for the situation forcing its way out of my brain. "Gee, let me see, dog not moving in cage. What do you think?" I asked.

"Yes?" Pete answered, more of a question than a statement. He was starting to edge away from me. I made a low growling noise in the back of my throat. "Has he even moved in the last couple of days?"

Pete looked back at the corpse in the cage and squinted a little, overclocking what few brain cells he had to their maximum tolerances. "Not really," he decided.

I reached into the cage and lifted a limp leg and let it drop. The rest of Peanuts body remained stationary.

"That can't be good," Pete summed up.

"Ya think?" I wasn't sure if my demonstration had sunk in. "Um, he's dead," I expounded.

Pete jumped back, as if Peanuts had just become contagious with Ebola. "You're kidding me," he said. Obviously the thought had never entered his mind.

"Afraid not, and by the look..." I took a brief whiff of the inside of the cage, "...and the smell of things, he's been this way for two or three days. He's well past the rigor mortis stage. You really mean to tell me you had no idea?"

"It's not like we have dogs die here every day," Pete said in his own defense.

"How would you know?" I asked with exasperation.

Pete stepped a little closer, peering around me into the cage. "How did he die?" he asked. "Could it have been suicide?"

I turned to look at Pete and confirm the serious look on his face. Where did Betty find these kids?

"Well," I answered, "I don't see a note."

"They can write notes?" he asked.

Way too easy. "Go get Betty or Kirby," I directed, holding in my frustration and desire to pop him a good one on the back of his head. The boy turned with a shrug and let in a brief spasm of canine noise before closing the door behind him. I opened my medical bag and pulled out a pair of rubber gloves. Careful to breathe only through my mouth, I started to examine the little beagle.

Despite his hypothyroidism, Peanuts had been one of my "no problems" patients. I'd see him in the spring for his annual check up, thyroid test, heartworm preventative, and vaccines. Then again in the fall to recheck his thyroid hormone levels. Like most beagles, he was a barker. That loud, high-pitched, piercing bark that cuts through your head like a knife. But he was excellent with the Johnson's three children, allowing himself to be dressed up, carried around, and have his tail pulled without even baring his teeth.

I looked in the mouth first. Nothing obvious there. His airway appeared fine, but I could only see to the front of the larynx with my penlight.

I palpated along his neck and body, trying to see if there were any enlarged lymph nodes or other growths that had appeared since his last physical. It was all normal. I put my hand around his abdomen, feeling for anything abnormal. It felt squishy. Not the best medical term, but it was an adequate description. Undoubtedly there was some fluid in the belly. I pulled a ten-cc syringe from my bag and attached a large bore needle to the end. I then inserted in below the navel and aspirated. Instead of the negative suction that usually occurred with a normal belly tap, I ended up sucking out a syringe full of reddish-brown fluid.

"Yuck," said a voice from behind me. I turned to see Betty Cunningham staring over my shoulder. "Is he really dead?"

I capped the needle and put the syringe in a plastic lab bag then tucked it into my medical bag. "Why didn't you call me when you first noticed he wasn't doing well?" I asked.

"Why? Lots of dogs just mope around. They're depressed that they're not with their owners. We're busy here, we can't do a physical exam on every dog every day."

"I'm not talking about a physical. The dog has been lying here, decomposing for the last two or three days."

"That's your opinion," answered Betty. "When I called your girl this morning, he was probably still alive. It took you forever to get here."

I almost started to defend myself, but realized it was wasted on this woman. "Was he vomiting?" I asked.

"I'd have to check with Pete." Great, the kid who had been trying feed a dead dog for two days and was relieved when it didn't want to go out for walks.

"Do you have a phone number for the Johnsons? I need their permission for a postmortem exam."

"I'm sure it wasn't anything we did. I can't help it if people bring sick and dying dogs here. The thing was on medication."

"Thyroid supplement for his hypothyroidism. Hardly a life threatening condition. I'm pretty sure the Johnsons wouldn't have left Peanuts here if he was sick."

"Listen, you don't know how he died so you better keep your mouth shut. My nephew is a lawyer and we'll sue you so fast your head will spin."

That seemed a pretty severe reaction. I would expect a concerned kennel operator to want to know what happened to a dog in their care. Then again, we're talking about Betty Cunningham.

"Besides," she continued, "we have medical care responsibility while the pet is here. I'll call the Johnsons and Happy Acres. Send us your bill, if you think it's worth charging us just to say he's dead."

I was dumbstruck. I don't think I ever truly understood the meaning of that word until then. "You can't just have him cremated without a necropsy. We need to find out why he died. What if there is an infection? Something that may affect other pets here?"

"No other dogs are sick," she said. "For all I know, this dog died ten minutes ago. If you had come when I had called maybe he would have lived."

"You've got to be kidding me. Take a whiff in that cage and tell me he's been dead for ten minutes," I dared her.

She remained still. "I don't need to," she said.

I looked at her. Her sense of righteousness transcended reality. My mouth moved, but no words came out. I looked back at Peanuts. Poor dog likely didn't deserve to die like this. Alone, surrounded by dozens of barking dogs and indifferent staff.

I closed up my bag, making sure the syringe of abdominal effusion was still there. I'd have Sheila track down the Johnsons. They could ask Happy Acres to hold the body for me.

I made my way out the way I had come in. My appearance in the next room set off another round of barking and yipping. I started out trying to ignore it, but the morning was conspiring against me and even the sustenance I had ingested at Danny's couldn't diminish the headache that was brewing between my eyeballs. I stopped in the middle of the room and as loudly as I could I yelled, "QUIET!"

The silence was instant and profound. Dozens of pairs of canine eyes stared at me, confused. It was as if no one had ever asked them to stop barking before and their first instinct was to obey. Pete stood at the opposite end of the room, his jaw hanging open, apparently amazed at the effect I had. I walked over to him and reached into my inside jacket pocket, pulling out one of my business cards. I kept a few in there with my cell phone number written on the back. I handed it to him. "If Betty changes her mind, have her give me a call at the number on the back," I told him. He took the card numbly. His mouth was open and his gaze was slowly taking in the ranks of attentive dogs standing patiently at their kennel doors, presumably waiting to see what I was going to do next. I rolled my eyes. I was so glad I stopped at Danny's first. I continued to the back door, the silence persisting until I was out in the parking lot.

As the back door closed the spell ended. Barking broke out like a prison riot after the inmates were told that the television would not be on during the Jerry Springer show. I could hear Pete's voice among the din yelling his own "quiet." It had no effect. Forget the dog whisperer. I am the dog screamer.

I put my bags in the back of my Escape and speed dialed "1." If Sheila was going to keep ruining my morning, I was going to make sure she didn't get any rest either.

"What's up with Peanuts?" she asked in place of hello. Curse caller ID.

"Dead," I said.

"Dead?"

"For at least two or three days," I continued.

"And they were just calling you about it?" she asked.

"They didn't know he was dead."

There was silence on the other end.

"Listen, I need to try and get hold of the Johnsons. They're out of town, but maybe you can track them down for me."

"I'll give it a try. Can't you get the emergency number from Bark and Breakfast?"

"They won't give it to me."

"Why not?"

"They're afraid I'll do a necropsy, find out how he died, and blame them. They've already threatened to sue me."

"For what?"

"Exactly." It was beginning to sound like an Abbot and Costello routine.

"I don't think you should let your patients board there anymore."

"I've never recommended the place, but this is the first time that Betty Cunningham has turned so nasty. Kirby wasn't there. He'd probably be on my side."

"Okay, I'll work on it. Where are you going?"

I glanced at my watch. It was now seven forty-five. I'd been out for nearly two hours when I would normally just be waking up. "I'm going to head home. With luck I can get there in less than half an hour, get a little beauty sleep in and get ready for my regular day."

"Good thing you don't start until ten today," she added.

"But if Mrs. Jeffries calls, or you get hold of the Johnsons, call me right away."

"You won't bite my head off?" she asked cautiously.

"Depends on what I'm dreaming of. If Meg Ryan makes an appearance you'll be in trouble."

"Which movie?"

"Joe vs. the Volcano".

"You are a sick man, Atty."

"You want to be my nurse?"

"Give me five minutes before you take off. I want to see If I can get the Johnsons now. I'd hate to think that Betty would get away with killing him if it was their fault."

"Roger."

"How was breakfast?" she added.

"Heavenly," I answered.

"At least one step closer," she sneered. "Bye."

"Bye." I start to put my bags in the back of the Escape when I heard the Bark and Breakfast's back door open, accompanied by a crescendo of plaintive wails. Pete stumbled out with a cardboard box. On the side it claimed to be a Home Theater Blu-Ray Player of some brand I didn't recognize. He put it on top of one of the dumpsters in the alley then headed back in.

The proverbial light bulb lit over my head. It couldn't be this easy. I walked over to the dumpster and unfolded the tucked flaps of the top. Inside was a white plastic garbage bag. On top of the bag was my business card. The odor was muted by the plastic, but the form confirmed that it was the remains of my late patient, Peanuts. I folded the top closed again quickly and placed the box next to my supplies in the back of the Escape. I jumped into the driver's side and started the car up feeling more like a thief than a vet. Gravel spun under my wheels as I backed out quickly, hoping that no one would come out of the Bark and Breakfast to correct their oversight. I drove a half mile northwest on Lincoln Avenue before feeling comfortable enough to pull over and get out my cell phone.

I speed-dialed Sheila. She picked up before the ring even finished. "Atty? What is it?"

"Did you get in contact with the Johnsons?"

"Their answering machine was on. Hopefully they'll check in today."

"I got Peanuts," I told her.

"What? How? I thought they threatened to sue you if you did an autopsy."

"Necropsy. They put him in a box and left him on the dumpster as I was leaving."

"Eww."

"Eww, but good. I've got an airtight cooler at home. I'll pack him with some ice and when the Johnsons call back I'll get my necropsy."

"Do you think the Cunninghams killed him?"

"I don't think so, but he was a healthy dog and his abdomen had some ugly fluid in it. Probably peritonitis. It would be nice to know what happened. His thyroid hormones were perfect on his supplement, but even if they skipped a few doses, that wouldn't cause this to happen."

"Well, I'll let you know when they call back."

"Great."

I hung up and pulled back onto Lincoln. Even if the Cunninghams noticed that Peanuts had gone missing, they had no way to know that I took him. It could have been some ally pickers.

If you have something in your garbage that has any value, these guys would take it. It wouldn't be more than an hour before one of them drove by in their beat-up pickup trucks. The truck beds were modified with two-by-fours and sheets of plywood to extend the sides up eight feet or so. They could then load the truck up with old appliances, bicycles, metal chairs, window blinds, scraps of pipe and wire; anything they found useful or saleable to a scrap dealer.

I dreaded ending up behind one of these trucks on a main street. When they were fully loaded, the suspensions were stressed to their limit, the truck's bottom scraping the pavement with every pothole. The backs were often laced with rope in an effort to keep the file cabinets, old toilets, folding tables, even old computers, from falling out. It always looked like one good jolt could send a cascade of junk onto an unsuspecting driver behind them.

They had a good eye for what they wanted. They could speed along the alleys at twenty to thirty miles an hour, honking their horns when they reached a street to let any unsuspecting cars or pedestrians know they were crossing to the next alley. I always wondered what happened to the trucks with all the abuse they were put through. Perhaps they were also turned into scrap after a few months or a year of torture. The fact that these entrepreneurs could make a living picking through the garbage amazed me. If there was a niche, it would be filled, just like my own business.

I had started out working at a veterinary practice on the south side. I was fresh out of vet school, naive, hopeful, and ready to start saving lives. I interviewed at three practices in the Chicago area. At the time my mother still lived in the area. My sister Harley still does. I had three job offers and decided to go with New Vision Animal Hospital in the Beverly neighborhood of Chicago. I was promised the moon and instead given a piece of American cheese, or rather the pasteurized processed cheese food that came in those individual plastic wrappers that weren't really cheese, but made awesome grilled cheese-food sandwiches in college.

Dr. Bender, my new boss, quickly made me aware that his "new vision" happened twenty years before and he was much more interested in using the profits to buy escorts and fancy cars, rather than the new digital x-ray machine and surgical equipment he had assured me was coming on a monthly basis. After six months, I had seen the light. I gave him two months notice as per our contract. He didn't take it well and gave me two minutes to clear my stuff out. I didn't argue. The thought of spending another two months there horrified me. As a concession he waived the non-competition clause in the contract, allowing me to seek employment in the neighborhood if I wanted.

I set up interviews and during the course of my visits with various practices, many of them very nice, some even shabbier than New Vision, I found there was a huge demand for temporary help. Relief veterinarian they called it. Basically, a lot of solo practitioners needed someone to babysit the practice while they went on vacation. I was quickly making twice as much money as I had with Dr. Bender and working half as hard. Vets paid good money just to have a warm body in the clinic while they were gone.

At the same time, a few of my clients from New Vision tracked me down and I started seeing their pets in their homes. It was an education learning the business side of veterinary medicine on the run. They didn't teach that in vet school and working for Dr. Bender I wasn't involved in setting fees or paying suppliers.

I bought a second hand laptop, got a bare bones software package to write up invoices and keep medical records and printed up a thousand business cards.

I took off more quickly than expected. Within two years I dropped the relief work altogether and concentrated on the house call practice. It was the perfect way for me to practice. I didn't have the overhead of a brick and mortar practice, so I didn't have to see as many clients per hour as my colleagues. I could charge a premium for my service and keep the hours I wanted.

I reached Montrose when my cell phone chirped again. "I'm almost home," I moaned. I pulled over and checked the caller ID. It was Sheila. Maybe she had news on the Johnsons.

I had often debated the benefits of getting an earpiece for my phone, maybe even one of those wireless things that clipped over the ear. But the thought of people seeing me talk to myself driving down the road was a bit disconcerting. Plus I didn't always trust myself to be able to concentrate on a conversation and drive at the same time.

I tapped the answer button on the screen and put the block of black plastic and glass to my ear. "You found them?" I asked as a way of greeting.

"Um, no. Haven't heard from the Johnsons yet. I assume that's what you meant. Hello to you too."

"Hello, my sweet," I added. "Then what?" I asked. My heart began to sink in my chest. That wasn't just an expression. I could feel it get heavier. "Sheila, no," I begged.

"Atty, you know I wouldn't put you through this if there was another way."

"Come on, I'm three blocks from my bed and an hour more of sleep."

"It's Dave Harrison," she explained. "He says you owe him one and there is no one else he can call."

"That's because they're all sleeping or eating Fruit Loops in their robes and pajamas."

"You like Fruit Loops?" she asked. "You know they are like fifty percent sugar."

"And fifty percent artificial colors and flavors, I know. But they are so good. They make the milk turn an interesting neon color. That cereal milk at the end is awesome," I explained.

"While I'd love to expound on all the reasons why you shouldn't be putting that junk into your body, Dave says that they have a dead dog at the international terminal. They need someone to check it over."

Years ago I had supplemented my house call income by providing services to the O'Hare International Airport on an as needed basis. Occasionally pets that were traveling with their owners, or as baggage, needed medical attention or an updated health certificate. I was able to charge even more than my regular exorbitant fees for the convenience. On rare occasions they had animal medical emergencies. Dave Harrison oversaw the transport of animals as one part of his job and we had become friends over the years, taking turns winning twenty bucks off each other at monthly poker games.

When my mother had been detained after slapping a transportation safety officer who was patting her down on a random search, he pulled some strings to get her out of detention and on her way back to L.A. I did owe him. More than the comfort of my bed and another hour of sleep was worth.

I sighed loud enough for Sheila to hear and with misery and frustration in my voice I said, "Tell him I'm on my way."

"That-a-boy Atty. I already did. After what he did for your mom I'd think you'd be out there in the middle of the night." One of the annoying, or rather, the only annoying thing I've discovered about Sheila (so far) is that she doesn't just schedule appointments and check on how my patients are doing, she talks to people. They, unfortunately, tell her everything.

"He told you about that?"

"That and more, although I don't blame your mother," she said. "Some of the TSA people can get a little frisky," she added.

"Personal experience?" I asked

"Maybe," she teased.

"I always wondered what you did on those vacations you take."

"Usually I'm out on a hit, but sometimes the CIA just needs someone to get information, in whatever way possible." Her voice had turned to the sultry tone she knew drove me crazy.

"Ow," I said.

"Down, boy," she added before hanging up. The thought of some TSA agent patting down a well-built blonde was now in my head. Curse you, Sheila.

CHAPTER 5

At this time of the morning, driving out to O'Hare was going to be a nightmare. The airport was technically part of the city of Chicago even though suburbs surrounded it. A thin strip of land, along which the CTA train tracks ran, connected the airport to the rest of the city.

I had a couple of options. I could take the Kennedy expressway, but the traffic going out of the city was becoming worse than that going in. Reverse commuters they called them. People who lived downtown, but worked in the suburbs. Weird.

I could go back to Irving Park Road and battle the traffic lights and road construction, but that wasn't much better. The expressway won out and I continued North on Lincoln. As my Escape reached the turn for Sunnyside Avenue, I fought the reflexive urge to make the turn that would take me home. Later, I promised myself.

I followed Lincoln all the way to Foster Avenue and continued west. Traffic wasn't too bad on this stretch and Neil Diamond was singing "Solitary Man". Most people were heading east to Lake Shore Drive, as were the buses pulling out of the CTA yard near Kedzie.

After ten years of navigating Chicago streets, I had a pretty good sense of where the quickest, shortest and most efficient routes lay at various times of the day. After St. Louis Avenue, things sped up quite a bit. Northeastern University's athletic field, then the Bohemian National Cemetery followed by some forest preserves filled the north side of the street. The lack of cars turning north gave the traffic a nice flow.

Another mile and I was on the expressway. I stayed in the right lane, followed it until it branched off to the airport. I followed the signs to the international terminal and pulled into the parking lot. I grabbed a parking ticket from the box at the gate, fully intending to add the fee to my bill.

What a morning it had been so far. A sick dog that could die. A sick dog that was dead. And now a dead dog. But with most of a dead pig, some undeveloped chicken embryos, shredded fried bulbous roots and some roasted, crushed, boiled beans in me, I was ready to face it.

Heck, maybe this might even be a dead dog that is really not quite dead and I end up saving it. There's that joke about the restaurant patron who ordered a rare steak. When he complained that it wasn't rare enough, the waiter explained that a good vet could still save that animal. While I have never brought a steak back to life (and have no desire to do so) I have had my share of miracles.

My car's clock told me it was 8:30 a.m. I got out and headed to the back. I grabbed my bags and walked to the terminal building. I probably looked like another one of the travelers heading off for a business trip to Frankfurt. I turned to the arrival area just outside customs and found Dave Harrison talking to a female cop. She had a blonde ponytail poking out behind her cap, her upper body was encased in a combination of a black jacket over a sky blue bulletproof vest.

"Morning, Dave," I said, emphasizing the morning part of my greeting.

"Wow," said Dave, "you made it here fast." I had a sense he would have been happier if I had taken another fifteen minutes or so. The female police officer nodded at me and returned to her patrol of the terminal, seeking out terrorists in the form of veterinarian's mothers, children with Pokemon backpacks, and old men with tattered briefcases. Actually, that wasn't a fair thing to say. Pokemon hasn't been that big of a deal for years, maybe if they had a Minecraft backpack... My nephew, Desmond, was always going on about his Minecraft server and his latest mods, whatever those were.

"I was already up and out, my friend."

"This early? I thought you had a strict no appointments before 10 a.m. policy."

"Didn't stop you from calling," I pointed out.

"True, true," he added. "New rules. We get a dead animal we need to make sure it wasn't some biological or chemical agent that was meant for passengers of the human variety. Give it the once over and we'll get you on your way. Technically, for the next few minutes, you are under contract to the Department of Homeland Security. We have the body in the Quarantine Room."

"Quarantine Room?" I asked. "You get a lot of people and pets that need to be quarantined?"

"Actually, it's for food."

"Food?"

"Yeah. The EPA is worried about beetles, flies, trichenella, mad cow. We confiscate food items that don't go through the normal inspections and store them until the USDA sends over a truck to dispose of them."

"How much of that stuff do you get?"

"A day?"

"Sure, how much in a day?"

"About three hundred pounds."

I stopped in my tracks. That was a heck of a lot of food.

"That's only what we find. The USDA guys think there may be three times that much smuggled through in people's luggage."

"That's insane."

"Tell me about it."

"So you have a dead dog in a room with apples and sausages?"

"No apples today, but there are a couple crates of mangoes, and some peacock jerky."

"And that has to be destroyed."

"Every bit. If USDA hasn't inspected it it ain't getting in."

"So, any chance I can try some peacock jerky?"

Dave stopped, glanced around, then leaned in to me speaking softly, his words barely audible over the din of the airport terminal, "you don't want to try the peacock jerky," he said. "Trust me on that." He looked around again as if Officer ponytail might have overheard and continued on. I stared at the back of his head in a moment of disbelief before shuffling to catch up.

The Quarantine Room was appropriately labeled, "Laundry Supplies".

"What's with the sign?" I asked.

"Keeps people from pilfering the peacock jerky before the USDA gets here."

"Well, not everybody," I corrected him.

"Don't know what you're talking about," he said. A large key chain emerged from his pocket and the appropriate key unlocked the door.

There were plastic milk crates filled with everything from bananas to steaks. The odor was a strange mix of sweetness, decay and staleness fighting against one of those plug-in air fresheners, but the odor from the dead dog helped to overpower it completely. I was back to Peanuts' cage at the Bark and Breakfast.

I put my medical bag on the table next to the dog and pulled out a pair of gloves. My exams of dead animals were outnumbering those of live ones today. I dearly hoped that the trend would reverse by the end of the day.

I started my exam at the head. The body was cool, but movable. Rigor mortis had come and gone. "Any idea how long she was dead?" I asked.

"Could be a day. The flight was delayed in Paris due to mechanical problems. No one thought to check on the animal passengers or didn't notice." I could believe the latter, particularly if Pete had some French relatives.

"Where was the flight coming from?"

Dave pulled out his smart phone and tapped it a few times. I watched as his eyebrows raised, crinkling his forehead into a washboard. "Kazakhstan."

"What, like in the game 'Risk?'"

"Is there another?"

"Hmm. Okay. Why is someone shipping a dog from Kazakhstan to Chicago?"

"Someone's pet, I think. I mean, it looks like just a mutt."

"Where is the owner for this dog?"

"Don't know. No one has shown up, but that's not unusual especially since the flight was delayed."

"Did it have a health certificate?"

"Yeah." Dave pulled a sheet of paper from his folder. "The Chicago Police are trying to contact the consignee. It might be a fake name and address. We are waiting to hear back from Kazakhstan about the information on the sender."

"Undoubtedly someone is interrupting a Kazakhstani vet's dinner to find out."

"Undoubtedly," echoed Dave.

I continued my exam. No enlarged lymph nodes. The abdomen

was distended, but with gas, not fluid like with Peanuts. I palpated as best I could, but with the intestines inflated like those long balloons you twist into animal shapes, it was hard to tell any abnormalities beyond that. It was a female dog and she likely had puppies at one time. I looked over the body for any wounds or surgical incisions. There were none.

"Do people smuggle drugs in dogs?" I asked wondering if that might be a possibility.

"Sure, but it's not as reliable as in people."

"Why not?"

"The condoms tear more easily. They have to use smaller more sturdy balloons or implant the drugs surgically which leaves telltale signs," explained Dave. "So, genius, what killed the pooch?"

"In my opinion?"

"Do I have any other choice?"

I snapped off the latex gloves, "I have no idea."

"Great, glad you came."

"What did you expect? It could be a dozen different things. I certainly can't rule out an infectious disease or toxin by just looking at her."

"So, what will it take to get a definitive diagnosis."

"I'll need to do a post-mortem, get some lab tests."

"So, go ahead."

"What? Here?"

"Why not?"

"I don't have the equipment."

"Go get it."

"Better idea," I started, "I just take her with me."

Dave grimaced and made a sucking sound with his breath, "That's a lot of paperwork."

"For me or you," I asked.

"No other options? I mean can't you run one of those Star Trek things over it and scan her?"

"A tricorder. Sorry, left mine in the twenty-third century."

"There's also the whole chain of custody thing. If there are drugs in the dog, although I don't have any idea what they might smuggle out of Kazakhstan, we need someone present to witness and take possession of whatever you might pull out of this dog."

"Well, if you want a definitive answer, that's what I need to do."

"Let me think about it."

I closed my bag and headed for the door. I needed to get out of that room. The smell was beginning to get to me. Not that I couldn't handle the occasional bad odor. There is the ever potent anal gland, the stinky mouth with the teeth held in by the tartar, and my favorite, the cocker spaniel chronic yeast infection in the ears. That smell stays on your hands for hours even after scrubbing with antibacterial soap for two minutes.

A poster on the wall by the door caught my attention. It was labeled "Disease From Potential Bioterrorist Agents."

"Cool," I said.

"What?" asked Dave.

"This poster, you guys see a lot of anthrax and botulism in fresh fruit?"

"Oh we got that a few years ago. Someone thought we ought to put it up somewhere and the Quarantine Room won."

"I think I got one too. I didn't have a place to put it so I tossed it. It's mostly livestock diseases anyway. The closest I get to livestock is driving by the barn at the Lincoln Park Zoo."

Dave laughed. "Not into cows and pigs, eh?"

"Sure, just on bread after being blasted into their component hydrocarbons on the grill," I answered.

"What kind of vet are you? Aren't you supposed to love all creatures, great and small and all that stuff?"

I ignored the remark and let my eyes drift over the poster. It was broken into two sections, human and animal. The disease went from anthrax to Rift Valley Fever, Plague, Brucellosis, Psittacosis, and a number of nasty sounding toxins. I doubted a terrorist would ever think to use Tularemia as a bioterrorism weapon, but apparently the Center for Food Security and Public Health did.

As far as I could remember, Kazakhstan was not a hotbed of Ebola or Lassa Fever. In fact the only thing I did remember was that apples originally came from there. Some people speculated that the original Garden of Eden was there, tree of knowledge and all.

We walked out of the Quarantine Room.

"When could you do it?" asked Dave.

"The necropsy?"

"Yeah, whatever you call it."

"Well, this afternoon I have a break around one o'clock."

"Okay. Let me get the dog packed up for you."

"What about chain of evidence and all that stuff?" I asked.

"I think I have an idea." He pulled out a walkie-talkie that was clipped to his belt and hit the talk button, "Avers."

"Avers here," said a woman's voice.

"Bring a box and an evidence kit to Quarantine."

"How big a box?"

"Big enough to hold a dead dog," he answered.

"What are you going to put in it?" asked the woman.

Dave looked at the walkie like he was looking at the person on the other end herself. He pressed the talk button, "A dead dog."

"Roger," she answered.

"She seems pretty with it," I observed.

"Oh she's okay. Cops have a different thought process. They question everything and take nothing at face value."

"She's not the cop you were talking to when I came in, is she? The blond with the ponytail?"

"Real cutie pie that one. She's already threatened to use her cuffs on me. Meow."

"Really, Dave?"

"Hey, women love me. It's embarrassing sometimes how shamelessly they throw themselves at me."

"Hi, Dave," said a voice from behind him. The cop was standing still, holding a cardboard box, a smile on her lips.

"Officer Avers, we were just talking about you," he said.

"Yeah, I heard."

"I need you to pack up the body for transport then you can meet Dr. At here for the autopsy later and maintain that old chain of custody."

"It's a necropsy, Dave."

"What's the difference?"

"An autopsy assumes you are doing a postmortem exam on a member of your own species. Necropsy implies it is an exam of a dead creature."

"So all autopsies are necropsies, and some necropsies are autopsies," he summed up.

Officer Avers put down the box that had once held some paper towels and pulled some supplies from inside. A roll of yellow tape with "EVIDENCE" imprinted on it continuously in big black letters, a sticker with evidence log written across the top and a large black plastic garbage bag. "I brought the garbage bag in case it starts leaking."

"Good thinking," I added.

I held out my hand, "You can call me Atty."

"Atty At?" she asked. She shook my hand. Despite being almost a foot shorter than me, her grip was frighteningly powerful and she nearly wrenched my shoulder from the socket as she shook. Undoubtedly, a suspect would have little chance if they underestimated her strength. "What kind of name is At?" she asked. "Chinese?"

I thought about throwing back my line about the Charlie Chan remake, but figured it would soar over her head like one of the 747s taking off outside the terminal. "It's German," I answered, skipping over the full entomology.

"His first name is Atticus," added Dave.

I shot him a "why did you do that?" glare. He knew I hated to be called Atticus.

"Marcy Avers. You can call me Marcy."

"Nice to meet you Marcy."

We gently transferred the remains of my latest patient to the plastic bag. Even in death I insisted on making sure my patients were well treated and comfortable, a habit that was hard to break. I pressed out the extra air and Marcy wrapped the top with evidence tape that she initialed and dated. We then put the dog in the box, curled up in a fetal position which she also sealed with tape. She then placed the label on the box and wrote in some information before stepping back, satisfied with her work.

"Where are you taking her?" she asked.

"There is an emergency and specialty clinic near Western and Addison. I use their facilities for x-rays and surgeries sometimes," I explained.

"I know that place," Dave said. "I had to take my cat there for an abscess on the side of his face. Cost me five hundred bucks. What a rip off."

"Would you rather have the abscess rupture in your living room? Blood and pus dripping all over your couch?"

"You put it that way it sounds like I got off cheap."

"Call me next time. I'll give you the professional discount."

"What's that?"

"Well, it's more like a barter arrangement. I trade my services for an appropriate number of rounds of golf."

"Really?"

"Sure."

"How many rounds does an abscess on a cat's face go for?"

"Probably three."

Dave appeared to do some mental calculations in his head. "Nine or eighteen."

"Eighteen," I said, trying not to sound offended.

"Ahem," interrupted Officer Avers. She held up the box with the dead dog. "Shall we get going? I assume you have a way to get this evidence to the clinic?"

"My car's in the lot."

"You still driving that ugly green thing? That Vue?"

"I've upgraded. Got me a Ford Escape."

"Green?" he asked.

"Avocado," I corrected him.

"Green," he corrected back.

"It's distinctive." I picked up my bags. "Follow me," I instructed Office Avers.

"Finally," she said.

"Later, Dave," I said.

"So long," he said and locked up the Quarantine Room behind us. He smiled as he headed towards the administrative offices, probably off to play "Solitaire" until the next "emergency" required his attention.

Officer Marcy Avers quickly caught up to me and it was soon evident that her pace was quicker than mine. I was soon staring at her back. Her ponytail bobbed as she walked, giving brief glimpses of a slender neck. I almost had to jog to keep up. I am not a jogger. I don't understand joggers or runners. If a hungry beast is chasing me, sure, I'll pound pavement, but otherwise I like first gear. Plus, I didn't want to give Danny's breakfast any reason to be upset with me. It deserved a decent digestion for all the pleasure it gave me.

We glided past the customs lines and Marcy nodded to some TSA sentries on our way to the exit, a long glass walled hallway that dumped us to the short term parking lot.

"Which way?" she asked.

"To the right," I answered. I could hear a car alarm shrieking in the distance. "Shouldn't you do something about that?" I asked.

She nodded at the dog in the box, "I could throw this at the car thief?" she suggested.

Why did car companies bother with those things? In my neighborhood, they went off at least once a week and the only response they ever got was obscenities yelled from the neighbors instructing the owners to turn it off before they turned it off for them in very colorful language.

I caught up and was walking beside her and noticed the alarm was getting louder. "Sounds like that might be near my car," I pointed out.

My Escape came into sight around the back of a large blue minivan halfway down the long row of cars. Something wasn't quite right about the back hatch. It looked like I might not have closed it all the way. I always used the button on my key fob to activate the power lift to open and close the back hatch. Maybe something had stopped it from closing all the way.

As we walked the annoying car alarm was getting louder and the remains of Danny's breakfast were forming a knot in my stomach. I stopped and put my medical bag down. I reached in my pocket and pulled out my key fob. I pressed the red alarm button and the sound stopped.

"Oops," said Office Avers in response.

I quickly did a mental inventory. Most of my equipment was with me, but my laptop was in the car. My data backed up automatically last night so I would only have to reenter my visit with Mrs. Jeffries. The rest of the supplies, medications, dog toothbrushes, and supplement were replaceable, but not cheap.

I grabbed my bag and found myself jogging to my car. Who knew? Office Avers followed.

When I reached it I put down my bags and lifted the hatch. It pulled up easily. I scanned the bags and cases in the back. I had several plastic tool boxes that had supplies for every conceivable medical need. One had supplies for IV fluids, another for bandaging wounds, a third for supplies for lab samples. Milk crates held a supply of flea and tick products, heartworm preventatives, vitamins supplements and medications. I quickly spotted the black bag that held my computer. It appeared unopened. The milk crates and toolboxes all seemed intact. I let out my breath with a sigh of relief.

"What did they get?" asked Officer Avers.

"Everything seems to be here. The alarm must have scared them off," I said.

She laughed at my assessment. "Car alarms don't scare people. Maybe someone came along and interrupted them?" She put the cardboard box with my Kazakhstani dog on the edge of the rear bumper and dread came over me with the weight of a wet blanket. I closed my eyes. The Blu-Ray box was gone. Someone must have thought it actually contained what was pictured on the side. I looked at Marcy and said, "Peanuts."

CHAPTER 6

"I can think of more colorful things to say, but then again I'm a cop," said Avers.

"No, the dog. I had a dog in here. He's gone. They took Peanuts."

"There were peanuts with the dog? Aren't they supposed to be toxic or something to dogs?"

"That's raisins," I said. "The dog's name is Peanuts."

"What kind is it? I can get on the radio and have a Fido Alert put out."

"Fido Alert?" I asked.

"It's like an Amber Alert, but for dogs."

"Really?"

"No," she groaned. "I'm pulling your leg, stupid. But I can put out the word to be on the look out for him."

"Well, I don't think whoever took Peanuts thought they were stealing a dog."

"What did they think they were stealing?"

"A Blu-Ray home theater system. A nice one, 7.1 surround sound."

Marcy's expression of confusion was appropriate. Without being in on my visit to the Bark and Breakfast earlier this morning (it was hard to get used to the idea that after all I had been through, it was still morning) and knowing that the dearly beloved Peanuts was recently departed, my explanation made no sense.

"He was in the theater system box," I pointed out.

"What? With air holes?"

"No..."

"I'm missing something," she realized.

"Yes you are. My fault. I have failed to explain that Peanuts is in fact dead. Probably happened in the last couple of days."

"You've had a dead dog in your car for days?"

"No. No. He died at the kennel. I got him this morning."

"So they called you to pick him up?"

"Not exactly, they called to find out why he was sick."

"And it took you two days to get there?"

"No." I was frustrated that her questions kept interrupting my explanation, but I could see from her point of view that it was more than strange. "They didn't know he was dead."

"This kennel had a dead dog in a cage for two days and didn't know it? How does that work?"

"I'm still trying to figure that out myself," I said.

"Didn't they have to feed and walk it? Wouldn't that give them a clue?" If only Pete had the sharp, inquisitive, deductive mind that Officer Marcy Avers possessed.

"Well they put food in his cage, but since he wasn't moving, they didn't bother to walk him. Which they couldn't have done since he was dead. The kennel boy wasn't the sharpest knife in the drawer."

"So they gave his body to you in a home theater box," she realized. I didn't see the need to correct her on the "they gave his" part of her reasoning.

"Right."

"So some guy thought he was stealing a Blu-Ray home theater system. Samsung?" she asked.

"What?"

"Was it a Samsung?"

"I don't think so. Why?"

"Oh, I'm thinking of getting one and I heard they were good."

"I need to find him."

"Good luck," was Officer Avers contribution.

"What do mean? What about putting out the word?"

"What do you think is going to happen when they open up that box? He'll end up in the nearest dumpster. And trust me, there are a lot of dumpsters between here and Western Avenue."

"You're a cop. I've been robbed. Do your cop thing. Maybe someone heard my car alarm and saw what happened? Shouldn't you like, canvas the area or something?"

Officer Avers almost broke out laughing at that one. "You watch too many cop shows, Dr. At."

"Okay," I conceded. "How about video surveillance? This place must be riddled with cameras looking for terrorists and old ladies traveling to California."

"Excuse me?" asked Marcy, confused at my last remark.

"Long story."

"Yeah, there are cameras, but we really don't have the time or manpower to chase down someone who stole a dead dog."

"They broke into my car. That dog may have died from something contagious. There might be a public heath concern," I pointed out.

"Sounds a little thin," considered Marcy.

"Please," I begged. "There is a family on vacation who lost their pet. Their family member. I don't want to have to tell them he was stolen and likely dumped in the garbage. Anything you could do would . . ." I stopped myself. This cop didn't owe me anything. It was kind of ridiculous to think that CPD would drop everything to track him down. "I get it," I said. I pushed the button to close the hatch. "This day . . ." I started.

I felt a hand on my back. "Doc. I'm sorry if I came across as not caring about this. I do. Listen. I can asked the video guys to go over the camera feeds. Maybe we'll get lucky."

I looked at her. I knew it was a long shot, but I appreciated her effort. I pulled a card from my jacket pocket and handed it to her. "Here's the best way to reach me if they come up with something. Thanks." She took my card and slipped it into a vest pocket.

"Protect and serve," she added.

I walked to the front of my car and unlocked the doors with my key fob and slipped in. The passenger door opened and Officer Avers slid into the passenger seat. She pulled on her belt. I looked at her. She seemed to be right at home. She turned and looked at me.

"You going to put your belt on, Atty?"

"Are *we* going someplace?" I asked.

"I've been thinking. It's much easier if I just stay with the dog. Don't want someone stealing this one."

Ow. That hurt. "I thought you were going to meet me there. I'm not going to do the necropsy right away. I have appointments this morning."

"No problem," she said, "I'm used to sitting around in court waiting to testify in cases that never get tried. Stop by a Jewel or Walgreens. I'll get a paperback."

"You're going to sit around in my car all morning with a dead dog?"

"And a paperback. It'll only take me a minute to run in. I know just the one I want to get."

"Don't you have to work? Patrol the airport, catch terrorists?"

"I did that yesterday. This will be a nice change of pace. Hey, look at it this way," she added. "No one is going to break into your car while I'm in here."

She had a point. She also had a gun, so I decided not to argue. I fastened my seat belt and started up the Escape. I pulled out of the lot and got a receipt for my parking fee. I headed back on to the Kennedy expressway into the city. The traffic was terrible. Rush hour. Rats.

"You remind me of someone," Marcy said after some time. I glanced at her and saw the puzzled look on her face while she looked at me. I put my eyes back on the road.

"Oliver Platt," I prompted her.

"What?"

"I remind you of Oliver Platt."

"Who's he?" she asked.

"The actor?" I said in a suggestive tone.

"No," she drawled, "That's not it. I'll get it. Give me a few minutes."

I took another quick glance at her drawing down the corners of my mouth to a grimace. What a cool word, grimace. I grimaced at her. She leaned over and clicked the microphone on her shoulder. "This is ORD thirty-four."

"Whatcha need, Marcy," asked the dispatcher.

"I need someone to go over the security camera footage at the international terminal parking lot for anyone breaking into a green Ford Escape or possibly leaving the area with a box."

"Are you serious?"

"Joe owes me a favor. Tell him it's important he check it out as soon as possible."

"It may take a while. What did you do for Joe?" asked the dispatcher.

"I went on a date with his cousin."

"Nimble Neil?"

"Yeah," groaned Avers.

"He try to grab you?"

"Several times. We went to a Cubs game. Thought I'd be safe in the crowd."

"That's definitely worth a favor. I'll make sure Joe does it," the dispatcher assured her.

Officer Avers turned toward me. "Okay?" she asked.

"Thanks," I said. I was kind of impressed she'd call in a favor like that for a dead dog. I checked the time. It was 8:50. "Rats," I said out loud.

"Where," said Marcy, grinning at her own joke.

"I've got an appointment at ten and I still need to get home."

"Don't forget my paperback," she reminded me.

"You can pick out something from my house."

"You got any Janet Ivanovich?" she asked.

"Janet who? Don't think so. I've got some good Sci-Fi books."

"Eh, I'll stick with Janet. What exit you taking?"

"Austin to Foster," I explained. Lawrence was horrible in the mornings.

"There's a Walgreens by Milwaukee. It'll take a minute."

"I better not be late."

"You won't be. Trust me."

By the time I got on my exit the dashboard clock read 9:05. It was rush hour at its finest. Officer Avers made sure I took the detour to Walgreens. I pulled into an empty space in the lot and left the motor running. As soon as my passenger closed the door my phone rang. I glanced at the caller ID. It was Sheila.

Oops, I thought. Now would not be the time for the Johnsons to be rushing home to see their dead dog which I managed to lose and had little hope of finding despite Joe's eagle eyes.

"Please tell me the rest of my appointments have canceled this morning," I pleaded.

"No, but you did get a message from the Bark and Breakfast."

"Oh, yeah?"

"Yeah, they said they wanted you to call them right away."

"About Peanuts?"

"No, some other patient. Something about getting a refill on some medication."

"That's weird. Did they mention Peanuts?"

"Not a word."

"Did the Johnsons call yet?" I asked. Part of me prayed they hadn't. I didn't know what frightened me more, telling them or telling Sheila that Peanuts was in the wind.

"Nothing yet. I can't find out where they are staying, but I put three more messages on their answering machine. Hopefully they'll check in today and I can fill them in on what's happened and you wanting to do the autopsy."

"About that," I started.

"Atty."

"Just a little problem."

"You never seem to have little problems, Atty." That certainly seemed true today, I agreed.

"I, uh, kind of lost him."

"Lost him?"

"Well he was stolen," I corrected myself, as if that sounded better.

"Stolen?" she asked, her voice rising in tone and incredulity.

"Someone took the box he was in out of my car while I was parked at the airport, which as you may remember, you made me go to despite my weak, pathetic protests."

"At the airport?" she questioned again. It felt like I was trapped in a bizarre version of Jeopardy. I'll take Stupid Criminals for two hundred dollars, Alex.

"He was in a Blu-Ray player box. The thief probably thought he was getting a home theater system. They didn't even bother to take any medical equipment, just popped the hatch and walked off with the box."

"Didn't they look inside? Or better yet smell it?"

"Apparently not."

"What are you going to do?"

"The police are looking at surveillance tapes. I'm sure they'll find him."

"Atty, how could you lose a dead dog?" she asked. I could feel the disapproval and her head shaking from side to side through my phone.

"Hey, the Cunninghams lost him first. Technically they're responsible," I suggested.

"Don't even go there. You better hope the police find him."

"Yes, ma'am," I answered.

"Were you serious about canceling your appointments?" she asked.

Marcy picked that moment to open the passenger door of the car. She pulled it closed and said, "Let's roll."

"Who's that?" asked Sheila.

"Gotta go," I said. I glanced at the clock. I still could make the ten o'clock even with traffic. "I'll get back to you on that."

"Atty, do you have a woman in your car?"

I looked at Marcy. She was unwrapping a Three Musketeers bar and flipping open her book. "She's a cop and she's just riding along with the evidence. It's a long story."

"What evidence?" asked Sheila. The confusion in her voice had gone from being measured in teaspoons to gallons.

"The dead dog?"

"I thought he was stolen? They got him back already?"

"No, it's another dead dog. From Kazakhstan," I added.

"Atty, you are not making sense. Not that you usually do, but what is going on?"

"Girlfriend giving you a tough time?" asked Marcy.

"She's not . . . ," I started then shook my head. "Sheila, I got to go. We'll talk later."

"Later, Romeo," she said.

It was stereo harassment. I put the car in reverse and pulled out on to Milwaukee. I hit the on button for the media player and silenced Marcy's protest with a finger before she was able to utter one syllable. Neil sang "Song Sung Blue".

"Kill me," muttered Marcy. I smiled.

I turned onto Lawrence and followed it to Lincoln Avenue then south to my Sunnyside. I followed the alley to the garage. My neighbor was thankfully not out polluting her lungs. I pulled in to the garage. The dashboard clock read 9:35. Plenty of time to get to my appointment. No time to catch up on missed sleep or even relax. I had already figured out my bill for the Department of Homeland Security for my "consultation." It would help compensate me for my lost morning. I opened my door. "Wait here," I told Marcy.

She waved me off and returned back to her story.

I went out to the alley and through the gate into my backyard up to the back porch. I fumbled my keys out and walked through the door. I fought the urge to head to bed. A five-minute nap would be so nice. Beaker met me at the door, squeaking a complaint as he walked over to his empty food bowl. I reflexively searched for his box of cat food on top of the refrigerator and filled it. I stepped into my office and plopped myself into the chair in front of my desk. I could feel the caffeine draining from my brain, seeking out my kidneys. Likewise, the adrenaline that had been assisting it faded away as well. I yawned.

I am not a morning person.

I sat perfectly still for five minutes. Half of the time my eyes were closed as I hovered near sleep. Perhaps it was psychological more than anything else, but that seemed to reenergize me. I stood, let out the stale air from my lungs and started to gather what I needed: the files for my day's appointments, some vaccines from my mini-fridge that I transferred to a cooler with some ice packs, and some other supplies for blood tests and anything else I might encounter.

I found myself thinking about Darla. The reason why my day had started so early. I wondered what it was she had gotten into. A lot of times my patients try to eat bees or wasps. Once in a while I'd see the same sort of reaction to a vaccine. Occasionally it might indicate an infection or tumor interfering with the blood drainage from the head. I looked at my printer. Sheila had sent an updated schedule with a recheck for Darla squeezed in. I looked at the ninety minute gap that was my usual lunch break. No lunch today, I would be dissecting a dead dog instead.

I also was thinking about Peanuts. What was worse? Dying alone in a cage where nobody noticed you had died, or being stolen out of the back of an SUV, confused with a home entertainment system. Telling the Johnsons would be the worst part of it for me. Part of me held out hope that the CPD would come through.

My arm loaded with files, the other hand clutching my six-pack cooler full of supplies, I let myself out the back door. Beaker was just sitting in front of his food bowl, a good portion of it gone. His eyes were closed and he was doing a cat grin wide enough to inspire Lewis Carroll. Did he just sit there all day nibbling away at his stash whenever the mood hit him? I locked the door behind me.

I was almost to the alley gate when I heard an emphysemic cough breaking bits of tar out of Mrs. Hornby's alveoli.

There was no way I'd let her waylay me this time. I undid the gate latch with my knee and pushed out in to the alley, ready to ignore any greeting from my eccentric neighbor. My eyes focused straight ahead, but a murmur and a giggle caused me to risk a glance. I stopped. Officer Avers was standing on the alley side of Mrs. Hornby's gate. Mrs. Hornby was dressed in a flowered purple house dress that had gone out of style in 1967. A thick gray sweater hung from her bony shoulders. A lit Marlboro was perched in one hand, inches from her lips, ready to provide a fresh cloud of smoke with her next breath. The other hand pulled her sweater tight around her. It was still a bit chilly, even with a sweater. Next to her stood a little boy, perhaps ten. His brown hair hung around his head in an old time bowl cut. He wore round, black, plastic-framed glasses on a narrow nose and was pushing them back up it as he fidgeted in the cold wearing a down vest over a sweatshirt.

Marcy reached over and gave the boy's head a good tousling. She then looked at me, "Hey, I thought you fell asleep on me."

"We have to get going," I said.

"Mrs. Hornby was telling me how her grandson, Griffin here, wants to be a vet. But his mother says his allergies are too bad. That kind of stinks. I wanted to be a vet when I was a kid, but I never had good enough grades."

Surprise, surprise, I thought. The voice in my head doing a pretty good imitation of Gomer Pyle.

Officer Avers continued, "Maybe you could take him along, you know, let him carry your stuff and have him watch."

Griffin looked from his grandmother to me, an expression of hope and pleading on his face. All I could think about was this asthmatic kid going into anaphylactic shock on me.

"What about his allergies?" I asked.

"He's got his inhaler, don't you Griffy?" asked Mrs. Hornby.

The boy reached into his pocket and pulled out the device.

"I don't think it would be a good idea," I said.

Officer Avers shook her head in agreement, "Probably not, Griffin. Besides, we have a dead dog in the car and it stinks."

"Eww," groaned Griffin, disgust taking his face by surprise. He looked over the fence to the car in my garage and his face squinted as he pushed up his glasses one more time. He looked at me. "Can I see it?" he asked.

"What?"

"The dead dog, can I see?"

"Uhh, I, uh," I was fumbling for a good reason other than it was a bad idea. "She might have something contagious. I really need to keep the body sealed until we can do a necropsy."

"Did it have Leishmaniasis? I read that dogs get that and then sand flies give it to people. Did you see any sand flies? You know, people can die from that. It eats their spleen and gives them really gross sores. Did the dog have sores?"

"A virtual encyclopedia," said Marcy.

Griffin continued, "Marcy let me see her gun. She even showed me the bullets. You got a gun? You know, for like, dogs with rabies that attack you?"

"She did, huh? Well, no, I don't use a gun. And I don't think the dog had Leishmaniasis. This dog came from Kazakhstan. No sand flies there." I looked at Marcy. "I need to go, so you need to go."

"Bye, Griffin. Nice to meet you, Mrs. Hornby," she said.

Mrs. Hornby halfheartedly waved her cigarette and she and Griffin headed back into her house. Marcy headed for my car and I followed, still carrying my gear. I went to the back and popped the hatch and loaded up. She let herself in the passenger seat and settled in with her book.

I closed the hatch and got in my side, starting the car.

"Don't you like kids?" she asked.

"Sure I like kids."

"What, boiled?"

"Ha, ha."

"She's an interesting lady. I was just sitting in the car when they came out. I figured I'd say hello."

"Very nice of you," I said as I pulled into the alley and waited for my garage door to close behind us.

"Griffin's mother had to take her other son to a doctor's appointment. Makes you think."

"Uh, huh," I agreed.

"No, really. Mrs. Hornby has been smoking five packs of Marlboros a day for forty-five years. Never goes to the doctor. Her grandkids are kept in a practically sterile environment and they've suffered from everything imaginable; allergies, asthma, ear infections, the works."

There was actually a bit of logic to Marcy's assessment. Constant exposure to a low amount of nasty things did help the immune system keep the big stuff in line. "You're probably right," I said, "but I wouldn't say Mrs. Hornby is in the greatest shape. Did you hear that cough?"

"It was a little frightening," she agreed.

"Frightening? Sometimes I think her whole lung is going to splatter on the pavement. She'll spit up a wad of phlegm while I'm talking to her like a cowboy in a saloon. I once made the mistake of looking at it." The thought still makes me shudder.

I reached Ashland Avenue and turned. Marcy returned to her book and I clicked on Neil. My dashboard clock read 9:58 by the time I hit Clark Street. I was going to be late. I didn't know if speeding with a cop in the car was asking for trouble or getting permission, so I kept it at the speed limit. Rush hour was not really a factor now, but stoplights limited my progress.

At Devon Avenue I turned right and left another two blocks later. The street was lined with tall maple trees and brick apartment buildings that each held six units. I pulled up to one in the middle of the block and parked behind a red Mustang convertible and in front of a blue VW Beetle. We made a colorful lineup.

"I'll be about a half an hour," I said.

"I'll be here," Marcy answered.

"Could you check to see if they have anything on Peanuts, the stolen dog?"

"Sure," she said as she continued to read her book. I stared at her and she turned to me, "What?"

"The dog?"

"As soon as I finish this chapter. I want to see if Stephanie manages to blow up this car."

I stopped and looked at her. "She blows up cars?"

"She's a bounty hunter. They usually get blown up by other people."

"Okay," I said, enunciating the syllables to show my bafflement.

"See ya," she muttered and turned another page.

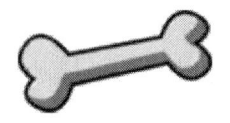

CHAPTER 7

I closed my door and headed for the back. I opened the hatch and started to load up. I put my computer bag on my right shoulder and picked up a supply bag with my right hand that contained medical equipment that didn't fit into my medical bag. It was fairly light, but bulky. I picked up the bathroom scale I used to weigh larger dogs and tucked it between my right arm and my body then picked up my black medical bag with my left hand.

A lot of people are surprised when they see the bathroom scale when I first visit them. They wonder how I am going to get the dog to stand on it. It's actually much easier than that. I weigh myself (an almost daily reminder of a lack of exercise, improper diet and apathy to do anything about them) then pick up the dog and weigh us together. The trick is to lift with the knees. Come to think of it, that is a sort of exercise.

I closed the hatch by thumbing the key fob in my right hand.

What was supposed to be my first appointment of the day, before my unscheduled emergencies, was with Mr. J. W. Pennyworth (as the label on his doorbell buzzer proclaimed) and his dog Bruno. Bruno would lighten my mood. Bruno loved me.

I walked up to his building and pushed open the heavy glass and oak door to the tiny foyer. I had to wedge myself into a corner, encumbered with my bags, to let the door swing shut. A small bank of mailboxes was imbedded in the wall on the left side of the entrance way, and next to them was a column of labels and buttons. I pressed the one labeled "J. W. Pennyworth." I glanced at my watch. It was 10:10.

"Yes?" came a quavery voice over the intercom.

"It's Dr. At," I said. "Come to see Bruno."

"Come on up. Third floor," he added. I had been to his apartment dozens of times, but he always made sure to tell me that I needed to come to the third floor. A loud buzz signaled that the door lock was disengaged. I would have a second or so to pull open the inner door to the stairway. I reached for it with my right hand, disengaging my index finger to grab at the handle and pulled the door. My grip on the handle was tenuous. I started to twist around to open the door, but the computer bag slung over my back wouldn't let me get past the mailboxes and I lost my grip. I tried to slip my left foot between the door and the jamb, but was too slow. The heavy door closed and the lock clicked.

I groaned. I put down my medical bag and pushed the buzzer again.

"Hello?" asked Mr Pennyworth again. I thought it unlikely that he was expecting another guest this morning, but I reintroduced myself.

"It's Dr. At again. The door closed on me. Could you buzz it again?"

"Of course, Dr. At," he said. "Third floor," he reminded me. I grabbed the handles of my supply bag with my left hand that was also holding my medical bag, leaving my right hand free, even though my right arm was still clamping my scale next to my body. I was ready this time. The door buzzed and I grabbed the handle. This time I pulled hard and was able to swing the door open almost all the way having shifted myself into the near left corner of the room. My scale slipped and bounced off the mat on the floor to the near right corner. I put my left foot out as a door stop and started to crouch down grasping for the scale, inches beyond my reach, with my now free right arm. The weight of the door trying to close, my total lack of balance due to the computer bag slipping down my right shoulder resulted in my falling against the outer door and the inner door once more clunking shut. I wondered if that security door was a distant relative of Mrs. Jeffries' building's elevator.

Okay. It was going to be like this then. I took a moment to gather myself and hoped Marcy was too busily engaged in her book to be watching my antics through the outer doors' window.

I put down my medical bag, and readjusted my shoulder strap over my head. I put the scale under my left arm this time, and grabbed both bags with my left hand. I now had everything on the left side, right arm free and unencumbered. I pressed the button for the third time.

"Hello?" asked Mr. Pennyworth. Either he was getting early Alzheimer's or he normally had a lot of visitors.

"One more time, Mr. Pennyworth," I said.

"Dr. At? Is that you?"

"Yes."

"Where are you?" he asked. Perhaps a logical question since he had already buzzed me in twice.

"I'm downstairs. I keep getting stuck in the door, but I have it figured out now."

"I'll buzz you in," he said.

We both said, "Third floor." Thank you Abbott and Costello.

As soon as the buzz started I flung the door open hard with my right hand and managed to slip into the small landing in front of the stairs as the door crashed closed.

Success. Well, at least partial success. I still had the stairs. In all I'd say I was carrying thirty pounds of equipment. As I looked at the steep stairway curving up and around the narrow stairwell it felt like sixty.

These old Chicago six-flats always baffled me. The angle between the front door and the inner security door and the narrow steep stairs always made me wonder how people ever moved their furniture in and out. Perhaps they sold the apartments furnished or winched them up through windows. I sometimes suspected there was a roomy freight elevator in the back of the building that the tenants shared and kept for themselves. Maybe the rear porches were a bit roomier, but with stories of porch collapses making the headlines every year, I was wont to trust them very far to support my slightly excessive weight.

The stairway itself was typical for these buildings as well. The musty, old odor was a distinct notch above unpleasant, approaching, but not quite making unobjectionable. There was a flavor of mothball, rotting carpet, mold and insecticide. The woodwork was solid oak covered in layers of patinated shellac that had a glossy, but scratched finish. A runner of dark, red carpeting ran up the stairs. It was worn and stained and ragged in the edges. In some places the yarn had been scraped away by decades of footsteps to the woven backing. The parts of the steps not covered showed signs of extreme wear as well; the finish worn off leaving impossibly smooth wood pale gray with age. The first few steps were triangular, curving around and up. It made walking up them with a load tricky, especially where the runner was getting a little loose.

I heard a door creak open above me and Bruno began barking in anticipation of my arrival. I'm sure it was enough to disturb anyone else at home. I worked my way up the tight staircase occasionally yelling, "Coming Bruno," to the loud barks awaiting my arrival.

When I reached the third floor, the apartment door closed and I heard the security chain slide off its groove. A moment later the door opened a bit and it was enough for Bruno to wedge his face in and force it open the rest of the way. He was jumping up on me and my bags before I even had a chance to get in the door. This was what I lived for.

"Down, Bruno, down," Mr Pennyworth commanded with the effectiveness of a butterfly making its way out of a hurricane. I pushed my way in, working against eighty pounds of slobbering bulldog. Mr. Pennyworth added a few "oh dears", but was otherwise unhelpful.

Still, I kind of liked the way Bruno greeted me. He was never less than exuberant on my visits. Most of my patients have developed a "what is he going to do to me this time" sort of attitude. Not Bruno. His body language seemed to say, "bring it on, Dr. At, I'll take whatever you got, buddy."

I managed to slough my equipment onto the Formica table with chrome legs that served as Mr. Pennyworth's dining table. I then shed my coat, the sleeves of which were covered with glossy patches of saliva. Then I was able to kneel down and give Bruno my full attention. Bruno was a bulldog and had a face that only a bulldog owner (and his vet) could love. He did what he wanted to do most and started licking my face. Yeah, it's kind of disgusting, but it was his way of showing his love and I wasn't going to deprive him of that. Some pets would be all calm and cooperative then try and bite my ankle as I was leaving. I almost lost my balance a few times, but eventually his excitement wore off, fading to just a manic wiggling in the curved stump of a tail he sported.

I pulled myself up, sans Bruno, his tongue, far too big to fit in his mouth in my medical opinion, draped itself to the left side as he panted away, content that his affection for me was properly shown. I turned to Mr. Pennyworth. "Sheila just said there was something wrong with Bruno. He looks pretty happy now. What are his symptoms?"

"Well, Dr. At," began Mr. P. He paused and his mouth puckered as if he was trying to swallow some sour bile. He looked very worried. His hands were held just below his chin and he wrung them persistently, dissipating nervous energy as efficiently as Bruno dissipated his excitement. "It's not so much that I noticed any symptoms, but he has, I'm afraid, developed a tumor."

"A tumor?" I asked. I was back on my knees, this time I was all over Bruno, he was still recovering from my greeting so was uncharacteristically calm as I started running my hands over his body. I was feeling for any sizable lump that may have alarmed Mr. P. "Where is it?" I asked. I had done a cursory search, but on a dog the size of Bruno, a sizable mass could elude a quick exam, especially around the skin folds covering his face and neck.

"It's by his ear, Dr. At," explained Mr. Pennyworth. His voice was weak and cracked on the word ear. "His left ear, just behind it."

I turned my attention to Bruno's massive head, scooting to his left side as I let my fingers slide over the skin behind the ear, feeling for the growth that I half expected to be some ulcerated, bleeding mass eating into the poor dog's skull. I worked at it for a half a minute or so. Where was it? He did say the left ear, didn't he?

Finally I came across what felt like a tiny nodule, perhaps the size of a pencil eraser. The hair around it stood up and barely visible was a small, gray, bleb. "Bleb" was a good word to describe what I was seeing. It was smooth and firm. As I felt around it, Bruno kept up with his panting and butt shaking. I showed it to Mr. Pennyworth. "Is this it?"

He leaned closer, pulling on his reading glasses which were hanging by a string around his neck. "Oh dear, that's it. It wasn't there two days ago, I could swear. I heard the faster a tumor grows, the worse it could be," he added. He stood up again, pulling off his glasses, wiping them with a handkerchief.

"You're sure it just appeared yesterday?" I asked.

"Oh, yes. I'd know if something that massive was present on my Bruno."

I looked at the tiny bleb that had taken me a minute to find and I knew where I was looking. I've removed larger balls of lint from under my toe nails. I leaned in closer and gently pushed the hair around the bleb to the side. I smiled. The bleb had legs. Eight of them and they were wiggling.

"Mr. Pennyworth, has Bruno been in the woods lately?" I asked.

"Excuse me, Dr. At?" he asked.

"Have you taken him to the forest preserve or the park where there is some tall grass?" I continued.

"A couple of days ago, when it was so warm, we went down by the river," he confirmed. Meanwhile I was opening my medical bag and rummaging through one of the upper compartments for a hemostat. I found the instrument and returned to my patient. He tried to lick my hand as I focused my energy on trying to find his little guest.

"Bruno has a tick," I explained.

"A tick?"

"Yes, a female by the size of the abdomen."

"Abdomen?"

"What you are seeing is the engorged abdomen of a brown dog tick. She's probably been sucking blood for a day or two, getting enough to create a few hundred eggs. And these," I pointed to the tiny limbs waving in a slow version of panic with my hemostat, "are its legs." Mr. Pennyworth leaned in for a closer look.

"Oh dear," he said.

I could tell he wasn't as greatly relieved at the news as I had hoped.

"He could get that Lyme disease, couldn't he?" pondered Mr. P.

"It's possible," I said. "It's mostly up north in Wisconsin and Michigan, but I've had a few patients test positive around here. Most never get sick. We'll take a blood test today and recheck in about six weeks. If there is any sign of antibodies developing we'll put him on antibiotics. But in my experience, his risk is very low. Have you been using that tick preventative I gave you in the spring?"

"I thought with it so cold it wouldn't be a problem if I stopped. Oh, Dr. At, if I've done anything to harm Bruno I'll never forgive myself."

"Bruno's a tough guy," I reassured him. "He's going to be fine once I remove the tick."

"Will it be painful?" he asked.

"I promise," I said with as straight a face as I could muster, "I won't feel a thing." It was a joke usually saved for kids who were worried about their pets getting their vaccines. It took Mr. P. a moment to absorb it, but then he smiled a puckered grin, rolling his eyes.

"Oh, Dr. At, I should have known you would never do anything to hurt Bruno."

"Of course not," I agreed. I opened the jaws of the hemostat and working it next to Bruno's skin, trapped the tick's neck between the tips.

There are a lot of misconceptions about removing ticks. Some people say you can dab a little gasoline or lighter fluid on them. That is supposed to deprive them of oxygen and force them to back out of their cozy little home in their host's flesh.

Other people swear that touching their rear end with the glowing tip of a blown out match will shock them to release their jaws and seek a less inhospitable environment.

While both these methods have mixed success, it is when the former is followed by the latter that trouble can ensue usually ending up in a trip to one or more emergency rooms.

There are dozens of implements designed to facilitate the easy removal of a tick without leaving their tiny head stuck under the skin. In truth, all it takes is some gentle pulling, opposite the direction the tick has buried its head, and some patience.

I pulled and sure enough, after about ten seconds, she released her grip and I pulled her out. I held up the trapped tick to make sure I could see all the parts. Nothing had been left behind.

"Excellent, Dr. At. He didn't even flinch. You are a gifted healer," complimented Mr. Pennyworth.

I didn't know about gifted healer. Pulling a tick is not something that requires years of schooling and an innate ability to know what is bothering an animal, but I took the compliment with a smile.

I rummaged through the upper compartment of my bag for a small, red topped vial I usually use to collect blood samples. I used my thumb to flick off the rubber stopper onto the table with a small pop as the vacuum inside sucked air. I dropped the tick inside and replaced the top. She was already starting to move around, disturbed from her feeding. I popped the vial into my shirt pocket and turned back to look at Bruno's wound from the tick bite. Just a tiny red welt remained. That would be gone in a day or two.

I gave Bruno a scratch behind the ears. I loved it when a problem could be solved so easily. "I just need a little blood for the tick-borne disease screen and we'll be done."

"Whatever you need to do, Dr. At."

"I'll have the results tomorrow," I told him. His anxiety did not seem to diminish. From experience I knew Mr. P. was always worrying about one thing or another about Bruno. If it wasn't Lyme disease then he'd be concerned about immune mediated hemolytic anemia or proliferative histocytic gastroenteritis. Whatever they might be featuring on those vet shows on Animal Planet. You had to like those shows, they made us vets look good and they were always good for a few extra appointments from the Mr. Pennyworths of the world.

I setup my computer on the dining room table and entered my astute medical findings along with a bill for the house call and blood test. Tick disposal was free. He was more than happy to pay it. I had saved Bruno's life after all.

Just as I finished packing up, my cell phone rang. I took a quick glance at the caller ID. It wasn't Sheila. In fact, I didn't recognize the number at all, which was pretty unusual. The only people who had this number were Sheila, my mother and my sister. My mother rarely called me on my cell, she was afraid it would give me brain cancer.

I had a land line at home. Attached to it was an answering machine. Occasionally the red light would flash and I would press the little "delete" button. My clients' calls were handled by Sheila and if someone really had something important to tell me they could call when I was home or even come see me in person or write a letter. They never did, so I figured none of those messages were very important.

I was tempted to let it go to the voice mail, but my curiosity was high enough to risk killing a cat or two. I answered it and put the phone up to my ear. "Hello?"

"Hello," repeated the voice on the other end.

"I said it first," I retorted. I smiled at Mr. Pennyworth and shrugged my shoulders. Probably a wrong number.

"Who is this?" demanded the voice on the other end.

"You called me, don't you know who it is?" I asked.

"Are you," the voice paused a moment and came back tentatively, "Dr. At?"

"Who is this?" I asked this time.

"You're sick, you know that? You think you're funny? Some sort of jokester? More like a creep."

I held the phone away from head and looked at it with puzzlement. I'd never been further out of the loop than I was now. I did not recognize the voice and had no idea what he was talking about. Sick? Creep?

"Who is this? What are you talking about?" I demanded.

"I almost threw up. What were you going to do with it? Or was it some weird practical joke. I got to tell you, Dr. At, or whoever you are, it isn't funny."

I was prepared to hang up on this guy, but I was still curious as to who had gotten my number and how, not to mention I still had no idea what he was talking about.

"What if I had opened the box when I got home? In front of my wife and kids? Huh? Would that be funny, funny man?"

Funny man? "I really don't know what you are talking about," I assured him. "What box?"

"This home theater system I bought on Western Avenue. Guy said it was one of those refurbished things, you know, someone opened the box and returned it. I get it to my car and open it up and there is a dead dog in it with your little business card on top and this number. You laughing yet? I ought to call the police."

I remembered the card I gave to Pete, the kennel boy, being stuck inside the box that contained Peanuts. It was making sense. "You got the box where?" I asked.

"Some guy on Western, had a van full of stuff."

"You bought a home theater system from a guy with a van on Western Avenue and you're mad at me?"

"Hey bud, I don't care if something is a little used or if the remote is missing a couple of buttons, but I draw the line at dead animals."

Who wouldn't. "That animal was being taken in for a necropsy. He was stolen from my car a couple of hours ago."

"Stolen? Who steals a dead dog?"

"Who buys one?" I asked back. There was silence on the line.

"I need him back," I said.

"Well, give me fifty bucks and it's yours," he said sensing my desire to get Peanuts back and an opportunity to cut his losses.

"Fifty bucks?"

"That's what I paid for what I thought was a Home Theater and Blu-ray player. You make me whole and the dog's yours. Otherwise I'm putting it in the dumpster."

"It's not yours in the first place. Talk to your friend on Western if you want a refund. That animal is a family pet."

"Well, fifty is what I want. I should tack on another fifty for my time. Now I have to go out and buy another home theater system. That's my time, bub."

In case you are wondering, "bub" was when I really got angry. "I'll call you back," I said.

"Ten minutes," he said. "In eleven the pooch will be rat food."

I hung up. Mr Pennyworth was looking at me. "Little mix up," I explained, slipping my phone back into my jacket pocket.

Mr. Pennyworth seemed content to remain oblivious to the events behind my phone conversation. Thinking about it, it must have sounded pretty strange hearing just my end of it.

"I'm sure, Dr. At. Thank you again for your wonderful care and attention to my Bruno." Bruno thanked me with a slobbery lick of my hand which I wiped on his fur. I loaded up my bags and Mr. P. held the door for me. I headed for the stairs and hoped a loose runner wouldn't cause me to break my fall with my laptop.

Getting out of the building was easier since I had to push the inner door to leave the stairwell and another tenant was gracious enough to hold the outer door open for me. I could see Marcy reading her mystery, her jaw muscles working furiously on a piece of gum.

I made it to the back of the Escape and put down some bags to let me fish out my car keys. I popped open the back hatch with a click of the remote and was met by a faint whiff of decomposing dog. I stowed my gear, clicked the key fob to close the hatch, god, I loved that feature. There are just some technologies that make sense. A hatch that closes itself is one of them. Right along with automatic coffee makers. I walked up to the driver's side door and let myself in.

Marcy stopped chewing and folded her book closed, her left thumb bookmarking her place. "I have good news and bad news," she announced.

I wondered what sort of news she could have gotten just sitting there, but I took the bait nonetheless. "Good news please."

"They found the guy who stole your patient. Turns out he's been arrested before for stealing from cars in the airport lots. He has some sort of electronic transmitter that broadcasts thousands of codes. He wanders the lot waiting for one to pop open. Your code came up. I mean the odds are pretty against it, but nothing is perfect."

I picked up her story, "And the bad news is he didn't have the dog on him. In fact he had just sold the home theater to some guy."

Marcy looked at me with what was as much of an astonished look as she would allow herself to show. "How did you know that?"

I pulled out my smart phone and went to the call log. I pointed to the number at the top of the list. My dissatisfied home theater customer who thought I owed him fifty bucks. "That's the guy's number. My card with my cell phone number was in the box with Peanuts. Apparently this guy was shocked that something he bought off a guy in a van on Western Avenue was not what it was advertised to be."

"Why was your card in the box?"

"I had given it to the kennel boy at the boarding place where the dog died. It must have dropped into the box when he was packing him up." I decided to leave my own felony out of the events. Best she concentrate on the real criminals. I handed over the cell phone. "I told him I'd call back to arrange picking up the dog. He wants fifty bucks," I added.

"Fifty bucks for a dead dog?"

"He said it was cheap considering the trauma it caused him and now he still had to go out and get a new home theater system."

"He hasn't seen trouble," said Marcy. She took the cell phone and jotted down the caller ID number in her little notebook. Then she used her finger to scroll the call log up. Most of the calls were from Sheila and said "Sheila" for the caller. "Sheila your wife?" she asked.

"She's my remote receptionist."

"Remote?"

"She handles my calls and scheduling. She works over the phone from home. She has other clients she handles as well."

"So you don't even see her," she realized.

"I've never even met her."

Marcy gave me a stare that said, "what kind of idiot are you?"

"You want me to check her out for you?" she offered.

"Check her out for what?"

"You know, a background check, criminal history, aliases, credit problems, et cetera."

"Et cetera?"

"Hey, she could be some sort of scam artist. Getting information on your clients, identity theft, all that."

I laughed at the idea. "Not Sheila," I said.

"You just told me you don't really know her. This is how it happens."

"No thanks."

"Suit yourself." She handed back the phone. She unclipped the microphone from her shoulder. "I'll have the precinct track down this number and send a car over. Where should we bring the dog when we get it?"

I thought about it for a moment. It might be hard to meet up with them and carrying two dead dogs around would probably leave a permanent odor in the back of my car. "Have them bring it to where we're going, the specialty veterinary clinic near Western and Addison. I'll call and let them know to put him in the cooler until I can reach the owners."

She made her report, giving the phone number of the man who had Peanuts and the location of the clinic. I pulled out from the curb.

"Serious case?" she asked once she was finished, nodding her head in the direction of Mr. Pennyworth's building.

I turned south on Clark Street to head south for my next appointment.

"Excuse me?" I asked.

"Your last appointment."

"Oh, just an ectoparasite," I answered.

This earned a glance up from her book. "Sounds spooky," she shivered.

I reached into my shirt pocket and plucked out the slim glass tube containing the tick. I placed it in the middle of her open book. She picked it up and held it close, trying to get a glance at the contents. Suddenly there was a shriek and the glass vial went flying up onto the dashboard. I swerved to the side of the road and hit the brakes.

"What's wrong?" I asked.

"That thing moved," she said.

I sighed and shook my head. "My god, I thought you saw something I was going to hit in the road."

"You gave me a live ecto-whatever it was?"

"Relax," I said as I reached onto the dashboard for the vial and slipped it back into my pocket. An angry cab driver passing on my left waved with only one of his fingers as I pulled back into traffic. I love Chicago drivers. "It's just a tick. It's so full of blood it can barely move. It's not going to attack you or anything."

"It was trying to get out."

"What kind of cop are you? It's just a tiny arachnid. It can't get out of the tube and if it did, I doubt it would do more than just fall onto the floor."

"They have diseases. Lyme disease and all that stuff," she answered, shifting away from me in her seat, her eyes glued to my pocket. "You can die from that, you know."

"I thought you were going to shoot the thing."

She shook her head and relaxed back into her seat. She retrieved her book from the floor and flipped back to where she had left off. I started to pull back onto Clark when her radio sputtered. I could make out a voice, but really couldn't tell what they were saying. Marcy smiled when she heard it.

"Ten-four," she answered. "Meet you at clinic in twenty." She turned to me. "They got your Peanuts. The guy is pissed, but they managed to convince him not to sue you in return for not going to jail for receiving stolen goods."

"You understood all that?" I asked.

"A thank you would be nice," she added.

"Thank you. That was fast," I realized.

"There was a squad car a block from the guy's location. They're going to meet us at that emergency clinic in a little bit."

"What now?"

"You got to be someplace else? You were all worried about this pooch all morning."

"Yeah, but I have other appointments this morning. My next break is at 12:30. That's when I was going to do the necropsies."

"When's you're next appointment?"

"Eleven," I said. She looked at the clock on my dashboard. It read ten thirty-five.

"Where is it?" she asked.

"On Sheridan, near Touhy," I answered. "It'll take me twenty minutes to get to the emergency clinic, ten minutes to get the remains put away, then thirty to get back to my appointment."

"You can't be late? Besides that one in the back is starting to really get ripe."

She did have a point, but my next appointment was with Donna Melton. She had half a dozen cats and I was usually over once a month. She and I had a mutually beneficial arrangement. Like me, she was also an entrepreneur. She took her business to other people's homes, like I did, but also had one of her two bedrooms of her apartment set up for work. She usually paid me in barter. Her services for mine. "Why don't you have them meet you at my next stop and you can take Kazakhstani dog to the emergency clinic. I can have one of the techs there meet you and get things set up. She can take care of Peanuts too."

"I'm supposed to just hang around and wait for you for two hours?"

"You were just going to sit and read in my car. At the emergency clinic they have a lounge with a microwave and coffee maker. One of those fancy one-cup-at-a-time ones."

She considered the proposition. "What's the address of your next appointment?"

"Seventy-one, fifty-five north Sheridan," I answered.

She leaned over and spoke in to her shoulder mike. A static-filled reply answered her. "We're set," she said. "You'll be at the emergency clinic at 12:30, right Doc?"

"Sooner if I can."

She continued to read and I turned on the radio. Traffic wasn't bad enough to justify Neil and sometimes it was nice to hear what "the kids" were listening to nowadays.

After about twenty minutes I could see Donna Melton's high rise just past the light at Touhy. There was a black-and-white Chicago police car parked in front. Marcy had her window open and made a motion to the driver. The trunk of the cruiser popped open. I reached over and released the back hatch of my Escape.

"I'll see you later, Doc," she said. After she closed the door she leaned back in the open window. "I figured out who you look like," she said.

"Who?"

"Jack Lord. You know the guy from the original Hawaii Five-O." That was a new one.

"It's the sideburns," she told me. She leaned in a little closer.

"They're cute," she added. She headed to the back of my car to get Kazakhstani dog.

Cute, I thought. I heard my hatch close and Marcy carried the box to the police car. I drove across the street and into the driveway of Donna's building, the black and white heading south in my rear view mirror.

I took out my phone and hit speed dial five for the emergency clinic. I reached Margaret, the day receptionist. During normal business hours the building was used by veterinary specialists. An ophthalmologist, a dermatologist, a cardiologist, and an oncologist. "Chicago Veterinary Specialty Center," she greeted, "how may I help you?"

"Hi, it's Dr. At."

"Oh," she said. The disappointment was readily apparent.

"The police are going to be there in about fifteen minutes," I started to explain.

"The police?" There was a pause. "Do you think that is really necessary, I mean, can't we talk about it?"

"What? They're bringing in some deceased animals for necropsies. What are you talking about?"

"Nothing," she quickly answered, her tone restored to her normal indifference. That was weird.

"Are any of the emergency techs hanging around?" I asked. Sometimes, the techs, who worked from either 6:00 p.m. to midnight or midnight to 8:00 a.m., or when really busy, all night, would just hang out and sleep at the clinic if they were going from a late shift to an early shift. There was a shower and a lounge with cable, a Blu-ray player, fridge, microwave, and of course, the coffee maker.

"I don't know," came Margaret's apathetic response.

"Can you check, please?"

I could hear a deep sigh. "Just a minute." She didn't bother to put me on hold. I could hear the handset clunk on the desk.

Half a minute later I heard, "None of the techs are here right now, but Allie's car is still here, maybe she stepped out for some lunch."

"Can you ask her to stick around if you see her? I'm going to need some help this afternoon."

"If I see her," she said. I gave my message a fifty-fifty chance of reaching Allie's ears.

"It's important. You can have the police put the dead animals in the freezer until I get there."

"I don't work for you, you know," she said.

"Please?"

"Whatever." The line went dead. I put my phone away and got out of the car. I went around the back, the hatch already opening as I fingered the key fob button to open it. I pulled out a small insulated bag and loaded some vaccines from my cooler, grabbed my black medical bag, my pediatric scale, and my computer bag. It was a relatively light load. I was going to give Dolly, one of Donna Melton's cats, her annual exam. In exchange, I would get a half hour of Donna's services. I was glad Officer Marcy Avers wouldn't be around to quiz me after this visit. My arrangement with Donna was my business, not hers.

Frank was waiting to hold the door open for me. Thank God for doormen. Last Christmas I had tipped Frank with a one-hour session with Donna. I was now his favorite person in the world. I would never have to fumble with my bags through a door in this building.

"Good morning, Dr. At," he greeted.

"Good morning, Frank," I returned.

"Up to see Ms. Melton?" he asked, winking at the same time.

"Her cat Dolly is in need of her annual exam," I said.

"I envy you," he said. "You're here at least once a month. Are you getting her services as well every time?"

"Only as part of a professional transaction," I answered.

"Well, see you in a bit," he said. I could sense the slight jealousy tinged with a bit of envy in his words. It was easy to understand. After one had enjoyed some time with Donna Melton, it seemed like nothing else could match it.

Frank had rushed over to press the elevator button for me and when the car arrived he reached in to press eight for Donna's floor. He was working for another Christmas tip and he would get it.

The speed of the elevator was a nice change from the slothful transit of those in Mrs. Jeffries' building. That reminded me, I would have to call after my appointment to see how Darla was doing.

When the door opened on Donna's floor I was pleased to see her standing in the doorway waiting for me. Frank must have called ahead for me. She was wearing shorts and a nice halter top. Her hair was pinned back in a ponytail and her bright smile was the perfect accent to her natural beauty. If only she wasn't so young I'd consider making a move. But her work would always make me jealous of her clients. Better that things were left at a professional level.

"Hi, Atty," she said. "I have Dolly in the carrier. Almost couldn't find her this morning. She seems to always know when you are coming."

"They pick it up from you. Probably noticed the carrier was out. She's no dummy."

"Tell me about it," she replied. She graciously held open her apartment door while my bags and I squeezed through. I found myself sucking in my belly a little bit. Donna had that affect on me even though I was sure she didn't care if I had a few (dozen) extra pounds on me.

She closed the door behind us. "I don't know why she hates it so much. You are so gentle and calm with them. At my previous vet it seemed like it took two people to hold her down and she screamed like she was being tortured."

We walked into her kitchen and I set my gear down on the table. "Well, if you take your time and use very fine needles, this should be no more stressful than getting petted." The carrier was on the table as well and I could barely see Dolly, she was cringing in the back.

I took off my jacket and set up everything I needed. The scale, my vaccines, my otoscope, ophthalmoscope and stethoscope. I then opened the carrier door and reached in for Dolly, scratching her behind her ears before gently extracting her from her bunker.

Dolly was a white Persian. Her fur was immaculately groomed and I didn't care that she was going to leave large patches of it on my lap as I settled her there and petted her for a moment. My exam was half scratching and petting and half poking and prodding. I was careful to be generous with the former and judicious with the latter. The only thing I noted that was a problem was some tartar buildup on her upper back teeth and some redness along her gum line. "She'll need a cleaning," I said as I pointed out the problem to Donna. She leaned in to look, her hair ending up right next to my nose. Boy, that smelled good. Down boy, I told myself.

"I tried to brush them like you showed me, but she hates it."

"That's fine. Most cats do. It's absolutely normal to need a cleaning every year or two. It's not often that I find a cat that has perfect teeth."

"Then I won't beat myself up about it. But we will schedule it as soon as you can, okay?"

"Absolutely," I assured her. A dental cleaning was worth about three one hour sessions. One would go to Frank at Christmas.

I picked up one of the two vaccines she was due for and lightly pinched her right shoulder. The needle was in before she knew it and I pushed the vaccine in. I had the second one in under the skin by her right hip before she started to get too mad. The whole thing was over in seconds.

"Did you just give her her vaccines?" asked Donna with amazement. "I hate myself for ever using that other vet. And the fact that you let me barter your services. Don't ever retire, Atty."

She had nothing to worry about there. I'd keep coming to see her pets long after I stopped having a practice.

Dolly turned and looked at me, as if to say, "is that your best shot, Doc?" Then yawned and started cleaning her paws, in no hurry to leave my lap.

"Now that it's over she doesn't even care you're here," observed Donna.

I lifted Dolly down to the floor, packed up my medical gear and set up my computer and printer, sitting back down to type in my notes. As I worked Donna came up behind me. She put her hands on my shoulders and started to work at the tight muscles I didn't even know I had. What's that expression? It hurt so good. I actually groaned a little.

"You are very tense, Dr. At," she said.

"You would be too if you'd had my day so far," I answered.

She kneaded a little harder and I stopped typing for a moment. A moment later I felt her hair brush by the side of my head. "Poor Atty," she whispered in my ear, "anything you want to talk about?"

"Three emergencies and one annoying cop," I summarized.

"What sort of emergencies?" she asked as her massaging extended below my shoulders. "No, wait, skip to the annoying cop."

"I'll just say it's been a long day. And the annoying cop is off annoying someone else right now."

"What time were you up?"

"Five-thirty," I sort of lied.

"Poor baby," she said sincerely. That was what I needed, some sympathetic words.

"It has been pretty stressful," I added.

"Well," she said, "maybe I can make it a little better. Are you almost done?"

I tapped out a few more things and soon the printer was spitting out two copies of the exam for Dolly. The cat had jumped back on the table when she heard the noise and started batting at the pages as they came out. "Just finished," I said. I closed the laptop as soon as the printer finished. I left a copy on the table for Donna's records and put my copy, the printer, and laptop into my computer bag.

Donna pulled my chair back and I got up. She took my hand and we headed for her "office", the second bedroom of her condo. A dim colored lamp in the corner lighted the room, barely. She tapped on the screen of an iPod sitting in a Dockable speaker and soft, relaxing music finished the mood. I was already taking off my sports coat and tie, hanging them on the hooks behind the door.

In the middle of the room was what I had been looking forward to since early this morning. Donna Melton's massage table. "I warn you, I might fall asleep on you," I said as I took off my shirt.

"If you don't then I'm not doing my job right. I'll get all that stress out, Atty." She smiled and I lay on the table. I felt her drizzle some of the heated massage oil on my shoulders and she began her payment on my bill for services rendered.

CHAPTER 8

I must have fallen asleep because the next thing I knew Donna was brushing the hair away from my right ear and softly saying, "Time to get up Atty."

I turned my face so I could see her. "I told you," I said.

"You needed it," she answered. She was toweling off the excess oil from my back. I got up and it almost seemed like I floated off the table. I didn't realize how stressed I was until after it was gone. If the rest of the day proceeded as it had started, the effects of Donna's magical fingers would be far too short-lived.

Donna switched off her iPod and left. I put on my shirt, tie, and jacket and was soon back in the kitchen, loading myself up with my bags. "Thanks," I said.

"Thank you for taking care of Dolly," she said. She looked over at Dolly, sitting on one of the kitchen chairs, posed like a sphinx, her eyes closed, her cat smile seeming bigger than usual. "Dolly thanks you too."

"We'll see how thankful she is when I clean her teeth."

Donna let me out and I rode the elevator down. Just as I reached the lobby, my cell phone rang. I put down my bags to answer it. I looked at the caller ID. It was Sheila. I answered. "Hi, Sheila, baby, what's up?"

"'Sheila, baby?' You must have just gotten your payment from Ms. Melton."

"Jealous?"

"You're a sick man, Atty. Making that poor girl touch you."

"She doesn't mind."

"Because she gets paid to do it."

"You can't spoil the moment. Why are you calling?"

"Well, I've got good news and bad news. Which do you want first?"

I hated this game. "Give me the bad," I decided.

"Darla is no better. In fact, Mrs. Jeffries is convinced she is worse."

"Rats," I muttered.

"What's the matter with her?" she asked.

"I thought she had a straight forward allergic reaction. She should be better by now. Are you sure she's not just exaggerating? Maybe Darla wouldn't eat her scones or something equally as non-serious."

"She said the swelling around her face looked worse and she was making some wheezing sounds."

"Rats," I muttered again, this time much louder. Frank even looked over at me. I waved.

"Atty, you really need to get some good curse words in your vocabulary. 'Rats' just doesn't seem to cut it most of the time."

"How about, gosh darn it?" I offered.

She tsked me over the phone. "I don't think so," she said.

"Do I have time to go over there?" I asked. I'd need to make time it sounded like.

"Well, if you had been answering your phone the last half hour you could have seen her instead of letting Donna Melton do whatever it is she does to you."

"Without Donna, I would not be back to my usual cheerful self."

"Remind me to play you the tape from this morning."

"You don't really record me, do you? I think that's illegal."

"Not if you have a warrant," she replied.

I went over my schedule in my head. My next appointment was close to my house and I was originally planning on getting home for lunch back when this was still going to be a normal day. "Can you call Mrs. Finley and reschedule her for the end of the day? I'll catch her on the way home. I'm not far from Mrs. Jeffries now."

"She said that would be fine," Sheila informed me.

"What would I do without you?" I asked.

"Your business would fail, you'd live half your life at Danny's, half at Mullen's Pub, and die a fat drunk."

"A happy fat drunk," I corrected her.

"Hey, what's the good news?" I asked, almost forgetting the

possibility there was an, albeit tarnished, silver lining hidden somewhere.

"What good news?" she asked.

"You know, you had good news and bad news," I reminded her.

"Oh there wasn't any, but I didn't just want to come out and say Mrs. Jeffries needed to see you."

"Thanks," I said, a bit of sarcasm dripping from the corner of my mouth.

"That's my job."

"Actually, it isn't, but I appreciate the effort."

"Mrs. Jeffries is expecting you in ten minutes," she added.

"Aarrgghh," I said before hanging up. I picked up my bags after stowing my phone in my jacket pocket and headed for the door. Frank opened it with a smile and a wink.

I loaded up the Escape and got into the driver's side and decided to make a quick call. I pressed speed dial three which connected me to the specialty Clinic.

"Chicago Veterinary Specialty Center, how may I help you?" twanged Margaret's annoying nasal voice.

"It's Dr. At," I said.

"The police are here and they're sitting in my waiting room," she said.

"Okay. Is Allie there?" I asked.

"Somewhere," was her answer.

"Can you get her for me?" I asked.

"Hold on," she droned. The phone dropped on the desk again. I heard heels click off into the distance. I don't know why she never put me on hold. I wondered if she knew the phones had a hold button. I wondered what they played for their on-hold music? Neil Diamond? That'd be sweet.

A minute later the phone was picked up. "Dr. At?" asked a too bright, too cheery voice.

"Allie, how's it going? Didn't you work last night?" Allie was my favorite tech. She was well-experienced for someone in her mid-twenties, worked well with the animals, and didn't mind hanging around for a few hours in the morning after an overnight shift to help me with my surgeries.

"Hey, what did you do? The police are crawling all over this place. You kill someone?" she asked.

"Crawling?" I asked.

"Well, sitting in the waiting room. But there are two of them. One has a home theater system and the other some paper towels. We've been betting on what they're for."

"That's actually what I need help with," I started to explain.

"Please tell me the home theater system is for the break room. The Blu-ray player here sucks."

"Sorry to disappoint you. Those boxes actually have two dead dogs in them. One is evidence, one a patient. They both need necropsies."

"That's even better," she said.

"Is Dr. Thomas there today?"

"The dentist? No just the eye lady and the skin guy." Someone listening on her end of the conversation only had to be thoroughly confused by now.

"Great, can you stay and set me up in the surgery room for the necropsies?"

"Why in surgery?"

"The dog in the paper towel box may have something contagious. That's the only place I can think of that is fairly well contained other than the isolation ward and there is no room in there to work."

"Wow," said Allie.

"Can you get radiographs and blood from both of them? I'll be there in about forty-five minutes."

"No prob," she said and I heard the phone hang up. Okay, that was easy. I ended the call and started up the car.

As soon as I was on my way toward Mrs. Jeffries the phone rang. I pulled over and put the Escape in park. I checked the caller ID. It was the specialty clinic. Maybe Allie had another question.

"Hello?"

"Doc At, I got a little problem here," Allie announced.

"What is it?"

"No problem getting the home theater box dog, but the chick with the paper towels is giving me a hassle."

"Oh yeah, she'll probably want to stay with the dog. It's evidence, remember?"

"Oh. So you're okay if she just watches or whatever?"

"Sure. You want me to talk to her?"

"I got it. She seems pretty cool."

"Great."

"Awesome." The phone was dead again. Problem solved. It took a moment for me to realize that Marcy would now have unfettered access to Allie and would turn on the interrogation full speed. Suddenly "awesome" didn't seem like the word for it. Well, I'd just deal with it when I got there.

I waited for the traffic to clear again and headed for Marine Drive and then south to revisit my first stop of the day. When I pulled up I looked for any sign of Henry or his mop bucket. I hoped after this morning he'd be a little less of a stickler, but I was in a hurry. Claire was manning the front desk. Billy's shift had ended at 8:00 a.m. I put on the flashers and clicked the hatch open before stepping out of the Escape.

I had been thinking about what was going on with Darla over the last five minutes. The antihistamines and cortisone should have worked by now if it was just an insect sting. Other possibilities had flooded my mind. One was a black widow spider bite. They can cause massive tissue damage with edema similar to an allergic reaction. Henry's plant filled atrium came to mind. I might have to pop in and check for spider webs to see if I could spot one.

I grabbed my black medical bag and left the computer in the car. I didn't want to take up too much time printing up my bill and odds were that I'd be back tomorrow or worst case, taking Darla to the clinic with me.

I considered a possible infection or even worse, a tumor that was obstructing the jugular vein causing fluid to pool in her head. Infection was the most likely. I grabbed a prepacked vial of cephalexin capsules from a milk crate and slipped them into my pocket. I might consider another cortisone injection to help with swelling, but that decision would have to wait until after my examination.

Claire was up from behind the desk and holding the door open for me as I entered the building. Claire was a fairly large black woman. Her width almost matched her height, but to assume she couldn't move when she had to was a mistake. Like all the door-people at the building, she knew me well. I smiled as I squeezed by her.

"I just called Mrs. J. to tell her you were on the way up," she told me.

I walked to the desk to sign in.

"Don't bother, Henry went home sick," she added.

I stopped and looked at her, "Sick?" He seemed fine this morning.

She shrugged. "Probably the flu. Goes through these old people like castor oil through a baby." The image made me grimace.

"You were here this morning. What's the matter, you couldn't fix that lady's dog then?" she taunted.

"She probably just misses me," I teased back.

"Is that all it takes for you to come running? My doggy is wheezing?"

"That and a check," I explained.

"I don't think I could afford you, Dr. At," she realized and laughed a deep hearty laugh at her own self amusement. She held the door to the elevator lobby open and I walked into an open waiting car and pressed the button for Mrs. Jeffries' floor.

All the way up I was trying to figure the best route to take me past Danny's to grab lunch before hitting the emergency clinic. A double cheeseburger would go a long way to making this a better day. Almost as good as Donna Melton's hands. But time was getting short today. Best to just get to the specialty clinic and get the necropsies done.

I stepped out as soon as the elevator doors gave me enough space to. With only one bag, it was considerably easier to maneuver about. Mrs. Jeffries' door cracked open and as soon as she got a peek at me, it closed enough for her to release the security chain. Who was ever going to get by Claire I had no idea.

"Hello, Mrs. Jeffries," I said as the door started to open. "Darla still not feeling well?"

The door was all the way open and Mrs. Jeffries' face gave me my answer. She had a worried look and she was clasping her hands around a lacy handkerchief. They hung by her waist, tired and weak. A cough, as delicate as she was, brought the ivory fabric to her mouth. "Please excuse me, Dr. Klammeraffe. I am so glad you could come by so soon. That wonderful woman, Sheila, told me how worried you've been all day about Darla and that you'd be here as soon as possible. She said you even had her reschedule patients. You didn't have to do that. But I do appreciate it."

Sheila's Christmas bonus just went up ten percent.

"Darla and I got you a little gift," she said.

"That's very nice. Totally unnecessary, though."

She went on, "You did say to call if she was having trouble breathing, well, she's making an awful sound. Won't even touch her Rice Krispies."

I didn't give a second thought to the Rice Krispies. I had no doubt that if offered dog food, Darla would turn her nose up at it and wonder what sort of creature would eat that stuff. "Let me take a look at her," I said. She led me to the bedroom.

Darla was in the middle of the bed, her puffy face between her front legs. Her eyelids were so swollen she could barely see through the slits that were left. The edema had gotten worse and from what I could see of her breathing, it was getting worse as well.

I pulled out my stethoscope from my bag and sat on the bed next to Darla. She tried to lift up her head, but the extra weight and her weakened condition, combined with the antihistamines I had given her earlier, made that impossible for her. I listened to her chest. There was considerable wheezing, but it was coming from her upper airways, not her lungs. Her heart rate was slow, about sixty.

I put my Vet-Temp in her ear and it flashed 103.5 after a second. Up from this morning.

Suddenly she started another wheezing fit which quickly turned into coughing and then I saw some bright red dots appear on the bedspread in front of her. I looked at her nose and mouth. Fresh blood dotted her nostrils and lips.

Okay, not an allergic reaction. My mind was racing with alternative possibilities, wondering what I had missed, but more importantly what to do next. I was concerned that the fluid building up in the tissues in her airway might be the source of the bleeding and her increased respiratory effort. I felt gently along her lower jaw and neck down to her shoulders. Both the lymph nodes under her lower jaw and the nodes in front of her shoulder were very enlarged and firm, but I found no other masses. They could be enlarged secondary to the edema, an infection, or possibly a tumor, but I didn't want to think about the latter. The fluid buildup now extended all the way to her shoulders. Quite a bit further than this morning. Was it only this morning that this had started?

It couldn't be her heart. Mrs. Jeffries had me run ECGs every three months. Usually edema from heart failure started in the rear legs. I checked her legs and abdomen. No swelling or signs of fluid in her abdomen that might also signal heart failure.

Well, either it was an infection or maybe she did have a mass in her neck or chest that was interfering with blood flow back to her heart.

"Is she going to be alright, Dr. Klammeraffe?" asked Mrs. Jeffries. She had collapsed into a chair near the bed. Another cough required the attention of her handkerchief. It was nothing compared to the alveoli busters of Mrs. Hornby, but I suspected the whole ordeal was taking its toll on her.

I smiled as best I could. I didn't know if she was going to be alright. I was worried enough about her breathing to know that she needed to be hospitalized. "You're right that she has gotten worse. I'm glad you called. I think, as a precaution, I should take her to the clinic and we can run some more tests on her. I'd like to get a blood sample and maybe some x-rays."

"Of course, Dr. Klammeraffe, please do whatever you need."

I usually brought a carrier when I knew I had to transport animals and I knew I didn't have one in my car. "I'll need something to carry her in," I said.

"Oh, I think I have a box in the other room. I'll put her bed in the bottom. There should be room," she added. She pulled herself up, perhaps a little slowly even for her.

"I'll go get it," I offered.

"Nonsense," she reprimanded me, "I'm not that decrepit. You stay with Darla." I waited for Mrs. Jeffries to accomplish her task, stroking Darla's soft, fluffy, orange fur. She sighed and settled into the bed.

I'd get her a shot of antibiotics and something to help with the fluid buildup as soon as we got down to my car. Hopefully Allie and I could get her stabilized and start on some diagnostic work before we attended to the necropsies. Definitely no lunch today.

"I hope this will do," said Mrs. Jeffries. It was a color inkjet printer box, plastered in glossy yellow and blue corporate logos and a picture of the printer that had once occupied it. I wondered where it came from. I had never seen any sign of a computer, let alone a printer in Mrs. Jeffries' place.

In the bottom was a velvet dog bed, a Darla shaped indentation compressed into the padding. I lifted Darla carefully and put her in the box. There was plenty of room for the tiny creature.

"This will be perfect," I said. There was little to no chance Darla would be trying to escape.

"Please call me as soon as you know anything," said Mrs. Jeffries. "Do you want to take your gift with you now?"

I was a bit curious as to what she and Darla had gotten me. "I'll get it when I bring her back," I said. Between Darla and my medical bag I really couldn't carry anything else.

"I'll give you an update as soon as I get some of the test results in an hour or so. In the meantime, I'm going to give her something to help with her breathing and some antibiotics in case she has an infection."

"You don't think it is an allergic reaction after all?"

"It may be, but I have to rule out other things as well."

"Could she have gotten the flu? It has been going around the building you know. I got my flu shot, but those things hardly ever work. I feel like I'm starting in with it myself," she added, punctuating with another cough.

"Dogs don't get the same flu as people," I assured her. "It's unlikely that she picked it up from another dog. I suppose she could have picked it up from a horse. Has she been out galloping with horses again?" I asked. I hoped the mild attempt at humor might lighten the mood and give some optimism to Mrs. Jeffries.

"Oh, Dr. Klammeraffe, you are so wicked. I assure you she has not been around any other animals, other than myself. Now you take good care of her."

"As if she were my own," I assured her. She knew I meant it.

"Thank you," she said, then coughed again.

"And you take care of yourself," I added. I gathered the box and with my fingers snagged the handles of my black bag as Mrs. Jeffries led me out. She even walked with me out into the hall and pressed the elevator button for me. I wasn't gone long enough for the car to be called away and the elevator chimed almost immediately.

Mrs. Jeffries reached into the box and gently let one bony, arthritic finger stroke her dog softly between the eyes. "Don't you worry, Darla, Dr. Klammeraffe will take very good care of you. Brave heart, my love."

I stepped into the elevator. I lifted a knee to help support Darla and freed up my right had to press the lobby button. Mrs. Jeffries stood outside staring at the inkjet printer box as we waited for the elevator doors to close. Finally, they did, but not before Mrs. Jeffries touched the corner of each eye with her lace handkerchief.

CHAPTER 9

When we did reach the lobby, I saw Claire jump up from her seat and move over to the lobby door where she held it open for me. She saw Darla in the box.

"What's the matter with that old pooch?" she asked as she tried to peer closer at Darla. "Looks like she's been through ten rounds with a super heavyweight."

"I have to take her in for some testing. Please check on Mrs. Jeffries every once in a while for me, okay? She might be coming down with that flu and with her worrying about Darla here, she may not take very good care of herself."

"Can do, Dr. At. We all love that old lady. She's not like most of the cheapskates around here. Always has an envelope for us desk people every Christmas and never forgets to say please and thank you. I'll keep an eye on her."

"Thanks." I looked out at my car, still blinking away in the fire lane. "I need to go. If you talk to Henry, tell him I said I hope he feels better."

"That old codger?" Claire was one of the few people I knew who used the word "codger."

"He's not that bad. I saw his garden earlier this morning. I didn't even know that place existed all the years I've been coming here. None of my clients have apartments overlooking it. I had thought maybe Darla had been stung by a bee or wasp."

Claire nodded. "He did do a fine thing with that atrium, I'll give him that."

I headed for the front door. She jumped ahead to open that door for me as well. Again with the assistance of my knee, I held the inkjet printer box and fumbled out my keys. In a moment, the back hatch clicked open. I put my black bag down and then Darla. With what must have been super-canine effort she lifted her head to look at me, her glossy brown eyes peering from between the swollen lids, pleading. "You'll be safer in the back," I explained to her.

I pulled out my little injectable drug box and found a bottle of furosemide and Baytril. The first would help with the fluid buildup in her tissues, the second was an antibiotic. Darla whimpered and managed to lift a paw to the edge of her dog bed. "Stay in there, Darla," I told her. Her paw slipped back and her head, heavy with fatigue, fell back onto her front legs, her eyes closing the last little bit. I pulled out two syringes from my medical bag and drew up the doses of the medications. She didn't even flinch as I gave her the injections.

I reached for the button to close the hatch. I looked in the box. Her breathing was heavy. I could hear the wheeze. She started a whine with each breath, high pitched and plaintive. Her expression was doleful and sad. "Okay you little drama queen," I relented. I lifted up the box and the whining ceased. I hated when women know how to manipulate me so easily. I took the box and Darla to the passenger side of my car, opened the door and put her on the seat. I moved my files and recently updated schedule to the floor and pushed the box tight to the back and pulled the seat belt around the front to help hold it in place. It was better than nothing. It was certainly better than Darla whining and trying to crawl out of the box as I drove.

I jogged around to the other side. Big mistake. I am not a jogger. How much time did that actually save? My stomach let me know with a lurch and grumble that lunch was far overdue. I tried to tell it that Danny's was not in its immediate future, but it ignored my pleading. I got in and started up the car and turned off the flashers. It was now 12:15. My next appointment was at two o'clock with my twelve o'clock shifted to six o'clock. God, I hated emergencies. I hated anything that ruined my nice, neat schedule. But they happened and it was part of the job. If I received a call after 6 p.m. about a pet who had eaten their owner's antidepressants or cut their foot on a glass shard at the dog beach or had been vomiting for three days, but tonight it really seemed sick, I (or usually Sheila) sent them to the emergency clinic. But, if it occurred during the day and it was something I could handle, I felt obliged to see them. I was a little upset that Sheila had expanded the definition of "during the day" to slightly before sunrise, but she had been right that I would want to see Darla.

I called the specialty clinic again. Margaret answered. "It's Dr. At, I..." I heard the receiver clunk on the desk. I waited a moment. "Hello?" Another moment. "Anyone there?"

"Hey Dr. At," said Allie's voice. "You piss in Margaret's corn flakes?"

"Apparently."

"Got your x-rays done and the blood tests are running. What's up?"

"You want to help me out with a live patient as well this afternoon?"

"You bet. You're just a busy little bee today, aren't you?"

"Buzz, buzz," I said. "Be there in ten."

"I'll be waiting."

I hung up, put the phone away, then sped out of the driveway and onto Marine Drive. We'd work up Darla first, then on to my necropsies. I was already planning what tests we'd do for Darla and treatments to get started on her to try and stop the symptoms and reverse them, as well as get to a diagnosis.

It wasn't often that I didn't know what was happening in a patient, but it seemed like it was more frequently that there was little I could do to make it better or speed recovery.

For Darla I was dreading the possibility of a tumor. Nearly as bad would be a spider bite. With a dog Darla's size, it could be fatal. I still held out hope it was an allergic reaction, although it should have responded even a little to the medications I gave this morning. Allie and I might have to shave off some of her beautiful orange fur to look for signs of a puncture to help rule out an infection.

I turned right on Addison. The traffic was picking up, the usual lunchtime surge. From 12:05 to 12:55 people would be trying to run errands, picking up take-out from fast food joints, or fitting in a lunch meeting at some sit-down place. It all meant more headaches for me. I looked over at Darla. She was exhausted, but I could tell she just couldn't get comfortable. My injection of furosemide might take a little longer to start reducing the swelling. The antibiotics would take hours to start having a noticeable effect, provided it was an infection and it was susceptible to the Baytril. She needed some oxygen to help with her breathing and an IV to keep her hydrated and prevent her from going into shock.

I pulled into the empty lot next to the emergency clinic that served as their parking lot. I saw Allie's Jeep and a few other cars belonging to the doctors and staff and probably a few clients. There were no police cars. I wondered if Marcy had taken off after all.

I went around to the passenger side to get Darla. I folded the top in a little, just in case she decided to get a burst of energy. I walked around to the front of the building. Allie was sitting in the waiting area and jumped up to open the door when she saw me.

While I had gotten used to Allie's appearance, for many people their first look at her was a little disconcerting. Although it changed on a monthly basis, her hair today was half green and half black. It was plastered up into a ridge that ran down the middle of her head. Each ear was perforated with a dozen earrings. Each eyebrow had three gold rings through them and a diamond stud decorated her left nostril, a small ruby on the right. Although she wore scrubs, under her shirt was a black and neon concert t-shirt and poking up from under that collar were the edges of tattoos I could only imagine.

Her eyes were heavily lined and she had on a very dark green shade of lipstick to match her hair. She was fairly tall, about five-ten, and thin. She was the best assistant I had ever worked with. She had started working at the specialty clinic as a kennel helper. Occasionally the doctors would need an extra hand and she proved to be better than many of the certified technicians. The animals almost seemed to be calmed just by her presence.

The first time I met her I had brought a cat to the clinic for a spay. She asked if I needed help and explained that she worked midnights at the ER. At that time her hair was done up in about a dozen purple and orange spikes and she had only one ring in each eyebrow. While I was thinking about it she had opened the cat carrier and was scratching Matilda behind the ears.

I had spent twenty minutes getting the cat in the carrier and she had hissed at me the entire drive over. Now she seemed to have overcome her fear and was accepting some affection from a stranger. Allie reached in and pulled Matilda out, cuddling her and rubbing under the cat's chin. I figured if the cat liked her, she had to be okay. Since then, I used Allie as much as possible. I did surgeries on Wednesdays when the surgeon at the specialty clinic was doing consults and rechecks. I would start after nine o'clock to give Allie a chance to run down to the 7-eleven to get a Super Big Gulp sixty-four ounce jolt of caffeine-laden Dr. Pepper. Despite not having any formal training, she was a fast learner and always seemed to know what I wanted.

"Ah," she noted as I walked past her, "an inkjet printer. What a collection of patients today. Run out of pet carriers?"

"Ha, ha," I said. Allie let the door close then pulled back one of the flaps to look down at Darla. She scratched her behind the ears then took the box from me.

"What's her name?" she asked.

Allie always seemed to know whether a cat or dog was male or female, even when it wasn't obvious. "Darla," I answered.

"Pretty bad edema. She already get the shotgun treatment?" she asked.

"The shotgun" was a term we used when we had no idea what was going on, so we treated for everything possible, in Darla's case, steroids, antihistamines, antibiotics and a diuretic. "Yep," I answered.

"Let me put her in an oxygen cage first, before we do the x-rays. She's looking a little stressed out."

I glanced into the box and could see her chest heaving a little more heavily than before. Why wasn't she getting better? "Great idea. You have the x-rays on my other patients?"

"The home theater and the paper towels? Can you call them patients when they're dead?" she asked.

"Peanuts Johnson and Spot Doe," I answered. "And yes, dead animals can be patients. They need to be diagnosed."

"A Spot Doe, eh? Where did she come from?" she asked. Spot Doe was a name we used for unidentified dogs, cats were Tigger Doe.

"Kazakhstan," I answered.

She looked at me, squinting her left eye into the evil eye look. "Kazakhstan? Like in the game 'Risk'?"

"She was shipped here from Kazakhstan and died on the flight. No one picked her up. I got a call from the airport this morning."

"I guess that explains the cop," said Allie. "Boy, did she give me a look."

"Everyone gives you a look," I pointed out.

"True, but her look was creepy. She even insisted on wearing a lead apron and watching while I took the x-rays."

"She gets like that. You see anything interesting?" I asked.

"You're the doctor," she answered, "you tell me."

"Let's go check them out while Darla gets oxygenated."

"Roger," she answered. She glanced over to the reception desk separated from the waiting room by a thick pane of plexiglass. She nodded her head at the door to the exam rooms and treatment area and Margaret buzzed the lock. I pulled the door open for her and followed her in.

"Is Officer Avers still here?" I asked Margaret as I passed behind her desk.

"Can't leave the evidence, Doc," said a voice from behind me. I must have jumped quite a bit because she started to chuckle a little. "Scare you, Doc?"

We continued down the hallway to the radiology suite as Allie turned into the ICU. "A little," I conceded. "Listen, thanks again for getting Peanuts back for me."

"Are you kidding? They're going to be talking about that one at the station for weeks. Glad I could help."

"You can wait in the employee lounge, have some coffee."

She appeared to consider my suggestion before answering. "I thought I'd watch you guys. I'm going to have to be there when you cut that dog from the airport up anyway. Chain of evidence and all. I'm actually looking forward to my first dog autopsy."

"It's actually a necropsy," I informed her.

"A what?" she asked.

"Never mind. I have a live sick dog to take care of first, then we can do the autop-" I stopped myself, "necropsies," I said.

"So have you seen, like a real, autopsy on a person?" asked Allie, her words dripping with curiosity. She had reappeared from the ICU after settling Darla in.

"Tons. There was this one guy, he was strangled with piano wire, the head was barely attached."

"Awesome," said Allie.

She turned toward me. "Darla's breathing the good stuff. Let me show you those x-rays." She led the way to radiology. Marcy leaned close to me, "You want me to run a check on that girl?" she asked.

"What? No. She's fine. Sheila is fine. If you want to check someone out, check out Margaret, the receptionist. I've always thought she was a little shady."

"You got a last name?" asked Marcy. She pulled out a note pad from a pocket on her vest.

"Harvey," I answered. "With an E-Y." I wanted to say I was just kidding, but it would give her something to do. What harm was there anyway. She was just an annoying receptionist.

Marcy followed me into the x-ray room. Allie sat at the desk with the computer. The specialty clinic had long switched to digital x-rays. No more giant sheets of film to mess with. I pulled up a chair and sat next to her. Two large LED monitors hung from the wall above a computer keyboard and mouse. Each had x-rays displayed.

"Spot Doe is on the left screen, Peanuts on the right screen. Got lateral and VDs of the chest and abdomen." Lateral views showed the patient laying on their side, VD or ventro-dorsal views showed them on their backs. "Something weird going on in both of their abdomens," she added.

The screens were set to display all four shots from each of the dogs in a 2-by-2 grid. I clicked on the side view of the abdomen for Spot Doe to enlarge it to full screen. I set the cursor to magnifying mode which created a small rectangular area that I could move around with the mouse to more closely examine areas of interest. I was immediately drawn to a round white spot in the middle of the abdomen.

"That doesn't look like it should be there," said Allie.

"What?" asked Marcy. I was sure that the radiograph looked like a garbled mess to her.

I moved the magnifier out of the view and pointed at the white sphere, likely a foreign object lodged in the intestines. "Probably swallowed something and got an obstruction. Her intestines leaked or ruptured and she died of peritonitis."

"You think it's drugs?" asked Allie.

Marcy gave her a look. "Maybe."

"Probably just a ball, or maybe a rock, or a trichobezoar..."

"A tricho-what?" interrupted Marcy.

"Trichobezoar," said Allie. "One of Doc At's favorite words. I've seen them get bigger than this. We had one in a rabbit last month the size of a tennis ball."

"What is it?" asked Marcy.

"It is the medical term for a hairball."

"Then why didn't you say hairball?" she asked.

"I paid too much for my education to not use my fancy words," I said.

I scanned through the other images. The object was just as round on the other view where the dog was lying on her back.

I then moved over to Peanuts' images. After looking at the smaller pictures, I once again enlarged to the sideways view of the abdomen. It was obviously filled with fluid. There were very few details visible apart from occasional pockets of gas, some fecal material, and a clump of whitish material close by where the stomach should be. "You see that?" I asked Allie.

"I did. Check out the VD view."

I pulled up the front to back image and centered on the anomaly, this time enlarging the entire image.

Marcy leaned in to see what we were so interested in. "That's inside the home theater box dog?" she asked. "Is it what I think it is?"

"She must have eaten it," said Allie.

"Didn't chew it," I pointed out, "It's pretty much intact."

"Ew, Ick," said Marcy.

"Cause of death?" asked Allie.

"I have no idea, but we're going to find out if Sheila ever gets a hold of the Johnsons." I left the enlarged image centered on the screen. I was seeing a perfect skeleton of a mouse. Little skull, tiny ribs, long tail, and the bones of the legs, all where they should be. Did Betty have her staff feed the mice they caught in traps to the dogs? Great way to recycle, I guess.

"I'm going to check on Darla," said Allie, "see if she is stable enough so we can get her x-rays. Can you set up the computer for her?"

"As you wish," I answered. She popped out to the ICU and I entered Darla's information into the computer.

While I waited for Allie I wondered if perhaps the mouse had been poisoned and Peanuts had died of secondary poisoning. It happened. People left out rat bait, the dogs ate the rats and absorbed the toxins from them. It seemed unlikely since the mouse was largely intact.

"So, that's a mouse in that dog's belly," said Marcy.

"That's what it looks like. And he swallowed it whole."

"Weird," she added.

I put on one of the lead aprons and fastened a thyroid shield around my neck as well. As I was slipping on the lead gloves, Allie returned with Darla. Her face was still swollen. When she saw me through the little slits of her eyes, her little legs started pumping and she nearly jumped out of Allie's hands. She looked like she was feeling a little better. "Take it easy, kid," I told her. "You're going to get too excited." I slipped a hand from one of the gloves and ruffled the fur over her shoulders. She calmed down.

"She's happy to see you, Doc," said Allie. "So, some weird sort of allergic reaction?"

"I thought it was, but she got worse after steroids and antihistamines," I answered. "She's got me worried."

"You want x-rays of her head?"

"Head, chest, abdomen; I don't want to miss anything. If we don't diagnose the problem maybe the radiation therapy will cure her."

"Ha, ha," answered Allie. "As long as her breathing is okay, we'll keep going, but first sign of respiratory distress and she's back in the oh-two."

"Aye, aye," I said. I turned to Marcy. "You'll have to wait in the hall." She turned and left with no argument. Allie suited up and we quickly snapped off our pictures, each loading up onto the computer. Darla remained calm and cooperative. She had been through this before when Mrs. Jeffries had been worried she had eaten her pearl earrings, mistaking them for breath mints. The earrings had turned up between some plastic-coated cushions on her couch, but not before Darla had been thoroughly scanned for the lost items.

Allie took off her apron, gloves and thyroid shield and I handed Darla to her. I removed my radiation shielding. It always bothered me that we were required to cover out body, hands and neck. What about our elbows? Heck, what about our heads? What use would our hands be if our elbows sloughed off. Sometimes I closed my eyes in an effort to convince myself I was getting an extra skin layer of protection from the x-rays. "Blood samples next," I said.

"What do you want?"

"The works: CBC, chem screen, electrolytes. We'll send some serum out for titers too; leptospirosis, tick panel, fungal panels, whatever else we can think of," I told her.

"Jeez, that's a lot," said Allie. "Think she'll have any blood left when were done?"

"If the radiation doesn't cure her, there's nothing like a good, old-fashioned blood-letting."

"Better than leeches, I guess," conceded Allie.

"Besides, money's no object with Mrs. Jeffries."

"With your clients I believe it," said Allie. "When the people who come to emergency at 1:00 a.m. say it, it usually means, money is no object because we don't have any!"

"I want to do a quick check of these radiographs. I'll be in to help you in a minute."

Allie took off with Darla and I started to look over the images. The shots of her head and neck showed severe soft tissue swelling, but no sign of any foreign objects or pieces of metal buried in the skin. No fractures that may have caused a blood clot, no signs of infections around the tooth roots or in the bones.

The images of her chest did show some fluid in the front part of her lungs. I could also make out white fluid lines between the lung lobes as well. Her heart was its normal size and I didn't see any nodules or other signs of tumors in the lungs. The abdomen was the least exciting. No organ enlargement, no fluid, no signs of infection. Overall they did little to answer my question as to what was causing this in Darla, but did create some new ones. Why were the symptoms mostly in the front half of her body? Most likely it started at the head and moved back.

"Let's go Doc, I'm ready," came a loud voice from the treatment room down the hall.

When I got to the treatment room, I could see Darla sitting in one of the two oxygen cages. They had plexiglass doors that effectively sealed the cages while a regulator pumped one hundred percent oxygen into the cage to make it easier for a patient to breathe when their lungs were in trouble.

Allie had everything set up to place an IV catheter and collect enough blood for all the tests I wanted.

"I assume a jugular stick is out the question," Allie said referring to the technique of drawing blood from the jugular vein in the neck. It was quick because it was a large vein, even in small animals, and it did require a somewhat cooperative patient, but in Darla's case, her neck was way to swollen to even try to feel the vein.

"Even I'm not that good," I said. I looked around the room.

"Where's Marcy?"

"She went to the lounge. Probably reading a back issue of Guns and Ammo or Soldier of Fortune. What's the deal with her? You into her?" asked Allie.

"What? What are you talking about?"

"I don't know, she seems to be into you. You know, the looks and stuff."

"What looks?"

"You know, looks. Jeez, you're beyond unaware."

"Nah," I protested, "besides, she's way too young for me."

"You're only as young as you feel," Allie said.

"I don't feel that young," I admitted.

"Maybe she could feel a little older and meet you halfway?"

"Get Darla," I ordered before it got further out of hand.

Allie took a look at Darla before opening the oxygen cage door. She seemed comfortable, but on one hundred percent oxygen, she should. She turned off the oxygen flow and opened the door, collecting the ball of orange fluff into her arms. She was carefully placed on a towel on one of the exam tables. "You got five minutes Doc, then she goes back in whether you're finished or not."

I accepted the challenge. Allie had everything laid out. While she soothed and cooed Darla, I clipped a section of fur from her front leg, all the way around. I grabbed the antiseptic soap-soaked gauze squares and cleaned the skin, wiping it with some antiseptic-soaked gauzes to finish up. We didn't want to add to her problems with an infection around her IV catheter. I opened the catheter Allie had set out and while she grasped Darla's front leg, acting as a human tourniquet, I could see the vein on top of her leg swell with blood. I laid my left thumb along the side of the vein to hold it steady while poking the skin with the tip of the catheter and sliding it into the vein. Darla was so used to my pokes she didn't move. At least I hoped that was why she didn't move. A crimson flash of blood appeared at the back end of the catheter and I slid the little white Teflon-coated tube into the vein over the steel stylet. Once it was completely in I pulled out the stylet the rest of the way.

To collect the blood samples I attached a short piece of tubing that fastened to a Vacutainer adapter, a small plastic cylinder with a needle inside attached to the tubing. We then started filling up blood tubes by pushing the rubber stopper into the needle. The vacuum in the tube then sucked blood from the catheter. It went slowly. I had to keep massaging her paw to get the blood to fill the constantly depleting vein, but soon we were done. It did seem like a lot of blood. Four tubes altogether.

"Dracula," Allie accused.

"She's not my type," I joked in my best Transylvanian accent.

I removed the tubing from the catheter and Allie handed me a cap to take its place and tape to fasten it in place. I then flushed the catheter with some heparinized saline in a syringe to keep blood clots from forming.

"Let's put her on a maintenance fluid rate," I told Allie, "I didn't like the look of the lungs. We don't want to drown her."

"Meds?" She asked.

I listed off four IV medications and doses knowing that Allie would remember them. She glanced at the clock. "Four and half minutes, Doc."

"Was there ever any doubt," I asked. "Do you think she'd tolerate some fine needle aspirates of her lymph nodes?"

"No," she considered as she carried Darla back to the oxygen cage. "Give her a little more time and you can try. You thinking cancer?"

"I'm thinking that those lymph nodes are filtering everything coming out of her head and if answers are to be found they'll be in those lymph nodes." A fine needle aspirate consisted of poking a needle into the tissue of interest and applying some suction with a syringe to collect cells which were then smeared on a slide and stained for examination under a microscope.

"We'll try in fifteen, twenty minutes." She attached a long line to Darla's catheter and taped it in place. The tube led out through the cage door to a bag of fluids and an IV pump. She then closed the door and turned the oxygen flow back on and Darla sighed before letting her head rest between her front legs. Allie set up the pump and it started its quiet cycle, a drop of IV fluids falling in the chamber every few seconds.

Allie gathered up the tubes. "We probably wouldn't have gotten that much blood with Dr. Cooper," she said.

"Dr. Cooper still a little hesitant?" I asked. Dr. Arnold Cooper had started working emergency shifts a month ago. Most vets started working emergency for one of two reasons; money, or in some cases, money. Because most of us regular practitioners had put the midnight emergency farm calls of the James Herriot days far behind us, and working on holidays and weekends cramped our style, emergency clinics were the only game in town if your pet needed care after hours. Accordingly, as the limited supply demanded, they charged a hefty premium for those services. They needed to do so to pay enough salary to attract people to work the crazy hours, and more importantly to work with the crazy clients. The pace could get insane during a full moon. A dozen patients an hour at peak times could show up and you had to assess, treat, and sometimes sneak in emergency surgeries while the rest of us enjoyed our beauty sleep.

As a result, burnout was high. A thirty-six hour shift on a weekend was profitable, but tough on the soul. Some managed to thrive, most did not. It didn't sound as though Arnold Cooper was going to be a thriver from what I heard from Allie and the other techs. Still, you didn't see me doing it. I had filled in a few times and each time resolved never to do it again.

"He tried to get a catheter in a great Dane the other night," she started to explain. "After three tries, I convinced him to let me have a go at the last leg. He's all thumbs when it comes to working with the animals, especially under pressure. You know what it's like here on a Saturday night. You need to be able to slip that catheter in while we're wheeling the dog to x-ray."

"Sounds like he won't be around long."

"You want to know the weirdest part?"

"Duh. Of course."

"Margaret likes him."

"No."

"Yes."

"I thought she hated humanity in general."

"Apparently not." She grabbed up the blood tubes and started labeling them. "I'll get the serum tubes spinning in the centrifuge, then we can start on the necropsies."

"Great, I'll get changed."

When I did surgeries I put on scrubs. Since this was likely to be as messy as a surgery, I wanted to be prepared. I headed down the hall to the locker room. I grabbed a set of green scrubs from the extra-large pile and peeled off my house call uniform. Once I was dressed, I slipped on a pair of paper shoe covers and grabbed a paper hat and surgical mask.

As I walked into the hallway, Marcy was leaving the women's locker room. She too was wearing a set of green scrubs. "We're twins," she observed.

"Except for the loaded gun attached to your hip," I pointed out. "What are you doing?"

"Allie said that if I was going to watch the postmortem exam I should get changed, so here I am."

"You could have watched through the window," I said.

"Nah, no fun in that," she answered. "Besides, technically if you do find drugs in that dog I need to be there to preserve the chain of custody."

"Chain of custody, eh?" I asked.

"Darn lawyers, they're pretty picky about stuff like that," she added.

I looked into her face. Her smile melted into a serious expression, obviously trying to mock me. "Don't touch anything," I warned. "We still can't rule out some infectious disease."

"Trust me, I won't be doing anything, but watching."

I brushed past her down the hall and entered the scrub room where we usually washed up before entering the surgery room. She followed on my heels.

"You want to get in on the pool?" she asked.

"Pool?"

"Yeah, I called in what we saw on the x-ray. The guys at the district headquarters are having some fun trying to guess what it is. Someone even has money on it being an artificial testicle."

"Ouch," I said. "Don't tell me, it was you, right?"

"Hey, maybe she was an attack dog, went after a guy with plastic nuts and bit one off, swallowing it whole."

I shook my head and rolled my eyes.

"Come to think of it, you probably shouldn't be in, if you were to win the guys would think you had some inside information, no pun intended."

"Are you always this witty?" I asked.

"Always."

Allie bumped in through the swinging doors holding up two sheets of paper. Lab reports from the emergency clinic's in-house blood analyzer. "Which one first, home theater or paper towels?" she asked.

"Peanuts," I answered.

She handed me the top sheet. "Looks like he had a pretty serious infection on top of liver and kidney failure," Allie said. The numbers agreed with her assessment.

I was hard-pressed to find a number in the lab results that fell in the normal range. The white blood cell count topped fifty thousand, three times normal. The creatinine and BUN, measures of kidney function, were ten times above those in an animal with normal kidneys and the liver enzymes were all elevated as well, indicating ongoing damage to the liver cells causing the enzymes to leak into the bloodstream. "It fits with peritonitis," I said.

"Perito-what?" asked Marcy.

"Infection in the abdomen. And the fact that his organs were shutting down tells me this didn't happen yesterday. He was suffering for a while."

"Why didn't the owners call you sooner?"

"He was boarding at the Bark and Breakfast. They claim he wasn't sick until this morning. When I got there he had to have been dead for days."

"Gross," said Allie.

"Sad," was Marcy's assessment. She was right.

Allie handed me the next sheet. This one was a little more difficult to interpret. There was some evidence of dehydration, which I would have expected with an intestinal obstruction. The dog was probably vomiting everything she ate and anything she thought about eating. The pancreatic enzymes were up as well, but probably more due to the dehydration than an infection in the pancreas. The protein levels were low as was the blood sugar and BUN. Most likely the dog hadn't been eating well, if at all. No wonder it had swallowed something that got stuck inside her.

The phone on the wall of the scrub room chirped and Margaret's voice bleated over the intercom. "Dr. At, it's your girl, Sheila, where are you?"

I picked up the extension and hit the answer button. "I'm in surgery scrub. Transfer her here."

"I'm not your secretary, you know," Margaret answered.

I rolled my eyes. "Could you please transfer the call here? I've been expecting some important information."

"Line two," she said and as her voice clicked off the light under line two started flashing. I pressed the button, "Sheila?"

"Atty, I found them."

"The Johnsons?"

"The Johnsons. But they seemed a little confused."

"Confused?"

"They said that Betty had called and that Peanuts had died of natural causes and they had made arrangement with Cozy Acres for her cremation."

"Natural causes, eh?"

"That's what they said."

"Did Betty happen to explain how they were going to have Peanuts cremated since they no longer had custody of his remains?"

"I think that detail slipped her mind. Maybe she thinks he's still out by the alley, waiting for the pet cemetery people."

"Do you have the Johnson's number?" I asked. She read it off and I jotted it on the small dry erase board with the marker attached by a short string. "I'll call them now. You didn't happen to tell them where Peanuts really is, did you?"

"I figured I'd leave that to you," she said. "How was lunch?" she asked, knowing full well that I didn't have time to get any yet.

"Not funny, Sheila," I told her before hanging up.

"Good news?" asked Allie.

"I have a number for Peanuts' owners. If they are up for it, we'll definitely be doing that necropsy as well."

"Awesome," said Marcy. Allie and I both looked at her. "What? Two dog postmortems. Wahoo. Besides, I got him back for you." She had a good point.

"Fine," I said. "Suit yourself."

"Jeez, he's pretty touchy today," she muttered to Allie.

"He gets that way when he doesn't have lunch," Allie explained.

"I'm not any way," I shouted. "I'm just trying to do my job here."

Allie rolled her eyes and Marcy nodded. "No lunch," they said in unison. My worst fear had come true, they were teaming up on me. Things could get ugly. I turned to the phone and dialed the number Sheila had given me, written on the white board.

It rang twice before Mary Johnson picked up. "Hello?" her voice wavered. I could tell she had been sobbing. Perhaps still was.

"Hello, Mrs. Johnson, It's Dr. At," I said.

"Oh, Dr. At, Sheila said you were trying to get a hold of me. I'm sure you did everything you could for Peanuts, even if you weren't able to get there right away. I know how busy you are," she added.

That sounded odd. "Excuse me? What do you mean?"

"Betty Cunningham explained how you arrived shortly after Peanuts died."

Shortly after? Betty was covering her butt. Should have seen that coming.

"She said that Peanuts probably had a heart attack. I guess those can happen to dogs, just like people. I've told Andy to stop giving her buttered toast, but he's more difficult to train than a dog," she continued. "Anyway, there probably wouldn't have been anything you could have done if you had gotten there when they called you."

Heart attack? Wow, why would Betty make that up? I was beginning to think they had done something to Peanuts and were trying to cover it up.

"I want to ask your permission to do a postmortem exam," I explained.

"Like an autopsy?" I refrained from correcting her. Grief and all. "Well, I'd hate for you to go all the way to the pet cemetery if it was just a heart attack."

"No, no, no. I have Peanuts' remains with me," I told her.

There was a long pause. "I don't understand."

"There has been a serious miscommunication, Mrs. Johnson. I did go see Peanuts this morning shortly after Betty had called. In fact, I was already out on another emergency." It didn't hurt to make myself look like the good guy here. "When I got there it was obvious that Peanuts had been dead for some time." I didn't want to tell her it had been for days. "I did a quick exam there and found fluid in the abdomen from an infection. It wasn't a heart attack."

"Why would Betty Cunningham tell me all that then?"

"I don't know, but I think that once we do the postmortem we may find out."

"You think that something happened to Peanuts at the kennel?" she asked.

"I don't know. Animals do die suddenly, but something feels weird here. I got Peanuts remains from one of the kennel workers and brought her to the clinic where I do my surgeries." No need to fill in the details of Pete not actually handing the remains to me and the merry-go-round Peanuts had been on for a big part of that time. "I've run some preliminary blood tests and we did x-rays, all at my expense, and the postmortem will go a long way towards figuring out what happened and if something did happen to him there, preventing it from happening to other pets."

I could hear Mary conferring with her husband, Andy. "Dr. At, we've always trusted you. Please find out what happened to our baby," she said.

"I'll call when I have some information. And I truly am sorry for your loss. You know how much I loved Peanuts as well."

"We do. Thank you." She hung up.

"Sounds like the kennel is trying to hide something," observed Marcy.

"You think?" I responded, dripping a little too much sarcasm.

"If they did do something, you going to arrest them?" Allie asked Marcy.

"You betcha. I love dogs too."

"Great. Now that that's all settled let's get started."

"This is going to be fun," said Allie, "in a sad sort of way since a pet died, but it's not often we get three medical mysteries in one day."

Before gloving up, I decided to make one more call. I picked up the phone and dialed Sheila. "It's me."

"What's up?"

"I'll be here a while. See if my two o'clock can reschedule for tomorrow."

"Already done," she said.

That didn't surprise me. Sheila was often one step ahead. "Maybe you should have cut that visit with Ms. Melman short." she added.

I let that one go. I deserved that massage. I could still feel her magic fingers melting the knots in my shoulders.

"Let Mrs. Jeffries know that Darla is stable and I'll call her when I get the blood test results."

"I tried calling her a little while ago, but no answer."

"That's weird. I'd think she'd be glued to the phone. It wasn't busy?"

"No. I'll keep trying."

"Check with Claire, maybe she went out."

"She's really okay? Darla I mean."

"Yes, she's hanging in there."

"You take care of her," she ordered.

"Yes, Ma'am," I answered. She hung up. No one was pulling for that little dog more than me. If she went, who knew what Mrs. Jeffries would do. I shuddered to think. Allie was right, it was a medical mystery. I hoped I was up to it.

CHAPTER 10

I slipped the receiver back onto the hook. Darla's mystery was the most important one to solve. She was still alive. I hoped the blood tests would show something. If her symptoms continued to progress, the edema would essentially choke her to death.

I turned and smiled at the two scrub-clad ladies. "Okay, let's go," I said as we entered the surgery suite.

Allie quickly had Spot Doe on the table with her legs tied out of the way. She shaved the belly a few inches on either side of the midline. We weren't worried about sterility, but the long hair could make closing her back up a lot harder. The table was split down the middle and had been set up in a flattened V-shape. This left a little gap that drained into a trough that led to a bucket. Great for catching any built-up fluid in the abdomen that would leak out.

I wheeled over the instrument stand that had a surgery pack laid out, the scalpel handle was loaded with a fresh number ten blade and ready to go. I slipped my mask up over my face. The girls followed suit. We didn't have to worry about the patient getting an infection, but conversely, we didn't want to inhale anything dangerous that might be inside her.

I started my incision just below the breastbone and cut all the way down to the pelvis. My first cut was just deep enough to go through the skin. There was little body fat beneath it. I started to cut deeper through the muscle. Once I was through it and could see the glistening intestines through the cut, I swapped the scalpel for a pair of Metzenbaum scissors and extended the abdominal incision the length of the skin incision.

Like a mass of alien worms, the intestines pushed their way up through the incision, a foul smelling fluid leaking out as well. I looked at Marcy. Her eyes betrayed a bit of unease, but she was hanging tough. I didn't bother checking out Allie, she had seen worse. I could immediately smell the stench of leaking bowel. I started pulling on the intestines laying them over on the opposite side of the dog. Allie had a suction tube and was sucking out reddish brown fluid, similar to what I had aspirated from Peanuts' abdomen at the Bark and Breakfast.

Marcy leaned in for a better look, but rolled back on her heels when she got a good whiff of the abdomen. "That smell can't be right," she correctly deduced.

"No," I answered. I kept pulling out more intestines as well as the spleen, laying them over on the pile I had started. The abdominal cavity was becoming just that, a mostly empty hole. It was looking like Hannibal Lecter had decided to extend his homicidal tendencies to animals. I still reminded myself that this dog was someone's pet. That someone had cared for it at one time. I was trying to be respectful and considerate, but there was only so much one could do during one of these exams. I had to get a good look at everything.

Finally, I externalized the piece of small intestine with the obstruction. The bowel bulged nearly twice its normal size. It looked like a snake that had swallowed a golf ball.

"What is that?" asked Allie. We both noticed the "that" at the same time. An eight inch white tendril was protruding from inside the intestine through the tissue into the air.

"Eww," groaned Marcy. "Is it alive?"

It wasn't moving, but it had the same appearance as a roundworm, long, white and pointed at the end. I didn't know what parasites were prevalent in Kazakhstan, but ascarids, as us veterinarians call roundworms, were pretty much ubiquitous. I reached out a gloved finger and touched it.

"Ow," I screamed and pulled my finger back. The girls jumped back involuntarily. I couldn't help, but chuckle. It earned me a pair of evil glares, but was well worth it.

"Jerk," commented Allie.

"It's not a good idea to mess with me like that," added Marcy.

"Why not?"

"I have a gun," she pointed out.

I remembered how she reacted to the tick in the car. "Touché," I said.

"What is it?" asked Allie. She was poking it now. "It feels stiff."

"That's what she said," I added.

"Ha, ha," said Allie. She had heard that one a million times. There seemed to be no end to the situations we encountered where that famous line from *The Office* applied.

I gently grabbed it and pulled. It seemed to be attached to whatever was causing the obstruction. "Let's see what it is," I said. Allie handed me my scalpel.

I sliced the intestinal wall over the bulge. The edges of the cut pulled away revealing a brown sphere studded with scores of tiny spikes. There was a crack running along the circumference of the object and from that protruded the stiff white tendril that had poked through the intestinal wall. I grabbed a pair of Allis tissue forceps and got a hold of the foreign object and pulled, backing the tendril through the intestines where it had found its own way out, through the incision I had made.

Allie had a stainless steel basin filled with water and I placed whatever it was in it to wash off the intestinal contents. I swished it a bit, still holding it with the forceps. Those spikes looked nasty. I held it up and we got a better look.

It was the size of a golf ball and in spots the spikes were covered with what looked like patches of flesh sticking to the object. The circumferential crack went about three quarters of the way around and inside the crack a smaller white ball was visible.

"What in the world is that?" asked Marcy.

"If I were to guess," started Allie, "I'd say it was a seed."

"A seed?" asked Marcy.

"Yeah," I agreed, "It looks like a giant seed. That's the root coming out. I've never seen anything like this."

"Makes you never want to swallow a watermelon seed again," said Allie.

"Jeez," whined Marcy, "all this for a stinking seed? Where are the drugs? Heck, I'd settle for some diamonds or rubies or something."

"Sorry, Officer Avers," I consoled. "It looks like this dog swallowed a seed that got lodged in its intestines. It looks like it started to germinate after the dog died. With all those spikes on the outside it's a wonder it got that far."

"I wonder if it was all covered with that soft fleshy material. The dog couldn't have known it was covered with spikes. Just swallowed it whole," suggested Allie. "I've heard that some seeds are spread around by getting a free ride from the alimentary canal of different animals."

"Reminds me of that cat poop coffee they sell for a thousand dollars a pound," said Marcy.

"They're civets. And don't knock it till you've tried it," I corrected her.

"You paid that much for coffee?"

"No, but one of my clients has a cafe on the north side where they serve it. She let me try some. The digestive process takes out a lot of the bitterness. Best coffee I ever had."

"You do know it was in poop," said Allie.

"They clean it up," I said.

Allie dumped the water from the basin in the bucket on the floor and I returned the seed to it. I had an idea who might be able to tell me more about this seed. It probably was common in Kazakhstan, but certainly a novelty here. I went back to digging around the abdominal cavity.

"What are you doing now?" asked Marcy.

"I have to be thorough. I don't want to miss anything." I followed the intestines to the rectum and back up to the stomach. Apart from some red splotches of inflammation here and there, no other foreign bodies were present. The pancreas, kidneys, and liver were all unremarkable.

"You want to go up into the chest?" asked Allie.

"Might as well," I answered. She handed over a set of rib cutters that looked like pruning shears. I cut up the left side of the breastbone through the cartilage that attached to the ribs then spread open the chest.

The lungs were nice and pink, the heart a deep red. No abnormal fluid. No signs of infection. "Well, Dave will be happy to know that the dog died of stupidity. Didn't know it couldn't pass that huge seed. Nothing that will affect national security or the health and welfare of the passengers," I said.

Allie handed me a large needle with a yard of heavy duty fishing line attached. I closed my incision taking full thickness bites with the needle that encompassed skin and muscle using a locking loop suture pattern that resembled a blanket stitch. Allie cleaned the outside of the dog while I stripped off my gloves. I helped her put the dog into a cadaver bag from the pet cemetery and I took her to the freezer near the back door while she got things ready for Peanuts' necropsy. The freezer was full. They must have had a busy night last night. I laid her on the floor. If the pet cemetery came by later, I'd transfer her in. Since she didn't have a tag they'd leave her here. There was still a chance someone would come to claim her.

Peanuts was strapped onto the table when I returned and a strip of fur shaved along his midline. I snapped on a new pair of gloves and Allie handed me a scalpel from a new surgery pack. She was standing by with the suction hose. We both knew there was going to be a mess.

I proceeded as I had with Spot Doe. After I made the initial incision into the abdomen, Allie put her suction tip inside and we removed about two liters of the red-brown, cloudy fluid. I then extended my incision and exteriorized the intestinal tract, running my fingers along every inch of it, looking for something abnormal. It didn't take long to find a hole. It was fairly small, about an inch across, but it was ragged.

"Looks like something chewed through," observed Allie.

"Let's not jump to conclusions," I said.

The dog that swallowed the hamster or gerbil and choked on it was a common urban legend, but I was hard-pressed to think that a mouse could survive being swallowed long enough to make it into the intestines and eat its way out.

I once again removed as much of the intestinal tract as possible, leaving a gaping space in the abdomen. The bottom (or rather top of the abdomen since Peanuts was on his back) still had quite a bit of fluid in it. Allie started sucking out the remaining fluid until we could see everything. At the space where the right kidney met the liver was what appeared to be a small brown string. I took a pair of hemostats and grabbed it, pulling lightly. Out popped a dead mouse by its tail.

I lifted it up.

"Again, ew," said Marcy.

"That is weird," said Allie. "How did it live long enough to do that? And poor dog."

"I don't know," I said, "but it's far cry from natural causes. Betty is going to have a lot of explaining to do."

"Do you think they were feeding their boarders live mice?" asked

Marcy. "That sounds pretty sick."

I remembered back to my visit to the Bark and Breakfast. There was a fresh bowl of dog food in Peanuts' cage. I didn't remember any mouse droppings around, but I wasn't really concerned about that at the moment.

"Maybe it crawled in his mouth after he died?" suggested Marcy, "looking for a warm place to hide."

"That wouldn't explain the peritonitis. If Peanuts died first, the infection couldn't have been cause by the mouse, but I found nothing other than that one ragged hole in the intestines. I just can't imagine a dog swallowing a mouse whole and it living long enough to chew its way out. It makes no sense."

"Well, that makes one out of three. Not doing well on our medical mystery solve rate," commended Allie.

"Not quite," I said.

"What do you mean?" asked Marcy. "Dogs eat weird things all the time. Sometimes they die."

"Yes, that's true. But why didn't the owner claim it at customs, dead or not?"

"Don't say that," said Marcy. "I don't want to spend anytime tracking down more leads on this dog. It's not national security or a police matter. The dog died from eating a weird nut. There's nothing illegal about that."

"Maybe," I said, raising one eyebrow with my best Dr. McCoy from *Star Trek* impression.

"What are you trying to do?" Marcy asked.

"Dr. McCoy. *Star Trek*. I'm a doctor, not a TSA Agent, Jim," I answered. I guess she wasn't a *Star Trek* fan.

"He gets a little goofy at times," Allie chimed in.

I turned my Dr. McCoy impression into the evil eye and directed it at Allie.

She bagged the mouse. I completed the rest of the necropsy exam then stitched him up after finding nothing else suspicious. Allie had snapped a pile of pictures with the clinic camera. I was glad Marcy had been there in case the Cunningham's nephew decided that we were trying to frame them or something. I didn't relish the phone call I would have to make to the Johnsons. We transferred Peanuts' remains to another large blue plastic bag provided by the pet cemetery and I wrote SAVE in large letters on the outside just to make sure they didn't collect him with the other pets.

Marcy had changed back to her cop uniform and was waiting outside the locker room. "Need any more help today?" she asked.

"I'll be fine," I said.

"I don't mind."

"That's okay."

"You really think there is something fishy with that dog from Kazakhstan?"

"I don't know. It's not cheap to ship a dog from halfway around the world. From the looks of it, the dog wasn't a champion purebred."

"Maybe the owner had some trouble or was sick himself. There are a lot of possible explanations," she said. "Maybe he was there when the flight was supposed to arrive and decided to come back later rather than waiting."

"Hmm," I hmmed.

"What's that mean?" she asked.

"Maybe they weren't shipping the dog," I said.

"Okay, you lost me. I'll admit I didn't go to school as long as you did, but it was a dog you just did an autopsy – sorry, necropsy on, wasn't it?"

"We were expecting to find something else in the dog, maybe drugs or a nuclear bomb. That's why you were here, wasn't it?"

"I came for the coffee and the company," Marcy answered.

I headed for the surgery room and she followed. On the counter, Allie had left the bag with the dead mouse and had also bagged up the germinating seed. I picked it up. "What if this is what they were shipping?"

"Why would they ship a nut inside a dog? As far as I know, It's not illegal to ship a nut."

"I don't know, but I may know someone who might."

"Who?"

"A friend of a friend."

Marcy shrugged. "Do what you want. My report will say the dog had an intestinal obstruction from swallowing a nut."

I glanced at my watch. It was 1:45. Four more appointments this afternoon and I needed to reschedule another for tomorrow, not to mention I'd have to now come back here after my six o'clock to check on Darla.

Marcy stood there silent. She smiled. I smiled. I looked at my watch again. "Thanks again for helping me get Peanuts back," I said. "That was amazing."

"Thanks for letting me watch. It was an education. What do you do with the Spot Doe now?"

"We'll keep her in the freezer for a week and if Dave has no one claim her she'll get cremated with the other dead strays."

I started to head back to the hallway. Marcy followed. "You headed towards Kimball and Lawrence?" she asked.

"Not really," I said.

"I suppose I could wait around for a black-and-white to give me a lift." She produced a business card from her pocket and handed it to me. On the bottom was written her cell number. "Let me know if your guy comes up with anything interesting," she said.

"I thought you wanted to get rid of the case."

"I can still be curious," she said and smiled.

Was that a flirt? I hated reading women. I never got it right. My cell phone rang. Saved by the bell. I looked at the caller ID. It was Sheila. Talk about not being able to read women. I answered. Before I could say anything she was talking. "Get over to Louis Weiss Memorial Hospital," she blurted.

"Up on Lake Shore Drive? What's there?"

"Mrs. Jeffries. Claire said they took her out by ambulance ten minutes ago. A friend had gone to check on her when they heard Darla was at the hospital and found her collapsed on the floor."

"What was it? A stroke?"

"Atty, I have no idea. You now officially know as much as I do."

"I'll need to cancel..."

"Already done. Go. I hope this isn't because of Darla. That little dog is her life. I could see her worrying herself to death over that little ball of fluff."

"Do you have a phone number for the hospital?"

"I texted it to you," she said.

"I'll call as soon as I know anything." I hung up.

"What's up?" asked Marcy.

"A client of mine was taken to the hospital. Her dog is that little Pomeranian I'm treating here. Sounds like she had a stroke or something."

"Can I help? You want me to come along?"

"Thanks, but I don't know what you could do."

"Police officers can get in places that regular people can't. I might be able to get some information if they think it is a police case."

"But it isn't."

"As long as it's a male doctor and he can see, I'll be able to get something," she added. "Come on, Atty, let me help."

I considered her offer. Maybe it would be helpful to have her along. It couldn't hurt. "Okay, but don't shoot anyone," I said.

"Deal," she agreed.

I pulled up Sheila's text and dialed the number for the hospital.

"This is Dr. Klammeraffe," I told the receptionist as soon as she answered. "I'm trying to find out the condition of a patient brought in by ambulance. Virginia Jeffries."

"Are you her physician?" she asked.

"Who's Dr. Klammeraffe?" whispered Marcy.

"Shh," I whispered back. "I am." I put the phone back to my face, "I'm, uh, a family doctor." It technically wasn't a lie. Marcy stifled a chuckle.

"Just a moment," she said.

I waited. The music on hold was playing "The Girl From Ipanema". It only took about ten seconds for me to start moving to the bossa nova rhythm and begin whistling along.

Soon Marcy was whistling along with me, unconsciously swaying to the beat with me. Allie came by with a printout and gave us both a strange look. "I'm on hold," I told her.

"You're on more than that by the looks of it," she added. "Better be careful, she's a cop," she said, nodding her head at Marcy.

"This is Dr. Fred," said a voice in my ear.

"Dr. Fred?" I said reflexively, confused at the familiarity of the appellation.

"Fred is my last name, P-H-R-E-A-D," he said. From his tone, it was not the first time he had been forced to explain it to someone.

"What's your first name?" I asked.

There was a pause on the other end before he answered, "Frederick."

"Fred Phread," I said.

"Who is this?" he asked, changing the subject.

"This is Dr. Klammeraffe," I answered. I wasn't about to admit to my more familiar appellation of At At. "I'm trying to get some information on Virginia Jeffries."

"Are you her doctor?" he asked.

"Not exactly," I answered.

"You told the receptionist that you were the family doctor."

"I take care of Darla Jeffries. I'm with her right now." I was really wading into murky waters now.

"Oh, is that her daughter? We haven't been able to contact any family."

I considered letting the deception run a little further. I didn't need to correct him. It wouldn't help if he knew I was a veterinarian and Darla was a dog. Gosh darn MDs looked down on us most of the time. Truth was they were just vets who specialized in one species: humans. "What can you tell me about her condition?"

"A neighbor found her collapsed. Initially we thought it was a stroke, but now it's beginning to look like an infection."

"Any edema around the face or neck?" I asked.

"Why?"

"Darla Jeffries presented with those symptoms this morning. They live together and I wondered if they might have the same infection."

"No. She is having respiratory symptoms, but no edema. Could be just a bad flu, but in these old folks that can be as serious as small pox. You have a diagnosis on the daughter?"

"Not yet. We're waiting on test results."

"So she's not at Weiss, then?"

"No." I saw no need to expound further.

"How old is Darla?" he asked.

"Thir-," I caught myself. I couldn't have Mrs. Jeffries with a thirteen year-old daughter. Think how everyone would talk. "Thirty-nine," I lied. As far as lies I was telling, it was a small one. "Any chance I can come see her?"

"Sure, she's in the ICU with respiratory difficulties. You have privileges here?"

"No."

"I'll alert the nurses you are coming. They don't like surprises here."

I spelled out my name for him, then hung up.

The printout Allie was holding was from Darla. She handed it over. The white blood cell count was twenty-five thousand. Way too high. There were some elevations of liver enzymes that weren't on her last panel and a low blood sugar.

"I switched her over to some D5W," Allie said.

"Good call." D5W was five percent dextrose in water. A quick way to get some sugar into Darla before she slipped into a coma. "I just got off the phone with Weiss Hospital. It seems that Darla's owner collapsed and has a respiratory infection."

"Any connection?"

"They're thinking flu. She did have a cough this morning now that I think about it."

"Could this dog have a bad case of the flu? I hear dogs get that too."

"Different virus," I said.

"There can't be that many things that affect people and dogs?" said Allie. "Lyme disease, tetanus, rabies..."

"Rabies?" interrupted Marcy.

"No," I chuckled. "Wrong presentation and time course."

"Is there anything that could cause such different symptoms in the two of them?" asked Allie.

"Probably, I'll have to do some research later. Probably quicker to wait for the lab results from the titers we sent out, but this is going to be gnawing at me."

"Maybe the old lady was distressed from her doggy getting sick and tried to off herself. Maybe a poison? Pill overdose?"

"Never," I said, "but if I have time, I think it might be worthwhile to go back to her apartment and look around. Darla could be having a reaction to something she was exposed to. I concentrated on the atrium garden earlier. But I didn't even think to give the apartment a going over. The place is immaculate. Plastic slip covers and all."

"Eww. My legs used to stick to my grandma's sofa. I hated that," said Marcy.

"Are you able to stay and keep an eye on Darla?" I asked Allie.

"Sure. I have another shift at six anyways. I'll watch her all night."

"No sleep then?"

"That's why they make Super Big Gulps. I'll grab a couple of cat naps between checks on her. She's doing quite well in the oxygen."

"I owe you," I said.

"I'll send you my bill," she answered.

Actually, Allie and I did have a financial arrangement. When I needed her help she was paid a handsome hourly wage in cash which

I easily passed on to my clients as a hospitalization fee. Worth every penny.

She started to head down the hall. "Oh, hey, you still want to do the fine needle aspirates on Darla? Try and suck some cells from a lymph node or two?"

I had nearly forgotten about that, but with Mrs. J. in the hospital, it made it perhaps even more important to get as much diagnostic information as possible. "If she is as stable as you say, let's give it a try." I looked over at Marcy. She said nothing, but her smile and wide eyes said that she wanted to watch.

I groaned. "Come on," I said.

We followed Allie into the treatment area. While she went to get Darla from her oxygen cage I gathered up some needed supplies. A stack of glass slides, several ten cc syringes and some inch and a half twenty-two gauge needles.

"What exactly are you going to do with that stuff?" asked Marcy.

"Fine needle aspirates," I answered. "I'm going to stick these long needles into her lymph nodes, suck out some cells, smear them on the slides, then send them to the lab to be stained and peered at under a microscope by someone who has been specially trained to peer at cells under a microscope and tell me what they are."

"Don't they teach you how to do that at vet school?"

"In fact they do, but they don't expect us to actually do it, that would put the pathologists out of business," I pointed out.

"Here she is," announced Allie. Darla seemed better, but nowhere near her usual bouncy self. "Her fever is down to 103. I think the edema is down too, but I wouldn't keep her out of the oxygen too long. Do your stuff, Doc, and I'll get her back as soon as you finish. Neck and shoulders?" she asked.

"Yep," I answered and our well-oiled machine went into action.

With the skill of an Aussie sheep shearer she used the cordless clippers to remove swaths of orange fluff from four spots on Darla, two under her chin and two in front of her shoulders. Before the clippers stopped rattling on the counter she had started scrubbing the areas like we had when we put in her IV.

I snapped on some surgical gloves and grabbed one syringe topped by the inch and a half needle. I tried to isolate the lymph node under her jaw on the left side under the thickened, edematous skin as best as I could between two fingers. I guided the needle in.

Darla remained either very stoic or apathetic. I couldn't tell which. In either case, she didn't move. When I felt I had gone deep enough I pulled back on the plunger and the vacuum that was created hopefully would pull some cells into the needle. The syringe sucked back. No blood or saliva. That was a good sign.

I pulled the needle straight out and twisted it off the end of the syringe. I pulled the plunger halfway back and reattached the needle. Moving to one of the slides on the table, I pushed the plunger and a small clump of cloudy tissue sprayed onto the glass. I grabbed another slide and used it to smear the cells on the slide by pressing it over them and sliding along the length. I got a nice consistent layer of cells that dried very quickly.

"Great job, Doc," said Allie.

I repeated the process under the other jaw and in front of either shoulder. I could feel the latter two lymph nodes more readily and they were enlarged as well. I expected that with all the swelling in the head. The great thing about lymph nodes was they trapped all the garbage that got into the tissue before it got sucked back into the circulation. A good pathologist should be able to tell me some idea of what I was dealing with, or at least rule out a tumor.

Allie wiped each of my aspirate sites with a little peroxide on a gauze sponge and whisked Darla back to her oxygen cage.

I labeled the slides with a sharpie and slid them into a plastic case. Allie took it from me when she returned. "Darla is none the worse for wear," she said. "I think we got some great samples."

"That dog just let you stick those huge needles into her. I'd be screaming like a baby," said Marcy. "Doesn't she feel that?"

"Sure, it's just not that bad. A little poke in the skin. There are no pain receptors in the lymph nodes," I said. I snapped off my gloves and tossed them. "I need to get changed, I'll be a minute then we can head to Weiss," I told Marcy.

I popped into the men's locker room and stripped out of the scrubs. I looked in the mirror, standing there in my plaid boxers. There was no way Marcy Avers was interested in this. I shuddered with the thought. She was just being nice. No love interest there. At least I could stop letting it bother me. I quickly put on my street clothes and popped back into the hall. I found the two girls giggling like school kids. I groaned.

"What's so funny?"

"Nothing," they both said.

That meant it was something.

"You ready?" asked Marcy.

"Yeah, let's go," I said.

"Don't forget your thing," said Allie. She handed me the bag with the seed in it. I looked it over again. The glistening root did kind of look like a worm. That spiked ball looked medieval. Why that dog would want to swallow it was still a mystery.

She had my slides in her other hand. "You want these stat too, right?"

"Yeah. Put my cell phone on the lab request so they can call me directly." I turned to Marcy, "Okay Cagney, let's roll." I headed for the back door that led to the employee's parking lot behind the building.

"Does that make you Lacey?" Marcy asked.

"You've actually heard of that show? I'd have thought it was before your time."

"They rerun it on the old-time television cable channel."

The ringing of my phone halted me in my tracks and kept me from having to come up with a snappy comeback. The caller ID said it was Sheila. I wondered briefly if there was news on Mrs. Jeffries. Probably bad. Usually I looked forward to her calls, the playful flirting, a nice diversion to a stressful day. Now I was tempted to send her to voice mail. I answered. "Hello?" I think my voice quavered a little.

"Are you on your way?" she asked.

"Um, no. Had to do a few more tests on Darla. Just leaving now."

"Well, then that's okay," she said

"Is that what you called about?" I asked.

"No, but it's nothing bad," she reassured me. Boy, she knew me well. "Well, not bad in terms of what it could be, bad in terms of what it is, which is actually relatively good considering all the badness of the day so far. Did that make sense?"

"Yes. In a strange way it did. What's up?"

"Betty Cunningham called. Not about Peanuts, which is what I was expecting. I don't think she has a clue about that yet. Did you find out what happened?"

"It looks like it was an inside job," I said.

"Inside job?"

"It looks like he swallowed a mouse or it crawled down his throat and its claws or teeth tore a hole in the bowels. Infection spread to his abdomen. How it got into him or if it was alive when it tore the intestine I don't know, but it is very weird."

"Nothing you could have done about it?"

"If they called me two days ago when he first got sick and was alive, maybe. But we digress. Betty Cunningham called," I prompted, "not about Peanuts."

"Right, she called earlier about getting a refill for a patient. She'd like you to take care of it now."

"Really? Who?"

"Jasper Kent."

"They ran out of his phenobarbital?" I asked. Jasper was doberman who had seizures. His twice a day medication prevented them. "He isn't due for a refill for a month or so," I said.

"She claims they did not send enough pills. She wants you to call it in to the CVS pharmacy down the street from them. I got the number, you ready?"

"Sure," I answered, patting my jacket pocket for something to write with before remembering I had left my little notepad and pen in the car. There was no whiteboard nearby this time. She started spitting numbers at me and I said them back, hoping they would stick in my head. As soon as I was finished I heard a tearing sound and Marcy was handing me a piece of paper torn from her own cop notebook with the number I had already forgotten neatly scrawled across it.

"Thanks," I mouthed to her before continuing with Sheila. "Weird that the Kents didn't send enough medication. They never let his meds get low. Always refilling a few weeks before they need to. They know what happens when his blood levels get low."

"That's what I thought too. Who knows, maybe someone at the kennel swiped them. Kids love to do that random prescription drug thing."

I thought back to Pete. Maybe. "I'll call it in now, then I'm heading to Weiss."

"Call me when you have any info on Virginia."

"You got it," I assured her. I clicked the phone off. I dialed the number and left a message on the CVS voice mail with the prescription info, then slid the phone into my jacket. "Okay, now we can go," I said.

As if on cue, the blare from a car alarm began to blast from outside the emergency clinic. It was eerily familiar. "No way," I said. I turned to Marcy as she turned to look at me.

"Not your day, Doc," she said.

"What's going on?" asked Allie as she popped into the hallway.

"Not Doc's day," repeated Marcy.

I stepped to the door and opened it. Bright sunshine burst in. It was a death match to see which of my senses overwhelmed me first, the brightness of the daylight or the piercing shriek of the car alarm. Marcy was beside me, her hand reflexively hovering over her holster.

I pulled out my keys and hit the alarm button. The sound stopped. Any last hope that it wasn't my car that was producing the alarm vanished.

Marcy scanned the alley. There was no one else there. She started to head for my car. I followed. So did Allie. Marcy had unsnapped the guard on the holster giving her ready access to her gun.

From where we were the car looked fine. I had parked next to Allie's Jeep. As we got closer I could see something strange about the back window. It wasn't reflecting the glare from the bright sunlight like Allie's Jeep was. Around the edges of the window frame I noted some shards of safety glass clinging to the rubber weather stripping.

Another noise punctuated the tension. I reached for my key fob again under some reflexive reaction that if it worked before, it would work now.

Allie had come out to join us. "It's your phone," she said as I looked confusedly at my keys.

It rang again. "Jeez," I sighed. Marcy was peering into the rear of my car as I pulled out my cell. The call ID wasn't a number I recognized. Marcy gave an all clear signal like she just cleared a hut in a Vietnamese jungle. I started walking to my car as I answered the phone. "Hello?" I asked more than greeted.

"Atty, it's Dave."

"Dave, what is it?" I pointed at the phone and mouthed "Dave" at Marcy. She held up her hand, flapping her fingers and thumb like a duck's bill, the universal sign for yapping. I don't know why I thought she'd care.

"Did she get hold of Sheila?" he asked.

I had reached my car and was half listening, half checking out the contents of the rear. "Did who get hold of Sheila?"

"The lady."

"You'll have to be a little more specific. Someone just broke into my car for the second time today. I'm a little preoccupied."

"Sorry, Atty. You call the police?"

"Office Avers is securing the area as we speak," I told him.

"Oh yeah?" He replied too snidely. "I'd let her secure my area any time."

I groaned. "What lady?" I prompted again.

"The lady with the Kazakhstani dog. She showed up a couple of hours after you left. One of the TSA people found her wandering around baggage claim. Said she was looking for a pet carrier and described our DOA."

"I told her it had died and that you had custody and were doing an autopsy..."

"Wait, you told her that I had the dog? Was that a good idea? What if the dog did have drugs in it? What if she was some drug dealer?"

"Well, I suppose that could be bad. She seemed nice. Did you find drugs?"

"No."

"There, problem solved." Another day in Dave World.

"Not solved. The dog had swallowed a weird seed that ended up killing it."

"Ooh. Is that bad?"

Marcy was standing in front of me now. "What's going on?"

I looked at her shaking my head. "Dave told some woman that I had the dog from the airport."

"And you're surprised, why?"

Dave went on, "So you think there was something fishy with the seed and the dead dog?"

"I'm wondering if she was trying to smuggle in the seed."

"Maybe," said Dave trying to be helpful.

"Do people do that?"

"Oh yeah. There are tons of plants on the watch list. Invasive species and all that."

"Well, I know a botanist, so I'm going to try and get him to look at it."

"Cool. Let me know what you find out."

Something clicked in my brain, "Wait, did you tell her I was bringing the dog to the emergency clinic? Because I'm looking at my car missing its rear window and wondering if she came here and thought it might be in my car."

Dave was silent a moment. "I might have mentioned your destination. To be honest, Atty, when I'm schmoozing a lady I never know what I'm going to say. I just go with the flow."

"Dave, you're an idiot," I told him.

Marcy yelled at the phone. "What he said."

"Hey," answered Dave, "at least you got a highly trained Chicago Police Officer as a bodyguard. I wouldn't mind her guarding my body, if you know what I mean." His mind was totally in the gutter.

"Bye, Dave," I said and hung up.

"Might not be Dave's fault," said Marcy.

"What do you mean?"

"How would she know it was your car?" asked Marcy. "Why wouldn't she just come in and ask for the dog? It might be that the dog just ate a seed."

Both very good questions.

The next sound caught us by surprise. A scream came from the open alley door.

CHAPTER 11

Marcy had her gun out of the holster. She was at the alley door in the blink of an eye and poked it into the building ahead of her. She slid in, her rubber-soled shoes silencing her steps.

"That sounded like Margaret," said Allie.

"You've heard her scream before?"

"No, but I'm sure it was her. Who else?"

Neither of us moved. We were more than willing to let Marcy be the hero. She did have a gun as she was fond of reminding me.

"What do you think is going on?" she asked. No further screams had emanated from the alley door.

"I think some Kazakhstani dog owner is upset that I took her dog and wants it back."

"You think whoever broke into your car is in there now?"

"Yep," I said, "but I'll wait to hear from Marcy before confirming that on my own."

Allie began to tap her foot impatiently. We heard a voice from inside. It sounded like Marcy had pulled out her cop vocabulary handbook. "I'm going in," said Allie.

"Are you crazy?" I asked. "Let Marcy handle it. She has a gun."

"Someone could need medical attention."

"Then she'll call an ambulance."

"This is technically an emergency clinic."

"For animals," I pointed out.

"You're the one always complaining that MDs are nothing more than vets who specialize in one species."

She had me there. I did say that a lot. "What if she shoots me by accident? Or not by accident?"

"What did you do to her?" Allie asked. Her anxiety had quickly been replaced by morbid curiosity.

"Nothing. Innocent people get shot all the time. I don't want to end up in an ambulance on my way to the hospital. Can't imagine trading a Danny Burger for a Jell-O cup."

Suddenly Marcy appeared in the doorway. "Come on in, what are you guys waiting for?"

Allie gave me her "I told you so" face.

"What's going on?" I asked.

"I need some help in here."

"Is it the lady?" I asked.

"What lady?" she asked.

"The Kazakhstani dog owner who smashed my car window in."

"There is no lady looking for a dead dog. Margaret screamed," Allie turned and stuck her tongue out at me, "because there is a guy in the waiting room with a snake on his arm."

"What's so scream worthy of a guy holding a snake?"

"No, you're not getting it. The snake is *on* his arm," Marcy explained unsuccessfully. "Also, Margaret fainted and is lying on the floor in the reception area."

"Cool," said Allie. She brushed past me and was in the building before I could ask another question.

"Come on, Doc," said Marcy as she tugged on my arm, "you really gotta see this."

I let her pull me towards the building. "I've seen snakes before, you know. And I'm sure that Allie can handle Margaret. I should really be getting to the hospital and I have to figure out what to do with my car window."

She was stronger than she looked and I stumbled for a few steps before giving in. She led me along the hallway. When we got to where Margaret was slumped on the floor behind her desk, I was confused to see Allie, Laura, the ophthalmologist's technician, and Dr. Rice, the ophthalmologist, all staring past the desk through the plexiglass window to the waiting room. None had the slightest interest in the unconscious receptionist.

I stooped down to check on Margaret. She was out cold, but breathing. I started to stand up again, "What's..." I stopped in mid-sentence as my eyes looked through the security shield into the waiting area. There was the guy with the snake on his arm. Only the snake wasn't draped over his arm like I was expecting. It's mouth was halfway up the guy's forearm. Twelve inches down the boa constrictor's neck was the bulge of the man's fist.

A moan from Margaret snapped everyone out of their wild-eyed stares and to her aid. Allie and Laura had her sitting up against the wall and Dr. Rice had gone down the hall to the water cooler to get a cup of water. Margaret saw Marcy and shifted away from her along the wall, "She was going to shoot me," she said.

"No I wasn't," said Marcy. "I heard a scream."

"Hello," said the man outside the glass in the waiting room. "I really need some help here." His speech was slightly slurred and as I watched he seemed to be wavering on his feet. An elderly woman holding a bug-eyed Boston Terrier, presumably waiting to see Dr. Rice, was huddled on a chair in the far corner of the room, her dog happily panting away.

He raised his arm as best he could with the snake on it. "Could someone get this off please?" The motion was enough to send him off balance and he collapsed onto the floor.

"Great," added Marcy. "Doc, I think you're needed out there." We left Margaret with the others helping her up and entered the waiting room.

Marcy knelt next to the guy. "Whew," she said, wafting away the alcohol odor drifting up from the man. She slapped him lightly a few times. "Hey, mister, wake up. Snap out of it, sir."

I checked his arm. The snake managed to inch itself up another few millimeters when I lifted it. I could see small rivulets of the man's blood dripping from around the snake's teeth, lodged deeply into his flesh.

"Does that snake think it can actually swallow this guy?"

"Good question," I answered. The snake was a six-foot boa constrictor. At least we didn't have to worry about venom. "Snakes usually don't try to eat things much bigger than they are."

"Usually?"

Allie popped out into the waiting room. She had the digital camera and had already snapped a couple of pictures before I could get her attention. "Hey, we need to do something here."

"Want me to shoot it?" asked Marcy.

"No," I said with enough gooey sarcasm to cover a cupcake. I turned back to Allie. "Get me ten ccs of ketamine."

"Ten ccs?" she asked.

"Come on, before this thing gets up to his elbow."

"Why doesn't it just stop and let go?" asked Marcy. "It must realize it can't swallow this guy whole."

"It can't let go," I told her. "Its teeth curve backwards to keep any partially alive prey from being able to crawl out."

"So what is the ketamine for? That's some kind of hallucinogen the kids take. Special K, they call it."

"It's actually an anesthetic. We'll sedate the snake and call for an ambulance and let the ER guys figure the best way to get the snake off." As I finished speaking the snake took another half inch of the man's arm.

Allie returned with a large syringe capped with an inch long twenty-gauge needle. Marcy spoke into her radio mike asking the dispatcher for an ambulance. A static-filled reply came back which she amazingly understood.

"Is this life-threatening?" she asked.

"Only to the snake," I answered. "This guy is so self-anesthetized he's not feeling anything."

"What do you mean, only to the snake?"

Allie handed me the syringe and I jabbed the needle into a particularly meaty section of the snake and pushed the plunger sending the ketamine into the muscle tissue. "If the snake makes it up to the shoulder it might end up suffocating itself."

Marcy replied to the microphone and listened to the reply. "Forty-five minutes to an hour," she said.

"What?" I looked at the clock in the waiting room. It was 2:35.

"Hey, there are only so many paramedics and lots of people trying to die."

"Great."

"Hey," said Allie, "can we get an x-ray? It'll be great for the x-ray contest that veterinary magazine has every year. You know, 'What did they eat?' We could probably win a thousand bucks."

"Allie," I groaned.

"Come on, they're both out. We got time to kill. It'll only take a minute. We cover the guy with a lead apron and snap the picture."

I looked at Marcy. Her eyes were gleaming with anticipation and excitement. "I need to get to the hospital to check on Mrs. Jeffries. I don't have time for all this."

"Tell you what, Doc," Marcy said, "Allie and I will help you get her x-ray. The girl deserves a thousand bucks. We'll pile snake guy into the back of your car and take him to the ER at Weiss. I'll drive. We'll get there in no time. Win, win, win, win, win."

"I'm sorry, which win is mine?"

"The third," answered Marcy.

"Please," begged Allie, "they won't x-ray him at the ER, they'll just take off the snake, or if they do, I'll never get a copy of it." Marcy stood next to her and they both put on the most pathetic hound dog expressions I had ever seen.

"Oh, why not, like this day could get any less strange." I looked down at the partially eaten man. He didn't seem to care one way or another. "Get the gurney, but as soon as you take the x-ray we load him into my car and we go to the hospital."

Allie dashed off and was soon wheeling the gurney they used to move large dogs around the emergency clinic. It was only four feet long. Big enough for most dogs, two feet short for this guy. We lifted him up, letting his legs hang down over one end and the boa draped over his chest. The snake was now feeling the effects of the anesthesia and was not creeping any further up the arm, but its teeth were still firmly embedded in his flesh. I considered the idea of trying to remove it myself, but the thought of something going wrong and the ensuing lawsuit dissuaded me.

My own malpractice insurance ran a little under two hundred bucks a year. I'm sure the emergency room's attending physician's ran about a thousand times that. I was also sure my insurance wouldn't cover me for a snake-ectomy gone wrong.

We pushed the gurney next to the x-ray table and lifted the arm with the head and neck of the snake up and positioned it near the center. She draped the rest of him with two lead aprons and tapped a button on the machine that lit up the area that would be exposed to the x-rays. She made sure the bulge of the man's fist and the snakes head were both in the frame.

We ducked around the corner and Allie had pulled the foot pedal that triggered the exposure with her. She set it down and tapped it with her foot, snapping the picture.

We all then raced back into the room to see the image that was downloading to the computer screen. "Well, I'll be," I said.

"Is that what I think it is?" asked Allie as she peered around my shoulder.

"The idiot must have fallen asleep holding it in his hand," I said. The bones of the man's hand were curled up around what appeared to be a chicken drumstick. The hungry boa had smelled the meat and started swallowing the man's hand. I wondered if the snake was also under the influence of some intoxicating substance. You wouldn't expect one to be so stupid normally. The fangs should have woken up the guy, but any attempts to pull the snake off would have made it swallow faster. Why he came here instead of the human ER or even calling an ambulance, I didn't know. It probably was due to his intoxication and stupidity.

"Burn me a CD, Allie. I'll take a copy to the ER."

She slid a blank disc into the computer and burned the image to it. It spit the disc out when it was done. Allie put it in a paper sleeve and wrote on it with her big black Sharpie, "SNAKE EATING MAN." I chuckled. She put it on the gurney.

"Okay, we have to go. If Mrs. Jeffries and Darla are suffering from the same thing, I need to know. What they find out about her may be the key to saving little Darla."

"What are you waiting for?" asked Allie, as if I was some sort of idiot. "Let's get this guy out of here." She put the arm and snake back on the man's chest and we pushed him out of the room, down the hall to the back door. Marcy had the door open. The bright sunlight was still a bit of a shock.

We bumped along the parking lot to my damaged Escape, careful not to jostle our cargo off the stainless steel cart. I pressed the button on my key fob by touch while it was still in my pocket to open the back hatch. Marcy started brushing glass shards out on to the pavement. I was moving my bags and cases to one side to make room for our passengers. Allie had run back into the clinic and returned with a big quilt that usually was used to pad the big caged areas for the dogs staying overnight at the clinic.

"Just in case," she added. A sudden release of this guy's bladder was not out of the question and a thick layer of padding would save me having to shampoo the inside of the cargo area.

Marcy had worked her way into the back of the car and was crouching down holding out her arms. "Hand him in," she directed.

Allie and I moved the cart right up against the back of my car and locked the wheels. We lifted him by his upper arms and heaved him back. Marcy grabbed him under the armpits and pulled. He slid back with a couple of attempts. We had to bend his knees to allow the hatch to close.

"I'll call the lab to see if they can pick up those samples from Darla early. The driver has a thing for me," said Allie.

"Who doesn't?" I shot back.

"Oddly enough, the pet cemetery guy refuses to respond to my obviously shameless flirtations. I think he's gay. Cute, but gay."

"Can't win them all."

"It's fun trying."

"Well, thanks again. I really owe you."

"We're past you owing me. I now own you."

"Be gentle," I added in parting.

"Keys," said Marcy.

I laughed. "Yeah, right." I thought she had been kidding about driving. She was standing by my driver side door.

"Seriously, Doc, you drive like a woman."

"And what do you drive like?"

"A cop."

She had a point. Furthermore, my morning coffee infusion from Danny's was just a faint memory and my fatigue was beginning to break through the adrenalin of the day's excitement. I looked enviously at the restful human-reptile chimera lying in the back of the car. I sighed, tossed her the keys and headed for the passenger side.

"Yes," she hissed.

"Later," said Allie.

"Call if any changes with Darla."

"Will do."

I got in the car. Marcy was adjusting all my mirrors. She then pressed the accelerator, revving the engine on my Escape. I think a look of terror crossed my face. As she turned towards me to peer out the back window I could see her evil smile. Yes, it was evil. Wicked, in a way.

I looked behind us as well. Allie had gotten clear and I felt myself pulled forward against my seat belt as squealing tires and the pungent odor of burnt rubber accompanied Marcy's exit from the parking space. She turned forward, shifted into drive and we darted from the driveway out onto Addison. There was little concern for traffic because she had her hand pushing firmly on the horn.

"Hey," I said, "this isn't a cop car. Take it easy."

"Tell me about it, it's got as much pickup as a whale."

She was revving through traffic, slipping in and out of openings between cars. I found myself gripping the dashboard. I forced myself to relax. She must have some special training in driving, right? I didn't want to ask. I let out the breath which I had been holding. She turned right onto Addison and we were headed toward Lake Shore Drive. Stop signs became something less than pauses and honks from offended motorists were met with a simple, but effective gesture from Marcy's left hand.

I finally began to relax a little as traffic thinned when we reached Lake Shore Drive. I was still terrified, but a little more relaxed. I found myself thinking about Jasper Kent's medication. Something about it bothered me.

"I wonder what happened to those pills," I said.

"What pills?" asked Marcy, her eyes never leaving the road. (Thank God.)

"The Kents are very particular about Jasper's meds. They would have sent him with extra pills if he was boarding. Those idiots at the Bark and Breakfast must have lost them or something."

"Maybe an employee took them," she suggested.

"That's what Sheila thought."

"Kids today will take about any prescription drug they can get their hands on. They mix them up and end up in the hospital or dead a lot of the time. Phenobarbital is probably pretty attractive."

"Really? It's a tranquilizer. They'd just fall asleep."

"You mix it with a stimulant and you can get some interesting effects."

"I suppose." Then a thought occurred to me. I should have thought of it earlier. It suddenly explained some of the questions about Peanuts. "They didn't," I wondered out loud.

"Didn't what, Doc?" asked Marcy.

"I was just thinking, what if they didn't lose the pills or someone didn't take them? What if they used more pills than they were supposed to?"

"So one person gave him his meds then someone else thought they were supposed to and gave him another dose? Wouldn't that cause a problem?"

"It could make him a little drowsy. Phenobarbital is a sedative at higher doses. Thing is, Jasper is about ninety pounds."

"So?"

"So, what if they weren't giving Jasper the extra doses? Peanuts was getting a thyroid pill twice a day. What if some, oh let us say, idiot, who couldn't read a prescription bottle, was giving Peanuts Jasper's meds. Peanuts was about twenty-two pounds. It would knock him for a loop. I doubt he'd even be able to stand after a few doses."

"So you think that maybe Peanuts was so sleepy that a mouse did crawl into his mouth and get lost?"

"That or someone put it in the cage and scared it into going in there."

"Can you prove that? I'll go lock up the whole bunch right now."

"No. But I can have the lab check his blood for Phenobarbital. If it is positive they'll at least be negligent."

"That won't be good for business."

"Probably not. I better call Allie and have her order it."

"I like that girl," said Marcy.

"You wanted to run a check on her before," I pointed out.

"I still do, but that doesn't stop me from liking her. She certainly knows how to put you in your place."

"We've worked together for a while. I let her get away with it."

"Uh huh."

I pressed my speed dial button for the emergency clinic.

"Chicago Veterinary Specialty Clinic," answered Allie.

"Where's Margaret?"

"Laura and Dr. Rice are reviving her in the lounge. What's up?" she asked.

"I need to send out some blood on Peanuts. You have any left from the tests you ran before?"

"A cc or so. What do you want?"

"A thyroid level and phenobarbital level."

"Phenobarbital? Was Peanuts epileptic?"

"No. Another of my patients at the Bark and Breakfast seems to be low on his seizure meds. I'm wondering if it ended up in Peanuts."

"Oh, no."

"Oh, yes."

"Well, that would explain the mouse. I'll make sure it goes out with Darla's samples. She's still the same, I was just checking on her.

You at the hospital yet? I didn't know your car could spin out like that."

"Not yet, but I'm not so sure we won't end up getting there by ambulance the way Marcy drives." A hard fist punched my left arm.

"Ha, ha," said Marcy.

"With that guy in the back they might just end up bringing you back here. Any more of him disappear?" she asked.

I turned and took a peek. The snake still seemed fairly sedated. "No, they're both sleeping it off."

"Later," said Allie.

I clicked off and slipped the phone back into my jacket. I could see the hospital a block ahead. I stared at the dashboard clock; 3:20. Marcy turned in at the emergency entrance and pulled in under the canopy that protected the ambulances from the weather as they unloaded their patients.

As we stepped out, another police office emerged from the automatic sliding glass doors. He seemed pretty agitated that someone would dare to park in the ambulance-loading zone. Marcy stepped out and as soon as he saw her he was all smiles.

"Marcy Avers, what's up girl?"

Marcy gave him a roundhouse punch to the shoulder. "We're going to need a gurney. We got a guy being eaten by a snake. Then my friend," she pointed behind herself at me, "needs to go see a lady up in ICU."

"No problem," said the other officer. "I'll just get..." I could see his brain catching up with what Marcy had just told him. "Did you say a snake was eating a guy?"

"Marcy led him to the back of the car and pointed through my broken rear window.

"Wow," he said, "just when you think you've seen it all you get something like this. How'd it happen?"

"We think he fell asleep drunk with a chicken leg in his hand."

"That'll do it," agreed the officer, obviously competent to assess such situations. Probably part of the Police Academy training.

He disappeared back through the sliding doors and in less than a minute two scrub-clad orderlies were wheeling out the gurney. Even they had to take a second look when they noted the snake nearly to the man's elbow.

"The snake is sedated with ketamine," I told them as I handed over the CD with the x-ray on it. "Here's the x-ray."

"He's a vet," added Marcy to make sure my information was received with the austerity it deserved.

"We better head up to the ICU," Marcy said. "Go on in, I'll take care of the car."

I took my orders and slipped in before the glass doors could close after the gurney laden with the partially eaten man. It must have been a slow morning in the ER because pretty soon about fifteen people were gathered around the gurney. One of the doctors, apparently filled in by one of the orderlies, walked over to me. "You're the vet?" he asked.

"I'm the vet," I told him. I held out a hand. "Dr. At."

"Dr. Windsor," answered the clinician. "So you sedated the snake then brought them here?"

"I didn't want to try and remove it myself. Figured I'd leave that fun for you."

"Any advice?" he asked.

I liked this guy. He knew I was a vet and didn't even dismiss me.

"Well, the teeth curve backwards, so you'll need to slide the jaws a little forward to disengage them and keep in mind that they aren't hinged at this point. With some gentle continuous pressure you should be able to loosen up the muscles. Judging by the size of the snake and its progress, I doubt the hand is far enough in to start getting digested."

"That's a relief."

I turned and looked out the doors. Marcy was handing my keys to the other officer and jogging in toward me.

"I need to go see someone in ICU," I said.

"Don't tell me you have a patient here?" he joked.

Marcy arrived and smiled at the doctor. He smiled back. "I'm with him," she said. "Which way to the ICU?" she asked, her eye lids fluttering. I waited to see if that was going to work.

The doctor pointed down the hallway. "Turn left at the end of the hall and take the elevator to the fourth floor. ICU is all the way to the left as you get out."

"Thanks," said Marcy and with a flip of her ponytail we were fast walking down the hall.

"Wow," I said.

She raised her eyebrows then stepped up the pace until I was almost jogging.

When the elevator arrived, we let a nurse with a wheelchair-confined patient out and Marcy and I slipped in. The number four had ICU printed next to it. Part of me was hoping to find Mrs. Jeffries doing fine, sipping a cup of tea, worrying about her dog. Another part of me expected her to be just a frail old body amongst a sea of other frail old bodies, waiting to die.

The elevator made it to four nonstop and as we were leaving a short, bald, white-coated MD was walking straight into us, his attention focused on a hand-held computer he was tapping at furiously with a little stylus. I noticed his name tag. "F. Phread, MD"

"Dr. Phread," I said.

He stopped long enough to lift his head and take us in. I got a full up and down glance, but with Marcy his gaze stopped at eye level; his eye level, not Marcy's. On Marcy, his eyes came up to about the level of her police badge pinned to her chest.

CHAPTER 12

"I'm Dr. Klammeraffe, this nice young woman with the gun is Officer Marcy Avers. I spoke to you earlier about Mrs. Jeffries. Any change in her condition?"

"Huh?" he stammered as he shook his attention back to me. I glanced at Marcy who was smiling.

"Mrs. Virginia Jeffries, she was brought in this afternoon after she passed out in her apartment. You told me on the phone you thought it might be the flu."

"Oh, the respiratory distress in four-eleven." He tapped on his hand-held again. "Not the flu. Tests came back negative. Still not sure what's going on. You're treating the daughter, right? How's she doing?"

I didn't correct his assumption that Darla was her daughter. If you asked Mrs. Jeffries, she'd say she was. "Not well. I'm still waiting on some additional tests and some lymph node aspirates."

"Lymph node aspirates?"

I wondered if I said something wrong. Didn't MDs do lymph node aspirates?

"As I mentioned on the phone, her head and neck are swollen. I've been treating for a possible allergic reaction, but I'm beginning to think it is some sort of infection. If Darla's infection is in her neck and Virginia's is in her lungs, we could be dealing with the same disease."

"Virginia?" asked Dr. Phread.

"Your patient, Mrs. Jeffries," I prompted.

"Right, I'm not that good with names," he admitted. I was liking this guy less and less.

"I'd like to see her. See if she can think of anything that they both would have been exposed to. Someplace they went together. At first I thought Darla had gotten stung by a bee or wasp in the atrium of their apartment building, but when I checked it out, I couldn't find anything suspicious."

"You went to her building? Must be nice to be in private practice and have all that time on your hands," muttered Phread.

"He does house calls," offered Marcy.

"House calls? I didn't think doctors still did that. Do your patients pay you in chickens?" He chuckled. My affection was waning more and more.

"Can we see her?" I asked.

"Sure, I'll take you in. You said you didn't have privileges here. Where do you work out of normally?"

"There's a small hospital on Addison," I told him, forgetting to mention it was for four-legged patients only.

Dr. Phread paused a moment. "I really shouldn't let you in. The ICU is limited to family and the attending physicians."

"I'm sure she'll want to know how Darla is doing. It might cheer her up to get some news."

"Come on, Fred, give the guy a break. He's been having a tough day."

"And why are you here?" he asked. I couldn't tell if he was suspicious or flirtatious. That didn't feel right.

"Dr. At has been helping with a Homeland Security matter. I go where he goes," she said.

That seemed to do it. He led us down the hall to the entry to the ICU. A pair of sliding glass doors separated the unit, but unlike the ER entrance, they didn't open automatically. Dr. Phread scanned his ID badge over a white rectangle set into the wall. The doors slid open and we walked up to the nurse's station.

There were two nurses working there, both seemed very engrossed in their work. We stood in front of them, even Dr. Phread seemed afraid to disturb them.

"Yes," muttered the older one, not even glancing up.

"Dr. Klammeraffe and Officer Avers are here to see four eleven."

"The old lady who doesn't have the flu?" she asked, almost making fun of Dr. Phread. Her attitude reminded me of Allie.

"Go ahead," the nurse said, indicating the proper direction with a flip of her head. "We just did her hourly check. She's awake. Asking about her dog, keeps muttering its name."

"Thanks," I said quickly and scooted Marcy off to the direction she indicated. Phread followed, glued to Marcy like she had a leash on him. All I needed was for Fred Phread to realize now that I was a veterinarian. I needed to see Mrs. Jeffries. I had to know if there was a connection between their illnesses.

I knocked on the door to four-eleven and cracked it open. I wasn't quite ready for the sight that greeted me. All the life had left Virginia Jeffries. Her normally well-coiffed hair was splayed over her pillow like a rat's nest. Her skin seemed papery and dry, her fingers gripped tightly to the edge of the blanket and sheet covering her, the tips white. A nasal cannula was wrapped around her face, the pure oxygen sucked in with every rattling breath.

"I wouldn't spend too much time. She really needs to rest," offered Dr. Phread.

"Can't you do anything else for her?" asked Marcy.

"I assure you, we are doing everything we can, old people get sick," he said. I glared at him with one raised eyebrow. I would need to find out who was her regular physician and get him involved. Dr. Phread was too involved in tests and technology to have any sort of bedside manner.

I walked along the right side of the bed and was soon standing near Mrs. Jeffries. Her head rolled toward me and her eyes opened. They were dull, unfocused, blood-shot. "Who's there?" she asked.

"It's Dr. Klammeraffe," I told her.

"Oh dear, Dr. Klammeraffe, I'm such a mess. They haven't brought me any of my things."

"I'll let Claire know, she'll take care of it."

"We'll get your things to you," said Marcy.

"My, who are you?" asked Virginia.

"This is Marcy Avers. She's a police officer. I was helping her with a police matter today and she offered to come with to check on you."

"Oh how sweet, my dear. You do know that Dr. Klammeraffe is available, but maybe not. He is so delicate regarding those matters. I have to pry things out of him. I can't for the life of me figure out why he hasn't found anyone yet."

I smiled at Marcy and tried to warn her not to say anything.

"Our relationship is strictly professional," Marcy said with all seriousness.

"Well, you can't be 'professional' all the time," she answered. "Tell me, how is Darla? You mustn't let her know I am like this. She will worry too much and not get better herself."

"She's holding her own," I answered, trying to spin my inability to get her better into a positive light. "I'm waiting on some tests that I sent out. Allie, the nurse from the specialty clinic is watching her. Sheila and I are more worried about you right now."

"That's good to know, Dr. Klammeraffe," said Virginia.

"I need to know if there is anything that you and Darla may have been exposed to that may have made you both sick. Someplace you went, someone else you know who isn't feeling well."

"I thought Darla had an allergic reaction?" she asked.

"So did I, but I'm beginning to think it is an infection."

"Oh dear. I really can't think of anything. We really haven't been anywhere except around the block and of course to Henry's atrium in the last week or so. Mrs. Peters in nine-thirteen had a stroke two weeks ago, but I don't suppose that's what you mean."

"Not exactly. Tell me everything you can remember in the last few days. You said your nephew brought you some plants? Did Darla try to eat them?" I asked.

"Eat plants?" asked Dr. Phread, his attention being drawn to the incongruous question, at least incongruous in his perception of the situation.

"Oh, she would never do that. In fact, she helps me take care of them. Reminds me to water them. I don't think I'm being much help. Everything seems so foggy. I'm so tired."

"Then I will let you rest. I understand Henry is sick too. We're going to see him and maybe he can put it together."

"Henry? That poor sweet man. Pretends not to like Darla, but I can see she's wearing on him. I hope he doesn't have what I have. I do so hate being in this hospital. The nurses are so efficient."

"I'll check in on you later, and let you know how Darla is," I promised.

"We'll try and get your things to you then," added Marcy.

"Thank you my dear, thank you to both of you. It was so kind of you to drop in on me."

"I think that's enough then," said Dr. Phread. It was unnecessary since we were leaving, but I let it slide. He was nice enough to let us in and I wanted to make sure that continued.

We left the room. Dr. Phread waved at the nurse's station to let them know we were leaving and got a very slight head nod in acknowledgment. The doors to the unit slid open automatically, no card needed to exit and we all walked silently to the elevators.

"Not much help, huh?" commented Dr. Phread.

"Actually, quite a bit." I looked at Marcy who smiled and looked at Dr. Phread.

"If they were exposed to something, it's in her apartment or in her building. That narrows things down quite a bit."

"And if Henry has the same thing, well, that probably puts our agent in the atrium."

"Unless Henry poisoned Darla," surmised Marcy.

"You're just looking for someone to arrest, aren't you?" I asked.

"Hey, it's a cop thing," she explained.

"I wouldn't mind you putting the cuffs on me," added Dr. Phread. It was all I could do to stop myself from bursting out laughing. I looked at Marcy who managed to keep a straight-face.

"Have you been a bad boy?" she asked.

Dr. Phread's mouth dropped open as Marcy rubbed the top of his head with her right hand. "Your head is so smooth," she said. "You want to touch it?" she asked me.

I shook my head furiously and bit down on my lip. This was too much. She leaned into his left ear and whispered something too low for me to hear, her hand falling down the side of his face, along his chest stopping over his heart. She pulled back from him and turned and walked into the waiting elevator. I followed her. Dr. Phread had drool dripping onto his chin. He continued to stare at her, even as the doors closed.

"What did you say to him?" I asked.

She looked at me and smiled. That was all the answer I was going to get. Part of me didn't want to know. A crackle from her radio broke the moment. An unintelligible voice spoke. She clicked the transmit button and said, "Roger that."

"Roger what?" I asked.

"You're just full of questions, aren't you?"

"Uh, yeah."

"You'll see," she answered.

The elevator let us out in the lobby near the ER. Marcy's smile got us past the receptionists into the treatment area that led to the ambulance bay doors. Too bad she was too young. Too bad she was too much of a cop. Too bad she was too – Marcy. Oh, well.

"Doctor," shouted a voice from my left. I stopped and turned. Dr. Windsor was jogging over to me. "We've run in to a little problem," he told me.

I looked around in confusion. "Are you talking to me?"

"Yes, we need your help, come quickly." He turned and headed for a hallway lined with treatment rooms. Marcy pushed me from behind and I was doing my best impersonation of a jog behind him.

"They need your help, doctor," she said. I could hear the smile in her voice.

The ER Doc held the treatment room door open and I felt Marcy bump up behind me as I stared at the scene in the room. Two of the biggest orderlies I had ever seen were trying to unwind the boa constrictor that had previously been crawling up snakeman's arm from around the neck of a woman. She had on pink scrubs. Her fingers were trying to pry between the snake's massive body and her own neck. It was only by the gasping sounds that were coming from her mouth that I knew she was able to get any air in.

Marcy moved past me and had her gun out.

"Don't shoot," shouted everyone in the room.

"Just a head shot to the snake," she said.

"Give me a minute," I told her. The ketamine I had given must have worn off some. It was warm in the room and from what I remembered about reptile physiology that would speed up its metabolism of the anesthetic. Still, why the snake would go for the nurse's neck was a mystery.

"You have any ketamine around here?" I wondered. Another dose would knock it out again, but unless I hit a vein, it might take longer than we had.

"We can order some from the pharmacy, it'd take a few minutes."

"Don't have a few minutes," I surmised, as the nurse's grunts were getting weaker, and those of the orderlies were getting louder. Even worse, the snake's head was hovering over the woman's face, it's forked tongue smelling her and causing her panic to increase. "Have someone go get it anyway, I want to try something else. Why in the world did it attack her, anyway?" I asked, scanning the room and seeing what I wanted in the corner.

"It didn't," explained Dr. Windsor. "We got it off that man's arm, pried the jaws open with a large Weitlaner retractor and slid it off with a lot of KY jelly."

"Ew," said Marcy.

"Nurse brainiac thought it would be fun to wear the snake as a boa, no pun intended, and it just started to slither around her neck and squeeze."

I stepped over to the anesthetic machine in the corner and pulled it close to the snake. I looked at the mask that was attached. Unlike veterinary style face masks that were long and cone shaped, this was designed to fit over a human face, flat and contoured for the mouth and nose. Useless for a snake. I had to think fast.

"Get me a bag of fluids," I ordered.

A nurse stepped into action, pulling a bag of saline from a metal shelf. She ripped off the plastic outer coat and grabbed a drip set and started to open that as well.

"Just the bag," I told her. "And some bandage scissors." Confused, she handed over the bag then pulled a pair of large bandage scissors from a pocket of her scrub pants. She glanced over at Dr. Windsor, but he just nodded to me. He was just as confused, but apparently didn't have any better ideas.

I held the bag out and cut the top off. Salt water spilled all over the floor, a good portion soaking my Topsiders. I did the same to the bottom creating a plastic tube, open at both ends. "White tape," I said, hoping they knew what I meant.

A hand holding a roll of one inch white adhesive tape thrust at me and I started pulling off the end. I ripped the mask off the anesthetic machine and put one end of the bag over the tube. I folded the corners and taped it as tight as I could. "Turn on the gas," I ordered the nurse who had gotten the fluids for me. "Full blast, five liters a minute."

I then slipped the open end of the bag over the snake's head and started taping it tight behind the skull. The nurse was now silent and turning blue. If this didn't work quickly, I would have to kill the snake.

"Is it going to work?" asked Dr. Windsor.

"The snake should still be a little sedated from the ketamine I gave earlier." Seconds ticked away like hours. I felt sweat dripping down my forehead.

"It's coming loose," shouted one of the orderlies. He was unwrapping the tail from the one side. A strangled gasp came from the nurse as her own airway opened a little. I was holding the snake's head tight, trying to keep it from pulling away from the improvised mask, but I could feel it getting weaker with every breath. Another thirty seconds later and the orderly's strength overcame the weakening reptile and they unwound it from the nurse completely. She collapsed into another nurse's arms and soon she had her own oxygen mask delivering one hundred percent O_2 through her bruised larynx.

I saw a laundry hamper and asked one of the orderlies to empty it and pull it over. We slipped the tail of the snake inside then I removed the tape from the bag over his neck and let him slide in completely. The laundry bag had handy draw strings and I cinched them tight and knotted them excessively. "It'll wake up just as quickly," I warned them.

Dr. Windsor put a big hand on my back. "Dr. At, good work. I would have never thought of that."

"Oh sure you would have, I think that was on an episode of ER."

"Fast thinking, Doc," said Marcy. "I was really hoping I wasn't going to have to shoot it."

"I had no idea you were such an animal lover."

"It's not that. Do you know what kind of paperwork we have to file whenever we fire our guns? I'd have been at the precinct until dinner time."

"Right," I said, not completely taken in by her cynicism.

I felt a tap on my shoulder and the previously snake adorned nurse was looking at me. Her eyes were a little wet and she threw here arms around me. In a Lauren Bacall rasp she said, "Thank you."

"Snakes don't behave normally when they are sedated. They can get disoriented and confused just like people. It just was acting reflexively, I'm sure it didn't mean to hurt you."

I turned back to the staff in the room. "Gotta go. Glad I could help." One of the orderlies stepped in front of me and thrust the laundry bag containing the boa in front of me.

"Not mine," I said.

"But you're a vet."

"Right. A vet, not an animal shelter. Besides, I'm sure the guy who you took it off of would appreciate it back. These things aren't cheap."

He nodded and shrugged, taking the bag back.

"All right people, let him through. Dr. At has places to be. Things to do. Lives to save," said Marcy in her best Chicago Cop voice. The crowd parted reflexively. I was surprised to see another twenty or thirty people in the hall. Applause broke out as Marcy escorted me out. "Enjoy it while you can," said Marcy.

We walked past the reception desk then towards the ambulance bay. The doors slid open and we exited the insanity of the hospital.

"Got a surprise for you, Doc," said Marcy. As we stood on the sidewalk near the circular drive, my Escape pulled up next to us.

"What service," I said, thinking this was the surprise.

"Over here," she said. She led me to the back and it took a few seconds before I realized the back window had been replaced.

"Wow."

"I know a guy over on Lawrence with an auto glass shop. Bobby ran it over."

Bobby got out of the car and came around to hand the keys back to Marcy.

I shook his hand. "Thanks. How much do I owe you?" I asked.

"Ask Marcy. Apparently her guy owes her."

I raised an eyebrow at her, but she just stared at the window, running a finger along the weatherstripping. "I'll write you a check," I promised her.

"Not necessary," she said. "I think I like having *you* owe me one."

"Right," I figured. "I wonder how the auto glass guy ended up owing you one."

She shrugged and then turned to me and smiled.

"Thanks," I said. I really appreciated what she had done.

"Don't I get a hug?" she asked.

I looked back at the window. It actually did deserve a hug. I hugged her. She hugged back. We hugged. Then we unhugged.

"I need to make a quick call then make a couple of stops. Can I take you anywhere?"

"Yeah. With you. Do you think I'm going to let you out of my sight? I can't wait to see what happens next."

"Nothing's going to happen. I'm going to see a botanist then get Mrs. Jeffries' things."

"That's what you think," she said.
That is what I thought.

CHAPTER 13

"I'm still driving," she said dangling my keys in front of my face. I reached to grab them, but she saw me coming a mile away and smiled as they disappeared behind her back.

"Come and get 'em," she taunted.

Tempted, yes. Going to, no. "Okay, why not? You drive. I need to make a phone call anyway."

"You should get one of those Bluetooth thingies."

"Be amazed I have a smart phone."

"Technophobe?"

"No. I just have to have a really good reason to do it. Being able to look like I'm talking to myself doesn't meet my standard."

"Right." She turned to Bobby. "Thanks a lot. And whatever they say about the snake in there, it's all true." She gave him a wink and his eyes opened wide. We pulled open our respective doors and slid into the Escape with Starsky and Hutch efficiency.

I reached in to pull out my phone only to have it ring at me. That was weird. I looked at the caller ID before answering it. It was Sheila. Suddenly I felt a little ashamed. Like I had been caught cheating, only I hadn't been cheating and what did it matter to Sheila anyway, she wasn't my...

The phone rang again and I snapped out of my internal argument to revisit reality. I pressed the send button and said, "Hello."

"Atty, any news?"

"We just saw her and..."

"We?"

Okay. Was she jealous? "Officer Avers and I. She helped get me in. It's kind of handy having a cop around." Marcy smiled and her foot slammed onto my accelerator. The four-cylinder engine did its best to respond to her request.

"Where to?" she asked as she braked just as quickly at the end of the curving driveway.

"Don't know yet, I need to get an address."

She slipped the car into park and turned to me with the best hound dog expression she could muster. "Let me know when you're ready." She turned back to facing Marine Drive and gunned the engine.

I put the phone back to my ear. "What's going on?" asked Sheila.

"Just a little whiplash," I answered.

"Hmmm."

"Hmmm," I answered.

"From what Allie tells me Officer Avers might come in handy for other things as well. Way to go Atty."

"No," I argued. "Nothing like that."

"Tell me about Mrs. Jeffries, is she going to be okay?"

"Well, it's definitely not the flu."

"What is it then?"

"Unfortunately ruling out one disease among thousands doesn't quite allow me to pin it down further for you, but if I had to guess, it's related to whatever is making Darla sick."

"Then you better go figure out what's wrong with Darla."

"I'm waiting for the lab tests."

"So Allie says."

"You've been talking to Allie a lot."

"Were you going to tell me about the guy whose snake swallowed his arm?"

"I haven't had time to finish telling you about Mrs. Jeffries."

"She doesn't have the flu."

"She wants me to get some of her things for her."

"I'll call Claire and have her get one of her neighbors to get some together for you."

"Great. I also need to get Henry's address."

"Atrium Henry? What for?"

"I have a plant question for him."

"What does this have to do with Darla or Mrs. Jeffries?"

"Absolutely nothing. I have a botany question."

"There is nothing more you can be doing for Darla right now?"

"Not until I get some test results."

"Okay. I'll call back in a minute."

"Thanks." I clicked off.

"Which way?" asked Marcy.

"I'm waiting. I don't know which way Henry's house is. For all I know he lives in Mrs. Jeffries' building."

"Which is where?"

"Marine Drive and Montrose-ish," I answered.

"Ish?"

"That area. But Sheila is going to call back and then we can go."

"What should we do until then? Look for some animals in distress?"

"I don't think I want to go looking for trouble right now. I'm tired. I'm hungry, now that I think about it. And because I rearranged my schedule I'm going to be way too busy the rest of the week."

"Try dealing with crabby airline passengers. After a few thousand you get a little frazzled as well."

"Touché," I said. My phone rang. The screen flashed Sheila.

"Sixty-five seventy-five North Sheridan," she told me.

I relayed the address to Marcy and with a screech of my poor tires we were heading north.

"Thanks."

"You keep that little dog alive. She dies, then Mrs. Jeffries dies."

I had thought of that as well. She hung up and I put my phone away. My car clock told me it was just after 4:00 p.m. I hoped Marcy was up to the rush hour traffic. It was starting to begin again.

"You know," I said, "That's up right on the lake. Those homes aren't cheap."

"You think Henry is holding out?"

"We'll see." I had driven down that stretch of Sheridan hundreds of times. There were several condos where I had patients further north, but I couldn't remember what buildings were in the sixty-five hundred block.

"You know, this little car isn't that bad," she said after a couple of minutes of silence.

"I could get used to having a driver. Maybe not you, but a driver would be nice."

"You could afford that?"

"Well, I could do phone calls and other things between

appointments and not have to worry about people breaking into my car."

"And not have to worry about the Bluetooth thingy."

"You get a Bluetooth thingy if you want one so bad."

"Take it easy, just a suggestion."

"All I'm saying is that a driver would make me more efficient, and I could see more patients and make enough money to pay them."

"So basically, you're working more to make the same amount of money ultimately, just more efficiently," Marcy pointed out.

I thought about it. She did kind of make sense. That is probably why I worked alone most of the time anyway. But I kind of wished she didn't have to be right.

"Here we are," she announced, pulling in to a driveway off Sheridan Road. We stopped in full view of the home. I had driven past it many times. I thought it was some sort of museum or historical building considering how out of place it was.

The house took up maybe a two hundred foot lot. A big hunk of lakefront for just a house. It was surrounded to the north and south by high rise apartments and condos. The driveway continued past the south side of the house to what could be described as a carriage house. A two story structure with three large ten foot high garage doors.

"This guy is a gardener?" asked Marcy.

"Retired," I answered. "Worked at the Garfield Park Conservatory before taking the janitor job at Mrs. Jeffries' building and he only took that because they let him landscape their atrium."

"This thing is a mansion."

"It's got to be worth four or five million sitting on the lake like this. I'm surprised it hasn't been taken down for another condo building."

"Probably has landmark status or something. Maybe he just caretakes it. Stays for free and keeps up the lawn or something. I bet he lives in the apartment above the garage."

"Let's go check," I suggested. We got out of my car and Marcy beeped the lock and alarm. "Let's see what the name on the mailbox is." The front porch was probably thirty feet across with wide wooden steps. Dozens of planters lined the sides, the fall and winter foliage adding unexpected color to the landscape.

The mailbox had no label on it, but there was some mail inside. I lifted the lid and saw Henry's name on the top letter. "If he does live out back, his mail gets delivered to the main house," I told her.

Marcy rang the bell. A loud Westminster chime echoed through the inside. I figured it might take someone a minute or two to get to the door if they were upstairs or at the back. After a while Marcy rang it again. "No one home. Maybe Henry wasn't that sick after all. Playing hooky or something."

"That doesn't sound like something Henry would do," I said, but in truth, I really didn't know him that well.

Marcy walked along the porch and shielding her eyes peeked into one of the windows. "What's Henry look like?" she asked.

"Medium height and build. White hair. Tanned skin. Why?"

"Darn it," she semi-cursed.

"What?"

She walked over to the front door and tried the knob. It was locked. She took a half step back, then kicked at the door near where the latch entered the frame. A loud splintering of wood and slam of the door smacking into the wall obliterated the normal street sounds. "More paperwork," she said.

I looked inside. On the floor, Henry was sprawled on the floor at the bottom of a winding staircase. From the front porch, he looked dead.

CHAPTER 14

"I told you something was going to happen," she said. "You're a doctor, go check on him," Marcy ordered.

I looked at her with my best Oliver Platt stunned expression. "You're a cop."

"I break down the doors, you can feel for the pulse."

Someone had to. I walked in the door. Henry was about twenty feet away at the base of the stairs. Was his chest moving? I inched my way over. I could feel Marcy creeping along behind me. I really didn't want to find a dead Henry. Not only would it be disgusting, but I didn't know who else to ask about that seed. Dead animals I could do. I started to taste a little breakfast mixed with stomach acid in the back of my throat. I reached the body and knelt down near him, reaching out my right hand to check for his pulse. I looked back at Marcy. She was standing over us, gun drawn and pointing up. "What are you doing with that?" I asked.

"The murderer could still be here."

I put a finger over his carotid artery. The pulse was strong and steady. "Sorry, he's not dead yet. There goes your murder theory," I told her. "Please put that away," I added, nodding at her gun.

Marcy holstered her gun and radioed for an ambulance. The dispatcher announced that one was on the way. Apparently an old man at the bottom of the stairs, or perhaps it was this neighborhood, warranted an immediate response.

"Do you think he fell down the stairs?" she asked.

"It looks more like he was trying to go up and maybe passed out. I'm not going to move him until the paramedics get here."

"Good idea. I'm going to look around."

"You really think someone else might be here?"

"Don't know."

"What do you hope to find?"

"Clues," she suggested. She headed out of the entryway into what looked like a dining room.

Henry groaned. "Henry," I said. "Can you you hear me?"

"What happened?" he asked. He tried to move, but I put my hands on his shoulders.

"Best to stay still until the paramedics get here."

"Is that Dr. At?"

"Yep."

"What are you doing here?"

"I had a plant question and Claire said you went home sick. I'm kind of glad we decided to stop by."

"We?"

"I'm here with a cop, Marcy Avers. We've kind of been helping each other out all day."

Henry coughed and his whole body racked with spasms. It was almost as bad as Mrs. Hornby, but I was pretty sure he didn't smoke. I pulled out my handkerchief just as he was taking in another breath to start another cough and held it over his mouth.

"Thanks," he muttered after he finished. I started to slip the handkerchief back into my jacket when I noticed the red specks of blood.

"How long you been coughing?" I asked.

"Started yesterday, really got bad today. I couldn't get any work done and I was too tired to even try. The flu is running through that building. I had my shot, but they say it doesn't take in everyone."

Flu. They thought Mrs. Jeffries had the flu, but it wasn't flu. I remembered her saying almost the same exact thing about her flu shot. With my luck it was Ebola or something weird like that. I'd be sure to get rid of the handkerchief as soon as possible. "It looked like you passed out."

"I was feeling dizzy. I was just going to go upstairs to lie down."

"Is there anyone else here?"

"No. I live here alone." He tried a laugh. "I bet you're surprised to see this is where I live."

"A little. Well, a lot. Well, yeah."

"My grandfather made a fortune in the stockyards. Set up the house in a trust that takes care of the taxes and utilities and upkeep. Can't sell it or rent it out. I'm the only one in my family interested in living here, so I get to stay. Plenty of space for my plants."

"So you're rich."

"Nah, just have the house. I get by on my park district pension and the salary from the building. Most of that goes to my plants."

A siren crescendoed and stopped outside. Marcy stepped back into the entryway from the opposite side she had left. "No one else here."

"I know, Henry's awake."

"You okay, sir?"

"I've been better."

"I'll go get the paramedics. We'll get you to the hospital in no time."

"Is that necessary?" he asked.

"I think it's a good idea," I added and he nodded and relaxed.

Marcy showed the paramedics in with their gurney and I let them do their job. They put one of the plastic whiplash collars on Henry and rolled him onto a backboard. In no time they had in an IV, had run an ECG, and had him ready to go and up on the gurney.

"Where are you taking him?" I asked.

"Weiss," he answered.

"Make sure Dr. Phread sees him. Tell him he works at the building that the lady who doesn't have the flu lives. It'll make sense to him," I assured the confused paramedic. Marcy wrote a note on her pad and handed it to the paramedic.

"Make sure this gets to Dr. Phread," she said.

As they left I pulled out the handkerchief and showed it to Marcy.

"Doesn't look good."

"Coughing up blood usually isn't."

"You think it's related to the old lady and the dog?"

"I'm beginning to get suspicious. Darla was coughing up blood this afternoon as well. Too many coincidences."

"Did you ask him about the seed?"

"Rats, forgot all about it with him lying on the floor coughing up blood and everything."

"Understandable. What now?"

"Well," I started, looking at my watch, "saving lives deserves a decent meal. I haven't eaten since breakfast and I'm not going to deprive myself any further. We eat. Then go check on Darla, get Mrs. Jeffries' things and back to the hospital."

"I know a great diner on Irving Park Road. It's called..."

We both finished the sentence together.

"Danny's."

I didn't seem to mind her erratic, almost daredevil style of driving on our way to the diner. I wonder why that was? She found an open parking spot across the street and slid into it neatly with a tight u-turn I didn't know my car could do. The gurgle in my stomach proved this was the right thing to be doing. I fed the meter, jealous that it was eating while the smells of Danny's taunted me. The aroma of Carla's coffee and the odor of carbonizing beef and potatoes was stimulating my olfactory receptors into overtime. I wondered how anyone could walk past this building without being sucked in the door by that smell.

"I can't believe I've never seen you in here if you claim to come as often as you do," I told Marcy as I held the door open for her.

"Cop lunch hour is different from other people. Their lunch hours tend to be busy for us so we eat early."

"That would account for it, I guess."

Before I had my butt entirely ensconced on the red vinyl covered stool, Carla was pouring two cups of steaming, thick, coffee. "Hiya, Doc, Marcy. You two know each other?"

"Met today," Marcy confessed. "Professional capacity."

Carla gave us a strange look. "What sort of professional capacity would put you two together?"

"A dead dog, a stolen dead dog, a snake eating a man, a snake choking a woman, and a botanist who most likely doesn't have the flu."

That summed up our day pretty effectively I thought. "I need a double Danny burger, fries and a chocolate milk shake," I ordered.

Marcy nodded. "Sounds good, make that two."

I took a long look at her. How was it she looked like that and I looked like this. Some things just weren't very fair.

"So thanks for getting my window fixed, but I can't help wonder who broke it. Do you think it could have been the dead dog lady?"

"Possibly, but I have another idea."

"What's that?"

"I'd rather not say. I'm waiting on some leads."

"Come on, I've been letting you tag along with me all day, now it's my turn to venture into your world."

"I need to go back to the specialty clinic."

"We're already going there, so that's good."

"There is something I need to check out."

"You won't be anymore specific."

Carla brought out our burgers. The juice dripping from them was half grease, half blood.

"Not right now. Eat your burger."

"Yes, officer."

She smiled as she took a big bite of her own cholesterol delivery system. Grease dribbled down her chin.

We finished up. Carla gave us separate bills which was fine with me. Despite the fact that Marcy had some nice attributes, I didn't want this to turn into anything resembling a date. Or that our temporary partnership was anything more than professional. I looked at the time on the diner's clock. It was 5:25.

I thanked Danny and Carla and we headed back to my car. Marcy got into the driver's side automatically. She had claimed that territory and I wasn't in a mood to give her a fight.

Traffic had slowed even more and almost out of reflex I hit the radio button and Neil Diamond started pouring out the car speakers.

"Oh – my – God," said Marcy. "What in the world is that?"

"Oh, sorry, my traffic music. Neil Diamond."

"Are you serious?"

"Does it bother you?"

"The rule is the driver gets to pick the tunes."

"What rule is that?"

"The rule. You know, like home field advantage. Whoever is driving and has to deal with the traffic, and weather and annoying passengers, has the right to decide what sounds fill the inside of the car. And I do not want to listen to Neil Diamond. What else do you have?"

"Billy Joel?"

She gagged.

"Phil Collins?"

Choking sounds.

"Sting."

She pretended to vomit.

"What do you want to listen to?"

"Anyone from this century," she said. She clicked on the radio and had the tuner to a station that had never resided in one of my presets. She cranked the volume and started bopping in the seat like a teenager cruising on a Friday night.

Normally I might have given an argument, tried to work on a compromise, but as we were only two blocks from the specialty clinic, I decided to let her have her way.

We pulled into the parking lot and she stopped the car. The music ended abruptly and my brain began to stop shaking from the racket.

We exited the car. "Why don't you go check on your dog while I sniff around a little."

"Sniff around?"

"Police work, Doc. Police work." For a moment she reminded me of Barney Fife from the old Andy Griffith show, though I doubt she realized that was how she was coming across.

"Can't I sniff with you?"

She looked me over. "No offense, Doc, but you might be a little of a hindrance, if you catch my drift."

"Gotcha." Sounded boring anyway.

I went to the back door and pulled out my key. In twenty minutes the clinic would be shifting over to emergency mode. Animal emergencies, not guys with snakes on their arms. I walked toward the ICU to check on Darla. Allie was sitting in the ward in an aluminum lounge chair. She had a giant soda and a slice of pizza and was reading "Cosmo".

"Hey, Dr. At, want to take a quiz to find out what kind of lover you are?"

"Gosh, Allie, I really don't think I want to know."

"Come to think of it," she said, "neither do I. Darla is doing better, but still having some trouble. She nodded at my favorite patient in the plexiglass-fronted cage. The sealed environment kept her in one hundred percent oxygen.

"I don't suppose you have any of the test results yet."

"It's only been a couple of hours. They usually start sending out results around 1:00 a.m. You want me to wake you?"

"That's Sheila's job."

Allie knew that I had never actually met Sheila and that I dreamed of one day actually seeing her. As time went along, I was beginning to realize that the Sheila I liked, that I cared about, was not the idealized woman of my fantasies, but the caring, funny, witty woman on the other end of the phone line.

"I'd think that maybe Officer Avers would be taking over that role after today. You guys are getting pretty chummy."

I glared at her as best as I could. "Strictly," I reinforced, "professional."

"If you say so."

"I say so."

I walked over to the oxygen cage and unhooked the small round door to one of the access holes that let the vet techs and doctors access the patients inside the cages without letting out all the enriched atmosphere they contained. I slid my hand in and reached over to pet Darla between the eyes. She seemed to enjoy the touch; her eyes closed and she pushed her head against my hand. I could still see her fighting for every breath, but she did seem a little better.

"So what did you learn at the hospital and what happened to the incredibly stupid snake guy? Did they have to cut off his arm?"

"Do you really think they'd cut off his arm to remove a snake?"

"Maybe it had already started to digest and the skin was falling off and the bone was poking through the muscle."

"You watch too many horror movies."

"I live a horror movie," she corrected me waving an arm around to indicate the whole of the specialty clinic.

"Actually, they got the snake off just in time for the ketamine to wear down and it started to strangle one of the nurses. I had to gas it down before she lost consciousness."

"You had to?"

"Marcy wanted to shoot it," I said.

"Not a good idea in a hospital."

"That's what I told her."

"What about Darla's mom?"

"She looks pretty bad. They know it's not the flu, but other than that they're shooting in the dark as well. She's still awake, but compared to this morning she's deteriorating fast."

"Do you think she just might be pining away?"

"No. This is too much. I've seen her concerned about Darla. She's really sick. Then there was Henry, the janitor."

"Henry the janitor? What, at the hospital?"

"No, at Mrs. Jeffries' building."

"What about him?"

"Marcy and I went to see him."

"At Mrs. Jeffries' building?"

"No, at his house, he had gone home sick."

"You wanted to see if he had the same thing?"

"Actually, I wanted to ask him about the seed we found in the Kazakhstani dog. He's a botanist and I figured if anyone could tell me what that thing was, he could."

"So what did he say?" asked Allie.

"Nothing. Well, nothing about the seed. He was unconscious when we got there. Marcy broke down the door."

"Way to go, Marcy."

"We thought he was dead at first."

"With the day you're having that wouldn't have been too big a surprise."

"I suppose not. But it appears he might have the same thing as Mrs. Jeffries."

"You think they have something going on?" asked Allie.

"Why does your mind always find itself in the gutter?"

"It's trying to crawl its way out of the sewer," she answered.

"Good point. No, I don't think there is anything going on, but I am going to stop by Mrs. Jeffries' place and get her some things. I'll have another look around. If I know I'm looking for something, maybe I'll find it."

"What could make all three of them sick?" asked Allie. "I'm pretty sure it's not rabies. Dogs don't get the human flu and when they get dog flu, it's more of a respiratory disease."

"And they know that Mrs. Jeffries at least doesn't have the flu."

"So you said. Well, zoonotic diseases. Is it viral, bacterial, fungal or parasitical?"

"Good question. If we assume it is the same organism in all three patients, then we have to find something that produces flu-like symptoms on people and head and neck edema in dogs."

"They just sound too different."

"Not if there were different routes of infection."

"Meaning?"

"If Darla chewed on something that had the infectious agent, that would account for the symptoms around her head and neck. If Mrs.

Jeffries and Henry inhaled it, it would start in their lungs and spread systemically."

"Okay. Inhaled probably rules out most parasites."

"True."

"But that leaves fungus, bacteria and viruses."

"Viral is least likely. A lot of viruses are species-specific, apart from rabies and some encephalitis viruses. I doubt it's Ebola or one of the hemorrhagic fevers."

"Fungal would fit well," suggested Allie. "Blasto and histomycosis both hit the lungs. Both can have a subcutaneous lesion."

"We don't have Darla on any antifungals...do we?"

Allie smiled, "No."

"Then what sort of bacteria could it be?"

"*Bordetella*? *Brucella*? *Yersinia*?"

The last one caught me by surprise. "Plague?"

"Okay we don't see much of that in Chicago, well, we don't see it at all really, but you said the one guy worked in a garden. See any rats around there?"

"The antibiotics we have Darla on should take care of *Yersinia pestis*. I can see Darla maybe sniffing around a rat's nest, maybe biting one. I suppose some fleas could have gotten onto Mrs. Jeffries and Henry. But it's got to be low on the list."

"Maybe someone from out of the area brought it in."

That reminded me of the dead dog from the airport. Animals and people from all over the world moved around every day. Someone exposed to plague could take days to show symptoms. And I still wanted to find out about that seed. "Well, we wait for the aspirate results. Did you order a culture too?"

Allie gave me a sideways look. Of course she had. She was Allie, supertech.

"Here you guys are," said a cheery voice from the doorway. I turned to see Marcy leaning in the opening, smiling broadly.

"You look happy."

"Dr. At, I am happy. And you should be too. I found out who smashed your window."

"Really?" asked Allie.

"Well, I'm ninety-nine point nine percent sure."

"Darla has the plague," said Allie.

"What?" said Marcy. She nearly jumped out of her skin. She

immediately started wiping her hands on her uniform shirt.

"Well," continued Allie, dead-pan faced, still sitting in her lounge chair, "we're ninety-nine point nine percent sure."

Allie looked at both of us and began to shake her head from side to side. "Come on."

"It's a possibility we're considering," I explained. "Not that likely, but it explains the symptoms in humans and dogs."

"Really?" asked Marcy, this time with more curiosity rather than hysteria.

"Really."

"I thought animals just carried plaque and didn't die from it."

"She's not dead yet," I said waving at Darla.

"Sorry," Marcy apologized.

"So who smashed my car window? It was Margaret, right?" I joked.

Marcy nearly froze as she looked right at me. "How did you know?"

I laughed, assuming she was putting me on. "Come on, who did it?"

"Margaret. The receptionist," she answered me.

"Okay, we played our little joke, you've done yours. Margaret was sitting at the front desk when my alarm went off."

"It was her," Marcy insisted.

"How?" asked Allie before I could.

"Remember when I told you I was going to run a check on Margaret?"

"Yeah," I said cautiously.

"Some interesting things came up on her."

"Margaret?" said Allie. "I knew there was something fishy about her."

"Let me start with the really interesting part. That guy who came in here with the snake trying to eat him, he's Margaret's brother."

"Brother?" said Allie. "This is turning into some weird soap opera."

"Well, he has a bunch of DUIs and some B and E arrests."

"B and E?" it was my turn to ask.

"Breaking and entering."

"Geez, don't you watch 'Law and Order'?" Allie asked me.

"Silly me," I answered.

"So he broke into Doc's car?" asked Allie.

"No," Marcy answered. "Margaret has a little side business."

"Doing what?" I asked.

"She sells stuff on eBay."

"Lots of people do that," said Allie. "I've sold stuff on there. You'd be surprised to see what people actually buy."

"She sells animal tranquilizers. Ketamine and diazepam and something called xylazine."

"They don't let you sell that stuff on eBay. Don't they monitor for controlled substances."

"Yeah, but they don't monitor Beanie Babies."

"She puts the drugs in the Beanie Babies?"

"Yep. Apparently there are some keywords that these drug dealers put in their ads to let their clients know which of the items are the drug containing ones."

"Why haven't they arrested Margaret then," I asked. "Heck, why hasn't the emergency clinic figured out she's been stealing drugs?"

"Apparently she doesn't steal them. She just orders them using the doctors DEA numbers from the clinic and has them shipped here. She gets to them before anyone else since she is up front when they arrive, and probably just puts them in her purse or something."

"Sneaky," said Allie.

"I still don't get how she broke my car window or why she did."

"Well, you are one of the doctors whose identity she has been using."

"Me? Great, I'll lose my DEA license."

"Nah, they won't do anything to you. The DEA has been watching her for months."

"I knew there was something weird about her," I said. I was getting pretty angry about her using my DEA license to buy drugs. It would be pretty hard to practice without being able to get those medications.

"Her son is the one who broke your window."

"Margaret has a son?" said Allie with disbelief. "You mean someone had to grow up with her as a mother? No wonder he turned to a life of crime."

"Apparently he was supposed to put some of the drug-stuffed beanie babies in your car, not steal anything. You would call the police to report the break-in, the police would wonder about the cute

Beanie Babies in the car and check them out. There was even an anonymous tip to check your car that apparently Margaret placed."

"But there were no Beanie Babies in my car."

"No," Marcy laughed, "this is the funny part. He forgot to bring them with him to your car. He just had his tire iron and after he broke the window and heard the alarm, realized his mistake and went back to his car to get them. When he returned, he must have seen me in the alley and vamoosed."

"How did you find all this out?" asked Allie.

"Yeah, how did you?" I wanted to know.

"When I found out about the investigation into Margaret's drug dealing, I was really suspicious about the vandalism to your car. Part of me was thinking it was the woman from the airport, you know, the one Dave let slip about the autop..." she caught herself, "necropsy. I wondered if anyone may be around, watching the place, biding their time. They probably knew you were coming back. I came across a patrol car on Addison. They were sent to check out the Escape with the busted rear window, but since it had already been fixed, they had no reason to go looking for Beanie Babies, drug stuff or otherwise."

"But that was hours ago."

"Wasn't a priority call. No crime was being committed. You didn't phone in a report."

"Well, you were already there."

"Precisely."

"So did they catch her son?"

"Actually, yes. He was in such a hurry to get out of here he rear-ended an ambulance."

"An ambulance?" Allie asked.

"Yeah. Got the front end of his car wedged beneath its bumper. So he took off and went home. Unfortunately, he left a couple of the Beanie Babies in the car along with his registration papers. They picked him up about an hour ago."

"That's probably why the ambulance was delayed."

"Probably," said Marcy.

"What did her brother have to do with any of this?" asked Allie.

"Nothing. Other than being an idiot and falling asleep with the drumstick in his hand, they think the snake is stolen."

"Better call the hospital then. Good thing you didn't shoot it."

"When does Margaret get the perp walk?" Allie inquired.

"DEA wants to keep building their case a little more, so she stays free for now."

"What? Working here?" I asked.

"You can't let her know they're onto her."

"How much more evidence do they need?" asked Allie. "Sounds like they got a pretty good case as it is."

"They think she is working with someone else, but haven't figured out who yet. They are hoping she will lead them to her partner as well."

"Don't you think with her son arrested she might get suspicious and close up shop? Move away?"

"They are under the impression that the arrest will make her careless and she'll make a mistake. Personally, I'd like to lock her up now."

I looked at my watch; 5:50. "Well, she'll be leaving in ten minutes anyway when the emergency staff comes in. She may have left already."

"Geez, I need to get ready for work," Allie announced. She reached next to her lounge chair and pulled up a sixty-four ounce Super Big Gulp. With the power of an Oreck vacuum cleaner she sucked the last few ounces out and released a bodacious burp.

"Sexy," I said.

She gave me a wink and left the room with a smile.

Marcy looked at me, "If I'd have known that's what it took to get your attention I'd have gotten myself one of those Super Big Gulps."

"Wouldn't work. You're just too scary."

"It's the gun, isn't it," she surmised. She fondled it. That might work on Dr. Phread, but it wasn't going to phase me. "So the uniform doesn't do anything for you?" she asked, modeling in her best Vanna White pose.

"Still nothing," I lied. She was hot. And maybe the gun did turn me on...a little.

I turned my attention to Darla. The little dog had fallen asleep, but her chest still moved with exaggerated effort. I checked her IV line and picked up her chart. Allie had noted all the meds, as well as hourly TPRs; temperature, pulse and respiration.

"How's she doing?" asked Marcy, her concern genuine.

"Hanging in there. But not doing as well as I'd like. It's definitely not an allergic reaction and it'll take a bit longer to tell if the antibiotics are doing any good. I'd really like to get back to Mrs. Jeffries' place and check it out."

"Let's go," she said.

"I appreciate your sticking with me today, and all your help, but I'd be happy to drop you off someplace. Your shift must be long over."

"Yep, I had the guys sign me out a couple of hours ago."

"Really?"

"Yeah, this is fun. I'd still like to help you out. Maybe an extra pair of trained eyes might be of benefit."

"Maybe."

"Come on. We're a good team."

"Let's go, before I change my mind or something else strange happens."

CHAPTER 15

Marcy drove to Mrs. Jeffries'. Along the way I tried to get a hold of Dr. Phread, but he was apparently still busy with Henry. I called Sheila and updated her as well.

"Claire said she took care of getting Mrs. Jeffries' things. It's really sweet of you to do this for her," she said.

"Well, I really want to get a good look at her apartment. There has to be something I'm missing."

"You, uh, going to be searching her place, uh, alone?"

She must have talked to Allie again.

"Officer Avers volunteered to help."

"I bet she did," she snarled.

Yowza.

"You're welcome to come help too," I suggested.

She didn't take the bait. "Be careful," she said.

"I will," I answered not knowing if she meant in my search or of Marcy.

We hung up, neither of us in a mood for further play. I called the lab just to check if they might have Darla's results, but they didn't. I made sure it was a stat and asked them to add on several other titers if they had enough blood. The lab person assured me that they would be done. I verified that the cytology on the aspirates I took from Darla's lymph nodes were included in the rush order. Part of me wondered if I was irritating them and I hung up just as we pulled into Mrs. Jeffries' building. It was now 6:15 according to my car's clock. I went to the back of my car and grabbed a handful of sterile culture swabs from one of my bags and slipped them into my jacket pocket, just in case I found anything interesting to test.

The night desk clerk, Charlie, was on duty. Charlie was a college student, studying film writing at Columbia University. It was not unusual for me to make evening calls for Darla when Charlie was on duty, so he knew me well. Marcy pulled up into the fire lane area and turned on my flashers. She followed me into the lobby.

"Hey, Dr. At, Claire said you'd be coming by." His eyes wandered to Marcy. "Hello," he said with a seductive tone. It had no effect on Marcy.

"She has a gun," I pointed out. Marcy's hand slid conspicuously to the wooden grip, her forefinger tapping the leather of the holster.

"Yeah," he agreed and handed over a set of keys attached to a Pomeranian key chain. "This is to Mrs. Jeffries' apartment. Drop them off when you're done. I have a bag of stuff her neighbor packed for the hospital. I hear she's not doing too well. How's that little dog of hers?"

"Hanging in there. We're going to look around the atrium then head up to her apartment."

"What are you looking for?" asked Charlie.

"Something made them sick. Henry is in the hospital with what appears to be something very serious as well and I'm wondering if they all have the same thing."

"Probably the flu," Charlie guessed.

"Probably," I agreed, not wanting to get into an in-depth discussion as to the differential diagnoses. I grabbed the key and headed toward the atrium first. I walked to the door Henry had led me through earlier that day. I tried to remember if he was sick then. A little crabby in the morning, but that was usual for him. Maybe a little slow, easy to tire, but I could easily have put that off to his age.

"What are we looking for?" asked Marcy.

"Hey, you're the detective," I said.

"Not yet," she corrected me.

"I'm looking for something toxic or infectious. A plant that may have a poison in it, a box of tainted chocolates, a moldy sandwich. Anything that all three of them may have been exposed to."

"Well, that narrows it down," she said sarcastically. "One of those, 'you'll know it when you see it' type of things?"

"Exactly."

It was dark outside and the atrium itself was lit by stray light from the apartments ringing the green space. We walked around the entire area. No one else was there. Marcy was shining her flashlight in every crevice she could find. The floor around the fountain was paved with bricks set in a herringbone pattern. Benches were strategically placed around the fountain, flanked by large cement planters artfully planted with colorful and aesthetically pleasing plants.

The mermaid was still getting her shower.

"She's just a statue," Marcy said. I was probably staring at the mermaid a little too long.

"Yeah, yeah. Just look around."

The garden beds were well tended. There were no weeds and the soil, where visible, was a rich, dark loam with specks of white perlite which I assumed Henry added to help condition it. Around the bases of the larger trees was cypress mulch, adding a woodsy aroma to the space. It was a million times better than my backyard. I'd have to remember to have Sheila schedule me some down time after seeing Darla in the future, so I could enjoy a few minutes in here, especially in the winter. That was assuming I managed to save Darla's life.

While I couldn't imagine Mrs. Jeffries without a pet, I could quite easily see her fading fast if she lost that little orange fluff-ball.

I walked the entire perimeter, spending more time than I had earlier looking for plants I knew to be toxic or any that might have been chewed on. I was sure Henry wouldn't put any out, especially if residents brought their pets in there, but I'd be sure to ask him if I got to see him at the hospital.

At the far end was a door marked "Janitor". It was cracked open a bit. I pushed it and it swung in. The room was dark, but from what little light spilled in from the dimly lit atrium it looked spacious. I felt around the inside of the door frame for a light switch. Nothing. I looked into the darkness and could barely make out the naked bulb hanging from the ceiling. I held my right hand in front of me as I stepped into the murky darkness. I was feeling for a string hanging down that would let me turn on the light. A metal bucket went skittering out of the way as I kicked it. I stopped long enough to make sure that was all the damage I had done.

Marcy appeared at the door. "Here you go, Doc," she said as she shined a bright light into the room from behind me. I turned and was instantly blinded as the beam hit me square in the eyes.

"Hey!"

She moved the light, but the damage was done. All I could see were purple blobs of light as my eyes squinted shut against further damage. Suddenly, the room was filled with more light as Marcy found the switch I had missed.

The additional blast of light did nothing to help me regain my vision, "Hey," I shouted again.

"Take it easy. You're not blind." I could tell she was moving around me and indeed my vision was returning. "Looks like where he keeps his gardening supplies," she observed.

I found myself looking at a rack of hoes, rakes and shovels. To my left was an old workbench, chipped and scarred by decades of use. Various-sized clay pots were stacked up on the bench and on a shelf above it were canisters and bags containing fertilizers, plant food, and various other chemicals and supplements.

My gardening skills were limited to mowing my little postage stamp of lawn every two weeks in the summer and killing a few dozen flowers from Home Depot that I tried growing every year, confident that they'd bloom into a dazzling display this time, by golly.

A few more blinks and the purple globs faded and more of the room came into focus. There were some posters advertising various exhibits at the Garfield Park Conservatory where Henry used to work. Framed photographs of Henry among the greenhouses and some that seemed to be set in exotic locations – rain forests and jungles in far-off places with Henry standing next to some unusual plant, posing with some other more or possibly less important individual. In one corner was a worn and tattered recliner. A reading lamp and a telephone were on a small table next to the chair. Undoubtedly, he found small moments in his day to escape and retreat to a past full of memories and excitement, until a resident needed his services or some daily task beckoned to be done.

"See anything that might be our suspect?" Marcy asked.

I scanned the shelves. There was some lime and bone meal in old brown paper bags, for conditioning the soil I presumed. Newer bags had specific fertilizer mixes for roses, zinnias, and half a dozen other flowering plants. There were about a dozen old metal coffee cans with handwritten labels taped to the front, most faded, but some readable. One of them, located by a stained, but apparently workable Mr. Coffee machine, actually had coffee in it. A mug labeled "Garfield Park Conservatory" and Tupperware filled with sugar sat nearby. "Nothing is jumping out. It's all plant food. I suppose it could be toxic, but the three patients are showing symptoms more in line with an infection rather than a poison."

Marcy patted the recliner and a cloud of dust billowed into the air. "Not too clean in here. There could be anything around here waiting to infect someone."

"According to the presentation of symptoms, Darla was infected first, then Mrs. Jeffries, then Henry. I think we need to look at Mrs. Jeffries' condo and see what we can find up there."

We left Henry's hideaway and closed the door behind us. I walked slowly, taking in everything, hoping something would jump out, but nothing did.

We went back to the lobby and headed for the elevators. Charlie buzzed us through and I pressed the up button. While we waited I asked Marcy, "Any ideas on your end?"

"Suicide pact?" she suggested.

"Never mind."

"I'm not a doctor or a vet, but what if it's all a coincidence?"

"It's possible."

"I mean, Darla's symptoms don't match the old folks, right?" she asked.

"Not all diseases present the same in different species. A bacteria that may be fatal to one animal, may only cause mild diarrhea in another. And since there are hundreds of diseases that affect both people and dogs, it's not impossible that the same bug could be in both."

The elevator to our left opened. Gentleman that I am, I motioned for Marcy to enter first. I followed her in and pressed the button for Mrs. Jeffries floor and waited. Waited for Marcy to get impatient.

"Is this thing broken?" she asked,

"Wait for it," I advised her.

"Wait for what?"

"It's testing you," I said.

"Let's get another one," she said and headed for the doors just in time for them to start closing. Of course she tripped the electric eye and they slid open once more. She looked at me with a cop's eye of suspicion. "How did you do that?"

"Do what?" I answered, feigning ignorance and innocence.

Marcy jabbed at the lit button for Mrs. Jeffries' floor once again and hit the "close door" button a few times for good measure then settled in to wait for the doors to close. She turned to me. "Okay, what's the secret?"

I held up my hand as if to indicate she was about to witness a feat few had ever seen before. In a too loud voice directed to the ceiling of the elevator I said, "Looks like this one isn't working, let's go try another." I feinted for the doors and they began to close. I slid back just in time to miss the electric eye and the elevator began its crawl up.

"You're really weird."

I had no response to that.

As we crawled up the elevator shaft, one floor at a time, I tried to put it all together. I needed some positive test results. Either from Darla or Virginia. I couldn't imagine any fertilizer would make them sick. I didn't see any pesticides in Henry's workroom. Darla would be exposed to such things and probably Henry, but not Mrs. Jeffries.

We reached the twenty-third floor. Marcy stepped out of the elevator first, scanning the hallway in both directions, then giving me an all clear nod with her head. Cop thing, I guess.

"Which way?"

"To the left," I instructed. I led the way to Mrs. Jeffries' door and slipped in the key that Charlie had given me. As she stepped in she stopped in her tracks, her eyes wide.

"Wow, talk about visions of grandma's house."

"You get used to it."

"There's plastic on all the furniture," she observed with her omniscient cop eyes. "Who still puts plastic on all their furniture? I guess with the dog that makes sense, but still – ick."

"Let's get started. The sooner we finish and get back to the hospital, the sooner I can get home and get some rest." I was impressed that I was still going after getting up so early this morning. Had this all started this morning? It felt like days.

"I'm too excited to rest."

"Good for you. Come on." We split up and started to look around. I went to the kitchen first. Marcy went for the bathroom. I didn't think I was strong enough to check in all her bathroom cabinets.

Perhaps the bathroom would be less scary. I winced as I checked out some of the cupboards. Next to a box of dog treats, opened, but only a few missing, were almost empty containers of Bugles, Cheetos, butter cookies, a half-empty bag of mini-marshmallows, and a bag of shelled pistachio nuts.

I checked under the sink. There was a baby-proof latch, presumably for Darla's benefit, that hid the usual assortment of cleaners and cleaning supplies. I couldn't imagine Virginia doing the cleaning herself, most likely she had a maid in one or two times a week. That's what I needed. I hated cleaning as well.

I checked the refrigerator, opened every jar and container I could find, putting my nose to use for things that might even pass my smell test. I was known to shave an occasional green patch off a mostly unused block of cheddar or microwave the heck out of some week-old leftover pasta. In the bottom near the back I found Mrs. Jeffries' gift she had told me about. It was an Eli's Cheesecake.

"Cheesecake," I moaned in my best Homer Simpson. I let it be. I hadn't earned it yet. But talk about motivation.

I took some culture swabs from my pocket and collected samples of some of the more suspicious looking foods. I'd send them off the to the lab for testing later. At this time of night, it would probably be tomorrow morning before I could get them picked up. I didn't swab the cheesecake.

Next, I went to the living room and was drawn to the half-dozen pots of African Violets sitting on the window ledge. They were beautiful enough to take my attention away from the dusky shoreline of Lake Michigan. Those must be the plants that Henry had helped her with. Every single one of them was loaded with deep, purple blossoms. I was amazed, mostly because my attempts to grow plants on the window ledge over my kitchen sink (which had a view of my neighbor's brick wall), usually caused the specimens to end up in the garbage dried to yellow-brown husks of their former selves.

On one side of the row of flowers was a small Tupperware container, similar to the one that Henry kept sugar for his coffee in. A masking tape label indicated it was bone meal and I suspected the key to Mrs. Jeffries' botanical success. A small silver spoon lay on top of the container. I opened it up and looked at the white powdered substance. Calcium and phosphorus. Nothing deadly there.

"Anything interesting?"

"Only if you consider ground-up bones interesting."

"On certain days maybe, but today that doesn't even make me flinch."

"Any luck in the bathroom?"

"I could summarize her medical history for you, but I don't think we have a couple of hours to spare."

"I forgot to mention that she is a hypochondriac."

"Ya think? I could bust her on possession with intent to distribute with all the stuff she has in there."

"Too bad you're off duty."

"Yeah, too bad. Well, I'm thinking that if it was a drug overdose and she managed to poison Henry's coffee, they would have found that at the hospital. They must know about all her medications."

"Probably. I don't think she takes any of them. She just likes to have them around, just in case."

"That's why I have bullets in my gun. Just in case."

"At least I've ruled out a bunch of stuff. That can be helpful. Got some swabs of some questionable items in the fridge for cultures."

"Kind of like eliminating suspects in a murder case, eh Sherlock?"

"Yeah. Being a doctor does require some investigative work."

"Hey, take it easy. I wasn't trying to put you down."

"I know," I said, a bit sorry that I came across as defensive. "In a way, having you around is a help. Allie seems to help point me in directions I don't think of right away and you do the same thing."

"Thank you, Doc, I think."

"You're welcome."

"Are we done here?"

I scanned around the apartment one more time. "Yeah, we're done. Thanks for coming with."

She nodded and smiled. I hoped I wasn't leading her on in some way. Anyway, I had to be delusional if I thought she was really interested in me. Even if she thought I looked like Steve McGarrett.

We headed for the door. Somehow we both tried to squeeze out at the same time, the result being us wedged together. She looked up at me. "After you," I said, sliding back into the apartment. Her eyes stayed locked on mine as she went out, a slight smile on her face.

No, no, no, I thought. Not going to happen.

We waited for the elevator in silence. When it arrived with its soft chime I checked my watch. "6:45," I announced. "I better get back to Weiss then I need to stop back at the emergency clinic. Can I drop you somewhere?"

She confirmed the time on her own watch and seemed to think a bit as the elevator doors finally closed. "I live over in Albany Park near Lawrence and Kimball. If that's too far I can catch a bus or hitch a lift with a black and white."

"I can do that," I said.

"Great," she answered. "Where do you live?"

"Ravenswood. Over on Sunnyside."

"By the library?" she asked.

"A couple of blocks away."

"I like that branch better than the puny one by me. They have a much better selection of books on CD."

"Let me guess, Janet Evanovich."

"There are worse," she said.

"I'm sure."

"What do you read?"

"Stephen King. Dean Koontz. Occasional Tom Clancy and John Grisham."

"I like Dean Koontz too," she said.

"No way," I answered.

"Way," she said. We let the conversation die an uncomfortable death as we finished the elevator ride and stepped out into the lobby.

Charlie held the door open for us and handed over the bag of Mrs. Jeffries' belongings. "See ya later," he said. He took one last eyeful of Marcy and let out a deep breath.

We walked out to my car. "You know, I could tag along to the hospital. I don't have anything to do and I'm actually becoming very interested in this case."

"What case? I mean, I'm pretty sure that what's happening to Mrs. Jeffries is not a crime."

She tossed the keys over to me. I looked at them and at her. I was getting too soft in my old age. I tossed the keys back.

"You drive, I'm getting used to having a chauffeur," I said.

"Awesome," she said.

"I'll have to drop you off after that. I'm planning on staying at the ER for a while tonight. I'm hoping the test results might be in later."

"Can't Allie do that?"

"She's on the ER clock after six. They are usually too busy to monitor my patients too closely. Allie will check as much as she can, but I don't want her to get in trouble."

"That's sweet."

"I'm hoping to get a chance to talk with Henry as well. See if he might have some idea what might be making them all sick, as well as tell me something about that seed."

"What ever happened with the gal who was coming to claim the dog anyway?"

"Good question," I said. I was wondering too now that she mentioned it. "If she wasn't the one who smashed my car window, then I wonder if she even did come out to the clinic. Maybe she thought it wasn't worth the effort."

"Maybe. But most pet owners wouldn't give up that easily. You still have that seed?"

I pulled the Ziploc out from the compartment between our seats. "If Henry can't help with the seed. Maybe we could do a little research on our own."

My phone rang. "Pull over," I said.

"Why?" asked Marcy.

I pulled out my phone and thought a moment, "Sorry, force of habit."

"Good habit to have," pointed out Marcy with a smile.

The ID was Sheila. "What's up, Chuck?" I asked in an unusually chipper tone. Marcy rolled her eyes. Sheila did the same, I was sure.

"Dr. Nancy Manchester from the lab called. She needs to talk to you right away."

"Did she leave an extension?"

"Yes." She read off a four digit number.

I repeated it back. "Did she say what it was about?"

"I assume some lab work. She may have said some test or something, but I just block that stuff out, Atty. I figured you would know what it's all about."

"Did she say which patient?"

"I assumed it was about Darla. You really haven't done much else today."

"Not my fault."

"It never is, Atty."

"I did send some tests out on Peanuts."

"I thought Peanuts was dead. Are you hoping to reverse his condition?"

"More like confirm the COD."

"Hey," interrupted Marcy, "that's cop talk. No cop talk, unless it's a cop talking. Capisce?"

"Is she still with you?" asked Sheila after hearing Marcy.

"She's actually been very helpful."

"You bet your sweet bippy, I've been helpful!" said Marcy.

"Sounds a little tipsy, if you ask me," Sheila commented into my ear.

"I heard that," said Marcy.

"No you didn't," I told her.

"Well, I know what she was going to say."

"Anything else?" I asked Sheila.

"You're going to have a full day of it tomorrow. I had to book you a 9:30 and a 5:00 and no lunch break. Pack a sandwich."

"Rats."

"That's what you get for taking a day off."

"It's not like I've been goofing off. I probably won't get to bed until after midnight."

"I know. Just get that little dog better."

"Aye-aye, Captain." I hung up. At least the day couldn't get any stranger. I punched the speed dial button for the lab. I navigated the voice mail system to get to Dr. Nancy Manchester's extension. I hadn't ever talked with her before. There were a couple of pathologists on the lab's staff that I like to consult with on those occasional baffling cases, but she had never shown up as a pathologist on any of my reports prior to today.

"Dr. Manchester," answered a British accented female voice.

"Hi, this is Dr. At. My answering service said you called."

"Oh yes, Dr. At," she answered, a snippiness entering her tone that was unexpected. "You think I have time to play games?"

"Excuse me?" I turned to look at Marcy, my baffled expression returned.

"This sample you sent in, the aspirate. Don't think you're not going to be charged the full lab fee as well as the stat fee."

"What's the problem?" I asked.

"The problem is that you can get in a lot of trouble for this. Falsely reporting a reportable disease is a big deal."

"What did you find in the sample?" I asked. What was she going on about?

"Right. Okay. Like you don't know."

"I don't, that's why I sent it in." This was getting harder than extracting a mandibular canine tooth from a cat. Trust me, that's pretty dang hard.

"*Bacillus anthracis*, like you didn't know."

It took a moment for what she was saying to sink in. "Anthrax?" I asked. "Darla has anthrax?"

CHAPTER 16

I looked at Marcy. "Anthrax?" she whispered at me. Her mouth hung open in disbelief. I bet mine did too. How did a little fluffy orange dog who has never left the city block she lives on get anthrax?

"Just admit you faked the sample and I can get the lab administrator to get her knickers out of a twist," said Dr. Manchester.

"Are you sure it is my sample?"

"Of course," she spat back.

"Dr. Manchester, that sample is not a fake. I took it from a little dog with severe head and neck edema this afternoon. Are you sure about the diagnosis?"

"This isn't a joke?"

"No joke. You're sure?" I asked again.

"Everyone in the lab has looked at it. There is nothing else it can be."

"Then that means..." I turned to Marcy. She must have read my mind. We both said "Mrs. Jeffries" and she jammed on the accelerator and was weaving my Escape around the dwindling evening traffic with the precision of a penguin navigating a kelp bed off the west coast of South America. Okay, that simile is a little exotic, but that's how it felt.

"Dr. Manchester, do what you have to do, I have some calls to make." I hung up.

I had two calls to make. Both equally important. I'd have to do them quickly. I dialed up the emergency clinic. It had shifted to the night emergency crew and Gwen answered the phone after one ring. Gwen liked me. I brought her cupcakes. I brought Margaret a cupcake once and she just dumped it into the trash like I insulted her.

It was red velvet. Maybe she didn't hate me. Maybe it was the red velvet she hated.

"It's Dr. At. I need to speak to Allie," I told her.

"I think she's busy. Can I take a message?"

"Sorry Gwen, this is super important. Tell her it's about Darla and to get someone to take over. I need to speak to her, please."

"I'll see what I can do."

The traffic continued to whiz by. Oddly, I felt little fear from that. I could feel my heart thumping against the strap of my seat belt. Adrenaline was a great drug, but I knew I'd pay for the explosive vomiting of my adrenal glands when it wore off. On the other hand, hanging out with Marcy didn't give those little adrenals much of a break.

"Dr. At," answered Allie's voice. "What's up?"

"Are there any other patients in ICU?"

"A heart failure dog and a cat with kidney failure."

"Hopefully they'll be okay. Listen carefully. I still have another call to make, but time is of the essence. Darla's lab tests came back and she has anthrax."

"No way."

"Way."

"How?"

"Haven't figured that out yet, but I think there are two more cases. Human cases."

She managed to repeat the same phrase I had heard earlier from Dr. Manchester word for word. "What do you need me to do?"

"Start Darla on ciprofloxacin injectable. Then have everyone who came in contact start oral cipro, as well as the other patients that are in ICU." I spit out the dose hoping that it was the right one for anthrax.

"What about her other meds?"

"You can stop the antihistamines and cortisone, but keep up everything else. I'll be by later to check on her, but I need to get over to Weiss."

"On it," answered Allie and she hung up. When Allie was on it, I knew it was getting done. A blaring car horn dopplered off in the distance as we blew through a red light onto Marine drive. The hospital was a mile up the road, but I figured I'd better call anyway. I searched my phone's call history for the hospital number then had the phone redial it.

I asked for the ICU and had the nurse page Dr. Phread. By the time he picked up we were parked and walking into the emergency room door. "This is Dr. Klammeraffe. Have you checked Mrs. Jeffries for anthrax?"

"Right, we screen every old person with flu symptoms for anthrax."

"Her dog has anthrax."

"What?"

"I just got a call from the lab. They confirmed a lymph node aspirate for *Bacillus anthracis*." I could see the elevators ahead.

"Why are you talking about her dog's lab tests?" asked Dr. Phread with appropriate confusion. I had forgotten that as far as he was concerned I was a real doctor.

As we stepped in my phone started to crackle. "I'm her vet," I said.

"Her what?"

"Her vet-er-i-nar-i-an," I said iterating every syl-la-ble into the phone as the elevator doors closed. Marcy pressed the fourth floor button. There was silence on the phone. I looked at the screen and noted there were no bars. The call had disconnected. "Rats," I said.

"At least this elevator has some speed to it," added Marcy.

"Regular thrill ride."

I almost ran into Dr. Phread's bald head. Apparently he was waiting at the elevator doors for us.

"What are you doing here?"

"I came to see how Mrs. Jeffries was doing and to have you start treatment for anthrax. I just confirmed it in her dog."

"Her dog?"

"Darla."

"Darla is a dog?"

"Yes, and she has anthrax and I think Virginia got it from the same place."

"But you are Darla's doctor."

"Right."

I waited the few seconds for the current to make it through all the twisted connections in Phread's brain and for the light bulb to click on above his shiny head. "You're a vet."

"And Bingo was his name-o," I said.

"You're weird," added Marcy.

"Oh, hi," said Dr. Phread as he realized Marcy was with me. I was surprised she hadn't tripped his radar earlier.

"Is she on any antibiotics?"

"We started her on cephalexin just in case it wasn't viral."

"That won't touch anthrax. Get her on cipro."

"But you're a vet."

"He's still a doctor," Marcy said. I was surprised by her defense of my honor.

"It'll take a while to do the tests, then if it confirms it we'll switch her."

"She may not have a while. How is she doing?"

Phread considered this for a moment. "Not well," was his considered medical opinion.

"You have nothing to lose switching her. The cephalexin isn't doing anything."

"Please," added Marcy. "I would hate to have to shoot you," she said, her right hand fondling the grip of her revolver. Almost seductively. I shook my attention away from her near pornographic caressing of her sidearm. Dr. Phread's jaw was hanging open.

"Cipro," I said.

"Yeah, yeah. Good idea. Can't hurt," he said.

"Oh, and you have another patient from her building, Henry something. An ambulance brought him in a couple of hours ago. He collapsed in his house. The paramedics were supposed to let you know he lived in the same building as Mrs. Jeffries. He probably has anthrax too."

"Yeah, we just moved him to a respiratory bed."

"Put him on cipro too."

"Is this some sort of terrorist attack?" he asked.

"Unless Pomeranians and senior citizens have suddenly bumped up Al-Qaeda's target list, I don't think so."

"Could be a dry run. A test of some delivery system," mused Marcy.

"You think so?" asked Dr. Phread, his expansive forehead wrinkling in consternation.

Marcy shrugged then smiled. "Cipro," she reminded him as she shooed him away with her hand.

"Cipro," he parroted. We headed to the ICU doors, following Dr.

Phread. His ID opened the sliding doors and while he headed for the nurses station, we headed for Mrs. Jeffries' room.

I stopped when I saw her. In just the few hours since our last visit I could barely recognize her. "My god," I muttered.

I looked at Marcy. Her playful expression had melted away into a deep compassion. She wiped at her left eye, aborting the tear that was starting to form.

On the hospital bed Virginia Jeffries' frail body seemed overwhelmed by the thin white hospital sheets and the coarse blanket. Her head sank into the pillow like a fuzzy white raisin on a marshmallow.

Her head twisted on the thin stalk of her neck and a dry groan escaped from her lips. I moved toward the head of the bed. "Mrs. Jeffries?" I spoke almost too softly to be heard. "Virginia?" I added a little louder.

Marcy was on the opposite side of the bed. She took the paper-skinnned hand with the overwhelming pulse oximeter clip on the middle finger and carefully held it. The touch stirred Darla's mother.

"Who is that?" her voice rasped.

"It's Dr. At-Klammeraffe," I answered. "I'm here with Officer Avers."

"How is my Darla?" she asked. Her first concern was for her friend and companion. To think of Darla as her pet would diminish the relationship.

"I found out what she has and we're changing her medication. She should be fine."

"I knew you would help her, Dr. Klammeraffe. You are ever so clever."

Marcy looked at me and grinned. I looked back at the frail body in the bed. Her eyes were turned toward me and despite the fact I knew I was just a blur to her unbespectacled eyes I could see them moisten with tears at the thought that Darla would get better. It seemed as though strength was returning to her. "She's going to need you to get better to take care of her. We think you might have the same thing that she has."

"Oh, dear, did I make her sick?" worried Virginia.

"No, no, no," I assured her. "You both probably picked it up at the same time. In fact, Henry may have it too."

"Henry? That poor old man. He's been so kind to me and Darla. I should make him some cookies," she decided.

"You might have to wait a little bit," I told her, my eyes taking in her hospital bed.

"Darla is going to be okay?"

"If she doesn't get better, I'll shoot him," promised Marcy.

Mrs. Jeffries looked at Marcy and smiled a smile that matched Marcy's. "You know he isn't married yet, a fine young man like him. It's a real shame, darling." Her continued attempt at matchmaking two steps from death's door made me chuckle and smile.

"Marcy is just a friend," I assured her.

Mrs. Jeffries tsked and threw in a pshaw for good measure.

A masked nurse appeared at the door with a small bag of IV fluids. An orange sticker plastered over it labeled it as "CIPROFLOXACIN". "Perhaps you could let Virginia rest a while," she suggested. "I need to give her her cipro."

That was fast. "How did you get that so fast?"

"Protocol. We are required to have it in stock in all wards in case of a biological attack."

That made sense, I guess. Especially considering the part-time resident of Hyde Park who might make a tempting target.

"Let's go," I said to Marcy. I turned back to the nurse. "There was an elderly gentleman named Henry brought in earlier. Is he on this floor?"

"433. I just got his Cipro started."

"Is it okay if we talk to him?" asked Marcy.

Perhaps her uniform gave the request an official tone rather than just the curiosity I had about the seed.

"He's pretty out of it."

"We won't take long. He may have information where this anthrax infection came from," she added.

She considered my plea while setting up the antibiotic drip. "If he's awake you can try," she said. "And get some masks from the nurse's station."

We grabbed two surgical masks from a dispenser on the nurse's station and looped them over our ears. We followed the u-shaped ward until we came to room 433. I slid the glass door open and we walked in. The small bag with the orange sticker was already feeding into Henry's veins. An oxygen mask covered his face and his chest heaved with every breath. I hoped it wasn't too late.

I was trying to fit together the appearance and severity of the symptoms in these three patients. I knew that anthrax could be ingested, inhaled, and even get in the skin. Darla likely ate it, but Mrs. Jeffries and Henry probably inhaled it. That was the worst form it could take. But where the heck did they get it? I remembered from school that it had been known as Woolsorter's Disease. Why I remembered that I couldn't tell you. I also knew that Tularemia was called Rabbit Fever, and leprosy was called Hansen's disease. There was probably some mnemonic that burned those facts into my neurons, forever taking up space that could have been occupied by something more important like my bank account on-line password.

I hadn't seen any sheep-shearing gear in Mrs. Jeffries' condo. No dead carcasses in Henry's workshop. Henry seemed the worse of the three judging by his breathing. Despite his semi-retirement he was still younger than Mrs. Jeffries by at least a decade. He probably ignored the first symptoms, writing them off as a cold or the flu, until it overwhelmed him.

Anthrax lived in the soil. It had to be in that atrium somewhere. They'd need to gut the whole place as a biohazard. But why was it coming up now? Henry had been working in that place for years. Darla and Mrs. Jeffries had visited it hundreds, if not thousands, of times.

I felt the plastic bag containing the mystery seed in my jacket pocket. Marcy and I walked up on either side of the bed.

"He's out of it," said Marcy.

"Don't think I'll get anything out of him now."

"I'm going to have to make a report. They're going to need to quarantine that building and the emergency clinic."

"They're going to hate me for that."

"It's not your fault."

"I brought Darla there."

"Who are you?" asked a voice from behind us.

A tall woman stood in the door. Her mask covered her mouth and nose. Her eyes were green and slightly blood shot, like she was exhausted. Her blonde hair was cut short, just above her shoulders. She lacked the scrubs that all the other ICU ward personal donned and had a "Visitor" tag stuck to her blouse.

"Who are *you*?" asked Marcy, stepping forward, her gun hip thrust forward with little to no subtlety. Meow.

"Karen Wilson."

"What are you doing here?"

"What are *you* doing here?" she returned.

"I asked first," said Marcy. She had managed to step closer to the woman who had about four inches on Marcy. Dr. Phread would feel like he was surrounded by Amazons.

"Is my uncle in trouble?" she asked.

"Henry's your uncle?" I asked.

"Yes. I just got into town today. I went to see him at his home and the police there said he had been taken here. They said he had the flu."

"So you haven't seen Dr. Phread in the last ten minutes?" I asked.

"Little bald guy, creepy stare."

Marcy chuckled and relaxed. A bonding experience. "That's him."

"No."

"Henry and another resident in the building where he works have been exposed to anthrax." I nodded over at the bag of antibiotics. "They just started treating him for it."

"Is he going to be okay?" she asked.

"Hopefully."

I followed her weary eyes as they took in the frail body that lay on the bed. I never want to get old. It sucked. "I'm sorry," she said, almost as an afterthought, "and you are?"

"Oh, sorry. Dr. At." I held out a hand.

Ms. Wilson took it weakly and we shook. "You're looking after my uncle too?"

"No," I started, "I have another patient that was also likely exposed at the same time. We were hoping your uncle might be able to shed some light on it."

"Did he?"

"No. He was asleep when we got here and you came in right after that."

"If you give me your number I'll call if he can remember anything." I felt around for a card, but Marcy had hers out before I could succeed. I felt a slight evil glare from her. A warning?

"You can call me," she said.

Karen took the card.

"I was also hoping I could make use of his botanical knowledge."

"Oh?"

"I came across an unusual plant, well, seed, earlier today," I started to explain. "I was hoping he could tell me about it."

Her eyes widened above her mask slightly. "How did you come across this unusual seed?" she asked.

Further explanation was needed. "I'm a veterinarian. My infected patient is the dog of the other patient here from where Henry works."

"A veterinarian?" she asked.

"Yes. Um, long story short, dead dog appears at airport, necropsy shows death by foreign body ingestion and," I pulled the plastic bag from my pocket, "this was it."

"How did you get that?" she asked.

"Excuse me?"

"That's a *Corposeum korchenkii*." She grabbed the bag from my hand. She carefully examined it from all angles. "It's still intact."

"Did you say corpse?" asked Marcy.

"*Corposeum*," she repeated. She looked at the both of us. "I'm a botanist too. Spent too many summers following Uncle Henry around the Garfield Park Conservatory." She looked back at the bag. "I've only seen it in journals. They didn't know the extent of its culture until about twelve years ago."

"Its culture?" I asked, the botanical idiot in me rearing its ugly head.

"How it is grown. The conditions it requires. I should take this back to my greenhouse. It needs to be handled carefully."

Marcy carefully plucked the bag from her hands, almost having to tear it away. "It's evidence."

"Well, it's exportation is restricted. It has the potential for ecological harm. You know, expanding beyond its natural habitat unrestricted."

"Is it from Kazakhstan?" I asked.

"Is that where the dog came from?"

"Yes."

"You took the seed out? How long ago?"

I looked at my watch. "Six hours give or take?"

"Put it back in," she said.

"What?" asked Marcy.

"Put it back in the dog. Or something dead."

"Why?"

"Notice the spines on the hull?"

"Yeah. They caused it to lodge in the dog's small intestine."

"Exactly. The seed is normally coated in a centimeter or so of flesh which has the somewhat unique characteristic of smelling and tasting like meat."

"Meat?" asked Marcy.

"Meat," Karen confirmed. "A carnivore, usually a wolf, will eat it. The flesh part dissolves away in the stomach and then the seed lodges in the intestinal tract and begins to germinate.

"And then they pass it?" I hoped.

"The seed can only grow in the corpse of the animal that ate it. Hence, its scientific name. It still could be viable if you can get it back into the corpse."

"And then what?"

"It's a very valuable specimen. They don't exist outside Kazakhstan. Any conservatory would love to have it."

"I thought you said it was restricted. Something about it being dangerous."

"If it gets out into the environment, sure. If one of these plants gets established in an ecosystem that has no controls on its spread, it would wipe out any carnivore population, letting the herbivore population expand uncontrolled, leading to the overgrazing and destruction of the native plant life, not to mention the water contamination."

"Water contamination?" I asked, taking over the useful idiot position vacated by Marcy.

"The plant produces a chemical that leaches into the water. It kills other small animals in the area so the carnivores will be forced to eat the plant's seeds."

"Why hasn't it taken over Kazakhstan?" I asked.

"The plant's range is limited to a single valley. The water runoff is enough to dilute the chemical downstream. The wolves that are its main target usually stay in their valley. There are perhaps a hundred specimens cataloged in the wild. It's a very delicate balance that has persisted for millennia. In a controlled greenhouse you can prevent it from leaching into the water table and prevent the seeds from being spread by hungry dogs. It is a fascinating specimen. Such a unique means of seed propagation." Her eyes turned on the bag in Marcy's hand.

"Is it valuable?" asked Marcy.

Karen looked at her intently. "To a private plant collector, a million dollars wouldn't be too much to pay."

I looked at the seed in Marcy's hand. A million dollars. Whoa.

"If it's still alive. Otherwise it's an ugly paperweight."

"Who are these plant collectors?"

"I can think of half a dozen that would pay that amount in Chicago alone. Half of them are on the board of directors of the Garfield Park Conservatory. There are probably hundreds more worldwide. This really should be in a conservatory."

"Who knows how many other dogs were shipped out of Kazakhstan," I said mostly to Marcy.

Marcy added, "I'm not as worried about that as the woman who was expecting to get this one. Importing restricted biologics is a pretty serious offense. Whoever planned this took some serious risks."

"Sounds like it's good that we intercepted it," I said.

"I doubt that whoever intended to receive this is going to give up on it. They likely had a buyer lined up and are going to want it back," said Marcy.

"Like I said, I can make sure it gets to a safe place," said Karen.

"Sorry, it'll have to stay with me. It's evidence and now that we know what it is worth, we'll have to make sure we get it someplace safe."

"You need to put it back in that dog at the very least," said Karen.

Marcy handed me the bag. I held it up and looked at it again. "I've never put a foreign body back into a patient," I said. That probably sounded stupid. I compounded my stupidity. "Let alone a dead patient."

"So assuming we get this back into the corpse what do we do then?"

"Get a big plastic tub. Fill it halfway with topsoil, and lay the corpse on it. Keep the soil moist and pray."

"What do you think, Doc?" asked Marcy. She handed me the seed.

"I'm game." I turned to Ms. Wilson. "I hope Henry gets better soon," I said. She nodded. Marcy and I left and she moved to Henry's side. I closed the door behind us.

"Nice woman," I said. Marcy's open hand hit the back of my head, knocking off one ear loop of my mask.

"Men," she said.

I guess that ended that discussion. I changed the subject.

"Okay, let's get back to the emergency clinic. I'll call and have Allie defrost Spot Doe."

"I'll get a hold of Dave and see if he can give me any more info on the woman who came to get the dog."

As we stepped into the nurses area I saw Dr. Phread giving orders at the center station. "Hey," he called. "We confirmed anthrax. I have a lot of questions that need to be answered."

"I'll bet," said Marcy with her best smile. It seemed to disarm Dr. Phread for a moment, but when he noticed we were still heading out past him he snapped out of it.

"Seriously, there are protocols. Homeland Security needs to be notified and we need to find out anyone else who might have been exposed and get them started on antibiotics." We kept walking. "You can't leave."

"We have an emergency," I said as I held up the plastic bag containing the necrophilic seed for him to see.

"What's that?" he called.

"A million dollars," answered Marcy and we left the ward. We didn't look back, but I assumed we left Dr. Phread more confused than when we came in. I pulled out my phone as we headed for the elevator. Just as I was about to speed dial the specialty clinic it rang. The caller ID was the specialty clinic. "Weird," I said before answering. "Hello, this is Dr. At."

CHAPTER 17

We had reached the elevator and I halted, remembering how I lost my phone reception in there before.

"At. Tompkins here. Anthrax? Really?" Dr. Carl Tompkins was a vet that needed very few words to get across his meaning. He usually saved them for when a surgery went particularly messy.

"I talked to the lab a little while ago. It's confirmed," I said.

"Do you know what we have to do?" his conservation of conversation leaving him as the adrenaline kicked in.

I paused a moment. "No," I sort of squeaked.

"We have to shut down. Quarantine every animal in here and have everyone who was in the building called, get them to a CDC approved health care provider, get tested, put on antibiotics and questioned by the FBI. What were you thinking?" he asked.

"A bee sting?"

"What?"

"I though she got bit by something. She started having trouble breathing and needed intensive care."

"The dog."

"Right."

"This is a mess, At."

"Sorry."

"You need to get back here."

"On my way. I need to get the body of another dog I brought in today."

"More anthrax or maybe some botulism or bird flu? Maybe some hoof and mouth disease?"

"Could you ask Allie to pull Spot Doe from the freezer?" I asked tentatively.

I heard a growl over the phone and then was disconnected.

"Trouble?" asked Marcy.

"A bit," I said.

We entered the elevator and Marcy looked up at me. "Well, Doc, this has been the most fun I've had in ages. Most of my dates are more boring than this."

Dates?

I started to explain, "My days usually aren't like this and to be honest, I prefer them at a much slower pace without dog thieves, potential biological weapons and seed smugglers."

"I can see that," agreed Marcy. She seemed a little put off. Then it hit me. Oh jeez.

"But having you around has made it a much more tolerable experience," I added. "Almost...fun?"

She seemed to bite the corner of her lower lip as she considered my attempt to salvage her feelings. "Tolerable, eh?"

"Downright not horrible," I added. That earned me a stifled chuckle.

We made it through the ER without having to extract any people from animals or vice versa. Marcy was on her radio and had dispatch try to contact Dave for more details on the seed smuggler.

"It really is clever of them to smuggle the seed like that. If that plane hadn't been delayed in Paris the dog probably would have made it here alive and would be comfortably dead in someone's garden by now, spreading its deadly roots into a liver or spleen or something equally gross."

"She probably was just some stray," I added.

"What?" asked Marcy as we got into my Escape.

"Spot Doe. Some hungry mutt that would eat anything that looked like food."

"I'm sorry," said Marcy as we settled in.

"For what?"

"I forgot about Spot."

"Part of me thinks I should just chuck the seed and let her go to Cozy Acres with the rest of the strays and have a decent end."

"What do they do with the animals there?"

"Cremate them, spread the ashes around this meadow of wildflowers. I've been out there. It's pretty neat."

"So she'd still end up as plant food."

"I suppose."

"This way she can help the advancement of science."

We had reached my car and without question I entered the passenger side.

I smiled. "Let's go."

Marcy hopped in and revved my four cylinder engine before shifting into gear. She turned on the car's radio, blaring the latest from some girl named Miley Cyrus and we pulled out on to Marine Drive and the g-force slid me across my seat, straining at the belt. I didn't know the car had it in it.

We headed for Addison, staying off Lake Shore Drive and then turned right. Rush hour was thinning out and most of the people driving seemed to be listening to their own version of Neil Diamond or whatever got them through it.

We hit Western and made a sharp turn to the emergency clinic. We pulled into the parking lot at the back. I let us in the back door with my key. Allie appeared out of one of the doorways.

"Dr. At, Officer Avers. You've come to join the party."

"Where's Dr. Tompkins?" I asked.

"He's on the phone. He's mad," she said. I grimaced. "There's a nurse in the lounge to take blood samples and to give you your cipro."

"That was fast."

"You call Public Health and say anthrax and the hounds are unleashed."

"How is Darla?"

"Already better. I even got her to eat some dog food."

"Dog food?" I asked.

"Is that okay?" asked Allie.

"It's terrific. I don't think she's ever had dog food before."

"Well, she likes it. Swelling is starting to go down. No fever. I'm going to take her out of the oxygen later. Come on, I'll show you."

We went to the ICU ward and the previously lethargic lump of orange fuzz lifted her head and wagged her tail from side to side with enough energy to power her IV pump. I opened the examination hatch and scratched her head. It did seem as though the swelling was down. "This much improvement with just one dose of antibiotics," I commented.

"She wasn't really doing any better on the Baytril. Good thing you put that cytology in for stat results. You want to meet Nurse Ratchet now?"

"I really need to see Spot first."

"Right, Dr. T. mentioned something about that. We're at overflow so she never made it into the deep freeze."

"That's a bit of luck," I commented.

"Remind me never to go gambling with you if you consider that lucky," she said.

"What do you need her for?" asked Allie as we followed her to a room off the back hallway. Inside was a large chest freezer and several blue cadaver bags laid out neatly on the floor.

"Need to do a little surgery."

"You think you're that good?"

Marcy laughed.

"Surgery to do what?"

"I have to put this back in," I told her, holding up the seed in its bag.

"Why?"

"So it can grow."

"Of course," she said as if was the most natural thing.

"It's from a rare plant that actually requires the body of a dead animal to grow in," explained Marcy. "In fact, it actually makes the animal eat the seed and the process of it sprouting kills the animal."

"Makes the animal eat it?"

"Disguises itself as a giant meatball," Marcy explained.

"Cool," Allie added.

"Well, should be no problem. It's pretty dead here since we can't let anyone else in until the Department of Public Health clears us."

There was a table in the far corner of the room normally used for necropsies. The top was a giant shallow sink covered by a metal grate. If I hadn't been worried about infectious diseases, that's where I would have done my procedures earlier. It made clean up a lot easier.

We lifted Spot's bag onto the table and unsealed it. The odor was almost overpowering. We laid her on her back. Her legs were stiff, but I managed to get her positioned so I could easily reach the incision I had sewn up earlier.

Allie and I donned gloves, more for our protection than to prevent contamination, and snagged some surgical tools that were set aside for necropsies only. I cut through the sutures.

Once I had the body open I had Marcy open the bag with the seed and gently slipped the root and seed into the body cavity. I hoped I didn't need to reimplant it into the intestines. I figured since they had already ruptured, the whole inside of the abdomen was like the alimentary canal in a way. Allie opened me a suture pack and I closed up the abdomen.

We sealed her back into the blue body bag.

"Sharpie?" I asked Allie.

She handed me one from a pocket on her pants and I wrote in large letters, "SAVE."

"At," said an angry voice from the doorway. We turned. It was Dr. Tompkins. "What are you doing now?"

"Just finished."

"What?"

"A little botany experiment."

"Have you had your blood test and started your meds? You're the epicenter of this whole mess."

"On my way," I said throwing a salute that Dr. Tompkins did not find amusing.

He grumbled and looked at Marcy. "You here to arrest him?"

"Sure," she said without a second thought.

"Well, we're all stuck here until they clear us. Probably twenty-four to forty-eight hours."

"What?" I asked.

"That's the rules."

"I can't stay here two days."

"And I can? Go see the nurse."

Marcy shoved me from behind. She had her cuffs dangling from her left hand. "Don't make me have to use these," she threatened with a tone that was way too playful for me.

As we walked up the hall her radio crackled. It sounded like a response to an inquiry about Spot's so-called owner. She let me go ahead while she interpreted the staticky voice.

The nurse was set up in the staff lounge. I was directed to a chair next to a table after removing my coat and rolling up my sleeve. A thermometer was shoved into my mouth, probably more to keep me from complaining than to get data on my body temperature. The tourniquet was so tight every vein on my arm doubled in size.

Fortunately she hit one on the first try and took a couple of tubes of my blood. She slapped a cotton ball over the hole and taped it down, folding my arm up to help keep in in place. She shoved a vial of capsules in my other hand. "One every six hours," she directed with no hint of compassion. Allie was right to dub her "Nurse Ratchet".

Marcy was next. She received the same treatment and her own supply of ciprofloxacin.

"Uh, Marcy," interrupted Allie. "You might want to come up front."

"Why?"

"There is a guy outside yelling through the glass. He says he's here for the dog that died at the airport."

Marcy jumped up and headed for the door, one hand on the grip of her pistol. I waved my pills at her with my best "good luck" gesture.

After not hearing any gunshots my curiosity started to get the best of me. I headed for the reception area. I could see Marcy yelling in the waiting room. I almost went back to the relative safety of Nurse Ratchet's lair.

"Open this door," she yelled, pounding on the locked glass door. "I need to get out of here!"

Dr. Tompkins was soon at my side as we stood in the reception area behind the thick plexiglass shield that was the only thing between us and Marcy's gun. "He's running," she said.

"I thought it was a woman who asked about the dog," I said.

Marcy once again demanded the door be opened, this time with more of her cop vocabulary in use. Her gun was still holstered, but the way she was eying the locked front door I wouldn't bet on it staying there.

"Better open that door, Dr. Tompkins," I told him.

"Can't."

Marcy turned and just stared at him. I'm glad I wasn't in the way of that gaze. There was fire in her eyes. "Open," she countered with her own one word sentence.

"Quar-an-tine," he answered stressing each syllable.

"Bite-me," she retorted similarly.

I threw in my own syllabically limited two cents. "Back-door." I hit the buzzer to unlock the door to the reception area.

Marcy moved faster than Dr. Tompkins, and I managed to get

between them as she raced past him then ran down the hall. The back door slammed open as she burst into the parking lot. I followed down the hall with Dr. Tompkins behind me. I peeked out the door in time to see her round the corner towards the front of the building. Not knowing what to do and deciding it was safer with Marcy than Dr. Tompkins, I followed her. Dr. Tompkins started yelling after us while he stayed in the doorway, tethered by Public Health's invisible leash. I guess he had a greater fear of the Public Health nurse than a gun-wielding cop.

I caught up to Marcy at the street and found myself so out of breath I couldn't even speak. She scanned left then right then kicked the building in the bricks as she swore in a splatter of words that left a visible stain on the street.

"Who...was...it?" I finally spewed between gasps.

"I don't know. He saw me come into the waiting room and took off. Our lady dog owner must be working with someone."

"Why?"

Suddenly a voice yelled from the back of the building. "Stop!" It had to be Allie.

"Oh, no," realized Marcy.

"What?" I said still out of breath.

She took off back towards the short alley that led to the back of the building.

I found a bit of adrenalin left and jogged after her. I turned the corner. Marcy has stopped and her gun was drawn. A large black SUV was speeding down the alley directly at her towards the street. "Police. Stop," she ordered.

The SUV ignored the order and headed straight for her. I really thought she was going to fire, but she spun to the left and I dove back toward the sidewalk at the front of the building, my forehead colliding with the pavement. I turned my head slowly and saw the SUV screeching onto Addison, bumping the front fender of a taxi with its left side as it turned. There were two incredibly loud gun shots and the back passenger window shattered. The SUV sped away, weaving through the evening traffic.

"Are you okay?" asked Marcy. I was barely able to hold my head up. I was starting to feel the pain from my fall explode on my forehead along with a strange damp feeling.

"I'll be fine," I said, just before the blackness overtook me.

CHAPTER 18

Donna Melton was massaging my scalp. Her strong fingertips pushing the blood around, relaxing muscles I didn't know I had. I felt like I was waking up from a nightmare. Things like that never happened to me. I had a normal, non-exciting life, full of phone calls to return, dirty litter boxes, and a freezer full of lean cuisine. There were no cops chasing after corpse-stealing Kazakhstanis. Margaret wasn't really a drug dealer. Snakes didn't eat people's arms just because they fell asleep holding a drumstick. I had fallen asleep. I had dreamed it all.

I moaned. That only made her work harder. Suddenly she was slapping my face. "Atty, Atty," she almost screamed.

"What?" I answered. My eyes opened only partway, as if they had been glued shut.

"Wake up? Are you okay?"

"Don't stop," I muttered.

Another slap hit my right cheek.

"Stop that."

"Make up your mind," said Donna. Only it wasn't Donna. I cracked an eyelid. Red and blue flashing lights lit the area in the front of the specialty clinic. Marcy and Allie were kneeling next to me. I suspected it was Marcy who had been slapping me.

"Really?" I asked whoever was listening. It was not nice to tease me with visions of Donna Melton and her magical hands.

"You took a nice fall, Doc. Fortunately the sidewalk broke your fall," said Allie. She had an ice pack in her hand. She placed it above my right eye.

"Ow," I said.

"The ambulance is here," said Marcy.

"I don't need an ambulance," I assured her. After all who was in a better position to assess my condition? Me, a slightly unconscious veterinarian who had recently decided to crush part of his skull in with the sidewalk, or some paramedic who flunked out of med school?

"You were out of it," added Allie.

"You could have left me out for a little while longer."

"What?" asked Marcy.

"Never mind." It would be too hard to explain to anyone except Donna's doorman, Frank.

I tried to push myself up. Someone started hitting the front of my head with a hammer, probably one of those five pound sledges. "Stop," I said.

"Stop what?" asked Allie. She was still holding the ice pack to my disintegrated skull. I reached up and touched her hand. There was no hammer banging on my forehead. Her skin was ice cold, from holding the ice pack. I grabbed the pack from her and sat all the way up.

"You probably shouldn't move until the paramedics check you out," said Marcy.

"I'm fine," I said. I wasn't. Obviously. But for some reason that was what seemed like the right thing to say.

Things were coming back. The strange man at the front door, the quarantine, the SUV trying to run us over.

"The dog?" I asked.

"Gone," said Allie. "Apparently some woman decked Dr. Tompkins and grabbed it. Someone was nice enough to mark the bag with a big black 'SAVE'."

Oops. "Did you say a woman hit Dr. T?"

"Yeah, he kinda asked me not to mention that."

"Don't blame him."

"Hey, women can be tough," interrupted Marcy.

"You're not a woman," I told her. I could feel her icy glare. "You're a cop." Her gaze turned from anger to consternation. It seemed to appease her.

"What happened?" asked a voice from my left.

"He fell on the sidewalk," explained Marcy. "Got knocked out."

A bright light flashed into my eyes.

"Hey," I said trying to bat it away.

"Pupils responsive and symmetrical," said the voice.

I felt my hand and the ice pack lift from the gaping hole in my head. A gloved finger poked at the edges then the center. "Nasty bump, but I doubt you fractured anything," he said.

That was good news. I figured it wasn't worth mentioning the fact that it hurt twice as much after his poking and prodding as before. I returned the ice pack to the area.

"He'll have a nice knot and beautiful bruise. We'll take him to Weiss to get checked out for a concussion."

"No." I said. I didn't feel it was necessary to explain further.

"Marcy? Is that you babe?" he asked, distracted from his patent. Did every city worker know Marcy?

"Hey, Marco. How's Marina and the kids?"

"Great. Got a third one on the way."

"Way to go," she said.

I cleared my throat.

He nodded at me. "This guy really should go to the hospital," he said.

"Yes, he should. Little problem though."

"What's that?"

"We're under a little quarantine," she explained.

"Quarantine?"

"Yep."

"For what?"

"You're not going to believe this."

"Try me, I've believed seven things already this shift."

"Anthrax."

A clipboard was shoved in front of me. "Sign this to state you declined further treatment," explained the paramedic. He handed me a pen. I signed. I held the pen up for him. "Keep it," he answered.

Marco and his partner packed up and headed back to their ambulance. Pretty smart.

I tried pushing myself to my feet.

"Sit down, Doc," said Allie. "Take a minute."

"Sorry," I said.

"What for?" asked Marcy.

"For messing up your chance to catch those seed smugglers."

"Ah," she smirked. "As long as you're okay."

"Really?"

"No. I'll never hear the end of this one."

"Sorry," I repeated.

"You better be," she said and she smiled.

"Help me up."

Each of them grabbed an arm and I made it to my feet. The pounding in my head grew exponentially. I imagined the bump to now be the size of a watermelon. I reached up and touched it. It hurt, but was much smaller than the pain it inflicted.

The front door of the emergency clinic was still locked. A "Closed for Quarantine" sign embellished with the Public Health Department logo was taped to the inside of the glass door. Allie and Marcy walked me around the back. It was nice having them help me. My noodle-like legs appreciated it.

Dr. Tompkins was waiting at the back door. His own ice pack mostly covered up the nice shiner that was developing around his left eye. "Are you okay?" he growled.

"I'll live," I answered.

"Good, then I can still kill you. Why are psychotic criminals stealing dead dogs from my clinic?"

I wasn't going to point out that he didn't really own the clinic, just worked there. "I'm feeling a little dizzy," I said letting my legs buckle a little. Marcy and Allie helped shuffle me to the employee lounge. I could hear Tompkins slam the back door shut and twist the deadbolt closed.

Nurse Ratchet had finished with her samples and was working on her fingernails with a nail file, sharpening them, no doubt. The girls plopped me on an old leatherette couch, then sat on either side of me.

My phone rang. I fumbled with my left hand, trying to get it out of my jacket pocket, before switching the ice pack to my left hand and pulling it out with my right. The caller ID said it was Dave. I showed it to Marcy.

"I told him to call, I have some questions for him," she said. "I asked him to call your phone. I didn't really want him having my number."

"Good idea," I added. I accepted the call and put him on speaker. "Dave, old buddy, what's up?"

"Your hot little cop-ette wanted to talk to me, I think I've worn her down. Probably wants to give me a little interrogation, if you know what I mean."

"Hi Dave," said Marcy. "You're on speaker.

"Hey, Marcy," he said without missing a beat. "Didn't know you were there."

"I'm still here. Had a little run-in with a lady looking for her dead dog. She brought a friend."

"Oh really? They still want it?"

"It was growing a million dollar seed in its guts, Dave," I said, "they had a lot of reasons not to give it up."

Marcy added, "I'd like to find out a little more about the woman who came for the dog this morning?"

"Hey, like I said, once she found out the dog wasn't here she kind of took off. I couldn't keep her. I didn't know she was smuggling stuff."

"But you did tell her about me bringing the dog here," I said.

"Yes."

"Now I need you to think Dave," asked Marcy, "I know you can get a little laser-focused when confronted with a human being with breasts, but was she with someone else? A man?"

"You wound me, Officer Avers."

"Dave, think."

"She was alone. I suppose there could have been someone waiting for her outside or something. I mean, the carrier that dog came in wasn't that small."

"You said she was good looking, can you get specific? Hair color? Eye color? Tattoos? Jewelry?"

"She was a blonde. Shoulder length, but nothing fancy. Didn't see any tattoos anywhere. I think her eyes were green. I think she wore some small diamond studs in her ears, otherwise..."

Marcy and I looked at each other. "No," I mouthed.

"Dave, did she give a name?"

"No."

"Phone number, anything?"

"No. She did say something weird though."

"Weird?" I asked.

"Yeah, you know those planters at baggage claim with the plastic plants?"

"Those are plastic?" I said.

"You think anything would grow under those fluorescent lights?"

"What did she say?" asked Marcy, growing exasperated at our excursion into the inane.

"She said the flowers were the wrong ones for those plants. Like anyone cares."

"Thanks, Dave," said Marcy. She pressed the end button on the screen then looked at me. "Looks like your girlfriend has been busy."

"It might not be her?"

"Girlfriend?" asked Allie.

"First, she's not my girlfriend. Second, just because she's a botanist with short blonde hair and green eyes doesn't mean she's the dog smuggler."

"She tells us to put the seed back in the corpse. You oblige, and ten minutes later it's stolen."

"When you put it like that."

"We need to get out of here."

"No one is leaving here until we get the lab results," muttered nurse Ratchet, still honing her claws to razor sharpness.

"Speaking of which, did you notify public health about Mrs. Jeffries' building yet?" I asked.

"No," said Marcy.

"Building's already quarantined," announced nurse Ratchet. Boy, she had good hearing. She looked up at me, staring over her half-lens reading glasses. "You think we're stupid? Once I found out where that little orange dog lived, we had the building sealed up."

"They're not going to like that," I said.

"Don't care," said Ratchet as she turned back to her deadly manicure.

"Why were you asking about the building?" asked Marcy.

"Because, if our botanist-slash-seed smuggler is intending on planting that dog, what better place than that atrium? It's private, isolated, and at this moment, unattended."

"You think Henry could be a part of the whole plot," she said.

"No."

"Why not? He would have the contacts to sell the thing. Probably knows the board of the Garfield Park Conservatory by their first names. He as much admitted to being destitute."

"He lives in a mansion," I said.

"Eating cat food," pointed out Marcy.

"I didn't see any empty cans of Fancy Feast."

"Still, a share of a million bucks might be attractive."

"I suppose."

"But she can't take the plant back to the building now, not with the quarantine."

"She doesn't know it's quarantined."

"But once she gets there, she'll see the signs on the doors like this place. There will probably be some emergency vehicles there too."

"Yeah."

"She said all you need is a plastic tub and a couple bags of potting soil. She can get those at any Home Depot."

"Maybe we can trap her. Get the Public Health Department to back off and let her get into the atrium where we'll be waiting." Allie and Marcy both stared at me. "Where you will be waiting?" I amended the plan.

"No one is leaving," droned Nurse Ratchet and added, "again."

I ignored her. "We know her name, maybe you can have some other officers check out her home?"

"She's probably smarter than that, but I'll report it in. Maybe they'll find something at her place that could tell us where she might go. But I agree, the atrium is a definite possibility."

"Right," I agreed.

Marcy reported in on her radio. My ice pack was losing its iciness. I threw it on the table. Allie turned my head toward her and eyed my wound with her trained medical eye.

"I just want to stick an eighteen gauge needle in it and suck out all that blood," she said.

"Take it easy, Elvira," I said.

Marcy finished up and eyed Nurse Ratchet. She sighed. "Twenty-four to forty-eight hours," she said.

"Anyone up for Trivial Pursuit?" asked Allie. There was a copy of the game that amused the emergency staff during the rare slow periods. This was going to be a slow period.

"I left my book in the car," mused Marcy.

"No one is leaving," Nurse Ratchet reminded us.

We sat silent for a while. Dr. Tompkins peeked in, glared, then left. Probably to crash in the administrator's office. It had a slightly less disgusting couch in it. There were four other employees locked in the building with us. Gwen, the emergency receptionist; Dr.

Lowell, a first year, underpaid intern; and two other techs, Dave and Chris. I hadn't seen Dr. Lowell. Gwen was manning the phones, making sure to send people to the Northside Veterinary Emergency Center. Dave was parked on the lounge chair in ICU and Allie said that Chris was napping on the benches in the waiting room.

Marcy was tapping her fingernail on the handle of her gun. Tap, tap, tap, tap. It didn't seem like a good time to ask her what was up, but she appeared to be thinking.

"She wouldn't go in the front, would she," she said.

"What?"

"Your girlfriend. She wouldn't just waltz in the front hauling a bag with a smelly dog in it. The doorman would want to know what was going on. I doubt he'd let her in the atrium."

"So she wasn't planning on going back to that building."

"Well, it still is the ideal place to stash the plant. I mean, if she buried the dog among the other plants, we wouldn't know which it was."

"But you have dogs that can sniff out dead bodies."

"I'm pretty sure they just respond to dead humans. Otherwise they'd get too many false positives."

"Okay, but where does she go then?"

"Is there a back door?"

"Back door?"

"Another entrance."

"Maybe. But the Public Health Department would seal that door too."

"Hmm," Marcy hmmed.

"This is really bugging you," I said.

"We were so close. We were in the room with her. I didn't make the connection. Remember how she reacted when you pulled out that seed? She wasn't excited to see some rare seed, she was wondering how the heck you got it."

"It was hard to tell with that mask on her face."

"It was in her eyes. I just didn't put it together. She even said that she just got into town today."

"I didn't see it either."

"You weren't looking at her eyes."

Allie laughed.

"She might go in the loading Dock," I said.

"Excuse me?"

"The loading Dock. There's a big garage door at the north side of the building. It's where the trash gets picked up and there is a little area where large deliveries come. I think there is even a freight elevator back there."

"You're sure?"

"Billy parked my car there this morning. I've used it before. There's a code to open the big door from the outside."

"Do you remember it?"

I tried to look like I was remembering it, but that number had been erased when my bank password was looking for a home. "The doorman would have it."

"Right. Would Ms. Wilson have it?"

"Henry would know it."

"So she probably does. She could slip in and out and no one would know." Marcy pulled out her radio and asked for them to send a unit to check out the loading Dock. "They'll take forever," she mused. "Especially with the building under quarantine. You saw how those paramedics acted? You don't want to get caught up in a quarantine."

"Tell me about it," I said, gazing around our forced accommodations. "What else can we do about it?"

She lowered her voice. "I have to get out of here."

Allie leaned in and whispered. "We can create a distraction for you. Atty can fake a seizure or something."

"A seizure?" I whispered back.

"Or something," Allie added helpfully.

"No one is leaving," added the party-pooping nurse with the nails of death. So much for our plotting.

"I suppose I can use the rest room."

"Knock yourself out," she said.

"Again," added Marcy. Allie laughed.

"Help me up, you two," I said. They pulled me to my feet.

"I'll walk you there, but once you're inside you're on your own steam, Doc," said Allie.

Marcy chuckled this time.

Most of the weakness had left my legs, but I was still a little dizzy. We left the break room and stood in the hall.

"Don't need to go, Doc?" asked Marcy.

"I needed to get away from happy pants in there."

Marcy eyed the door at the end of the hall. No one was guarding it. She put a finger to her lips and we walked slowly and quietly down the hall.

Marcy carefully opened the deadbolt. I was afraid the dull click would grab the attention of our cheerful captor. She opened the door. Red and blue flashing lights spilled into the hallway. A cop stood guarding the exit.

Nurse Ratchet was probably smiling from ear to ear.

CHAPTER 19

"Marcy," greeted the cop.

"Seriously?" I asked her. "Is there anyone who doesn't know you?"

She looked at me. "What can I say, I'm a likable gal."

"How'd you end up in this place?" asked the cop in the alley. His cruiser was parked across the rear entrance.

"Long story, Steve. This is Dr. At. He's a veterinarian."

"Really, I always wanted to be a veterinarian," he said. Surprise.

"Really?" I said, feigning interest.

"Dragged home every animal I could find when I was a kid. Then my uncle took me to the firing range and that's when I wanted to be a cop."

"Wow," I said. Didn't take much to quench that dream, I thought.

"Hey, we need to get out of here."

We? I thought. I looked at Marcy.

"Doc here hit his head." She pointed to the goose egg sticking up from above my right eyebrow. "At the time we didn't think anything of it, but now he's really acting strange." She nudged me.

"Uh, are we going to the zoo, grandma?" I said. Allie and Marcy both stared at me. Too much.

"Thought I'd take him up to Weiss. The nurse cleared him."

"Sure," he said.

"Thanks, Steve," said Marcy with a big smile and a flip of her ponytail. That woman has superpowers, I thought.

"You want me to call an ambulance?"

"Nah, I've got the keys to Doc's car. Thanks."

"No problem."

I looked at Allie, she seemed like she wanted to bolt with us, but she stayed inside. "I'll take care of Darla," she said. I had almost forgotten about Darla.

"Call if she gets worse," I said. As I said it my phone rang. Allie laughed and closed the door.

I pulled out the phone as we walked briskly to my car. We weren't free yet. Allie could probably cover for us. I wondered what kind of excuse she would give for us both to be missing at the same time. The caller ID was Sheila.

I opened up my passenger door and got it and answered the phone. "Hello,"

"Anthrax?" she said.

"How did you find out?"

"It's on the news, Atty."

"What?"

"There are cameras at the specialty clinic. The reporters are wearing masks. Are you okay?"

"I'm fine." I covered my phone with my hand and whispered to Marcy, "Cameras out front." She nodded her understanding.

"Darla?" asked Sheila.

"Getting better once we put her on the right antibiotic."

"And Mrs. Jeffries?"

I paused. "We were just at Weiss."

"We?" she picked up on right away.

"Officer Avers is still with me. They confirmed anthrax in Mrs. Jeffries and she's on antibiotics as well. I'm hoping she'll pull through."

"Oh, Atty, how did they get it? They're saying it's a possible terrorist attack. That there was gunfire at the clinic earlier."

"That's a totally different thing," I said before I realized how bad it sounded.

"We've got to go, Doc," said Marcy. She gunned my car's four cylinder engine to life.

"You were getting shot at?" Sheila assumed.

"No, Marcy was shooting at the plant smugglers. Listen, I'll explain it all later." I clicked off. I'd hear about that later, but right now I had other things to think about. Like how I busted out of a quarantine and was on my way to where the bad guys who tried to run us over were.

Marcy spun my tires as she raced down the alley, heading toward Addison. It was kind of fun, actually. I looked at Marcy. She was smiling. I opened the little compartment where my CDs were hidden and pulled one out.

"No Neil Diamond," she warned.

"Oh, you'll like this."

I slipped the soundtrack from the Blues Brothers into the slot on the dash. In seconds the thumping bass from the theme to "Peter Gunn" was shaking my speakers followed by the drums and brass.

"Yeah," said Marcy. She coaxed a little more speed from my Escape and was weaving through traffic like clown fish through sea anemone tentacles. What can I say? I like aquatic similes.

The honks and obscene gestures faded behind us. We turned onto Marine Drive just as "Sweet Home Chicago" started playing. By the time we reached the condo, Cab Calloway had us bopping to "Minnie the Moocher."

Marcy turned off the CD player. There were half a dozen public health vans parked in the front. Totally blocking the fire lane.

"Go around the block," I told Marcy.

The street we needed to be on was one way going east so we had to go completely around the building to find the loading Dock entrance. Marcy pulled up slowly. Tucked in the loading Dock area was a black SUV. The rear right window was missing.

There were no free parking spaces since it was after five. Everyone was home from work.

On the far side of the street a fire hydrant left an open space along the curb. Marcy parked next to it.

"Hey, I'm going to get a ticket," I said.

"I'll take care of it," she assured me.

Marcy used her radio to update the dispatcher and they promised to send the new information along to the District Headquarters.

"Great," I said relieved. "They're probably rolling out right now. We can just sit and wait for the cavalry to show up.

"If the bad guys are still here by the time they show up," muttered Marcy.

"Block the drive. They'll be stuck. If they give you trouble, shoot them. I'll be behind that tree," I said, pointing to a fairly thick trunked oak on the parkway. It looked wide enough to hide me from sight.

"Block it with *your* car?"

"It's insured."

"Tempting. But I have another idea. Stay here."

"What?"

"I'm just going to do a little recon."

"What if they come out?"

"Like you said, I'll shoot them. I don't think they'll leave soon. They have no reason to believe we know where they are and if they came up the back way they may not know about the quarantine. And I suspect that it will take your girlfriend some time to plant her dead dog."

"I don't like this. Skipping out on overly protective public health nurses is one thing, but I've had enough of cars trying to run me down and being shot at."

"You weren't shot at."

"It was in my general direction."

"If the direction was New York and I was aiming at Los Angeles." Marcy looked at me. "Doc, relax. I'll be right back. I promise I won't do anything other than look around until help comes."

"Okay," I said, slumping down into my seat. I was actually missing Nurse Ratchet.

Marcy quietly opened the car door and closed it just as silently. She pulled her gun out, keeping it ready at her side. She slithered across the street and snuck up to the SUV, cautiously looking in the windows. She then scanned the area around the loading Dock. There was a large container for trash to the right, and a set of steps on the left that led up to the loading Dock level. In front of the SUV, up three feet from the ground a platform sat in front of the large sliding door. Trucks could back up and be right at the perfect level to unload. The hood of the SUV was just slightly above the platform. Just to the left of that was a regular steel door. Between them I could see a small light near the electronic keypad for the large door. As far as I knew, the smaller door was key only.

She came back to my car and slipped back in. "Okay. No one in the car. No dead dog. They must be inside."

"So you wait for backup and nab them when they come out."

"What if they go into the lobby and run into the Public Health Department people."

"Call and warn them."

"You think they'll listen to me? That nurse at the emergency clinic had no interest in what we had to say," she reminded me. "They'll probably try to go into the atrium and try and get them to give blood samples."

"True," I agreed.

Marcy tapped the steering wheel, her eyes burning through the large door with laser intensity. "I wish you knew that code."

"Yeah. I always had to call the doorman to get it when I had to come in that way."

She looked at me. "Why didn't you tell me that earlier?"

"What?"

"Call the doorman. The phones will still be working."

"No. Then you're going to go in there. Uh-uh. No way."

"It's just in case. Besides we will need it when the backup arrives."

That made sense. "You're not going in until the troops arrives?" I asked.

"I'm not stupid, Doc."

I pulled out my phone, squinting at her. I had a feeling that I lost this battle, but couldn't see how. I dialed the number for the front desk. It was answered on the first ring.

"Charlie speaking," said the voice on the other end.

"Charlie, it's Dr. At."

"Dr. At. Hey, hope you're not planning on coming over for a house call. We have a quarantine going on here."

"Yeah, so I hear."

"Yeah? Well how can I help you?"

"Um, what's the code for the loading Dock door?"

"Whatcha need that for, Dr. At?"

"Actually, it's the police that need it."

"Really?"

"Here," I punched up the speaker phone.

"This is officer Marcy Avers. Do you have the code?"

"Um, yeah." Charlie read off the code. Marcy had her little notebook out and wrote it down.

"You have a security camera on the loading Dock, right?"

"Yeah. Here let me...oh."

"What?" asked Marcy.

"It's not working."

"Fiddlesticks," said Marcy. I looked at her, trying not to burst out laughing. She punched the mute icon. "I've been hanging around you too long." She unmuted the phone.

"Can you get to the atrium from the loading Dock?"

"Sure. There is a door that opens right onto it, near that little office that Henry keeps. Good thing he went home early. He'd be pissed about now."

I didn't see the point in telling him that Henry was part of the reason for the quarantine.

"You want me to go into the atrium?" asked Charlie.

"NO!" we both shouted at the phone.

"Okay, okay."

"Are the public health people in the lobby?" asked Marcy.

"One of them is. The rest went up to twenty-three. They even took a blood sample from me and gave me some pills." Charlie wasn't the curious type. He probably just popped a pill and went back to reading his book. He once told me he read a book a night.

"But I got to warn you, if you come in, you're not getting out for a while. They have the whole twenty-third floor sealed off. Everyone else has to stay put. They seem a little scary."

"Oh, I don't doubt it, Charlie," I said.

"So what's going on?" he asked.

"Ongoing investigation," answered Marcy.

I looked at her. Like that line was going to work.

"Okay, no problem." He hung up. Alright, with anyone, but Charlie that wasn't going to work. Marcy handed me the phone and I slid it back into my jacket pocket.

"Okay, so you do nothing until the S.W.A.T. team shows up, right?"

"Doubt they'll send S.W.A.T.," Marcy answered.

"Why not?"

"It's a dead dog."

"Right," I said. Then I realized, "But they tried to run you down. That's like attempted murder or something. You're going to at least need hostage negotiators or something."

It was Marcy's turn to give me a look. "You watch way too many cop shows, Doc."

There was a tapping on the window behind me. I must have jumped two feet out of my seat or would have if the seat belt allowed me to.

A flashlight shined in the window. A man outside with a bulky helmet was making the roll-down-your-window-gesture with his hand. I opened the window, shielding my face from the glare.

"You can't park here, it's a fire hydrant," he said.

"We're not parked," I started to say, "we're waiting for..."

"Manny?" said Marcy.

I looked at her and exhaled with what I hoped was a sense of disbelief and exasperation. "Come on. Really, Marcy. You can't know everyone."

"Marcy? Hey. What are you doing here?"

"Why are you here?"

"Got a call to back up a unit staking out a robbery suspect. That you?"

"Yeah."

I looked back out my window. He was on a bicycle. I scanned him from head to toe. He was on a bicycle and was wearing bicycle shorts and those tiny athletic socks with black sneakers. His bicycle helmet was strapped neatly under his chin. He did have a gun. "You're the backup?" I asked.

"Yes, sir. Who are you?"

"This is Dr. At. He's a veterinarian," she said. I grimaced when she said that. She did it on purpose. We both waited for him to say what we expected him to say. Marcy was grinning. He didn't say it. Finally, someone who didn't want to be a veterinarian, or at least didn't want to admit to it. Thank heaven for small miracles.

He held a hand inside my window. I reached up and shook it. "Great to meet you. So you know Marcy?" officer Manny asked.

"Just today."

"That's all it takes," he said.

"So, what's the situation? The perp inside?" he asked. "I heard this building is under some sort of quarantine."

"Perps," Marcy corrected him. "I'm worried they might be destroying evidence though."

"No you're not," I interrupted. "You just want to go in there."

"If they are destroying evidence," said Manny, "we really should go in."

"No, no, no," I said. "This is wrong. Those people tried to hurt you earlier," I added.

"Ooh," grimaced Manny, straightening up on his bicycle,

unsnapping his chin strap, "attempted murder of a police officer. This really sounds serious. We can't possibly risk them getting away."

"What?" I asked incredulously. There was no credulousness in that word at all. "You need more than just you two. Can't you call in snipers or a canine unit?"

They both looked at me with raised eyebrows. I slumped. "Doc," said Marcy, "we are highly trained police officers. Yes, one of us looks incredibly hot in shorts; I won't say who, but take my word for it, but we are prepared for these situations. We can handle it."

"So, we going to flank them?" asked Manny.

I put my face in my hands and just shook it from side to side.

"I'll take Doc and go in the front. You go in through the loading Dock door." She tore off the code from her notepad and handed it across me to Manny, the bicycle cop. "Here's the code to the sliding door."

"What about the Public Health people?" I asked.

"They may give a little fuss about letting us in, but technically we are still supposed to be in quarantine anyway so this will even that out," said Manny.

"That sounds like an interesting story," said Manny.

"Your logic is beyond me, Marcy," I said.

"You want to stay in the car?" she asked.

"I want to go home."

Marcy put a hand on my shoulder. "I know, Doc. It's been a hard day. But I need to see this through. I can't let them get away. Please, you'll be safe in the lobby. If they're going to bolt, it'll be through the loading Dock. Manny is tougher than he looks."

I hope so, I thought. Manny squinted a disapproving look back at her.

"Hey, that's no way to talk to your back-up."

My face fell into my hands again.

Marcy got out of the car. Manny moved his bicycle and Marcy came over to my door. She squatted in front of the window and put her arms on the frame of the door. "Come on, Doc, we've been a great team all day. I'll feel better if you are out of the line of fire."

"That's just it. What if there is shooting?"

Marcy knocked on her bullet proof vest. I knocked on her bullet susceptible skull.

"I didn't think you cared, Doc." She stood and opened my door. I sighed. I had lost this battle the moment we left the specialty clinic. I pressed the button to close the window then stepped out.

"Let me know when you're in position," said Manny.

"Roger," said Marcy.

Marcy started to jog around the front of the building. I stared at her a moment before jogging after her. "Slow down," I whispered.

"Speed up," she whispered back.

When we reached the front of the building I walked the rest of the way to the front door. Through the glass front of the building I could see Charlie sitting in his chair behind the reception desk, reading a book. A man with a blue windbreaker, DPH stenciled on the back, was pacing the lobby, his attention split between the elevator banks and the front door. Marcy tried the door. It was locked. When the Public Health officer saw Marcy and me, he walked over.

"Quarantine," he shouted through the glass.

"Police business," Marcy shouted back, her hand on the butt of her gun. "I need to get inside."

They stared at each other for what seemed like minutes. There was no hair tossing or flirty repartee. Marcy meant business. He glanced over his shoulder at the elevators. Charlie was looking over at us. He smiled and waved at me. I waved back.

DPH turned to Charlie and waved him over. Charlie jumped up and pulled the ring of keys off the clip on his belt. He opened the door.

"You're not getting out," said DPH.

Marcy ignored him as she brushed past. I followed. DPH motioned for Charlie to lock up after us. He did.

Marcy clicked on her radio. "We're in," she reported.

"Roger," said Manny. "Entering code now."

"Stay out here," said Marcy. It was a totally unnecessary thing to say. She walked over to the atrium door. The DPH agent blinked in disbelief. As if he never noticed the door before. She opened it.

It was still dark inside. Marcy pulled out her flashlight and holding it with her left hand, used her right hand, gun at the ready, to steady it. The beam cut into the darkness. She entered and the door closed behind her.

"Who is that?" asked DPH.

"That is Officer Marcy Avers of the Chicago Police Department. A very fine policewoman, if a little overconfident in my opinion."

"What is going on?" asked DPH.

"A robbery suspect entered the building through the loading Dock," I said.

"Loading Dock?" repeated DPH. He glared at Charlie who just shrugged.

"Nobody really uses it at night," said Charlie.

"Who are you?" he asked me.

"I'm Dr. Atticus Klammeraffe," I told him. "You can call me Dr. At."

"You look like Oliver Platt. Anyone ever tell you that?"

"It's my curse."

"Are you with CDC?" he asked.

"No," I said proudly. "I am a veterinarian."

"He really is," added Charlie. I smiled a thank you at him.

"Why are you here?"

"I don't know," I answered.

"I'm going to have to call my supervisor," he said.

"Good idea," I said.

"Stay here," he ordered.

"Got no place else to be," I said.

I looked at the atrium door. Marcy had plenty of time to nab Karen Wilson and her accomplice by now. She and Manny the bicycle cop were probably reading them their rights at this moment. They were, after all, highly trained members of the Chicago Police Department. Capable and good looking in shorts.

I smiled.

I counted three loud bangs.

I don't remember dropping to the floor. I do remember thinking how clean Henry kept the reception area tiles. They gleamed in the evening light.

Charlie had had the opposite reaction of my own. He was standing up and looking around.

"Get down, Charlie," I told him. Charlie took my suggestion immediately. I think the DPH guy did too. I think I heard him get down.

I was lying in front of the reception desk. I couldn't see the atrium door from where I was.

"What was that?" asked Charlie from the other side.

"Gun shots," I said.

"Who was shooting?" asked DPH.

"How the heck should I know?" I answered, a little perturbed at the stupidity of the question.

"What do we do?" asked Charlie.

"Stay down," I suggested.

We remained quiet for what seemed like minutes, but could only have been seconds. I could see the floor fog up with my breath as I hyperventilated. This was why I didn't want to come. This is why I didn't want Marcy to go in there with just a bicycle cop.

"What's behind that door?" asked DPH.

"The atrium," answered Charlie.

"What's in the atrium?"

"Plants and a fountain. It's really quite nice. There's this naked mermaid and she's taking a..."

"Charlie," I interrupted, "not now."

"Right," he agreed.

More silence.

I heard a large vehicle pull up in front of the building. It had to be S.W.A.T. I shifted my view without lifting my head from the floor. It was a large white van. On the side was the Fox News logo for Channel 32. A woman popped out of the passenger side and knocked on the sliding side door. It slid open and a man holding a camera popped out. He handed her a microphone. She went up and tried the door. It was still locked.

I tried to shoo them away. I pushed air towards them in an effort to let them know they should leave. Admittedly, not my best move. The camera man was panning across the lobby.

Charlie had scooted along the floor and his head was popping out from behind the desk staring at me. He looked outside. "It's the news," he said.

"Great timing," I said.

"Go away," shouted DPH. "It's a quarantine."

"I think they know that," I said. "It's probably why they're here."

"Should I let them in?" asked Charlie.

DPH and I both answered, "No."

The woman reporter was now standing in front of the doors talking into the microphone. I couldn't hear what she was saying.

"Maybe you should go look in the atrium," suggested Charlie, his voice cracking a little from behind the safety of his desk.

"Why would I do that?"

"Someone could be shot, you're a doctor."

"I'm a veterinarian. If a dog was shot, I will jump in to help. But as far as I know, the only dog in there is dead."

"What?" asked DPH.

"Never mind," I told him.

"I'm going to look," said Charlie.

"No," I told him. "There are at least two people in there with guns."

"We have to do something."

"I am doing something. I'm staying safe and alive."

"I need to call my supervisor," said DPH. Again.

More silence. Another news van had appeared, this one from Channel 2. Terrific.

I looked at the atrium door. This was taking way too long, I thought. They're professionals, I told myself. She's okay. She's fine. But what if she's not?

My phone rang.

CHAPTER 20

"Is that her?" asked Charlie.

"I don't think she has this number," I said. I slipped my hand inside my coat and pulled the phone out, all while staying glued to the marble floor, thank you very much.

I looked at the caller ID. It was Sheila.

I answered and put it up to my ear. "Hello?" I said, hesitantly.

"Atty," she said. Well, she didn't just say it, she oozed it through the phone and managed to cover it with concern, anger, frustration, confusion, and urgency.

"Yes?" I asked.

"Is that you lying on the floor at Mrs. Jeffries' building?"

I lifted the phone from my ear and looked at it before putting it back. "How did you...?"

"I'm watching you on the news," she said.

I turned to look out at the cameras. There were now three reporters standing in front of the building doing their reports. I waved.

"Funny," she said. "Actually, Channel 32 is saying that it's Oliver Platt inside the building. Something about him being in town to film a Charlie Chan remake. You weren't playing any pranks recently, were you?"

"Oh. Yeah. Danny's," I said.

"Atty," she said again, this time with mostly concern.

"It could be worse," I said.

"How?" she asked.

"They could be telling everyone it's me."

"True. What is going on? They're saying the building is under quarantine too. That the anthrax attack started there."

"There was no anthrax attack," I said.

"They why are you on the floor?"

I refused to answer on the grounds that it might incriminate me.

"Why," repeated Sheila, "are you and those two other men on the floor?"

"Is that Sheila?" asked Charlie, apparently eavesdropping on my conversation. "Hello, Sheila," he shouted.

"Tell Charlie I said hi back," she said.

I looked at Charlie. "Hi, back."

He smiled, content.

"Men. Floor," she prompted.

"It's a long story," I said.

"You've got time," she pointed out.

"We figured that the dead dog with the rare plant in it..."

"Stop. Dead dog with a rare plant in it?"

"That call to O'Hare this morning for Dave. They had a DOA and it turned out to have been carrying a rare seed in its gut. The seed actually kills the animal that eats it and uses the body for nutrients."

"Poor dog," she said.

"The people who were expecting to pick up a live dog tracked it down to the specialty clinic, thanks to Dave."

"Was it a woman?" asked Sheila. She knew Dave too well.

"As a matter of fact, Henry's niece."

"No way."

"Way."

"She and a guy stole it from the emergency clinic and took off before Officer Avers could catch them."

"So you figured that they were going to plant it in Henry's atrium. Is Henry in on this?"

"Don't know. He's trying not to die from anthrax too."

"So why did are you there? I'm sure that Officer Avers could handle something like this without your assistance." Her contempt was palpable.

"She used me to get past the police at the other quarantine."

"How?"

"Said she was taking me to get my head checked."

"Good idea," she added.

"So the dog-slash-plant thieves did show up here. Officer Avers and her 'backup,'" my voice added the quotes to backup, "went into the atrium to apprehend them."

"And you are on the floor, why?"

"We heard some noise."

"Atty."

"Possibly gun shots."

"Possibly?"

"They could have been something else."

"Can't you just get out of there?"

"Quarantine," I reminded her. "The other guy on the floor is from the Department of Public Health."

"Perfect," she added. "Do you think she is hurt? Or dead?"

"I don't know."

"Stay down," she said. "The police can handle this."

"Staying down," I assured her.

Bang.

This time the noise came from the atrium door flinging open.

Marcy stood in the doorway. She looked at the three of us on the floor, and then her eyes widened as she saw the television crews outside. All their cameras had turned to her.

"Is that Officer Avers?" asked Sheila over the phone.

"Yes," I whispered back.

"Doesn't look dead," she said. "You never told me she was pretty."

"What are you doing?" asked Marcy.

"Huh?" I said.

"Why are you on the floor?"

"We heard gun shots," I explained.

"Oh yeah, had to blow the lock off Henry's office. Get up, I need you in there."

"What for?" I asked, still glued to the floor.

"Come on, Doc. I told you, Manny and I got this under control."

"Gotta go," I told Sheila. I clicked off before her inevitable protest. I stood up, carefully peering around Marcy into the dark atrium. "You caught them?"

"Of course," said Marcy. "Come on." She looked at Charlie and the DPH guy. "You guys can get up too." She looked again at the cameras. I wondered what they were speculating now? Oliver Platt, arrested in terrorist plot to infect Chicago with anthrax. I bet his agent's phone was ringing off the hook about now.

I followed her into the atrium, her flashlight illuminating the herringbone brick path back to Henry's little work room. Manny was inside, standing over the two cuffed figures on the floor. They were face down, their hands behind them. Near Henry's little reading chair was one of the body bags from the emergency clinic. The bag was slit open.

"Check this out," said Marcy. She shined her light into the bag. "That's the other dog, isn't it?" she asked.

I looked inside and there was Peanuts Johnson. The poor guy had been stolen twice today. Three times if you count my rescuing him from the garbage cans at the Bark and Breakfast. I remembered that I had written SAVE on his bag after the necropsy.

"They took the wrong dog?" I asked.

"Looks like."

"We didn't take any dog," muttered the man on the ground. "They planted it."

Manny chuckled. "Didn't I tell you you had the right to remain silent?" he warned.

"They heard us come in and locked themselves in this office. Not the smartest of criminals."

"We're not criminals," said a female voice. I recognized it as Karen Wilson from the hospital. "My uncle works here."

"I know," I said. "We've met before. In his hospital room. Is he in on your little plant smuggling operation?"

She turned her face from the floor to look at me. "You're the doctor from the hospital."

"Hey," said Marcy. "Cop. From the hospital too."

Karen looked at her. "Oh, yeah. Hi."

"Hi," said Marcy shaking her head.

"Now what?" I asked.

"Well, we take them out the back. Don't really want to deal with the Public Health Department again."

"They know you're in here," I pointed out.

"Get up, you two," said Manny. He helped them to their knees by grabbing the backs of their pants.

I lifted Peanuts off the floor and put him on the counter where Henry's planting supplies were. I stroked his head. I knew he wasn't in this body anymore, but I still felt the need to make him comfortable. Lying on the floor didn't seem right. Marcy came and stood next to me.

"I knew you'd want to take care of this guy," she said. "No reason for him to end up in an evidence freezer. We've got enough on these two to hold them for a long time. You don't get to try and run down a cop and a veterinarian without consequences," she assured me. She put her hand on my shoulder then leaned her head against my neck. I leaned my head back. My eyes were watering.

"Hey," shouted Manny.

Karen's accomplice had rushed the bicycle cop, sending him to the ground. His eyes appeared crazy. Karen appeared just as surprised as we did. He stumble on his feet then turned to head for the door, his hands still cuffed behind him. Marcy went to check on Manny.

"Get, him," Manny told her as she helped him up. "I'm okay."

I found a sack of plant food in my hand and without thinking about it (boy I wish I had thought about it) I flung it at the fugitive as he barreled towards the door. It hit his head and exploded in a giant puff of white powder. The man crumpled from the hit and was soon covered with the contents. He lay still on the floor.

"Nice throw, Doc," said Marcy. She went over to check on him. She put a finger to his neck to check a pulse.

I hoped I hadn't killed him.

"He'll be alright," she said. She pulled her finger away and looked at the white powder covering her finger. "What is this stuff, anyway?" She reached and picked up the tattered remains of the bag and read the label. "Bone meal," she said.

"Oh, yeah, that's what Mrs. Jeffries used on her violets. Said it really turned them around." I remembered seeing the little Tupperware container with the spoon in her kitchen.

Then something clicked. I think there was an actual click in my brain. My eyes widened as I realized what this could mean. "Don't lick your finger," I told Marcy.

"I wasn't planning on it," she said as she wiped the bone meal on her pants leg. "Why, is it poisonous?"

"More like contaminated."

"With what?" she asked.

"Anthrax," I said.

Manny and Karen took a few steps back involuntarily. Marcy

stood in the middle of the bone meal dust storm. "What are you talking about?"

"Anthrax gets into the tissues and even the bones of the animals it infects. If that bone meal came from an infected animal, it could be the source of exposure for Henry, Darla, and Mrs. Jeffries."

"That bag looked forty years old," point out Marcy.

"The spores can survive that long with no problem and still remain infective when they are exposed to ideal conditions. In the case of Henry and Mrs. Jeffries, they likely inhaled some of the spores. That's why the respiratory symptoms. Darla probably ate them. Mrs. Jeffries might have gotten some of the powder on her food by accident."

"So, what about me?" asked Marcy.

"You started your pills from Nurse Ratchet, right?"

"Yeah. She watched me take the first dose."

"Anthrax is eminently treatable, especially if you catch it early."

"What about me," said Manny. "I thought this whole anthrax thing was just some mysteriousy-white-powder-in-an-envelope scare. There really is anthrax?"

I took my cipro pills from my pocket and tossed them to him. "Here, take one now and I'm sure you'll be fine. Unfortunately..."

"Yeah," realized Marcy. "No getting around the Public Health Department now."

"But if they confirm this as the source of the infection then they should be able to wrap things up quickly."

"On the other hand, they are from the government," she pointed out. "Not all public servants are known for their speed and efficiency."

The man on the floor was beginning to stir. Judging by his exposure level he'd need to get a double dose of Cipro as soon as possible.

"You might as well sit down," Manny told Karen. She sat in the corner furthest from the door and the mess. From the slight white haze that had filled the room, I doubted she had escaped exposure. They'd probably have to strip the entire place bare to make sure to get rid of any contaminated soil. That was a shame, it was a beautiful space. Manny carefully stepped around the fallen criminal, keeping a wide berth of Marcy as well. "I'll go track down the Public Health people and let them know what's going on."

"There's a guy in the lobby," I told him, "but he'll have to call his supervisor," I added. Marcy looked at me funny. "I'm just saying." I answered her glare.

Manny made his way back to the lobby. I moved to Henry's chair and collapsed. No getting out of quarantine this time. I touched the lump on my head. It was beginning to hurt.

Marcy helped my bone meal victim to his feet and led him to the corner where Karen sat. She tried to scoot away from him. He still looked pretty dazed. "Don't move," Marcy told them. "Next time Doc is going to throw one of those trowels at you or something."

I chuckled. She came over and made a funny face as she looked at the bump on my head. "You really should get that looked at."

"I think I'm going to have no choice."

My phone rang. I pulled it out. It was Allie from the emergency clinic. I answered it right away.

"Is she alright?" I asked.

"What? Who? Oh Darla, she's fine," she said.

"What is it then?"

"Got some test results back from the lab. You're not going to believe what they found in little Peanuts Johnson," she teased.

I looked over at the little dog on the counter. I had almost forgotten about my suspicions of what really happened at the Bark and Breakfast. "Oh, I bet I can guess," I told her.

CHAPTER 21

The next thirty-six hours were bizarre. Marcy, Manny, the two perps (as Manny continuously referred to them) and I were confined to the atrium area until a decontamination shower could be set up in the lobby. Men, and probably women, I couldn't tell in the bulky, yellow, full-body, hazmat suits, ushered us one by one into the portable shower unit. As I entered, all my clothes were confiscated, I assumed, to be incinerated. I had just gotten those shoes to where they slipped on and off easily. Fortunately the sides of the shower were opaque and all the television cameras outside got were plumes of steam coming from the top. After I was thoroughly decontaminated, I was given a white jumpsuit to wear, along with some white boxers and plain white sneakers and socks. I was then ushered to the elevator lobby where once again my blood was taken and antibiotics were issued to replace the ones that were somewhere in Henry's office.

Marcy came in with the collar on her jumpsuit up. She was pissed that they took her gun. I doubted they would give it back either. With my hair wet and slicked back I looked a little less like Oliver Platt, but still the cameras remained trained on me.

Charlie came over and handed me a set of keys with a Pomeranian key chain attached. "You want to stay in Mrs. Jeffries' place? I'm sure she won't mind," he said. "It sounds like we're here at least for a day."

"Awesome," said Marcy.

"Who says you get to stay there too?" I asked, hiding the keys from her.

"Come on, after all we've been through?" she said. She batted her eyelashes at me. I laughed.

"You get Mrs. Jeffries' room. I'll take the guest room."

"What's wrong with Mrs. Jeffries' room?" she asked.

"Nothing."

"Right," she said with cop-like suspicion.

"What about Manny?"

"He can sleep on the couch."

"It has plastic on it," I reminded her.

"Then the floor."

"This is so ridiculous. We are not contagious. They've scrubbed any spores off that got on us in that office. This is totally unnecessary."

"Yeah, well, at least we're not under arrest for leaving the other quarantine."

"Really? You think they'd be mad about that?"

"Well, you did fake an injury." She jabbed at my goose egg.

"Ow."

"Baby," she taunted.

The atrium door had been sealed off with plastic and all the condos with views had to have their windows sealed off with plastic as well. They had about a dozen guys in hazmat suits with shovels and plastic bag-lined garbage cans taking out all the plants, soil, and every bag of fertilizer from the atrium and Henry's office. It would probably end up worse than before Henry got his magical green thumbs on it. I wondered if the mermaid would have to go too.

"Where are your prisoners?" I asked.

"They were transported out."

"What?"

"Apparently the feds have a biohazard detention facility. Who knew."

"But they know this whole anthrax thing wasn't a terrorist plot."

"I told them," she said.

I walked to the elevators and pressed the call button. Eventually an empty car arrived and I gestured for Marcy to enter first, gentleman that I was. We stood inside and waited.

"I'm going to get another one," said Marcy loudly and clearly. She walked to the door and stopped short as they began to close.

"You're learning," I said.

I watched the floor number display slowly change during the elevator's crawl up the shaft.

Finally we arrived at the twenty-third floor. We stepped out and I walked up to Mrs. Jeffries' door. I fitted the key and opened it. The room felt empty without the little orange fuzz ball to jump up and greet me, doing her best to lick my face. I smiled thinking about it.

The phone rang.

"Should I answer?" I asked Marcy.

"Do you think it's for you?"

"It may be someone calling to ask Virginia why her building is on television," I said.

"All her friends probably live here," said Marcy.

I picked it up. "Hello?"

"Atty," said Sheila's voice.

"Sheila. How did you know I was here?"

"Charlie told me."

"Right."

"Turn on the news," she said, "Channel 32."

"I've been living it, I don't need to see it," I said.

"Atty, please," she insisted. There was a level of fear in her voice.

"Sure," I said. I found the remote and turned on the television, clicking through until the local Fox News report was playing.

"Again," said one of the newscasters, "we can confirm, one of the victims of the anthrax outbreak today has died. Apparently it was the pneumonic form of the disease which we understand is the most serious and difficult to treat."

Marcy and I looked at each other.

"Atty," said Sheila, "I tried calling Weiss, but they won't tell me anything. Can you find out?" she asked, the tears and sobs audible through the phone.

"I'll call now," I said.

"Let me know as soon as you do," she said.

"I will."

I hung up the phone and sat in one of the plastic covered chairs. "She looked so frail when we were there," I said.

Marcy knelt in front of me and put her hands on my hands. "Doc, it might not be her. Henry was in bad shape too."

I picked up the phone and tried to remember the number for Weiss and ended up calling information. My own smart phone had been a casualty of the decontamination procedure. I had them connect me. When I got the switchboard, I told them it was Dr.

Klammeraffe calling for Dr. Phread. I was on hold for a couple of minutes. No "Girl from Ipanema" this time. Just some Barry Manilow.

"Dr. Phread," said a tired, and almost lifeless voice.

"This is Dr. Klammeraffe," I said. "I wanted to find out about Mrs. Jeffries."

"Right," he said. "She's..." I felt myself choking up as he paused. It couldn't be. I should have figured it out sooner. She could have gotten treated earlier, "hanging in there," he said.

I breathed. Almost panting. "The other patient? Henry?"

"No," he said. "He didn't make it."

"I'm sorry," I said.

"Nothing to be sorry about. I should thank you," said Dr. Phread. "Without your diagnosis they would both be dead. We're pretty sure the old man got it first. His disease was much more advanced. How is the dog doing?"

I was a bit surprised he remembered. "She's responding to treatment. She should pull through."

"Great. I'll let the old lady know."

"Thanks. That will definitely make her feel better."

"I got to go," said Dr. Phread.

"Right. Good night." I hung up the receiver.

Marcy was smiling at me. "I told you," she said. She lunged at me and hugged me. And we both cried for a while. Finally she pulled away. "You would make a great detective, Doc," she said.

"You think so?"

"Sure." She stood and moved to her own chair.

"I think I'll stick with my day job," I decided. "But I do have something I'll need you to help me with once we get out of here."

"Name it," she said.

"Later," I told her. "I'm actually pretty exhausted."

"Yeah, me too."

"I have to call Sheila," I told her.

"Call Sheila," she said. She kicked off her white shoes, leaned back into the chair, and closed her eyes.

Sheila picked up before the phone had even finished rnging once. "She's okay," I said before she could ask.

"Thank God," she said. Then she realized what that meant. "Henry?" she asked.

"No," I answered. "He didn't make it."

"That poor man," she said.

She didn't know that he could have been the mastermind of the plant smuggling operation. I was doubting he was involved, but I hoped Karen Wilson might still clear him.

"You did good, Atty. I'm proud of you. Oliver Platt will be a little pissed, they're still saying that he might be involved, but I'm proud. Too bad you're under quarantine."

"Why?" I asked.

"Nothing," she teased.

I shook my head. I had one pretty, but exhausted woman, spending the night with me, and one seductress taunting me.

"I called the cat sitter," Sheila added. I used a high school girl down the block from me to watch my cat and house sit when I went out of town on vacation or to a conference. "She's going to check on Beaker and try to smuggle you some clothes. Charlie is waiting for her."

"That'll be nice."

"Yeah, I saw you on the news in your nice white jumpsuit. Very sexy."

"Ha, ha."

"I ordered you a new phone, I'll see if I can get it in with your clothes."

"What would I do without you?"

"You'd get by, but not as well."

"True."

"I canceled your appointments for tomorrow and Saturday. You're going to be busy next week."

"No rest for the wicked," I assured her.

"Is she there with you? They showed you two going into the elevator. They think that police officer is an FBI agent and she's interrogating you."

"No interrogating going on tonight," I said. "She's crashed on a chair."

"Hmm," she hmmed.

"I'll talk to you tomorrow," I said. "Thanks for everything."

"You're welcome. Good night."

I hung up the phone. Despite my weariness I didn't feel sleep coming. I stood up. Marcy was asleep, or doing a good impersonation of someone sleeping. I walked to the large picture window with the view of the lake. I could see lights on the water. Some late night cruises. To the south was the bright glow of Navy Pier. I realized I was hungry. There had been no dinner. No thought of dinner through all the excitement.

I wandered to the kitchen and opened the refrigerator. I smiled as I stared at the shelf. There was the Eli's cheesecake. I noticed there was a small note taped to the top.

"For Dr. Klammeraffe, thank you for taking such good care of my Darla."

I choked up at the faith she had in me. Well-deserved faith, as it turned out. I licked my lips, this was exactly what I needed. I waited for a moment, half expecting Sheila to call and tell me to leave it alone. Maybe she knew I deserved it as well.

Thank you Mrs. Jeffries, I thought. I opened cabinets and drawers until I found a plate and knife and silverware and cut off about a quarter of the cheesecake. I figured I'd leave some for breakfast. I found some decaf coffee and filters and set up a pot to brew with her coffee machine.

I sat at the kitchen table and let the dense, creamy, dessert melt in my mouth while the aroma of the coffee finished my vision of heaven. I thought about waking Marcy to offer her some, but decided she needed her rest more than this delicious cheesecake. I needed this delicious cheesecake more than she needed it. I earned it.

***

The next morning I found a bag with a change of my clothes, a new smart phone already set up with Sheila at speed dial number one, and a grapefruit with a snack pack of cottage cheese. At least she wasn't mad at me. There was also a piece of paper with phone calls for me to make and messages to return along with copies of the lab work from Peanuts Johnson.

I turned on the news. Oliver Platt had been cleared of all wrong doing, but the identity of the man impersonating him had yet to be determined. He probably ended up in the biohazard detention with the seed smugglers I speculated.

Marcy came out of the bathroom wearing Mrs. Jeffries terry cloth robe. She twirled to model it for me. I showed her the grapefruit.

"Eww," she said appropriately.

I had hidden the remaining half of the cheesecake (yes, I had another piece sometime during the night) under some cans of Ensure supplement in the refrigerator, the Eli's logo carefully turned to the back.

We wandered into the kitchen. I was still wearing my white jumpsuit and white socks. It was actually kind of comfortable. The coffee maker had been re-purposed to producing "real" coffee and I rummaged through the fridge and found some Jimmy Dean sausage patties (which Darla should definitely not be eating) and eggs and tried to do my own version of a Danny's breakfast in a frying pan. It turned out to be not so bad. What it lacked in quality, I made up for in quantity. Who knew I would be so hungry after eating half a cheesecake. Well, to be honest, I kind of suspected I would.

As we sat, downing our third cups of coffee, I pushed the lab work for Peanuts over to Marcy. She glanced at it.

"So, there was phenobarbital in that little dog's blood."

"About four times the therapeutic dose. Poor guy probably couldn't even stand. On top of that his thyroid levels had bottomed out so he would already have been pretty lethargic."

"Then the people at that kennel killed him," said Marcy.

"Her nephew is a lawyer," I told her. "If I go accusing them then he'll probably sue me, just to get me to back down."

"Yeah, but I'm a cop. When we get out of here, we'll go pay them a visit," she promised. I didn't like the look in her eye. She was almost as angry as when Karen Wilson's accomplice tried to escape yesterday.

It was my turn to shower and chang. I was beginning to feel more like myself. The shoes needed breaking-in, but I was glad Sheila had gotten me a new phone before Saturday.

I called the emergency clinic first. Gwen answered the phone. She sounded tired. I asked for Allie and a minute later she answered. She was way too perky.

"Darla is doing great. I took her out of the oxygen this morning. The edema is all, but gone and she ate like a madwoman."

"Dog food?" I asked.

"No. She wouldn't touch that this time. But she did devour one of the jelly donuts the cop at the back door snuck in. He said we should thank Marcy for them."

"I'll pass it on." I wondered when she had time to reach out to her buddies to get donuts delivered.

"She's following me around everywhere. Doc, she's going to be fine."

"How about you?"

"Well, still waiting on our blood tests. We saw you on TV last night. Laughed our butts off when they thought you were Oliver Platt. They seriously thought he was involved in a terrorist attack. Now they're pretending like they never even suggested it."

"That sounds like the news people."

"They did say that someone died from the outbreak."

"It was Henry, the janitor at Darla's mom's building."

"How is Darla's mom?"

"She was holding on last night. I'll check again after I get off the phone with you."

"Did you see Peanuts' blood tests?" she asked.

"Yeah."

"I say we go set up a protest outside their front door, close them down."

"Don't worry, Marcy has something in mind for them."

"Ooh. Can I come?"

"We'll see."

"You call me. You owe me."

"Okay, deal."

I hung up.

I called the number I had for Weiss and had them page Dr. Phread for me. He took a few minutes, but was soon on the phone.

"Dr. Klammeraffe?" he asked.

"Yeah."

"I am happy to say that Mrs. Jeffries," I was glad he knew her name, "is doing very well. She is sitting up and eating and setting up the single nurses with you. Any update on her dog?" he asked.

"Just got off the phone with the vet clinic. She is doing great. Also eating and missing her mom."

"That will make her feel a lot better."

Marcy motioned for me to give her the phone. I handed it over.

"Dr. Phread?" she asked, "It's Officer Marcy Avers."

I couldn't hear the other end of the conversation, but was thinking that Dr. Phread was starting to calculate the odds that a tall blonde was in his future.

"Sure," she said, "let me write it down."

She wrote nothing down. I assumed it was his phone number. The guy was persistent.

"You will take very good care of Mrs. Jeffries, right?"

She waited for his answer.

"I take care of those who help me out," she added.

That had to drive him crazy.

"Bye, bye," she said as she hung up.

"Nice guy," she said. "Not my type."

"What's your type?" I asked.

I only got a sideways glance in response.

We decided to go downstairs. Marcy still had her white jumpsuit on. Apparently none of the clothes in Mrs. Jeffries' closet were suitable. A note taped by the elevators warned us that the quarantine was still in effect and we should remain in our apartments. We ignored it and took the elevator down.

There were still a large number of Public Health employees in the elevator lobby. About twenty or so residents were gathered, all with important reasons to leave the building. The DPH wasn't even letting them into the main lobby. They hoped to have the lab results back by tomorrow morning, but there were a lot to process and they wouldn't lift the quarantine until everyone tested negative. I didn't want to ask what would happen if someone tested positive. A few more days in Mrs. Jeffries apartment and the plastic would have to come off some of the chairs. Part of me was wishing I had rationed that cheesecake a little more carefully.

The cameras were still there. Sheila had sent a baseball cap for me to wear to help hide my identity. It seemed to be working. They were more interested in the men and women in hazmat suits in the lobby than us.

I gathered from the various conversations that I could eavesdrop on and from the answers Marcy was getting to her queries that the atrium was completely stripped of dirt and they were disinfecting the whole place. I tried to find out what happened to Peanuts. I assumed his body was contaminated when I exploded the bag of bone meal on the plant smuggler's head. I hoped that he hadn't been tossed in a barrel with a bunch of dirt.

We decided to head back up after grabbing a few bagels that had been brought in to quash the complaints of residents who said they had no food. I doubted that was true. Mrs. Jeffries' apartment was ready for Armageddon. She had hoards of canned goods, pasta, some extra cases of Ensure, at least ten pounds of coffee, and even a bag of dog food. I assumed that was for show in case I ever asked what Darla was eating.

A man in a suit caught us before we entered one of the elevators.

"Are you Dr. Klammeraffe?" he asked.

"Call me Dr. At," I said. I shook his outstretched hand.

"I am Michael Warren with the CDC. I understand you first detected the outbreak in a dog?"

"Yes," I said.

"Good, work, doctor. I am so used to working with large animal vets during disease outbreaks; it's nice to know that the dog and cat doctors are on their toes too. I understand you were instrumental in getting treatment started on the two human cases."

"As soon as I knew what it was I informed the doctor at Weiss, yes."

"And it does look like the bag of bone meal was the source of the outbreak. I believe you put the public health people onto that as well."

"Yes." He was making me sound like a genius. I liked it.

"Well, I'm glad you were here. If there is anything I can do for you, let me know."

"I don't suppose you can get us out of here before tomorrow?"

"Sorry. That is for the locals. I'll see if the lab can speed up the testing."

"One other thing, I don't know if you can help, but there was a dead dog in the office off the atrium that got covered with the contaminated bone meal. I was hoping that she could get cremated and the ashes returned to the owner."

"That I will check into. I will make a few calls."

"Thank you."

He shook my hand again.

"A regular hero, you are," commented Marcy as we got on the elevator.

I smiled. "Maybe they'll get Oliver Platt to play me in the movie."

"If he ever forgives you for putting him on the terrorist watch list. Hate to be around the next time he flies anywhere," said Marcy.

The elevator took us back to our quarantine.

We got the all-clear at seven the next morning. The rest of the Eli's cheesecake had been appropriately consumed the night before. I felt bad sneaking it behind Marcy's back, but I was the one who saved Darla and I earned it. There was no breakfast this morning, we were anxious to get the heck out of there. We headed downstairs. People were exiting the building and just standing outside. I guess just being on the other side of the glass was freedom enough for most of them.

Charlie saw us as we started to head for the back way out of the building. I didn't need the cameras catching another glimpse of the Oliver Platt impersonator. He held up a paper shopping bag and jogged over.

"Hey, Doc. That CDC guy brought this in for you late last night." He handed it to me. I smiled as I looked inside. It was a blue box with the gold Cozy Acres pet cemetery logo printed on top. Inside would be the metal canister that held Peanuts' remains.

"Is he still here?" I asked.

"Naw, he said he had to get back to Atlanta."

"Thanks, Charlie. You headed home?"

"Yeah. Can't wait to get all that overtime."

"That's why you didn't seem so upset."

"A guy's got to do what a guy's got to do," he said.

Marcy and I continued out the back way. I took a peek into the atrium from the back entrance before heading for the loading Dock. All the plants were gone. The planting beds were stripped of soil. The mermaid was dry. It was sad. Henry was gone and all the work he had done had been erased. I doubted that it would return to the state he had lovingly built it into, quickly or at all.

I let the door close and wiped the bit of moisture that had appeared at the corner of my eye. A bit of irritation from the disinfectant chemicals, I suspected. I noticed Marcy was having the same reaction. We exited the loading Dock door and stepped out into our own freedom. A fresh, empty, garbage container was present. Karen Wilson's SUV was gone. Police tape barred anyone else from entering the parking area. We just walked under it.

My car was still in its spot across the street. It had grown some strange appendages during my time in quarantine. As we crossed the street I could see seven red and white envelopes covered the windshield and my driver's side door. Most were citations for parking by the fire hydrant, one for parking in a street sweeping zone, and one was for parking too far away from the curb. I assumed that parking enforcement officer was just trying to be creative. I gathered them up and handed them to Marcy.

"Uh-uh," she said. "You shouldn't have parked by the hydrant; what if the fire department needed to get in there?"

"You told me to."

"Do you do everything people tell you to do?"

"When they have a gun, I do."

She laughed and took them. "Just giving you a hard time."

I started to get in the passenger side, but Marcy stopped me and handed me my keys. "My turn to get chauffeured."

"Where do you live?" I asked as I scooted to the other side.

"Near Lawrence and Kimball," she answered.

I mapped the route in my head. "You know what's kind of on the way," I said.

"Danny's," we both said together.

"My treat," I said.

"Is that where you take all your dates?" she asked.

"Not a date, just a thank you."

"Yeah, well, it'll help make up for not sharing that cheesecake with me."

I froze just before sticking the key in the ignition.

"I'm a cop, silly. You think I didn't know?"

"Yes?" I half asked, half apologized.

"We'll plan out what we're going to do for those lovely people at the boarding kennel," she added, "once I get a fresh uniform and a new gun."

"Yikes," I said. I popped out the Blues Brothers CD and had the MP3 player pull up Neil. Before she could complain, I reminded her, "Driver's choice." Then I remembered, "Allie wants to come along too."

"I think she'll like it," said Marcy. "Absolutely bring her along."

Neil began singing "Crunchy Granola Suite". The opening riff had me bopping as I pulled out into the street. I looked at Marcy. She was bopping too.

CHAPTER 22

"Where you been?" asked the gravelly voice followed by the sound of sucking air and the inevitable cough.

I was that close to making it through my side gate and safely into my house.

"Work," I answered Mrs. Hornby.

"That you on the news?" she asked.

"Which news?" I stalled.

"That was you," she concluded. "I knew you weren't a terrorist."

That was a relief. My reputation was intact.

"I got something for you. Wait here."

I waited as she shuffled into her house, the trail of blue smoke marking her path. I actually waited. That was pretty stupid. I could have gone in. Said I heard the phone ringing if she ever asked where I went. Which she would. It was easier to wait, I decided.

I heard her back door slam and a few hacks later she was back at her alley gate with a bag. "This is from my grandson, Griffin. My daughter took them back home last night. Glad to see them come. Gladder to see them go," she added. She thrust the bag at me, "He wanted me to give it to you."

"Really? What is it?" My curiosity had moved me close enough to take the bag from her outstretched skeletal hand. Her liver spots had age spots and vice versa.

"He made you something. Said it was a vet thing. All he talks about is being a vet now. Well, either that or a cop. Hard to keep it straight with him."

I smiled and held up the bag then turned to head back to my own home.

"Aren't you going to open it?" she asked.

"Um, I thought I'd open it inside," I said.

"Open it, it's some sort of invention of his," she insisted.

I opened it. Inside was an asthma inhaler and taped to the mouthpiece was a cone of paper.

"It's for cats," said Mrs. Hornby as she coughed something up which she immediately swallowed. Gross.

I took it out. Sure enough, Griffin had adapted his empty asthma inhaler to fit over a cat's face. I didn't have the heart to say someone else had already invented the AeroKat inhaler.

"Very clever," I said.

"Ah, it's a piece of garbage. But you're nice to say it." She waved me off and shuffled back towards her house.

Once I heard the door slam I slipped the bag into my garbage can. Life was back to normal.

Beaker was glad to see me. I was glad to see him. I gave him food. He forgot I existed.

My answering machine was flashing constantly which meant it was full of messages. I hated messages. That was why I had Sheila. I only gave this number to a few people. I pressed the play button. It was my mother. I pressed delete.

"Message deleted," confirmed my machine. I pressed delete again and held it down. "All messages deleted," it informed me. That felt good. I knew that Oliver Platt the terrorist had made the national news and my mother would want to know why the nice newsman was calling me Oliver Platt and ask why I changed my name without telling her.

My mail was sitting on the table by the front door. My cat sitter had once again exceeded my expectations and made sure the house looked lived in, except to nosy neighbors. I left the mail on the table. There was nothing that needed my immediate attention. I did have one more errand to run today. I would have to deliver Peanuts to his owners and fill them in on everything. I still couldn't help, but get mad when I did think of what happened at that kennel. Such a stupid mistake.

I felt the scruffy beard on my face and did a pit check. No time like the present. I went to the bathroom, shaved and showered, called my little bathroom scale a liar, then remembered the cheesecake and apologized.

I made a pot of coffee. Not that the three cups at Danny's hadn't woken me up, but in reality, that was just enough to prime the pump. I needed to get the motor going. I had the willpower to leave the bag of Bugles in the cupboard, despite their desperate pleas to be consumed. I told them to tell it to my bathroom scale. I took my double-sized mug to the living room and checked out what my DVR had recorded for me. I skipped past the cop shows and settled on that new romantic comedy sitcom everyone was talking about. I had six episodes recorded. That sounded good.

Just as I got started my phone rang. I pressed pause on the remote. It was the land line phone sitting on the coffee table next to me. From the way it rang I knew it was my mother. I sighed. I picked it up.

"Hello?" I said. It might be Sheila. I was hoping it was Sheila. I was disappointed.

"Atticus," said my mother, "I was so worried. I left you a bunch of messages."

"Oh, did you?" I asked innocently.

"My poor baby. Did they waterboard you?"

"What?"

"The CIA. I heard that they waterboard terrorist suspects to get information. Did you tell them anything?"

Those last two sentences required my brain to do a little gymnastic move to wrap itself around them. Apparently my mother not only believed that I was a terrorist, but that I had vital information that the government wanted.

"Mom, there were no terrorists. There was no CIA. It was a misunderstanding. Just a mistake," I tried to assure her.

"Are you going to have to go to Gitmo?" she asked.

"Gitmo?"

"Make sure you have sunscreen. You burn so easily, dear."

"Mom. I'm not going anywhere. I'm fine, I'm home, and I just want to sit down in a chair without plastic on it and relax."

"What kind of animals would do that to you? Plastic?" she said with perfect outrage.

"No, mom. No one was doing anything to me. There was a contaminated bag of fertilizer. No terrorist plot."

"Your sister said that it was a mistake too. She said it was all that Oliver Platt's fault."

"Oliver Platt had nothing to do with it," I said.

"I didn't like him in that one movie," she said.

"Which movie?" I asked.

"You know, that one where he was that weird guy and did those weird things."

"Oh yeah," I said knowing from experience that that was as specific as she was going to get. I tried to change the subject. "How is Aunt Eunice?"

"Oh, that woman has it tough, Atticus. Her bowling average has dropped five points in the last month."

"Uh huh," I muttered. Off one train wreck, on to another.

"I think she might be getting Alzheimer's too. She keeps forgetting to put the top back on the toothpaste."

"Sounds serious," I said. I was sure Aunt Eunice didn't have Alzheimer's. Most of the time she made more sense than my mother.

"Oh, and don't get me started about her and that shopping channel. A new gadget shows up at the house every day. Yesterday it was a rechargeable lantern of all things. She said we'd use it camping. We never go camping. I wouldn't know how to put up a tent."

"If it's dark you could use the lantern," I suggested.

"That's true dear. You always have such good ideas."

"I have to go, mom," I said. "I'll call tomorrow at the usual time," I added.

"You're sure you're okay?" she asked.

"Absolutely fine. I'll talk to you later. Bye."

She said, "bye," and I hung up. I picked up the remote and hit play.

It was funny. I settled in, my thumb on the skip button for when the commercials came on.

The phone rang again.

"Come on," I said to it. I was going to have to get a phone with caller ID on it. I was sure it was my mother again, calling to see if the CIA was still listening in on the call and wondering if I could tell her what really happened.

I answered. "Hello?"

"Atticus?" asked the female voice on the other end. She sounded like a bad impersonation of Judi Dench.

"Harper," I responded, in my best John Houseman impersonation. It was a thing we had. How could we help, but be strange? Have you met my mother?

"What have you been up to?" she asked.

"You wouldn't believe it."

"Well, from what I've seen on the news and mom's theories as to what the CIA believes you did, it's a little confusing."

"I just got in the middle of something. It's over now."

"According to Dr. Wilson from the CDC, who they interviewed on the morning news, you are credited with the successful containment of the outbreak and the lack of further loss of life thanks to your vigilance and quick thinking."

"No."

"Yes."

"That doesn't sound like me."

"He forgot to mention your modesty."

"To tell you the truth, Harley, I could have just as easily missed it."

"No you couldn't have. You're a good vet, Atty. Relax and enjoy."

"I'm trying to, but the phone keeps ringing."

She laughed. "Are you coming over for Thanksgiving?"

"Don't I always?"

"Yes, you do. Take care, Atty."

"See ya, Harley. Tell Desmond his favorite uncle said hello."

"Will do."

I hung up and unplugged the cord from the phone.

It was about three episodes later and half a bag of the Bugles (okay, they won their little mind game over me) when the doorbell rang. I paused my show and got up to see who it was.

I peeked through the little square panes of glass in the wooden front door. It was Allie and Marcy. I opened the door.

"So," said Marcy, "this is your place."

"This is my place."

"Very nineties, Doc," said Allie.

"Do you even remember the nineties?" I asked.

She shuddered. "I was little, but yes, I do."

Alright, I didn't have a degree in interior decorating, but it was functional if not fashionable.

"I'm beginning to see why you don't have a girlfriend," added Marcy.

I ignored her. "So, we're going to do this?" I asked.

"We're going to do this," said Marcy as she patted the holster on her hip. It was shiny and new, as was the gun.

"I'm driving," said Marcy.

I looked at the car parked in front of my house. It was some older model Mustang, very cool, very small. "Am I going to fit in that?"

Marcy considered the question. "You're driving," she said.

"Right," I said. "Follow me." I led them out the back door, grabbing my coat on the way. Allie stopped to give Beaker some attention. He seemed to have more affection for her than he did for the schlub who fed him.

I clicked the garage door opener and we made it into the Escape with no interruption from Mrs. Hornby.

"So what's the plan?" I asked Marcy. She took shotgun and Allie flipped up the seat on the passenger side in the back.

"First, this," she said. She handed me a CD. It was labeled "Traffic Mix."

"I'm afraid," I said as I took it.

"You'll be okay."

I sighed. "What's wrong with Neil?" The girls groaned.

"So," started Marcy, "we going straight to the Bark and Breakfast. I have some guys meeting us there."

"Guys?"

"A few fellow animal lovers, you could say."

"Awesome," said Allie.

I slipped Marcy's disc into the CD player. As I was pulling into the alley and waiting for the garage door to close, "Highway to Hell" was blaring from the speakers. Marcy turned it up. She and Allie were loving it. I smiled and drove.

The Beatles came next with "Drive My Car" and then Ray Charles with "Hit the Road Jack". We were all singing along to that one.

A block from the Bark and Breakfast, as Tracy Chapman was crooning to "Fast Car," I could see the flashing police lights. As we got closer I could see a half dozen police cars were parked in front and behind the building. Officers were standing everywhere. I pulled up to the front in an empty space between two squad cars. One of the officers came over to Marcy's window. She opened it.

"Marcy, this the guy?"

"This is doctor At. The green-haired girl is Allie," introduced

Marcy.

He stuck his arm and and shook my hand. "Billy O'Hara. Any friend of Marcy's is a friend of mine. We ready to move, Marcy?"

"Let's roll," she said. She got out and Allie and I followed.

I could see Betty Cunningham on the phone inside the window. Her expression changed from fear to rage when she saw me.

Marcy took the lead. Allie and I followed and three more police officers came in behind us.

"I should have known you had something to do with this," Betty said as we entered.

"Betty Cunningham, you are under arrest for the murder of Peanuts Johnson," said Marcy. "You have the right to remain silent. Anything..."

"You can't arrest me for that dog dying. It was his fault taking so long to get here."

I shook my head and just smiled at her denial.

"We have evidence that the guest in question was given the wrong medication which led to his death. We also have evidence of health code violations, specifically a rodent found in the remains of the guest is question."

"What is she talking about? That dog went for cremation two days ago."

"I got permission from the family to do a necropsy," I said.

"What's that?" muttered one of the cops behind me.

"It's an autopsy for animals," Marcy educated him.

"Why didn't he just say autopsy," he muttered back.

"You stole that dog from my kennel?" she said, trying to turn it back on me.

"Your boy Pete left him on the garbage cans and I took him."

Marcy stepped in, "If the remains were in the garbage, there is no longer an expectation of ownership or custody at that time."

It was my turn to vent. "You or your kennel people gave Peanuts the phenobarbital that was for Jasper Kent. You killed him."

"My nephew is on the way, he'll take care of this."

"I have lab tests, Betty."

"Please place your hands behind your back," Marcy directed her.

"You can't do this," she said. "Don't you touch me."

Marcy snapped her fingers and one of the officers behind her handed her a folded paper. "This is a search warrant. We have cause to believe that controlled substances are being stored improperly on the premises and believe there are multiple building code and health code violations."

"Wait," said Betty.

A sudden burst of barking and yapping accompanied the opening of the door to the kennel area. "What's going on?" said a man's voice. It was Kirby Cunningham. He seemed a bit flustered and confused.

"Kirby, go back to the kennel. I told you I have this handled."

"Are you Kirby Cunningham?" asked Marcy.

"Yes. Why?"

"You are also under arrest for the murder of Peanuts Johnson." She repeated the Miranda warning.

"I told you those meds got mixed up," he said.

"Shut up," snapped Betty.

Kirby ignored her. "I usually do the medications for the dogs. But I was gone for three days."

"Kirby," warned Betty.

Kirby was starting to cry. "We killed that little dog, Betty. It was our fault." He turned to me. "Dr. At, the kennel boy just got the medications mixed up. We hide them in the food and he just put the wrong ones in the wrong bowls."

I looked at Betty. "You knew what happened. You were trying to make me look bad."

Allie was standing next to Kirby, comforting him.

"Prove it," she said defiantly. "If that dog died it was Pete's fault. Arrest him."

I couldn't believe she was throwing that kid under the bus.

Marcy nodded her head and the cops behind us headed for the kennel area.

"Wait," she said before they could enter. I could see gears whirling in her head. I wondered if there was something back there she didn't want us to see.

"Five hundred dollars."

"What?" I asked.

"We'll pay the Johnsons five hundred dollars. No admission of guilt. It was an accident, but just to cover any expenses."

"Are you trying to bribe us?" asked Marcy.

"No one is trying to bribe anyone," said another voice from behind us. A young man in a suit was brushing his way past the two officers guarding the door. "Lyle Cunningham. I'm the Cunningham's attorney. They have nothing further to say," he said.

"We got another one," said yet another voice. My head whipped around to see Pete standing at the entrance to the kennels. "Oh, hey, Doc. You're here already. This way."

Betty was about to blurt out something, but a stare from her nephew silenced her.

"You don't have permission to go back there," he informed me.

"He can go back," said Kirby.

Marcy grabbed my arm and we followed Pete before any further arguing could occur. Allie slipped in with us.

Pete motioned for us to follow him into another room of cages. I was expecting another dead dog, rotting in its cage. I was wrong.

"Aww," said Allie. She reached into the open cage door and grabbed one of the newly born puppies. There were four there, mewling quietly, squirming next to the warm belly of their mother. "Get me some towels," she told Pete. He found some in a stack in the corner and brought them back. She started drying the puppy off.

"I think one is stuck, she's been trying to push it out, but nothing," said Pete.

I looked at the exhausted border collie lying in the cage. The other puppies were doing their best to blindly locate their first meal. Allie put the puppy she had cleaned off back in the cage and grabbed another. Marcy also grabbed a pup and a towel from Pete, copying what Allie was doing, smiling from ear to ear.

I went to the mother and lifted her tail and could see the rear end of another puppy stuck in the birth canal. I looked around for a rubber glove. "Any gloves?" I asked Pete. He shrugged. I took off my coat and rolled up my sleeves.

I reached in and felt a tiny pair of legs and was able to get them out. With just a little tug, mom was able to push the pup out the rest of the way. It was a little boy. Allie produced a pair of scissors from her pocket and cut the umbilical cord. I picked up the pup. It was limp in my hand.

I stood and grabbed a towel from Pete and started rubbing furiously at the puppy. I grasped it firmly in the towel between my hands, held the head down, then gave it a fling downwards, hoping to clear any mucus from the airway. Nothing. I started squeezing the sides of the chest, hoping to stimulate its little heart. I stopped to see if it was trying to breathe. It was still.

I brought its head up to my mouth and opened its mouth. I cupped my hand around its head and blew in trying to get the lungs to taste some good old oxygen.

"Gross," said Marcy.

I did it twice before resuming my fingertip chest compressions. I stopped. Allie was next to me and we both looked at the tiny black and white wet lump of fur.

"Come on," I said. "Breathe." Darn fumes. The kennel must use that same disinfectant that the public health department used at Mrs. Jeffries because my eyes were starting to water.

I gave it another breath and rubbed it vigorously.

"Mew," it said. Its legs began to swim around, stretching and moving. The chest moved with each cry.

I handed the pup to Allie. "I'll take care of these guys," she said. "You guys get back up front."

Marcy agreed and we went back to the entrance to the kennel.

"You're in charge?" asked Lyle to Marcy.

"I am."

"And you're really arresting my aunt and uncle for murder?"

"Yes."

"Of a dog?"

"Yes. A family member, trusted to their care. They just admitted to it."

"You can't be serious. Maybe negligent destruction of property," he started.

"You call that dog property one more time and you can join them," Marcy cut him off. "Now, we have evidence that Peanuts got the wrong medication and six witnesses that heard Kirby admit as much. Someone is going to have to be held responsible."

"It's my fault," said Kirby. "I shouldn't have left."

"Quiet, Kirby," ordered Betty.

"How are the puppies?" Kirby asked, ignoring his wife.

"One had a little trouble getting out, but he'll be fine. It was touch and go for a minute."

"Doc here saved that puppy's life," added Marcy.

"Thank you, Dr. At. I don't know what would have happened if you didn't show up. Betty wasn't going to call you. She said that dogs gave birth all the time, didn't need any help or a vet bill."

"Is she your dog?" I asked.

"Yes. It's her first litter."

I didn't know the Cunninghams were into breeding.

Marcy turned to Lyle. "I need Mrs. Cunningham here to make a statement taking responsibility for that dog's death and covering any expenses that resulted, including the cremation."

Betty let out a laugh, but was quickly silenced by a stare from her nephew.

"And the building code and health code violations?"

"If they cooperate, we don't have to do that today. An inspector will be here in one week. That should give them time to make sure everything is up to code."

"And what about all these police cars around here. People are going to talk."

"Yes. Yes they will," agreed Marcy. I knew that was all she really had. The search warrant was a receipt from my oil change place she had pulled out of the glove compartment. No one was going to get arrested for murdering a dog.

Allie and Pete came out from the back. Pete had the mom wrapped up in a blanket and Allie had the puppies in a cardboard box lined with towels. "Hey," she said to the cop who had inquired about my necropsy comment. "Can you give us a lift to the specialty clinic on Addison?"

"Sure," he said.

"I'm going to take these guys in," she told me. "We'll x-ray mom to make sure there aren't any more."

"Good idea."

"Good luck," she said, referring to the next stop I needed to make.

"Thanks," I said. "I'll come by when we're done.

"This was fun, Doc," said Allie. She looked at Marcy. "Officer Avers, let's do this again."

"You betcha," she said.

Lyle had finished talking with his aunt and uncle and pulled Marcy aside. "They'll do it."

"Good. It's the right thing."

He shrugged.

"I'll be back if this isn't taken care of," said Marcy. I followed her out.

Kirby brushed his way past us to catch up with Allie and Pete. "Wait for me," he called.

The police officers were patting Marcy on the back and shaking my hand as they headed back to their cars. Dozens of people were on the sidewalk, some staring into the boarding kennel windows, others watching as Kirby was ushered into the back of a police cruiser that contained Pete, Allie and the puppies. The onlookers would make what assumptions they would.

Marcy and I got back into my car.

"You don't have to come with," I said.

"I'm coming with," she said as she hit play on the stereo. As we drove to my next house call, The Clash bragged about their "Brand New Cadillac" and Tom Cochrane assured us "Life is a Highway". By the time I pulled up in front of the Johnson's home the Cars were just finishing up with "Drive".

"Nice job on the CD," I told Marcy.

"I knew you'd like it," she said. "There are some oldies in there." She couldn't resist the dig.

I stepped out and opened the hatch to the back and retrieved the bag with the container that held Peanuts' remains from Cozy Acres. I started up the walk to their front door. Marcy took my arm. I felt my eyes starting to water again.

EPILOGUE

I walked into my bedroom and felt myself sigh heavily. The stress of the last few days was catching up with me and demanding payment.

The weariness I felt was well earned. I had learned from Dr. Phread that Mrs. Jeffries would be heading home in a few days. Charlie had picked Darla up from the specialty clinic and was going to babysit her until her mom was home. The Johnsons had been reunited with Peanuts remains and the circumstances of his death brought to light. According to Manny, Karen Wilson's confession had cleared Henry of any involvement in the seed smuggling. The *Corposeum korchenkii* was being cultivated at the Garfield Park Conservatory with Spot Doe's remains providing essential nutrients.

Margaret was picked up at O'Hare trying to "flee the jurisdiction" as Marcy explained it. She was arrested with her accomplice, Dr. Arnold Cooper, who had about fifty vials of morphine on him. No wonder she had a soft spot for him.

I took off my robe and threw it over the chair in the corner of my room. I looked in the mirror, I ruffled my hair and massaged some of the tightness from the back of my neck. It seemed as though all of Donna Melton's good work had been undone. That could be fixed though. I smiled at the thought of that.

"Goodnight, Oliver," I said to the man in the mirror. He wasn't so bad. Even if he was a suspected terrorist.

"Goodnight, Atty," he said back.

Beaker bounded up on the bed, squeaking and rubbing his head against me. "No more food," I told him. He didn't care. He seemed to know that I just needed a cat right now.

I crawled under the covers. I made sure the alarm was turned off.

Tomorrow was Sunday. My fun day. My I-don't-have-to-run day. God, I was old. Lyrics from the Bangles were in my head. I wondered what important information had been sloughed to make room for those?

Beaker crawled under the covers with me and started purring. That cat could purr. I let my eyes close.

The phone rang.

"Really?"

It rang again. I should have unplugged this one too.

Another ring. I answered.

"Hello?"

"Hey, Atty," said Sheila.

"Hi," I said cautiously.

"Just wanted to say goodnight."

"How did you know I was just now going to sleep."

"I had a feeling."

"It would mean more if there was a good night kiss too."

She made her puckering sound on the phone.

"You did great, Atty. You should be proud. I'm proud to work with you."

"I'm surprised that I haven't been getting phone calls for interviews and stuff."

"Oh, you've been getting them. I've just been keeping them at bay."

"Bless you, Sheila."

"So you going to see Marcy again?" she asked.

"I knew there was another reason you called."

"Just curious."

"And jealous?" I asked.

"Should I be?"

I thought about it. It was a loaded question. "No."

"Sorry," she said.

"No you're not."

"She was kind of cute."

"Too young."

"Not for Dave, apparently."

"No one is too young for Dave," I pointed out.

"I can see where you might be attracted to a slightly older woman," Sheila mused.

"How old are you?" I asked

"Not too young," she answered.

I paused. I wanted to ask her the question. And I didn't want ask it. We worked well together. Why take a chance at ruining it? Yeah, the playful flirting was fun. We joked. We laughed. But as I lay here alone I wondered. Would I ever meet her? Woudl I get a chance to put a face to the voice on the other end of the phone? I let it pass.

"Goodnight, Sheila," I said.

"Goodnight, Atty," she said. I started to put the phone back. I could hear her voice from the handset. "Atty?" I put it back up to my ear.

"Yes?"

There was a pause. "Someday," she said before hanging up.

I smiled.

The End

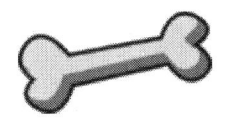

ACKNOWLEDGEMENTS

Thanks to Dan Mitchell, Rick Shoenfield, and Jennifer Sucharzewski for their help in reviewing the book and catching all those annoying typos.

Special thanks to all my own house call clients and patients who have indirectly contributed to the story. My experience with you inspired me to follow Dr. At on this journey in the first place. Hopefully, with more stories to come.

Cover photograph by me!

James Hosek

ABOUT THE AUTHOR

Dr. James Hosek, DVM was born in Chicago, IL, and grew up in Stickney, IL. He attended Thomas Alva Edison Elementary School and J. Sterling Morton West High School. He received his B.S. And D.V.M. degrees from the University of Illinois. After graduating veterinary school he did an internship at the University of Pennsylvania. He currently has a house call practice on the north side of Chicago and is the owner of Merrick Animal Hospital in Brookfield, IL. He is married and has two boys. He also has been adopted by two cats, Sonyonia and Hedwig. Apart from writing, he enjoys, gardening, woodworking, and photographing mushrooms.

Made in the USA
Charleston, SC
30 October 2015